The Ravine

A Novel

The Ravine

A Novel

For Cyd — Enjoy!

James Williamson

James Williamson

SUNSTONE
PRESS

SANTA FE

This is a work of fiction. The author intends no reference to any real person or event, and none should be inferred by the reader. The town of Tuckalofa, situated somewhere in the hill country of north Mississippi, does not exist.

Sunstone books may be purchased for educational, business, or sales promotional use. For information please write: Special Markets Department, Sunstone Press, P.O. Box 2321, Santa Fe, New Mexico 87504-2321.

Book and Cover design › Vicki Ahl
Body typeface › Adobe Garamond Pro
Printed on acid-free paper

Library of Congress Cataloging-in-Publication Data
Williamson, James, 1946-
 The ravine : a novel / by James Williamson.
  p. cm.
 ISBN 978-0-86534-887-5 (softcover : alk. paper)
 1. Civil rights movements--Mississippi--History--20th century--Fiction. 2. African Americans--Civil rights--Mississippi--History--20th century--Fiction. 3. Mississippi--Race relations--History--20th century--Fiction. 4. African Americans--Segregation--History--20th century--Fiction. 5. Political fiction. I. Title.
 PS3623.I5677R38 2012
 813'.6--dc23
                              2012014185

WWW.SUNSTONEPRESS.COM
SUNSTONE PRESS / POST OFFICE BOX 2321 / SANTA FE, NM 87504-2321 /USA
(505) 988-4418 / ORDERS ONLY (800) 243-5644 / FAX (505) 988-1025

For Reid

When from a long-distant past nothing subsists, after the people are dead, after the things are broken and scattered, still, alone, more fragile, but with more vitality, more unsubstantial, more persistent, more faithful, the smell and taste of things remain poised a long time, like souls, ready to remind us, waiting and hoping for their moment, amid the ruins of all the rest; and bear unfaltering, in the tiny and almost impalpable drop of their essence, the vast structure of recollection.

...the most terrible reality brings us, with our suffering, the joy of a great discovery, because it merely gives a new and clear form to what we have long been ruminating without suspecting it.

—Marcel Proust, *In Search of Lost Time*

PART I: 1990

1

Winter threatens. The December sky hovers low and heavy, socked in by stratus clouds. The fall semester of 1990 has been over less than a week, and already it is only a memory. The students have vanished for Christmas break, and the campus feels bleak, exhausted.

The intercom buzzes insistently somewhere beneath the pile of final examinations stacked on my desk. When I finally manage to unearth it, the Upper School secretary sounds skeptical. "Harry, you have a call from a Reverend Calvin Estes in Tuckalofa, Mississippi. He says it's important—that you'll know him."

I might as well have been punched in the gut. How remarkable that the old feelings could still lie so close to the surface. I hesitate before lifting the receiver, and when I do, I fear my voice is trembling enough to betray me.

"Hello, Harry," the deep baritone has lost none of its authority. The man must be well into his seventies by now, and I wonder if his hair is still oily and jet-black, brushed back above the high forehead to reveal a widow's peak. "I expect you're surprised to hear from me after all this time. You'd probably rather not hear from me at all. I understand that. But I was asked to call. I have some sad news to share with you. I'm afraid it's Miss Cordelia."

I've decided to take the old road south out of Memphis to Tuckalofa. No interstate this time with the headlights flashing in my rearview mirror as some SUV roars by, full of Ole Miss fraternity boys on Christmas break bound for a weekend of booze and strip clubs in the French Quarter.

The tightly stretched countryside drifting past on the outskirts of Memphis is flat as a road map. They say that near here is where the Delta begins—in Downtown Memphis, in the lobby of the Peabody Hotel to be exact. But just ahead lies the gateway to an equally fabled land, the Mississippi hill country. All that meets my eye so far, though, is a blighted wasteland of used car lots, barbecue joints, and derelict motels with names like "The Cloverleaf" and "The Rebel Inn." Sprawl is creeping beyond the outer reaches of the city, and it seems inevitable that before long, developer suburbs will replace even these relics of the past.

Once more I am on a journey to Mississippi to bury the dead. How many times before has a death in the family prompted a pilgrimage like this? I try to count the ranks of the departed—my mother and father, both sets of grandparents, numerous uncles and aunts—but the list fades into the recesses of memory. And now death, that most intimate of strangers, has called for the last of my parents' generation. Who wouldn't have thought Cordelia would live forever? But now she too is gone, although her memory still looms larger than life.

I travel alone. When I called to give my brother, Tommy, the Presbyterian minister in the "high steeple" church in the Atlanta suburbs, the news about Cordelia, he had sounded reluctant. "Tommy," I said, trying not to beg, "do you think you can make it for the funeral? It's not scheduled until Friday at the church, but I'll be driving down tomorrow. I want to give myself a couple of days to look over the house and see if anything needs to be spruced up."

"I don't know, Harry. I've got a big wedding scheduled—the clerk of the session's daughter. Besides, well, you know…"

"I do know. But you always liked Cordelia, didn't you?"

"Sure, but Cordelia wasn't the problem," he replied. "It was Tuckalofa— what happened to us there. I haven't been back since I was a kid, since that summer, and I don't know if I can bring myself to go now. It certainly won't make any difference to Cordelia."

"It would mean a lot to me to have you there."

"It's been such a long time, but it seems like yesterday. I don't think I'll ever get over it completely."

"No. None of us will ever get over it. But it's not going to be easy, being the only one there."

A long pause. "Okay, listen, I'll see what I can do. I won't promise, but maybe I can find somebody else to do the wedding. The minister over at First Church owes me a favor. But I'm sure I won't be there until the morning of the funeral. You'll do fine in the meantime. Give my regards to that old hypocrite, Calvin Estes."

My first cousin L.Q.C., the museum curator, is the only other family member I called. But his assistant informed me he was in New York organizing an exhibit on medieval tapestries at the Metropolitan Museum and couldn't be disturbed, so I left him a voicemail. There is no one else. It falls to me to make the arrangements.

There is something pleasantly hypnotic about driving alone, the steady stream of white stripes rushing toward the windshield. My mind eases into the rhythm of the road as the blighted landscape thins out. Between the body shops and truck stops I can catch glimpses of bright meadows nestled among clumps of dark woods and hillsides speckled with Black Angus. One by one the little towns glide by, their names tugging at me like the words to a forgotten lullaby: Olive Branch, Byhalia, Red Banks, Holly Springs, Oxford, Water Valley, Coffeeville, Grenada.

It is growing late when the road begins to descend between the two parallel ridges that gently enclose the little town of Tuckalofa like the hands of a man at prayer. Without preamble the highway transforms itself into Main Street. First the Masonic Temple, then the Gulf station. The abandoned Coca-Cola bottling plant huddles next to the bus station and pool hall where a dust-caked Greyhound disgorges a lone soldier in desert camouflage. He turns up the collar of his field jacket and swings an olive drab duffel bag over his shoulder, looking around blankly as though he's never seen the place before. I think of the summer I turned ten and my first bus ride to Tuckalofa all the way from Memphis. Of the scratchy seats, the freezing air conditioning, the smell of diesel fumes and stale cigarettes, and the half pint of bourbon protruding from the driver's coat pocket. And of the summer of 1958 when the town was filled with smoke and soldiers.

In those days on a Saturday two weeks before Christmas, Main Street would have been alive with farmers and townspeople, blacks and whites, carrying packages and calling out holiday greetings. Today, though, the street is virtually deserted. One or two snowflakes whirl past the windshield. Forlorn tinsel wreaths droop from the lampposts. At the Albemarle Hotel I turn and head up Lee Street. High up the hill ahead I can make out the corner turret of Cordelia's house. I wheel into the driveway, scraping the pavement as usual, and roll to a stop under the magnolia that shades the front porch. Any moment Cordelia should emerge, standing on the porch waving to me.

Instead, the front door opens, and a tall, powerfully built man in a dark suit steps from the shadows. As he closes it behind him, a loose pane of glass rattles in the frame. I shiver.

The black eyes have lost none of their power to hypnotize, and the hair, once a deep ebony, is gray and thinning but still brushed straight back above the domed forehead. He offers his hand, and after a long moment's hesitation, I take it. The grip is surprisingly strong, and his eyes bore into me.

"Hello, Harry. I hope it was all right if I let myself in. After they found her and called the sheriff, he asked me to come by with him and make sure everything was, well, in order, you know. And then after they came for her from the funeral home, I kept the key they found inside. I thought I'd just make sure the heat was on when you got here."

"Well, Mr. Estes, I won't pretend it's a pleasure to see you. I guess we both know it's not." He ignores my remark and now I regret it. Cordelia would not approve of my lack of civility. "But I thank you, anyway," I add rather lamely. "I gather she died quite unexpectedly."

"Old Dr. Elliot thinks her heart just gave out; she was ninety-two, you know. She was lying on the bedroom floor, probably collapsed some time the day before. Miss Martha Tutwiler next door couldn't get an answer on the phone. She and her yardman, Freeman, knocked at the door and then walked around looking in the windows and calling to her. Finally, when they knew something must be wrong, Freeman found an unlocked window and crawled in. He was the one who discovered her.

"Your aunt has surely gone to be with Jesus, Harry." He hesitates and then looks straight at me, the black eyes steady and piercing. "Could we say a little prayer for her?" He smiles in an apparent attempt at benevolence, and his huge, perfect, white teeth gleam. My God, I had forgotten those teeth—straight and white as tombstones and sharp like a predator's. I'm confused, a small wave of panic knots my stomach, and I feel his old power trying to exert itself over me again after all these years.

"No. Thank you, Mr. Estes; I think it's best if we not do that right now. I think I'll just get unloaded. There's a lot for me to do, you know."

The house is dim and silent, permeated by the odors of dust and coal and memories. A single lamp burns on the marble-topped telephone table in the entrance hall. It will be dark by 4:30 this afternoon. I walk through each room in turn, switching on lights. The stairs creak as I climb, sliding my hand along the oak banister, its varnish worn down to the bare wood by nearly a hundred years of my family's hands.

Cordelia's bedroom is as I remember it. Nothing is out of place. The four-poster bed is neatly made, covered with a brightly colored quilt, and her favorite leather-bound copy of Wordsworth rests on the night table. A tiny study separates her room from my Uncle Horace's old bedroom; I never knew them to share a bed. I take a seat in the corner rocking chair next to the fireplace where Horace used to nod off in the midst of reading a *National Geographic* or the poetry of his beloved John Donne. The fireplace still bears the dents left by his pipe as he knocked it out against the wood mantle.

The house has always seemed to pulse with an unseen energy, and somehow I feel compelled to frequent each of its quiet, secret places again, like a pilgrim returning to a shrine. The attic with its low-hanging rafters, the closet that plunges into the black recess under the stairs, the bulging kitchen pantry, the back staircase that spirals up in darkness from the kitchen, the window nook where Cordelia's pedal-powered sewing machine slumbers, the garage with its earthen floor like a tomb—they all stir my imagination now as powerfully as when I was a child.

These places are, in fact, far from extraordinary, and all are furnished with unremarkable domestic objects from the past. But for me, each glows with the aura of memory—the brass coal bucket on the hearth, a blue pottery mixing bowl, the tin laundry tubs with their sullen patina stashed in the pantry along with the washboards, the carved mahogany pineapple newel post on the stair landing, the cracked leather football helmet in the attic along with the gauzy ball gowns and the miniature minnie ball cannon.

In the summer the house would be alive with electric fans. The big silver Emerson in the living room hummed with stately urgency, like an old lady confiding secrets across a bridge table. The small green Hunter in my bedroom whirred with a rhythmic pulse. On the good nights when I could drift off into an easy sleep, its comforting moan merged with my dreams.

My secret world was not entirely benevolent though. I can see now that I projected my childhood anxieties onto the house. The eight-foot-high headboard of the imposing bed in the tower room had clearly been fashioned after the face of a goblin by some demented woodcarver. There were nights when I found it impossible to fall asleep beneath its malevolent glare, nights when the roses on the wallpaper commenced a convulsive dance as soon as the lights winked out. The mossy stain under the tap in the bathtub was a small crocodile, waiting to nip the toes of the unwary. On the parlor bookcase sits the pair of lamps decorated with scenes of a pine forest, bought by my grandmother at the 1904 St. Louis World's Fair. As an inner mechanism rotated, the lamps were intended to simulate sunrise and sunset. But to me as a child, they conjured up the terror of a forest fire projected onto the walls of the room. I feared flames might burst from the lamps and burn the house down.

Distinguishing between the real and the fantastic was not just a problem for children like my brother, my cousin, and me; the adults in my family seemed equally unable to do so. Or rather, they regarded it as an unimportant distinction. Behind the house stands the coal shed, a decrepit little hut clad in diagonal latticework. The roof sags and the brick foundation crumbles a little more each year.

"You know, of course, that Mr. Nobody lives in our coal shed," confided Cordelia one day when I was about five. My brother, Tommy, and I stared at each other.

"Oh, yes, I expect he's been there for years, since my parents built this house back in 1895. I imagine he's been with the family a lot longer than that, maybe since my great-grandfather first came here from North Carolina. Maybe even since our first ancestors came from England and Scotland.

"Who's Mr. Nobody?" asked my brother.

"Oh, goodness me, don't you boys know anything? He's one of the little people, just a few inches tall—about the size of a saltshaker, I should say. He dresses in tattered old clothes and wears a pointed cap. He has a wrinkled face and hands and long, shaggy hair. I wouldn't be at all surprised if he's hundreds of years old.

"Mr. Nobody's a shy, stay-at-home type. He plays harmless pranks and also does helpful deeds. He generally only comes out at night. He is awfully cunning and daring too. But he doesn't care much for rules or authority figures and doesn't put much stock in delayed gratification. Horace doesn't approve of him, at all."

"What's 'delayed gratification'?"

"Never mind that."

"Have you ever seen him?"

"Why, I should say I have, although mostly we just know he's there by circumstantial evidence."

"What's that?"

"I'll show you. Tonight, before we go to bed, we'll leave a bowl of milk out in the kitchen where he can find it when he comes in under the door. Mr. Nobody is quite fond of milk."

That night I lay awake under the glowering headboard, listening for the rustling of little people down in the kitchen. The sheer curtains coiled and uncoiled at the open bay window, and in the distance a train whistle wafted over the sleeping hills. The Ansonia clock downstairs on the parlor bookcase—the one with the bronze sculpture of Mercury in winged sandals—chimed the hour, and I began counting the bongs. I made it to seven, and it was morning.

I stumbled down the twisting back stair to the kitchen, feeling my way in the dark. Cordelia stood rolling biscuits on the kitchen table while Senatobia, the cook, cranked away on the coffee grinder. I rushed over to the back door and gawked at the empty bowl and the droplets of spilled milk, white as tiny ghosts against the weathered floorboards.

"Mr. Nobody must have been hungry," Cordelia commented, not bothering to look up.

2

I didn't ask to return. But Estes' call came as no less than a summons, not only to Tuckalofa, but back to what happened here. After that summer, we made a pact—Tommy, L.Q.C., Cordelia, and I—never to speak of it again. That's how it's been all these years. That's how it was meant to stay.

It has grown dark, and I realize that, driving straight through from Memphis, I missed lunch. I feel my way down the blackness of the back stair to the kitchen where I find a few odds and ends and throw together a simple supper. I unpack my things and then, not yet ready for bed, pick up the Wordsworth from Cordelia's room. I can't concentrate on the poetry though, so I try to sleep. But the past is too close, and I lie there, staring into the darkness beneath the glare of the goblin headboard.

I switch on the light and throw on my bathrobe against the chill. In a corner of Cordelia's bedroom stands the fold-down secretary, straight and severe as a wooden soldier, where, as a child, I used to watch her writing in a diary or planning one of her civic campaigns. On top of the desk rests a copy of last Sunday's *New York Times*, undoubtedly the only one of its kind in Tuckalofa. I rummage through the pigeon holes, crammed with paid bills and grocery receipts. In a drawer I find her old black Parker fountain pen, the one with the iridescent green sheen that I always admired. Uncle Horace's pocket watch lies next to a small black velvet box containing their son Frank's Phi Delta Theta fraternity pin. Another drawer contains her 1918 University of Mississippi yearbook, *The Ole Miss*, bound in worn leather with a program from a production of *Long Day's Journey Into Night* inserted inside the cover for safekeeping. The yearbook rests atop a legal-size manila envelope. A label on the front of the envelope, inscribed in a bold copperplate hand, reads, "Last Will and Testament of Cordelia Cunningham Coltharp."

I glance around the room. Where exactly did they find her body? She was 92, and by all accounts alert and spry to the very end. Did she go quickly?

Or did she suffer, perhaps lying there on the floor, helpless, desperately hoping someone would happen along?

Under these circumstances, alone in an old house, late at night, in a room where death has so recently called, I am not quite ready to face reading a will. And I am vaguely aware that I am avoiding something. Something buried in the past? I lay the envelope aside and return to the drawer where a packet of old letters tied with a ribbon is tucked into a corner. The small envelope on top is dated November 1943 and bears an official U.S. Navy censor's seal—World War II V-mail postmarked FPO San Francisco. I dig deeper, like an archaeologist excavating the layers of an ancient city, until, at the bottom of the drawer, I unearth a bundle of old photographs. In one, Cordelia and Horace smile back from a pair of lawn chairs in the backyard. Another shows the three sisters—Cordelia; my mother, Ellen; and my Aunt India—together on the front porch. My mother and India appear to be in their early twenties. While both are striking women, India is quite a beauty—the former Tuckalofa Okra Queen. Cordelia is a good bit older, in her forties perhaps, with a few streaks of gray in her hair. In the background a big black Packard sits brooding in the driveway.

In another picture, a steam locomotive idles in front of the depot. From the engineer's cab Horace waves. Next to him, peering over the windowsill, is the head of a little boy, their son, Frank. And finally there is a photograph of two boys—one, a white teenager wearing old-fashioned knickers, and the other, a little black boy, much younger. They are grinning for the camera. The older boy has wrapped his arm around the shoulders of the younger one. On the back is written, "Frank and Winston, 1936. Fast friends."

As I replace the photographs, I notice a small triangle of paper protruding from the joint between the side of the drawer and its bottom. Some forgotten document seems to have slipped almost all the way through the crack. I slide the drawer from the desk and hold it high enough to see beneath, but there is only the wood underside. Puzzled, I tug gently at the protruding paper, and to my surprise the bottom of the drawer lifts slightly. I pull harder and the false bottom lifts free to reveal a secret compartment.

An ancient handmade valentine is hidden there. Fringed in yellowed lace, the outline of a red heart has been carefully drawn with a paintbrush. At the top center, the artist has depicted the two halves of the heart intertwined, like the tendrils of a vine. In the center is inscribed "CC + RW, 1929." It seems obvious that CC was my Aunt Cordelia Coltharp. But who was RW? In 1929 Cordelia would have been in her early thirties. She and Horace must have been married for about ten years. And if RW was just a friendly acquaintance, why had Cordelia hidden the valentine? I run through a mental list of the family and friends whose names come readily to mind. There is no RW.

Another item is hidden in the secret compartment, a faded brochure from the Blue Ridge Hospital in Asheville, North Carolina. The cover features an illustration of a lush green lawn crowned by a rambling multi-storied white building wrapped by a porch. The building resembles a resort hotel, silhouetted against rolling mountains in the distance. Finally, there is a small leather-bound book. Inside the cover is a handwritten inscription: *Diary of Cordelia Coltharp.*

Mystified and intrigued by the odd assortment of mementos, I replace the diary, the valentine, and the brochure in their hiding place. I return to the bundle of old letters, secured with faded pink ribbon. Most seem to be V-mails dated 1943, and a quick glance shows them to be arranged in reverse chronological order. The letter on top is the last of the series. The single sheet is typed and bears the stamp of the navy censor. It begins, "Dear Mother and Daddy." The contents are mundane and obviously written in an attempt to reassure the folks back home. "Things are going fine here. We've been at sea a month now but have yet to see any action. I received the wool socks. Thanks for sending them, as it can be quite cold on watch." And so forth. It is signed, "Your loving son, Frank."

But her son was not to return. Across the bottom of the envelope, written in faded fountain pen in Cordelia's bold hand, is a simple notation— "Frank's last letter to us."

The story of his departure for the Pacific was one I had heard Cordelia tell countless times. She would lean back in her overstuffed armchair in front of the fire or on the front porch swing and a distant look would come into her eyes.

"We knew he was leaving early the next morning. He had received orders to report to a destroyer in the Pacific, part of Admiral Halsey's fleet. That night I planned Frank's favorite dinner: country-fried steak with cornbread and okra. We lit a fire—the first one of the season—and sat in the dining room trying to be cheerful and to think about something besides the war, since a lot of the news from the Pacific wasn't good in that first year.

"Senatobia would regularly appear from the kitchen to fill the tea glasses or clear the table. Frank and Senatobia were always fond of each other. She had practically raised him since he was nine, what with Horace constantly away on the railroad and most of my days occupied at work in the high school library. That night, Frank kept asking her if she wouldn't get on the train and come out to San Diego with him. 'Lawd, Mr. Frank,' she'd say, 'I ain't going to no California! The Almighty He put me here in Mississippi, and I 'spect that's where He be looking to find me when my time come.'

"I set the alarm clock for four o'clock, long before sunrise. I was down in the kitchen making the coffee, when I looked up to see Frank standing quietly in the door watching me. He was wearing his new dress blue uniform with the single gold stripe and gold star on each sleeve, and he was smiling at me. But it was as though a cold hand had touched my heart, and I remember wondering if it would be the last time I would ever see him.

"At breakfast we all made an effort to be bright and cheerful, with Frank making jokes and kidding everyone. But before long, Horace reminded us that Number Four always ran on time and that we didn't want to miss the train. So Frank shouldered his duffel bag, and we went out onto the porch together.

"I was resolved that we would walk with him down to the depot. It had gotten cold early that fall, and it was as still and black as a bucket of coal. A watery crescent moon hung low in the sky, and as we walked down the front steps, we saw that someone was there on the sidewalk, waiting in the dark. It was Senatobia, and standing next to her was her young son, Winston. He was pushing a wheelbarrow. I don't know how long they had been standing there—it could have been hours, and I'm sure they were frozen stiff. But as soon as they saw Frank, they both broke into big smiles.

"We loaded the duffel bag into the wheelbarrow and began our procession down Lee Street, Winston and the wheelbarrow bringing up the rear. We hadn't been at the depot five minutes when the train came rumbling up, pulled by one of the big steam locomotives like the one Horace drove. Of course, at that hour there were no other passengers and we had the platform to ourselves.

"We stood around for a few minutes, talking and putting on a brave face. Frank and Horace chatted with the conductor—I think it was Mr. Goodloe Pate. But then the whistle blew, and we knew it was time to say good-bye. Frank bent down and kissed me. He shook hands with Horace and started to shake hands with Senatobia too. I don't think he knew exactly what to do. But then she stepped forward and smothered him in a big bear hug, and I could see tears in her eyes.

"The conductor consulted his pocket watch, nodded to Frank, and climbed aboard, waving his flag in the direction of the engine. Frank lifted his duffle bag and pulled himself onto the first step of the Pullman car as the steam hissed, and the train jerked and began to roll. He grinned at us and waved. The train was picking up speed, and we were all smiling and waving, trying hard not to cry. And then I looked down at young Winston, between Senatobia and me with the wheelbarrow. He was standing at attention and saluting Frank, and Frank was returning the salute as the black coaches slipped away down the tracks and were swallowed up by the darkness."

I fold the fragile letter and replace it in the desk. I turn in again for the night, but when at last sleep comes, it brings feverish dreams.

3

Main Street is just beginning to stir. The pedimented portico of the Tuckalofa Funeral Home on Main Street boasts a row of Doric columns, mistakenly installed upside down, the shafts tapering downward. Imitation brass carriage lamps frame the paneled front door.

Stepping inside, I am encased in a cocoon of plush carpeting, flocked wallpaper, and velvet draperies.

"Why, good morning! How *are* you?" chirps the big-haired receptionist. Her cheerful voice is unsettling, too loud amidst the dampened acoustics. "I just bet you're Mr. Polk. Now you come right in here and have yourself a nice cup of coffee—we have regular or high-test—and make yourself at home while I tell Mr. Leonidas you're here. I think he's in the mortuary. I was *so* sorry to hear about Miss Cordelia. You know my daddy says she was his Sunday School teacher when he was just a little boy! Can you imagine that?"

I take a seat on the pale yellow Ethan Allen sofa beneath a reproduction of an English hunting scene. On the opposite wall behind the receptionist's counter hangs an Ole Miss Rebels football calendar. As a boy I would have committed to memory the date, location, and score of every game, but now I'd be hard-pressed to remember the name of the current head coach. On the desk, a little red ceramic statue of Colonel Reb, the team mascot, jauntily brandishes a miniature cane. Next to this curio is displayed a small sampler set in a wooden frame, hand-embroidered with the Ole Miss cheer:

Are you ready?
Hell yes! Damn right!
Hotty Toddy, Gosh almighty!
Who in the hell are we—hey!
Flim Flam, Bim Bam
Ole Miss By Damn!

"Harry—it's so good to see you again." The voice from behind me is soft and well modulated. A small, elderly man is smiling and advancing noiselessly toward me. I stand and take the out-stretched hand, startled by its softness, almost the hand of a child. He is immaculately groomed and dapper in a black suit, black tie, and black patent leather loafers that briefly reflect the brass chandelier hanging over my shoulder.

"I'm Leonidas Lovelace. The last time I saw you, you were no more than sixteen. Miss Cordelia was always so proud of you. Said you're a history teacher at a private school in Memphis, I believe. My, my!"

"I'm glad to see you too, Mr. Lovelace. I know our families have been friends a long time."

"Oh, goodness me, yes. I remember your Uncle Horace like it was yesterday, strolling down Main Street so tall and erect, always wearing a boutonniere, speaking to everyone by name. And did you know I escorted your Aunt India to the prom our senior year? Yep, Class of 1939."

"I don't get back to Tuckalofa much, I'm afraid. And when I do, it seems it's always for a funeral. But it's nice to know Cordelia will be in your care."

The undertaker clasps his soft, white hands together. The nails are perfectly manicured. "Well, now, just a few routine details to go over. I understand you're the official family representative?"

"Well, yes, I suppose I am. There doesn't seem to be anyone else unless my brother, Tommy, and my cousin, L.Q.C., can get here for the service, which seems unlikely. But I hope a few of Cordelia's old friends from here in town will show up."

"Oh, I'm sure it will be well attended. There is quite a lengthy obituary in the *Tuckalofa Tattler* this morning, and you know how widely respected your aunt was." Delicately he clears his throat. "Now I assume the remains will lie in state here in our chapel before the funeral? We are well equipped, you know, to efficiently handle all the, shall we say, associated logistics. And then there's the matter of selecting an appropriate casket."

"Actually, I had assumed that Cordelia would be at home for the visitation before the funeral, which we plan to hold in the Presbyterian Church. I asked Mr. Estes to speak to you about those arrangements. That's how our family has always done it. Cordelia was never one for funeral homes, I'm afraid.

"Oh, and one other thing too, Mr. Lovelace. I know Cordelia wouldn't want to be embalmed. I once heard her talk about it. She thought death was a perfectly natural part of life and that it should be accepted as such. Cordelia hated anything artificial."

Mr. Lovelace takes a small step backward. "Oh, dear! A visitation at home and no, er, preservative treatment? Oh, my. Really, Harry, I'm not sure you want to do that! It could be, well, unpleasant."

I feel sorry for Mr. Lovelace; he seems genuinely upset. But I am determined to stand my ground. "Oh, I shouldn't worry too much, Mr. Lovelace. It is December after all. And if we need to, we'll just open a window a little bit."

He gives a small sigh. "Well then, Harry, perhaps you would care to examine our casket selections." He almost whispers, taking my elbow and guiding me through a pair of double doors. He flips a switch and the recessed lights in the ceiling gently warm to a full glow. The large room is filled with coffins, the lids propped open for inspection. I gaze down at the one nearest us, the underside of the lid emblazoned with a full-color scene of a man in a boat reeling in a huge bass.

Mr. Lovelace steers me to the next row. "Now this is our finest model, the *Mount Vernon*." The pride resonates in his voice. "It's solid bronze with an imported damask lining embroidered with rosebuds. Strong but very feminine, very elegant—just like Miss Cordelia. Absolutely top of the line." He taps the side. "Listen to that. Solid as a Lincoln Continental, wouldn't you agree?"

I hesitate. "It's certainly impressive, Mr. Lovelace. But I don't want the casket open, and, as my brother said, Cordelia won't know the difference. So we don't really need any rosebuds."

"But, Harry, how can her friends tell her good-bye if the casket is closed?"

I try to be as gentle as possible. "I'm sorry, but I remember Cordelia once telling me that if I allowed an open casket at her funeral she'd come back to haunt me. We certainly wouldn't want that, would we?"

"Well, if you're sure you're not interested in the top of the line, then let me at least show you our *Monticello*. It's a very popular and economical model."

I know this is going to be hard for him, but Cordelia taught me the importance of speaking one's mind. "Actually, Mr. Lovelace, I think your plainest, simplest wood casket will do just fine. Maybe something in pine?"

As I make my way back up Lee Street, the fine, cold drizzle that settled over the town earlier seems to have let up. Instead of heading directly into the house, I make a detour around to the backyard. In the ramshackle coal shed covered with wood lattice and supported mainly by the remnants of an unruly mop of bare wisteria, lived Mr. Nobody. Next to the shed was once a well-kept garden plot, ablaze with orange daylilies in July.

Beyond the coal shed, the lawn slopes gently to a clearing where a little grouping of wicker armchairs once huddled in the shade. From there the terrain precipitously drops away. We call the region below "the ravine."

As a child, it seemed to me that just past the border of neatly mown grass began a world of another sort. Cordelia and Horace's world was all well-tended gardens, painted clapboard, and ordered respectability. But in summer the ravine was a chaotic jungle choked with honeysuckle, briars, and poison ivy. Ancient hardwood trees said to be hundreds of years old eclipsed the sunlight, and the faint burble of unseen running water could be heard far below. Red clay gullies yawned like wounds in the earth. The wildness of this place still both beckons and repels me. Although I have not set foot in its depths since the summer I turned thirteen, the ravine still figures in my dreams. And sometimes, even after all these years, in vivid nightmares.

On an impulse, ignoring the chill, I begin a descent by way of the steep, twisting path that starts at a far corner of the backyard. It leads downward through brambles and bare clumps of sassafras and sumac, and I stumble and slip on the wet leaves underfoot. Watery sunlight filters through the lingering mist and the soft gurgle of the creek grows louder. It is absurd, I know, but I would hardly be surprised to catch a glimpse of a gnarled satyr or a coy wood nymph laughing at me from behind one of the ancient oaks.

On the bank of Persimmon Creek I pause to gaze into the shallow current. The creek meanders through the town, disappearing into dank culverts as it passes under Main Street only to reemerge and continue to twist its way past deserted tarpaper shacks, forgotten sawmills, and abandoned railroad yards. Beneath the clear surface, the sandy bottom is etched with delicate ripples. The sun appears for a moment and dappled light plays over the tops of half-submerged logs, their moss-covered hulks protruding here and there above the surface. As children, we were warned of the treacherous bogs of quicksand said to await the unwary, and for a moment an old, half-forgotten fear grips my chest.

Making my way along the bank, the terrain gradually levels out into a broad, flat flood plain. Ahead stands Buzzard Bottom, the little enclave of weather-beaten cabins where the black people have lived as long as I can remember. Cordelia and Horace's house is no more than 200 yards away. Non-Southerners are often surprised to discover the close proximity, and in many cases the physical intimacy, which small town whites and blacks have always shared. But despite its short distance from Lee Street, Buzzard Bottom is still a ghetto separated from the prosperous white neighborhood not only by the depths of the ravine, but by the chasm of race. As a boy there seemed to be nothing remarkable about this. It was simply the way the world was constructed, a part of God's natural order. Until that summer, of course.

Wood smoke hangs low and a door slams in the distance, the sound carrying in the chilly air. A young black man smoking a cigarette, a sheer do-rag pulled tight over his head, is leaning against a car next to one of the shacks. He eyes me coldly from across the creek, flicks the cigarette to the ground, and angrily grinds it into the dirt. Cordelia told me that in Buzzard Bottom a few years ago, the quiet respectability of Lee Street was shattered by a drug-related shooting. I keep moving.

In a little fenced enclosure full of chickens stands a spirit tree, its naked branches festooned with old bottles of Thunderbird wine, milk of magnesia, and exotic patent medicines, all intended to keep the haints away. It is midday, and another brief ray of sun penetrates the bottles, casting sparkling splashes of purple and blue across the bare earth. A few fragments of cinder blocks and a forlorn brick chimney are all that remain of a cottage that once stood there. As a child, I would slip away from Cordelia's to the porch of that cottage. I half expect to hear Winston's deep laugh punctuating exaggerated accounts of marathon coon hunts, bloody cockfights, and bootleggers pursued by deputy sheriffs. I can see his beaming face as he waves to me from his Jitney Jungle delivery truck. And I recall his father, Robert, his demeanor quiet and scholarly, in the midst of some odd job up at Cordelia's. He unfailingly paused to greet me, inquiring how school was going and whether I had read any Homer that year. And always there was Senatobia, Robert's wife, a basket full of laundry under her arm, patiently climbing the wooded path that leads from the ravine up to Cordelia's.

I was once shown a plat of Cordelia and Horace's lot and was surprised to see how far into the ravine it extended. Winston, Robert, and Senatobia, it seemed, lived on my aunt and uncle's property, apparently rent free. It never occurred to me as a child to question this arrangement.

Directly across the creek from where their cottage once stood stands the Sweetheart Tree, its branches overhanging the water. Cordelia first pointed it out to me as a child, an ancient beech, its smooth, silver bark etched with the carved initials of a hundred long-dead couples. Now I examine it closely, looking for the names of families I recognize. There are a few Scots-Irish surnames like Cloyd, McCarthy, and McCorkle, but most are simply the given names of the boys and girls of the town—Buddy and Donna, Sissy and Floyd, Earl and Teasie. Others, perhaps the secret lovers, are recorded only by their initials. Some include dates; the oldest I can find proclaims *Ralph—1925*. Some are so high in the branches they can't be read from the ground. Perhaps they have slowly risen as the old beech has grown. There is also an ugly wound, now obscured by scar tissue, where long ago an inscription was violently obliterated. If all the carvings could be deciphered, they would surely provide an undiscovered history of the town.

"Hey, white boy! What you doin' 'round here?"

Startled, I spin around. On the opposite bank of the creek the young black man in the do-rag is ferociously glaring at me. In his hand I notice a metallic glint. Slowly, deliberately, he steps down the bank until his expensive Nikes are poised at the water's edge. He stands no more than ten yards away, his hard eyes filled with resentment. I stare back at what I can now see is a box cutter clenched in his fist.

"Hey, man, I ast you a question! You want me to come over there and teach you yo' manners?"

I turn and begin to walk away, not too briskly, I hope, back along the path. Behind me there is a splash as he leaps into the shallow water, and I know I'm in trouble. I glance over my shoulder.

But instead of pursuing me, he is motionless, a look of surprise replacing the hate. He has sunk up to his thighs in the muck. He flails about and sinks another three inches. "Hey, man! This shit's quicksand!" he cries, the arrogance replaced by panic. "Come on, man, you got to help me!"

Should I turn away and leave him to his fate? I could well save my life. It is then that a sort of vision flashes in front of me, one of the old nightmares I have worked so hard to forget. I can feel the sucking of supersaturated ooze and taste muddy water mixed with silt. How can I abandon this stranger when I know the secret to his survival?

"Hold on," I shout. "Try not to move." The man in the creek freezes, eyes wide with fear. He is still sinking, the water now up to his waist and rising. He knows he is about to die. "Look," I shout, "what you've got to do is float. Just like in a swimming pool."

He stares, uncomprehending.

"Okay, listen. It's easy. Just take a deep breath and lie back in the water. Keep your arms out straight. Keep your head tilted back, and don't move. You'll float; you won't sink. There's a spot a little further down where you can climb out on the bank."

Slowly, the man in the water does as he is told.

"Remember, keep your head back. When you start floating downstream and you feel your legs coming unstuck, don't try to stand up. Just keep floating, and let the current carry you away."

It's working, by God, I think to myself, as he slowly drifts free. Now his back is turned to me, and, seizing the opportunity, I scamper away from the path, beating a retreat up the hillside and into the trees.

Even though it has grown late and I am exhausted, sleep again eludes me. Finally, frustrated and wide-awake, I throw on my robe and return to Cordelia's desk. Downstairs the mantle clock strikes eleven as I remove the false bottom of the drawer, extract the old leather diary, and start to read.

By the time I have finished it, the night is over and through the window I can just make out the dim silhouette of the branches of the oaks against the sky. I'm exhausted and mystified by what I have read. But something has been awakened in me. The thing that has been allowed to lie undisturbed for so long has begun to stir. I know what I must do. It is time to look under the bed, clean out the attic, and confront the ghosts.

I allow myself a few hours of fitful sleep before stumbling down to the kitchen to make coffee. The funeral is not until tomorrow and the entire day is available for the task. Taking a lined legal pad and Cordelia's black fountain pen from her desk, I begin to write.

I have never revealed the whole truth about what happened that summer of 1958. Tommy, L.Q.C., Cordelia, and I promised never to speak of it again. And I know that despite my best efforts to record the events, the record will be incomplete—and not only because it has been over thirty years. There is something else, a part of the story held at bay just beyond my consciousness. With difficulty I think back to the fall and winter of that year, to the six months I spent in the hospital, and the kindly doctor with the thick, wire-rimmed glasses who kept coaxing me to try to remember. I never could manage to retrieve whatever it was he was after though, although I can still feel it lying there, a lump of something hard and heavy in my gut. Perhaps I am making a mistake trying to remember. Perhaps it is better to leave it all alone. Maybe some things are best forgotten. But after what I have read in Cordelia's diary, I know I must try.

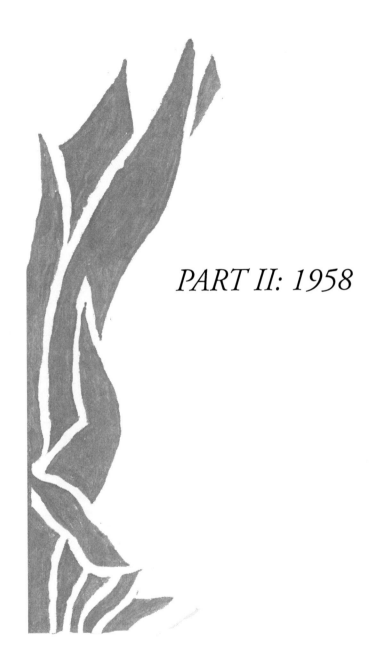

PART II: 1958

4

That June of 1958, summer beckoned. The summer I turned thirteen. The summer everything changed.

As our black Buick Special made its stately way south from Memphis, my father and mother munched on her homemade cheese straws. In the backseat Tommy, my ten year-old brother, and I joked and poked each other over the padded armrest. Behind us, in the trunk, two of my father's old army duffle bags bulged with T-shirts, khaki shorts, white bobby socks, and black, high-top Keds—our summer uniform—along with a single pair of blue jeans apiece.

"Hey, quick, it's almost ten; turn on the radio!" interrupted Tommy. "They're playing the top ten hits on WHBQ—maybe we'll hear 'Purple People Eater'!"

A few miles outside Memphis, not far past Capleville, I watched for the big magnolia blossom sign proclaiming, "Mississippi Welcomes You." As we crossed that invisible line, I heard my mother breathe a little sigh of contentment and watched my father's shoulder muscles tighten a bit.

A hundred yards further on a billboard urged "Impeach Earl Warren."

"Who's Earl Warren?" I asked.

"He's the Chief Justice of the Supreme Court, son," replied my father. "Some people here in Mississippi are upset that the court has ruled that segregated schools are unconstitutional—that Negro children have to be allowed to go to the same public schools as white people."

"He's a dangerous radical, that's who he is," interjected my mother. "President Eisenhower must have lost his mind appointing a liberal like that to the court. That ruling is going to tear the country apart."

"It's a simple question of justice," countered my father. "Things here will never change by themselves. The fact that Negroes have been treated like dirt for two hundred years doesn't make it right. The court had to step in, regardless of what all the rednecks think."

"That's putting it a little strongly, don't you think, dear? Not everyone—"

"A 'redneck'? What's that?" interrupted Tommy.

"Honey, I don't know why you resist going back down home so much," continued my mother, ignoring my brother. "Just look at those rolling hills and the farmhouses; they're really quite lovely."

"Yes, and think of all the foot-washing folk in those farmhouses," he replied, "coming home from Wednesday night prayer meeting to tell their children bedtime stories about the fires of hell, scaring the bejesus out of them. All God-fearing people, I'm sure, but perfectly capable of burning down some poor Negro family's house if the Grand Dragon of the Klan gives the word."

"Really, Harrison, you sound just like Cordelia. You know that's not fair. Almost everyone we know in Tuckalofa defies that description. They are kindhearted, gentle, hard-working people, still beaten down by the Depression, but who go out of their way to help each other. And things in Tuckalofa are friendly and relaxed. You know everyone and how you fit in—not at all like Memphis where no one gives a flip about who your people are."

"Let's just say I've spent most of my life trying to escape from Mississippi— all the narrow-mindedness and determination to resist change at all costs—and so I'm not as anxious as you to head back for every long weekend or Ole Miss home game."

"Now you know you like the change of pace in Tuckalofa. And I think you secretly enjoy football weekends in Oxford. You just don't want anyone to know it. You rather enjoy being contrary, pretending to be the only one in the family who doesn't live and breathe Ole Miss football. But I've seen you jump up and cheer like everybody else."

"The only time I've ever cheered at an Ole Miss game is when Mississippi State made a touchdown."

This change in my parents' mood bothered me. But clearly the reasons were more complicated than what appeared on the surface. My father's lack of enthusiasm for the Rebels seemed inexplicable. After my first football game in Oxford, seeing the dashing red jerseys, blue helmets, and Confederate-gray pants of their uniform; the beautiful college girls in their corsages; and the crowd leaping to its feet whenever the band struck up "Dixie," I had instantly become a dedicated Ole Miss fan. I had bought a Rebel flag that was now proudly displayed in my bedroom, along with a color photograph of the quarterback, who was already being mentioned as a future All-American. The team seemed poised for another Southeastern Conference championship, with another trip to the Sugar Bowl, and I could hardly wait for the season to begin.

I was vaguely aware of the controversy swirling about in the newspaper over integration, although I would have been at a loss to define the term. I knew my mother and father held diverging views about the Supreme Court and the rights of black people, some of whom seemed to be demanding far-reaching changes in society. I was baffled by most of this, however. All the blacks I came in contact with, like Rosie, our maid, seemed to be quite good-natured and content with life. They quietly went about their business cleaning houses, mowing grass, and picking up the garbage. When my mother drove Rosie to the bus every afternoon, she climbed into the backseat with no apparent distress. She never complained about riding at the back of the bus either, or sitting in the balconies of the downtown movie theaters, or about the separate water fountains in the bus stations and department stores. If the way things were was all right with the black people, why should the rest of us mind?

I had overheard the rumbles of disenchantment with the Democratic Party from my parents' friends and the dark rumors of the impending betrayal of "our Southern way of life." I had no real idea of what was meant by my Southern heritage—it was like asking a fish what it was like to be wet. My way of life hardly appeared to be threatened, so I dismissed these comments as nothing more than "politics," the most boring of adult preoccupations.

Rather than attempt to unravel all these complexities, I contented myself with gazing through the window of the Buick, concentrating instead on the landscape dotted with sharecropper shacks; barns sporting faded, painted advertisements like "Sweet Feed for Sale" and a string of signs sprouting along the shoulder:

Water Heater
Out of Kilter
Try the Brushless
Whisker
Wilter
Burma Shave

At Olive Branch we passed Maywood, an artificial lake where one could sun on white dunes of sand dredged up from the Gulf Coast and hauled five hundred miles north to create a tropical paradise here on the edge of the hill country. Near Byhalia, at the crest of a sweeping lawn shaded by oaks, sprawled a rambling building wrapped with deep porches.

"What's a 'sanitarium'?" asked Tommy, reading the letters above the gates.

"It's a sort of hospital," replied my father, "for people who drink too much or who suffer a nervous breakdown. They say old William Faulkner goes there to dry out about once a year.

"Now you boys know the plan for the summer," he continued, changing the subject. "You'll be staying with your Aunt Cordelia and Uncle Horace. And L.Q.C. will be there too—"

"And Sparkplug! Don't forget Sparkplug," interrupted my brother, who could think of little else but a reunion with Horace's dog.

"Yes, well I imagine you'll find plenty to do," continued my father. "Your mother and I are going home tomorrow, but she'll be back for a visit in a couple of weeks. You can send us a postcard from Carlisle's Drugstore and let us know how you're doing."

"Horace promised to teach me to drive and to shoot this year, as soon as I turn thirteen." I tried to sound casual but could not control the excitement in my voice.

"Learn to shoot? Horace said that? Oh, now, Harry, I don't know—" my mother began, but my father interrupted.

"Now, Ellen, the boy's got to learn sometime. Let me speak to Horace about it."

"You know how fragile he is, Harrison," she protested. "And how the doctor said he shouldn't take on too much. He wants him to take it easy and build up his strength this summer."

"Nonsense. What the boy needs is a good dose of fresh air and small town freedom, and I imagine Horace and Cordelia will see to it that he gets plenty."

"That's what I'm afraid of."

An uneasy silence settled between my parents.

For my part, I was sick and tired of being treated like an invalid. True, the last year had proven a difficult one for me with a mysterious, undiagnosed ailment that resulted in many days spent away from school recuperating. But

I felt much stronger now and looked forward to a summer away from home under the relaxed supervision of my aunt and uncle.

"Boys, just a little way over there is Abbeville," my mother observed after a few miles, turning to face us. "It used to be a lovely little town, a wealthy farming community, but it was burned to the ground during the Civil War. Lucius Quinctius Cincinnatus Lamar was from there...."

"Whoa! Was that really his name?" howled Tommy. "What did his friends call him?"

"People usually called him L.Q.C., as a matter of fact. He was a famous Mississippian—your cousin is named for him—a statesman who wanted the South to secede from the Union before the Civil War. But afterward he tried to bring the two sides back together again."

Further along as we swept around a curve, spanning the road ahead, stood a trestle-like structure painted with a grinning skull-and-crossbones, framed by the words "Danger!" and "Death!" Red warning lights covered the black steel truss. As we approached, the skull's red eyes and the warning lights began flashing and the shriek of a siren made my scalp tingle. From the flanking towers that supported the trestle, crossing arms rapidly descended, blocking our path.

"Stop, Harrison, for heaven's sake!" cried my mother, although he had already applied the brakes. A moment later a northbound freight train careened around the blind curve doing at least eighty, shaking the earth. In thirty seconds it was gone, the banks of kudzu that lined the roadbed fluttering in its wake.

"Boys, your Uncle Horace told me this is the most dangerous crossing in the state and that over a hundred people have been hit and killed by trains they couldn't see coming around that curve," my father said quietly. "Why, a couple of years ago before they put in the siren, Horace was at the throttle when a pickup truck stalled at the crossing. He blew the whistle and applied the emergency brakes, of course, and the truck driver was able to scramble out before the impact, but the train smashed that pickup like it was a can of sardines and then pushed what was left of it a half mile down the tracks before it could finally come to a stop."

I knew that in rural Mississippi people were killed by trains all the time. I had heard Horace's stories. But at that point in my life the reality of death, mine or anyone else's, was a purely abstract concept. No one in my immediate family had ever died. I had never even seen a corpse. In my mind, death was confined to remote railroad crossings and nursing homes.

I knew the way to Tuckalofa by heart. Now that we had reached Oxford, we were halfway and would be there by noon. Since it was a Saturday, the Oxford square was filled with country people come to town to meet their neighbors and do their shopping for the week ahead. The townspeople were out in force as well, running errands, exchanging views on the prospects of a successful football season, or taking in a matinee at the picture show. In the center of the square stood the graceful old courthouse, the symbol of the town's conscience and the repository of its collective memory. The lawn around it was crowded with farmers in faded denim and straw hats. Some lolled on the benches, chewing tobacco and gossiping, while others sat in the beds of pickup trucks backed up to the curb, tailgates down. The trucks overflowed with the first of the summer harvest from the surrounding hills—polished cucumbers, squash, sweet corn, and okra mounded in bushel baskets.

At Grenada I succumbed to the hypnotic hum of the tires and the rhythmic thump of the joints in the pavement. When I awoke, we were descending into the familiar valley nestled among the lush hills, the road into town lined with white clapboard bungalows.

Main Street in Tuckalofa was teeming. Cars and pickups were backed up, and we inched along past the two-story brick buildings that lined the street. The sidewalks were choked with shoppers, whites and blacks in equal proportion. The blacks jostled each other good-naturedly and exchanged raucous greetings. White teenagers lounged on the hoods of their cars at the curb. The girls, their eyes caked in heavy mascara, chewed bubble gum and made eyes at the boys. The boys, the cuffs of their jeans rolled up to display white socks, combed their ducktail haircuts with feigned indifference while casting admiring glances at themselves in the reflections from the store windows.

At the Albemarle Hotel we turned left, bumping across the Illinois Central main line and the bridge over Persimmon Creek. Twenty-five yards down the tracks, a freight train, pulled by one of the first new diesel engines, idled impassively, its headlight staring at us. An agile brakeman swung down from the caboose and sauntered over to a red and green switch. Thin and sun-browned, he propped one foot on the switch, waiting on the signal from the cab to throw the big lever and direct the train onto the main line.

"Horace says the diesels are a lot cleaner," mused my father. "But I'll miss the steam locomotives once they're gone. Probably won't be many more years until they're all cut up for scrap iron. By comparison the diesels just don't have much of a soul. They don't even sound like trains anymore."

Up the steep hill I caught my first glimpse of the graceful Victorian house with the wrap-around porch, pale yellow shake siding, and green-black shutters. The Buick turned into the driveway, scraping the concrete curb as my mother leaned over and tooted the horn. We piled out, waving to my mother's sisters, Aunt Cordelia and Aunt India, waiting on the porch. They wore flowered dresses and were smiling at us. The air was thick with the perfume of honeysuckle, and through the open windows of the kitchen, I caught the scent of freshly baked cornbread.

Down the steps sauntered L.Q.C., India's son and my first cousin. I hadn't seen him since last summer; he had shot up, although he was still chubby. Behind thick glasses his pale eyes shined with an owlish glint.

"Hi, cretin," he called, greeting me cheerfully.

"Well, if it's not Lucius Quinctius Cincinnatus!" I replied with glee.

He scowled and flushed momentarily, but then seemed to recover. "I brought my new nature collection; I've begun specializing in Lepidoptera and Coleoptera. And I brought the telescope I got last Christmas too—a three-inch refractor with equatorial mount and clock drive. Wait until you have a look at the Andromeda galaxy; the resolution is superb! And I've started a—"

"Now L.Q.C.," called India, "perhaps you could take a moment to ask your cousins how they are before you get too carried away! And perhaps you could be a gentleman and offer to help with their luggage.

"Honestly," she said glancing at Cordelia, "I've tried to get him interested in something besides science. Something more…normal. You know, like football. He has asked for a croquet set for his birthday in September. But croquet! Can you imagine?"

I was itching to roam through the big house once more, as though I didn't already know every closet, pantry, and window seat by heart. I couldn't wait to slip up through the darkness of the back stair that led to the attic with its ancient secrets. And, of course, there was the ravine that yawned beyond the backyard.

A knowing look from my mother warned me, though, that these would have to wait. First we would all sit together on the porch, catching up on the local news—the weddings, births, funerals, scandals, and romances—and inquiring after the health of an interminable roster of relatives. Then there would be dinner in the dining room. In those days nobody in Tuckalofa ate lunch.

"Well, Cordelia," began my father, "what's the news? And where's Horace? Don't tell me he's away on the road again. I thought he'd arranged to be home this weekend. I've got something to talk to him about; you know Harry's birthday is coming up."

"Don't worry," she replied. "Horace is due in on the 3:20 from Memphis."

"I want to go see him come in!" I exclaimed.

"Of course you may," replied Cordelia. "Why don't we walk down to the depot together?"

5

A few years later, when they took the railroad away from Tuckalofa, the town began to die. The local heroes—firemen, brakemen, conductors, and engineers—slowly faded into retirement, never to be replaced by a younger generation with different ideas about the dignity of hard physical work. The white boys, who wanted to be businessmen with nine-to-five office jobs, fled to Memphis, Tupelo, or Birmingham. The black boys, who simply wanted to be treated like men, fled to Chicago and Detroit. But in 1958, the railroad was still the town's chief reason for being, and its demise was one of those unforeseen tragedies that lay ahead.

Cordelia and I waited at the edge of the tracks—the main line of the Illinois Central Railroad, which ran through the valley parallel to Main Street, bisecting the town into east and west sides. In her brown and white Spectator shoes, Cordelia looked younger than usual, and it occurred to me that for an elderly lady, as she seemed to me, she was really quite pretty.

The whole place smelled of the railroad—creosote, sweat and coal smoke. The blue steel rails recessed into the wooden platform of the ramshackle depot glistened with oil in the summer sun. A black porter lounged against the depot wall, waiting to haul the baggage cart down the platform. We were all gripped by expectation, glancing down the tracks that led away to the world.

In the distance I could hear the low rumble punctuated by the syncopation of the pistons. Above the far-away treetops, black puffs appeared against the sky, and soon a small dark point shrouded in a veil of smoke materialized from around the bend. Then came a three-note whistle signal: two short trills followed by a long wavering howl that echoed across the hills.

The point grew and solidified with surprising speed until it was transformed, first into a smudge, then into something dark, angular, and faintly sinister. Finally, with an ear-splitting blast of the whistle, it became a black leviathan bearing down on us, polished brass glistening, smoke belching, bell tolling, water dripping from its innards. The towering drive wheels rolled to a stop, and with a prolonged hiss, a cloud of steam spewed forth from its belly enveloping the platform. Craning my neck, I gazed up at the cab perched behind the boiler, the numerals 857 painted in white on its side. Through an open window a man with a handlebar mustache wearing a blue bandana was smiling down at me and waving.

"Look, there's Horace!" I shouted to Cordelia, unable to contain my excitement.

Horace Clay Coltharp was the senior engineer in Tuckalofa. In over thirty years he had never been at fault in a serious accident or killed anyone at a crossing, which was highly unusual since very few of the rural railroad crossings were fitted with gates or warning lights.

"You know, Harry, they call him 'Main-line Horace.' He's a stickler for the rules of the road. Unlike some others, I might add. Take that Casey Jones, for instance. Horace was born up in Water Valley. Casey Jones lived there for a while, and as a little boy, Horace idolized him and the other I.C. engineers. But it has always made him angry that Casey Jones became a folk hero when his wreck was caused by disregard for a flagman's warning and the fusees burning on the track. Horace says that's the number one requirement for a good engineer— to always obey the rules.

"He's driven the same engine, Number 857, as long as I can remember. You've heard his trademark whistle signal, two shorts and one long. It almost seems to be singing 'eight-five-sevennn.' When it's time for him to leave on a run and the engine is fired up, his crew always gives his signal. You can hear it up at the house, and all over town for that matter. At night I sometimes lie awake and listen for that whistle as the 857 rumbles through town on the midnight run from Memphis down to Canton and back."

After a long wait there in front of the depot, we finally saw Horace climb down from the cab and step lightly to the platform. His coveralls were grimy with soot and his eyes were encircled by white rings where the goggles had masked them against the coal smoke. He wiped his face with the bandana, coughed deeply several times, and smiled at us through the enormous mustache, his blue eyes bright.

He greeted us in his soft-spoken way, removing his elbow-length gloves and shaking hands with me. "Why if it isn't Cordelia and Harry come to meet me! Welcome back to Tuckalofa, son. It's been too long since your last visit.

Better not get too close, Cordelia, unless you want coal dust all over that pretty dress."

"When are we going shooting, Horace?" I asked, unable to restrain myself.

He grinned. "Soon, I expect. We'll see...Well, Jethro, that's another run," he called to his fireman. "Better tell Eddie to put her in the barn. And tell him to have a look at the packing on that drive wheel bearing." He turned and disappeared into the depot.

I wandered alone along the platform, watching the occasional lizard scurry thorough a crack between the boards. Twenty minutes later, at the far end of the platform, I saw Cordelia greet a man in a seersucker suit and Panama hat, a banker or lawyer, I guessed. I was surprised when the stranger hugged her and then beckoned to me. As they strolled nearer, I recognized him. It was Horace, showered and transformed. I fell in behind them as we headed home down Main Street, bursting with pride to be the nephew of an engineer.

Horace's first stop was the florist shop. When he emerged, a red carnation boutonniere in his lapel flashed like a railroad lantern. Outside the picture show Mr. Buford, the insurance agent, stopped and tipped his hat respectfully. "Afternoon, Miss Cordelia. Have a good run, Mr. Horace?"

Horace smiled and nodded in return. "Pretty quiet today, Roscoe. Had a hotbox on one of the flatcars but managed to make it into Memphis. How's Miriam? Give her our regards."

A tall man with oily black hair brushed back to reveal a widow's peak stepped out of the barbershop. At his side stood a ravishing creature, a girl about my age.

"Good afternoon, Mr. Estes," my uncle greeted him. "You remember my nephew, Harry. Mr. Estes is our minister, Harry."

"Indeed I do remember him," exclaimed the preacher, flashing me a smile that was too big. "How do you do, Harry?"

He was handsome, and I could see why women would like him. But there was something about his black eyes that made me uneasy. "All right, I guess," I mumbled.

"And I hope you are well, Cordelia. Harry, this is my daughter, Blair," Mr. Estes said, still smiling so that his big teeth flashed. "Blair, this is Harry. And you know Miss Cordelia and Mr. Horace; Harry's their nephew. I hear he's spending the summer with them."

I was stunned. Could this be the same obnoxious, stuck-up brat, several years older than I, who I remembered from last summer when Mr. Estes had called on Cordelia and Horace? Now she had long, tan legs and was taller than I was. She was already growing breasts a year ago, but they had gotten a lot bigger since then. I tried not to stare at her chest.

Girls were a mystery to me. On one hand, they were pleasing to look at and to listen to. The ones in my class had begun to wear lipstick and bras, and on Sundays they appeared in church wearing stockings and high heels. More and more they seemed to be turning into grown women. I found all of this fascinating but a bit intimidating as well; it was particularly annoying that some of them had grown taller than I was.

Most of them seemed interested in topics I found boring in the extreme. Instead of Ole Miss football, war movies, model airplanes, or camping trips, they went on and on about parties and clothes or about who was "cute" and who was "conceited." I found it almost impossible to think of anything to talk to them about, and all in all it seemed simpler just to go about my business and ignore them as much as possible. The problem was that I was finding this more and more difficult to do.

"I've been meaning to tell you what a fine sermon that was last Sunday," Horace said. "You missed a good one, Cordelia—all about the importance of law and order in a godly society. Very appropriate for these times, I'd say."

"Oh, yes, that does sound interesting," replied Cordelia, "although I feel sure Mr. Estes would also agree that justice is equally important, and that there are times when blind obedience to an unjust law may conflict with our duty as Christians."

"Well, I, er—that's a very interesting question, Cordelia, and one I would need to meditate on…"

"Really? I should think the answer would be self-evident, based on the Gospels," she replied.

"Come on, Daddy," Blair broke in, "I've got to get home and get ready for my tennis lesson."

"Oh, yes, quite right, dear," said Mr. Estes, apparently with some relief. "We really must be off. Good-bye now, Cordelia, Horace. I look forward to seeing both of you in your regular pew tomorrow!"

"Bye, Harry. Come see us some time," Blair said, smiling at me. I stared into her dark eyes, realizing that she was holding my gaze. Then she turned away.

"You, know, Horace," Cordelia commented once they were out of earshot, "sometimes I think you've been with the railroad too long—all those orders and rules and regulations. I think you've got a little too much respect for authority."

"Why, Cordelia, what on earth are you talking about?"

"You know as well as I do that you're a stickler for going by the book. The only thing in all creation you like that flouts authority are those squirrels in our pecan tree. And honestly, the way you play up to Mr. Estes about his sermons! You know how shallow they are. He probably gets them out of some ministers' magazine—you know, some 'Sermon-of-the-Week Club.'"

I had heard Cordelia explain that Mr. Estes had attended Princeton Seminary for a year or two, but that he had found it to be too liberal and had transferred to some Bible college down in Jackson. His sermons were full of quotations from Billy Graham, and he often derided Supreme Court Justice Earl Warren, whom he thought ought to be impeached for his views on integration. When he went off on one of these tangents, Cordelia would give Horace a there-he-goes-again look or a little nudge with her elbow.

"Well, maybe he is shallow, but occasionally he'll make a good point," replied Horace. "Besides, you didn't have to challenge him so blatantly. Everybody in town knows you graduated from Ole Miss, and sometimes I think some of them resent it just a little bit, as though you think you're better than they are."

Just ahead, an elderly black man was slowly making his way toward us along the sidewalk. As we approached, he stepped off the curb, removed his straw hat, and, with eyes cast down into the gutter, waited while we passed. Horace nodded to him as we continued on our way.

Next to the fire station we came to the Sycamore Club, a tiny public park, where concrete checkerboards and benches encircled a gigantic sycamore tree. Most of the benches were taken by the regulars, a handful of retirees lounging away the day. Several of them nodded to us. There were no black members of the club, of course. They didn't play checkers, I supposed.

A tall thin man, younger than the others, stood, hitched up his pants, and sauntered toward us. He wore a Stetson hat and leather boots, a khaki shirt and trousers, and on his chest a silver badge gleamed. I recognized him instantly.

Everyone in Tuckalofa knew Sonny Fly, the Sheriff of Dancing Rabbit County.

"Afternoon, Mr. Horace, Miss Cordelia. This here must be one of your nephews from Memphis."

"That's right, Sonny," replied Horace. "This is Harry. He visited us last summer, you know. He and his brother, Tommy, and their cousin, L.Q.C.— he's India's son—will be with us again this summer until it's time for school."

"Howdy, Harry," the sheriff said, glancing down at me. He seemed friendly enough, but I stood there in silence studying the steel caps on the toes of his boots. There were little flecks of mud on them, as though he might have come from out in the country.

"Say, Mr. Horace, I just been out at Earlwood's discussing the prospects for the watermelon crop with him. Says he believes it's going to be a good year, what with all that rain back in the spring and hot weather now.

"What's the news up in Memphis? They still havin' trouble with them niggers up there? I hear they want to ride in the front of the bus and go to the zoo whenever they want. I'm worried they might be comin' our way, too, before long. Why, just yesterday I heared they still got that boycott of all the white businesses goin' over yonder in Tuskegee. Been a whole year now."

"Why, just think of it," Cordelia remarked, "the very idea that Negroes would be allowed to vote—to elect the sheriff, even—in a town like Tuskegee where they make up over 80 percent of the population!"

Fly looked at her with uncertainty, searching for any trace of sarcasm. I had heard a little something at school about an ongoing conflict in Tuskegee, somewhere way over in Alabama. But I hadn't paid much attention. What sort of problems was he referring to that were coming our way? Whatever they were, I had no doubt that our Sheriff Fly would take care of them. He was tall and wiry and certainly inspired confidence, like Gary Cooper in "High Noon." Should any troublemakers actually descend on Tuckalofa, I felt sure he would handle them with ease.

"I expect what Cordelia means is that it's not easy being an officer of the law. It's a heavy responsibility, especially these days. Isn't that right, dear?" Cordelia glared at Horace, but said nothing. "Well, I guess we'd better be getting along, Sonny," Horace continued. "I expect supper's about ready."

As we turned and started toward home, the sheriff called to us. "Oh, Mr. Horace, I've been meanin' to stop by and see you about that dog of yours. You know, I don't like to mention it, but I hear he's getting to be sort of a nuisance 'round the neighborhood."

"Why, Sonny," replied Horace in an even tone, "you mean our terrier, little old Sparkplug?"

"Yep, that's the one. Roy Donaldson says he runs out and nips at him every day when he makes his rounds delivering the mail. I seen him myself, runnin' loose and chasing cars up there on Lee Street."

"Well, Sonny, Sparkplug's always been a bit frisky, but he'd never attack anyone. I feel sure of that."

"Well, I hope you're right. But that's the U.S. Mail, and I got a duty to make sure there ain't no interference with it. You best keep him inside or up on the porch. And be sure he don't never try to take a nip at me. I'm warning you; I don't much care for stray dogs."

"Why, Sonny," interjected Cordelia, "you wouldn't do anything to poor little Sparkplug, now, would you?"

"Just keep him on a leash, Miss Cordelia. Just keep him on a leash."

We continued down the sidewalk, and after a block Horace turned to Cordelia. "He's right, you know. To tell you the truth, that dog really is a bit of a nuisance. If Tommy wasn't so attached to him, I believe I'd try to find him another home, but you know, that dog is the first one of us Tommy wants to see whenever he comes down for a visit."

"Rubbish!" she replied. "Sparkplug's not the real issue; Sonny's just trying to throw his weight around. I tell you, Sonny Fly may seem nice enough, but he's a bully, the type who'll abuse his power if he gets the chance. And he's jealous of you, Horace, and the respect you command in this town."

"Oh, I think he's just trying to do his job. It's not easy being a lawman in a sleepy little town and spending your time worrying about stray dogs, rounding up the occasional drunk, or breaking up Saturday night fights. Tuckalofa's not exactly Dodge City. Why the last thing that required his attention was that bat that got into Miss Corinne Jenkins' bedroom. Being county sheriff's not the kind of job that's going to attract another Wyatt Earp."

6

That summer men still wore hats. It would be several more years before President Kennedy upended the fashion world, standing bareheaded in the snow to take his oath of office, sending the hat industry into a nose dive from which it would not recover. But on that broiling day in June, not long after our arrival in Tuckalofa, hardly anyone in the little clump of men on Main Street was hatless. The white businessmen in short sleeved shirts and ties sported straw hats with finely textured weave and muted bands, brims turned up in back and snapped down above eyes hooded in shadow. A railroad man in a pinstriped cap streaked with soot struck a wooden match on his thumbnail, touched the flame to his last Camel, and dropped the empty pack at his feet. Beneath straw hats with green plastic visors built into the brim, the faces of the farmers, worn and faded as their overalls, were brooding and inscrutable.

The men stood in a loose circle in the street in front of the post office, heads bowed as if in prayer, anonymous in their solidarity. L.Q.C., Tommy, and I slipped around the perimeter of the crowd until we found an opening and managed to worm our way to the center. A foot or two from a cast iron storm sewer grate lay the biggest snake I had ever seen, as big around as my Louisville Slugger bat, so black it was purple, flashing in the sun with a fierce, iridescent sheen. It thrashed about in panic, trying to retreat to the safety of the grate. Several of the men held broken tree branches, and as the snake neared the grate, they poked and prodded it, laughing and taunting the creature. The snake pulled back into a half-coiled striking position and then darted in another direction, only to have its escape route cut off by its tormenters.

"Musta come up outta that sewer," a farmer in muddy boots, his sunburned forearms covered with little blond hairs, declared in the harsh twang of the Mississippi hill country.

"Yessir, I reckon that culvert runs straight into the creek," added a young man in blue jeans and a white T-shirt. He wore his long, dark hair slicked back in a ducktail thick with Brylcreem, like Elvis or James Dean—too cool to be caught dead in a straw hat. "Shore look like a cottonmouth to me. I betcha there's hunerts of 'em down there under the street, just waitin' their chance to come a crawlin' outta there!" He glanced down at me and grinned malevolently, then jabbed viciously at the snake. It had begun to bleed and streaks of reddish ochre stained the concrete.

"Aw, that ain't nothing but an old black racer," drawled a big, well-muscled young black man wearing a white apron. I recognized Winston, who lived in the ravine and made deliveries all over town from the Jitney Jungle. "They ain't poisonous; why not just let him be?"

Something shoved me from behind, and I stumbled and almost sprawled on top of the snake. A pair of legs in khaki trousers appeared, a blue bandana protruding from the hip pocket. The trousers terminated in a shiny pair of Red Wing work boots, the toes encased in steel caps, glinting dully in the sun. Next to the boots rested the stock of a shotgun, the barrel clutched in a meaty red fist. I smelled tobacco, gun oil, and cold steel.

"Gimme some room here!" ordered a voice from somewhere above the legs, and the spectators fell back in instant obedience. The boots advanced to within a foot of the snake, which began to coil again in self-defense.

"I ain't havin' no goddam snake on *my* Main Street!" A boot lashed forward, pinning the snake to the pavement just behind the head. A moment later the butt of the shotgun crashed down on the creature's skull. I heard the crunch of shattering bone as blood spattered in our direction.

Next to me L.Q.C. gasped as a spray of red appeared on his white socks just above his sneakers. "Holy shit!" he breathed as the snake writhed and twitched for a moment and then was still.

"Like I always say, snake's like a nigger. Only good one's a dead one. Now you boys break this up. Go on now, move along. Winston, you go get a sack and get rid of this here thing."

The crowd began to disperse, but Winston hesitated. "Aw, Mr. Sonny, you didn't have to kill that old snake. He was just a racer and—"

Sheriff Sonny Fly stepped toward Winston. "Maybe this boy getting soft in the head," he said to no one in particular, his voice hard with scorn. "Maybe he been eating too many of them cantaloupes he always totin' around town. Maybe he getting uppity and don't know what's good for him."

"Oh, nossir. Mr. Sonny, I didn't mean nothin, honest. I'm going to get me a shovel right now!"

The crowd had broken up, many of the onlookers swaggering down the street as though they had personally dispatched the deadly menace. We watched as the big black man in the apron returned with a shovel and scooped up the mangled carcass into a brown paper bag. "Po' old thing never hurt nobody," he muttered under his breath.

Holding the sack out at arm's length—everyone had heard a dead snake can still bite—he crossed the street and disappeared behind the Jitney Jungle as we stood staring at the pool of blood congealing on the blistering pavement.

7

My parents and Aunt India had departed and Tommy, L.Q.C., and I had begun settling into what would soon become our summer routine. It had been several days since Sheriff Fly had killed the black racer on Main Street. All three of us had been shocked by the sudden, unexpected violence. But what affected me more was the savage joy displayed by Fly and the others as they tormented the snake. And if I were honest with myself, there was the awareness that not only had we not tried to save it—after all, Winston had said it was harmless—but we had gone along. We had been swept up by the crowd. We had a pretty good idea of what Cordelia would say about that, and a secret sense of shame kept us from mentioning the episode around the dinner table.

I stood alone in the big backyard on the brink of the ravine. For me, the ravine had an enticing wildness, a powerful and not entirely benevolent aura, completely foreign to my suburban existence in Memphis. When I was wandering alone in the ravine I often drifted into a sort of waking dream-state, and it was easy to believe that in its depths dwelled all manner of things, seen and unseen.

I was thinking about the night before. Sitting between Tommy and me on the sofa, Cordelia had read aloud from an old edition of *The Knights of the Round Table*. She loved to read aloud from the classics, and though I was perfectly capable of reading the story myself, it was somehow more interesting, more comforting, to sit idly at her side listening to the cadence of her old-fashioned Mississippi voice, soaking up the life with which she instilled the characters, savoring the aroma of the old book and the presence of things that have lasted.

Now I saw myself seated at the Round Table, one of the knights around that magical table crafted by Merlin for King Uther Pendragon. It was the feast of Pentecost when miraculous events were to be expected. Now the room grew dark, and I heard a great wind rising outside the hall at Camelot. Thunder shook the castle, and then a strange quiet filled the gloom....

"Harry, what on earth are you doing out there?" cried Cordelia from the back stoop, interrupting my daydream. "Dinner is on the table, and everyone is waiting for you so we can have the blessing! Come in here at once before it gets cold!"

As usual, Cordelia sat at the head of the dining room table nearest the kitchen. Horace faced her at the other end, and Tommy and I sat on one side separated from L.Q.C. by the platters of vegetables, cornbread, and country fried steak. "You all save room for dessert now," instructed Cordelia. "Senatobia has made some of that boiled custard you like so much, Harry.

"And, Tommy, let's start the summer off right. I want you to hold that fork properly, not like some hoodlum about to stab an old piece of 'possum!"

The sunny room had grown dim as clouds gathered outside. Through the bay window we could see big raindrops thudding to the dry ground in tiny explosions of dust. "Oh, no! Not more rain," lamented Tommy as thunder growled in the distance somewhere out over the rolling North Mississippi hills, and a cool gust of air billowed the gauze curtains. They floated outward into the room like ghostly guests arriving late for dinner.

"Harry, will you return thanks?" asked Cordelia, and I groaned inwardly. "Harry, did you hear me?" she repeated, and I dutifully launched into a solemn Presbyterian grace, delivered without any special conviction.

"Can we read some more about the knights after supper tonight?" I asked when I finished.

"Naw, I'm tired of that," protested L.Q.C. "Cordelia said we could start *The Adventures of Huckleberry Finn*."

"Perhaps a bit of Mark Twain would be nice for a change," replied Cordelia. "He had a very progressive view of race relations for his time. The whole notion that the main characters, Huck and Jim, a Negro man, could be friends and treat each other as equals was hard for many people to accept. And it still is today. I had to fight hard to get that book placed in the library at the high school, and every other year or so there's a campaign to have it removed."

"Pretty darn naive, too, if you ask me," Horace said. "Why, I work with colored men on the railroad every day. I tell you, they just don't seem to want to get ahead. Half the time they're late for work, and when they do show up, they're hung over from the night before. I even found Sid, the fireman on Elroy Perkins' engine, asleep in a coal car the other day. Imagine that! Snoring away on a pile of coal just like it was a featherbed—at two o'clock in the afternoon!"

"Well, I expect if what you did all day long was shovel coal, you'd have a beer or two in the evening and catch a cat nap when you could!" Cordelia replied.

"You forget. I *have* shoveled coal. You don't start out on the railroad driving the engine! You pay your dues, obey the rules, and work your way up inch by inch if you don't want to stay a fireman all your life." I was surprised to hear what sounded like resentment in his voice.

"But, Horace, surely you'll admit that no Negro fireman is ever going to be allowed to sit at that throttle, no matter how smart he is or how hard he works."

"That's railroad policy, Cordelia. Those are the rules. We don't make them, but we sure have to follow them if we want to keep our jobs. That's the way it is, the way it's always been, and the way it'll stay. At least for my lifetime—and yours. And now, if you'll excuse me, I've got some paperwork to catch up on."

We all sat in silence as Horace balled up his napkin, pushed back his chair, and marched out of the dining room. Where had Horace's anger come from? I tried to remember if I had ever heard him raise his voice to Cordelia before.

"Now, boys," Cordelia said as we listened to him climbing the stairs, "Horace sometimes says things he doesn't mean, especially when he's tired or he's worried about things at work. He means well, and it's very important to him to be fair. But there's a lot of tension on the railroad these days. Men are worried about getting laid off with no pay or even losing their jobs altogether. There have even been some rumors about a strike. They're frustrated because no one listens to their concerns, and some are even blaming all the unrest on the Negro men who've begun demanding better working conditions. It's called 'scapegoating'—you blame your troubles on those who are the least powerful and least able to defend themselves."

I tried to make sense of the situation, but it all seemed very remote and abstract. But Horace had a point. I had seen the way the black porter at the depot lounged around between trains, sometimes slipping around to the back for a quick game of dice or a swig of bootleg whiskey. But I had also seen the way Sid and the other black firemen worked the steam engines, toiling constantly to feed the insatiable hunger of the great boilers with heaping scoops of coal.

They were sleek, lean men with bulging muscles in their arms and backs and a quick intelligence. They smiled often, and I had never heard one complain. So Cordelia was right, too.

What bothered me most was the discord between Horace and Cordelia. Ordinarily they seemed like the perfect couple, calm and respectful of each other, complementary in their interests and outlook on life. Now that I had seen them at odds, a shadow seemed to have fallen over dinner.

"What do you think is going to happen?" L.Q.C. asked her. "Will there be another railroad strike? I remember Horace was at home for a couple of weeks after the last one."

"Lord only knows," she replied in a preoccupied voice. "But Horace is a member of the union, and if there is a strike, then he'll have to take part along with all the others. Now, you boys go change your clothes and run on outside. It looks like the rain has stopped."

Wearing our freshly starched khaki shorts and white T-shirts, L.Q.C., Tommy, and I converged in the backyard. The grass shone after the brief shower, and as the endless afternoon stretched before us, the lingering tension from the dinner table seemed to melt away.

A commotion erupted from the bushes followed by a screech that would have shamed a banshee. In a flash of green and blue from under the lilac at the rear of the garage, half flying, half running, sailed Cordelia's peacock, Caruso. Her chickens in the little coop behind the garage were fluttering about in panic. Close behind Caruso exploded a blur of white, as Sparkplug, Horace's little terrier, charged after him, barking and nipping at his tail feathers. The peacock abruptly stopped, turned to face his tormentor, and with a great show of dignity spread his tail into an impressive fan. Sparkplug stopped in his tracks, intimidated by this show of defiance, and then in an apparent loss of interest trotted off to examine some enigmatic scent in the high grass at the edge of the ravine.

"Why does Cordelia bother keeping that old peacock anyway?" asked Tommy. "All he ever does is strut around looking important. He doesn't even lay eggs."

"He's her watch dog," replied L.Q.C. in a professorial tone. "More reliable than Sparkplug. Peacocks are territorial as well as decorative; if a stranger comes into the yard, old Caruso screams bloody murder."

It was my idea, inspired by our reading, to reenact the knightly quest for the Holy Grail. Tommy readily agreed, as long as he could bring Sparkplug along. L.Q.C. could hardly oppose the majority, although he insisted on playing the part of Sir Lancelot. Tommy was to be Sir Percival, as was only right since he was the youngest, and I appropriated the role of Sir Galahad.

We were cheerful enough as we began our descent into the leafy otherworld of the ravine, down through the briars and honeysuckle, past clumps of poison ivy and groves of sumac. Sparkplug scampered ahead on his own quest for a squirrel or a rabbit, pausing to cock a back leg and anoint his territory. But as we descended, the light filtering through the canopy of oak and hickory grew dim. Somewhere below, the muted gurgle of the creek was becoming a rush. L.Q.C. stumbled on a grapevine and cussed aloud in a most unknightly manner. I tried to ignore him and concentrate on my quest.

I was Galahad leaving Camelot where I had done better in the tournament than any of the other knights. Now I rode alone in search of adventure. I had to remain vigilant and alert, ready for any challenge that might come my way. Perhaps I would stumble upon some ruined abbey where I would be invited in by a gray-bearded monk to spend the night.

We arrived at Persimmon Creek and paused to gaze into the surging current. We had experienced several days of heavy showers and the water was opaque with churned-up silt. I tried not to think of the quicksand that we had been warned awaited the unwary swimmer. Normally the creek twisted amiably through town, its waters ambling along on their way to the lazy Skuna River, eventually finding their way via the Yalobusha and the Yazoo to the Mississippi. But its source remained a mystery, even to Horace. I imagined it arose in an enchanted Druid chapel hidden away in the hills, where in the cloister garden a magic spring bubbled from a bottomless well shrouded with moss, with eyeless snakes swimming in blind circles. Perhaps that was even the source of the black racer that had emerged into the sunlight of Main Street, the one Sheriff Fly had clubbed to death only days before. I could still hear the sound as the snake's head was shattered under the butt of the shotgun.

The path leveled out as we approached the little community of cabins on the opposite bank where the black people lived. The house nearest the water, where a spirit tree stood in the yard, was the home of Winston, the Jitney Jungle delivery "boy" as he was known. Winston lived there with his parents, Robert and Senatobia. I knew the little family well. Robert worked around Horace and Cordelia's house as a handyman, and Senatobia was their cook. Many times I had seen Senatobia eyeing a brightly colored empty bottle in Cordelia's kitchen in search of an interesting new specimen to take home for her spirit tree. Washed clean and hung over a bare twig, it would help keep spells and haints away.

"Let's wade across to Buzzard Bottom," suggested L.Q.C.

I hesitated; the water looked deep. "I don't know; maybe we should look for a shallow spot."

"Come on, this is a good place," he called, slipping off his sneakers and hanging them around his neck by the laces.

"Come on, Harry, I'll carry Sparkplug," Tommy said, scooping up the terrier in his arms and stepping into the current.

Something told me to refuse, but I resisted the inner warning. "Okay, okay," I muttered, giving in.

I had reached the midpoint of the creek, the water up to my knees, when the sandy bottom gave way. Instantly I sank up to my waist. As I tried to turn and wade back to the bank, I felt a powerful suction envelop my legs. "Hey!" I shouted to L.Q.C. and Tommy. "I'm stuck—I can't move!"

Losing my balance in the current, I almost toppled over; before I could find my footing in the muck, I had sunk deeper. When I finally righted myself, I was buried to my chest in brown ooze.

"Holy shit, it's quicksand!" exclaimed L.Q.C. "Quick, Tommy, run to Robert's house!"

I couldn't move, and I was slowly sinking. I tried to struggle, but that only seemed to make things worse. "Quick, throw me a stick or something!"

Tommy and L.Q.C. had both managed to reach the far bank. I watched helplessly as Tommy and Sparkplug sprinted for the cabin and L.Q.C. madly searched in the brush for a dead branch to extend to me.

Now I could taste cold water and the grit of sand as I sank up to my chin. I was sinking deeper, and, as the blackness closed over me, I could see L.Q.C. standing on the bank, tears streaming down his face. The chilly embrace of the mud enveloped me as I was drawn deeper and deeper into the bottomless hole. I gasped for air but only managed to suck in a mouthful of muck. So this is what it's like to die, I thought.

Then something seized me in a vise-like grip. In one powerful surge I was lifted free, sputtering and wheezing. Arms like tree trunks embraced me, holding me tight against a massive warm chest heaving with exertion. I was carried to the bank and felt myself laid gently on the grass. When I finally stopped choking and managed to open my eyes, I was gazing into a broad, caramel-colored face. Maybe I'm dead and this is my guardian angel, I thought.

I remembered Horace's remarks at dinner about lazy black firemen asleep on the job. If only he knew that angels were black.

8

It took a lot of scrubbing, but by the time I had finally washed off all the sand and slime in the big, claw-footed tub, been wrapped in blankets by Cordelia, and put to bed in the tower room, I felt all right. Just very, very tired, as though some part of me had been drained away in the creek. Now that it had dawned on me that I had almost died, the realization haunted me. I had somehow assumed that I was immune to death. I had thought that death only overtook old people shriveled away in nursing homes or drunken rednecks who managed to stall their pickups on railroad crossings. It would never happen to me, and certainly not on a clear summer day in a shallow creek in the ravine only ten minutes away from Cordelia's.

What would it be like to be dead? Mr. Estes, the minister, said that some people, like atheists, Communists, and Jews—all those who had failed to accept Christ—would go to hell, while others, like Presbyterians, would go to heaven. That seemed a bit extreme for God, who was also said to be about love. But who was I to question Mr. Estes or the Bible? And if everybody was automatically going to heaven, then what was the point of leading a good life? The other alternative, that there was just nothing at all, was hard to grasp. How could you even think about not existing?

I fell into a deep sleep, and it was then that the nightmares started, terrifying dreams in which I could taste the silt flooding into my mouth, the numbing cold of the water, and the greedy darkness sucking me downward. Weeks later, and even after I had ostensibly recovered, there were moments during the day when, without warning, the quicksand seemed to come for me again, leaving me trembling and gasping for air. I would have nothing more to do with the ravine, which had now become a place of menace for me, and invented some excuse whenever Tommy or L.Q.C. proposed an expedition there.

Cordelia insisted that I stay in bed. She asked if I wanted her to call my father and mother to take me home, but I had said no. That would surely mean the end of the summer in Tuckalofa. Of course, my mother heard about it and came anyway. From the moment she arrived, I could tell she was watching me closely, looking for any sign of complications.

I lay in the tower room listening to the fan, watching the sheer curtains billowing in the breeze, a pile of the latest comic books from Carlisle's next to me. "L.Q.C. picked them out," Cordelia told me. "There's a new *Blackhawk* and a *Superman* and I don't know what all."

Except for my mother's hovering over me, it was actually quite pleasant lying there like an invalid—as long as one didn't have polio or typhoid fever and wasn't missing an arm or a leg like some of the soldiers I had heard about in the VA Hospital in Memphis. During the day I amused myself imagining the billowing folds in the white bedspread as the mountains and valleys of a vast, snow-covered arctic landscape. In the evening I became the center of attention as my mother, L.Q.C., and Tommy gathered around my bed while Cordelia read to us, although no one wanted to talk about what had happened in the creek. Finally, on the second day of my recuperation, Cordelia knocked on my door.

"Harry, you have a visitor," she announced. "It's Winston. None of us will ever forget it was he who saved your life. He carried you up here to the house in his arms and wouldn't leave until the doctor had come and told us you weren't seriously injured."

"Hey there, Harry," called Winston, stepping into the bedroom, a bit hesitantly it seemed. He was wearing his white Jitney Jungle apron, grinning down at me. "I come to see if you got all the sand out of your ears! Miss Cordelia says there was a inch of goop in the bottom of that bathtub before they got it all off you. You know, they ought to post a sign or something down at that old sinkhole so's nobody else steps in there. Daddy once lost his old hound dog in that same spot.

"All you can do if you falls into quicksand is lie still and try to float. Then sometime you can get out. If you tries to fight it, it gonna win every time."

He sat down on the side of the bed and picked up my new *Superman* comic book. I stared at his brown hands and the muscles of his biceps beneath the tightly stretched sleeve of his white T-shirt. A wave of gratitude broke over me, and I remembered my astonishment as I was ripped out of the muck and gazed up at his face to discover that angels were black. Could Winston really be an angel? He certainly didn't resemble the pale, delicate creatures in the stained glass windows of the Presbyterian Church. He looked more like Superman to me, although of course there could be no doubt that Superman was white. But suppose Superman was just a type of angel? Maybe there were other angels around too, disguised as regular people like Winston and Clark Kent? What if the church had it all wrong? How many other people had ever encountered an angel anyhow?

"You like Superman too, huh? He's my favorite," Winston said.

"Yeah, this one's got a story about when he was a baby and he first landed on Earth in that rocket ship from the planet Krypton and he gets found by this farmer named Mr. Kent and they raise him like their own kid and...."

"Yeah," added Winston, "and later on it turn out there's this meteor made of green Kryptonite, and whenever ol' Superman get near it, he loses all them super powers."

As we talked, I was amazed to find that even though he was black, Winston knew more about Superman than I did. Soon we were deep in discussion about why no one ever got wise to Clark Kent or found his regular clothes in the phone booth where he changed into the Man of Steel. "He got a secret pocket in his cape where he keep his clothes," Winston confided.

After a while there was a cough at the bedroom door. "Wait here for just a moment, please," I heard Cordelia say. "He's right in here in the bedroom." She stepped into the room. "Winston was just winding up his visit, weren't you, Winston? I know Harry enjoyed seeing you."

Winston stood. "Well, good-bye, Harry. You come to see us now. I got some old *Supermans* you'd like. And I got to tell you 'bout this coon hunt last Saturday night. Just be careful crossing that creek, you hear?

"Come on now, give ol' Winston a hug." He leaned over and enveloped me in his arms, and once more I was crushed against the hard muscles of his chest. I flung my arms around his neck, pulling him down toward me, not wanting him to go. Then he grinned at me, stood up, and turned to leave. At the door Cordelia was waiting, and as he disappeared, I thought I saw her take his hand. Then I could hear the stairs creak as he descended.

I gawked as Mr. Estes, the minister, and his daughter stepped into the room behind Cordelia. Blair was wearing a little short tennis skirt that dared me to stare at those legs. I realized I was wearing my pajamas, and I felt the heat in my face and neck. As casually as I could, I stuffed the pile of comic books out of sight under the sheet.

"You all just pull up a chair by the bed," Cordelia said. "Harry, you remember Mr. Estes and Blair, don't you? They've come to wish you a speedy recovery, I expect."

"That's right, Harry." He smiled at me, displaying his great white teeth, just like Charlton Heston in *Ben-Hur*. "By the way, Miss Cordelia, I hate to say anything, but do you think it's a good idea to have nigras upstairs in the bedrooms?"

"Oh, you mean Winston? Why, Winston's just like…" she paused. "I mean, Winston's been around since he was a little boy. His father, Robert, has worked for us doing odd jobs for years, and his mother, Senatobia, has been our cook ever since Winston was born."

"Nevertheless, with all that's happening these days, we need to be careful about appearances, don't you think?" He glanced over at me. "Perhaps we could just chat with Harry for a few minutes. We won't be long."

Cordelia disappeared, leaving us alone. They both sat down facing me. Blair crossed her legs, and I shifted in the bed so as to see a bit farther up the tennis skirt without being overly obvious.

"I brought you a little something to cheer you up," she chirped. "It's a tin of cookies I baked for you. Your aunt says you like chocolate, Harry." Her smile was like the sun breaking through. All at once I felt like my old self again, and the bedroom had suddenly become a prison.

"Wow!" I gushed, instantly regretting my childish response. "I mean, they look delicious. Thank you very much."

"Well, Harry, it's good to have you back in town for the summer," began Mr. Estes. "But I hear you've been through quite an ordeal. You could have drowned, and we should give thanks to God for your safety. I understand you and your brother and cousin were down in that ravine where the nigras live."

"Sure, we go down there a lot. We were pretending to be knights and …" I stopped in mid-sentence. What a jerk I was, admitting in front of Blair that I had been playing make-believe like a little boy. "I fell into a deep spot and couldn't get out. It wasn't really so bad. I'm just glad Winston came along."

"Yes, well, nigras can sometimes surprise us. They are strong, of course, and loyal and devoted when they are managed firmly. Harry, I know you like

Winston. But you must have heard that here in Mississippi we are being forced to make some changes that go against our Southern way of life. We are being forced by the Northern courts and the federal government to abandon bedrock Biblical principles that have always guided us with respect to relationships with the nigras. Or perhaps I should say the 'Negroes'—since that seems to be the term of choice in some of those Northern newspapers down at the library.

"The future of our white, Anglo-Saxon civilization lies in the hands of young people like you and Blair. In your character, your courage to stand up for what's right, even when it is not popular. Even when it means refusing to obey the dictates of an oppressive government. Do you understand what I'm saying, Harry?" Mr. Estes' dark eyes bored into mine with hypnotic power.

"Well, I guess so. But Cordelia says it's unfair for colored people not to have good schools, or to have to use separate restrooms, or to have to sit at the back of the bus, or not be able to go to the zoo in Memphis except on Tuesdays."

"Ah! Does she now?" Mr. Estes leaned forward in his chair. "Well, your Aunt Cordelia does have some unconventional ideas.

"Harry, I know you are a fine Christian young man. Did you know the Bible warns us against mixing the races? Oh, yes, it most certainly does. Throughout scripture we are warned that God has decreed that there are to be masters and servants, and that the servants are to be obedient.

"And scientists have found that nigras are genetically inferior to whites. They came from Africa and are closely related to the apes. Their forebrains are not as well developed and that is why they are given to sexual promiscuity, suggestive dancing, and even criminal behavior. Did you know that? No, I don't expect you did, Harry.

"Did you ever think about why there are no big cities in Africa? Why all the great scientific and industrial advances have been made by white, Anglo-Saxon societies? I don't wish the nigras any ill. But I know that they need to be guided, to have their animalistic instincts restrained. That is why we must resist the integration laws, Harry. The courts and all those Communist judges are trying to force us to mix our blood with theirs, to make us all one!"

"Gosh, I didn't know all that," I stammered.

"And do you know that there's even a group of Communist students and faculty from that nigra college up in Holly Springs that's been riding around on a bus and showing up unannounced at white churches on Sunday mornings, demanding to be let inside? Demanding! Claiming to be there to worship! Why, I hope they show up at our church; we'll be ready for them!"

I heard footsteps in the hall and saw Cordelia at the door.

"Well, Harry, I expect it's time for your afternoon nap," she announced. "We do so appreciate your coming by, Mr. Estes, but he's on the brink of pneumonia from that freezing creek!" She seemed pleasant enough, but I noticed a fire in her eyes that hadn't been there before.

"Oh, of course, Miss Cordelia," Mr. Estes said. "We were just finishing up, weren't we, Blair? Come along; let's let Harry get some rest.

"Just remember what I've been telling you, young man. Perhaps we can talk again another day."

I glanced again at Cordelia, trying to tell how much of the conversation with Mr. Estes she had overheard. Blair waved to me sweetly from the door and turned away with a little swish of her tennis skirt.

Cordelia left me to my nap, but I only pretended to sleep. I could tell she was happy to see him go; I knew she and Mr. Estes didn't see eye to eye. But Mr. Estes had given me a lot to think about, such as why there were two of everything—black and white drinking fountains on Main Street, black and white restrooms, and black and white waiting rooms at the depot. Before, I had simply taken it all for granted, but now I saw that there were reasons, sound reasons it seemed, behind the separation of the races. God had ordained it, if you could believe Mr. Estes. And surely a minister wouldn't lie.

But it was confusing too. If God was fair and just, as my mother and Cordelia said, then why did colored people have to pick up white people's garbage and clean their toilets? Maybe they had committed some terrible crime and God was punishing them.

I was finding it hard to concentrate on these questions though. Every time I began to make a little progress, my thinking was interrupted by the recollection of the exquisite Blair. I imagined her on the tennis court, her tanned limbs flashing in the sun, little beads of perspiration on her upper lip, her breasts jiggling merrily as she sprinted for the ball. She had brought me a gift. Was it out of pity, or did she actually like me a little bit? If only I were three or four years older! Thank God I was tall for my age and my voice was finally changing. Maybe she assumed I was a lot older than I was.

I stared at the ceiling. It was better to stay awake than to give in to the nap and the dreams it might bring, but outside the window the lazy buzzing of the wasps in the eaves was luring me away. And then I was in the cold creek again, my legs encased in cement as the yellow water closed over me.

9

My first thought upon awaking, lying there alone in the rose-tinted sunlight of late afternoon, was of the lingering terror of the quicksand. It was followed quickly, however, by the memory of Blair's visit. Then I remembered that tomorrow was my birthday and that Horace had promised an excursion into the country where he would teach me to shoot. Sick of lying around, I dressed for the first time since my accident and, feeling a bit wobbly, ventured downstairs.

I found the house empty. From the back porch came an odd grinding noise. I went to investigate and found Cordelia on her knees cranking the White Mountain ice cream freezer. The sherbet had begun to solidify, and it was hard going for her. She smiled, pleased to see me up and about, and I offered to take a turn, but she refused. When I insisted, she reluctantly gave in, climbing stiffly to her feet and delicately dabbing at her forehead with the back of her hand. She sprinkled another layer of rock salt over the ice and took a seat on the porch steps where I could be properly supervised.

As I cranked, I took advantage of the opportunity to critically appraise my aunt. She was about sixty, I guessed, retired after almost forty years as a high school librarian—a living legend, beloved for her dedication to learning. Virtually everyone in Tuckalofa born between the early 1900s and the Second World War who ever heard of Chaucer, Shakespeare, Shelley, or Keats had first made their acquaintance in her library. I could remember a day spent with her as a child in that high-ceilinged school, the double-hung windows raised to admit a spring breeze and the smell of newly cut grass. On the wall she had hung a reproduction of a pre-Raphaelite painting of Sir Galahad in his flame-colored armor, kneeling in prayer. She sat at the front of the library, perched on a wooden stool, reading aloud to a group of students who had voluntarily gathered there during the lunch period. She was tall and slim and elegant with a commanding demeanor. Even the hulking football players and the chatty cheerleaders were silent, entranced by the soft cadence of her voice.

"Do you ever miss your library?" I asked, looking up from the ice cream freezer.

She was silent for a moment. "You know, Harry, I worked there all those years, but I absolutely despised most of being a librarian, keeping track of the books and trying to keep the place quiet. And I couldn't abide the Dewey Decimal System."

I was taken aback, given her reputation. "But, Cordelia, how in the world did you ever make it if you felt like that?"

"Well, I did love to read. So I spent a lot of my time just reading aloud to the students who would drop by. I saw to it that they could come to the library instead of study hall, and I developed quite a following. Most of the young people came from homes where no one ever read. They had never experienced the beauty of a poem or been caught up in a story. They had never heard of Robin Hood or Lancelot and Elaine or Tom Sawyer and Huck Finn. You should have seen their faces as I read *The Pit and the Pendulum*. Why when the bell rang, they wouldn't want to leave. So reading is mostly how I spent my time."

Out in the yard, Caruso, the peacock, was parading across the lawn with a commanding arrogance. Without warning, a blur of white exploded from under the garage as Sparkplug attacked. The haughty bird spun around and leapt into the air, wings fluttering madly, talons flailing. He uttered an unearthly shriek as Sparkplug gave a mighty leap, missed his target, and tumbled back to earth in a heap. Sparkplug looked around sheepishly, but Caruso had vanished.

The porch where we sat faced north. I cranked away at the freezer, grateful for the shade. Directly above us was Cordelia's bedroom where, as a young child, one cold, clear winter night, I had first discovered the stars. We had both been dressed for bed. Cordelia had switched off the lamp and beckoned to me to stand with her at the window. We took in the view over the backyard and the ravine beyond, the bare branches of the old oaks and hickories faintly silhouetted against the sky. She had pointed out the Big Dipper and then showed me how to follow the two pointers in the bowl to another star, suspended cold and alone, immobile above the pole.

"The slaves had their own name for the Dipper. They called it the Drinking Gourd, and they would follow it north to freedom along the Underground Railroad, the secret network of people who opposed slavery. And the Polynesians used the North Star to find their way to Hawaii; they discovered it when they first crossed the equator from the Southern Hemisphere. It was the one star that didn't move, and so they thought it must be a sign from the gods. Remember the Dipper, the pointers, and the North Star and you'll never be lost in the woods." Then she had shooed me off to bed, and as I closed the door to her bedroom, I could see her falling to her knees at the side of the bed to say her prayers.

The sherbet was beginning to freeze now, and I stopped cranking to take a breather. I felt a bit light-headed. "Harry, I'm a little worried about you," Cordelia said. "You've always been a sensitive sort, and sometimes you take things harder than other boys. You look pale, and I've heard you calling out in your sleep."

"I'm fine, really I am. Don't worry about me!" I protested, resuming cranking the sherbet a little more vigorously to demonstrate my fitness. Cordelia sat watching me in silence.

"Harry, what were you and Mr. Estes talking about up in the bedroom? I noticed that as soon as I came in he stopped."

"Oh, nothing much. He was just explaining about niggers and how we need to be careful about them, you know."

"Harry! We don't use that word in this house!"

"Well, maybe not," I said, "but so what? It's what everybody at school says."

"I don't care. Only common hoodlums say that. We don't say it in our family. It's crude and offensive. You may say 'Negro,' or 'colored,' if you prefer."

"Yes, ma'am," I replied meekly.

"Very well. So what else did he explain, Harry?"

"He said it was up to young people to save civilization, even if we had to disobey the law to do it."

"Hmm, when he talks about disobeying the law I doubt he's defending the civil rights activists we've been reading about. Breaking the law because you disagree with it is a serious business that can only be justified in the most extreme cases. And then what?"

"Well, he told me about how the Bible says the races shouldn't mix together and how colored people are descended from apes."

"So, tell me, Harry. What did you say to Mr. Estes after he said that about the Bible and Negroes?"

"Not much," I admitted. "I tried to think of something to say, but I couldn't think of anything. I mean, he's a minister and he knows what the Bible says. And after all, colored people do come from Africa, just like apes do. I hadn't thought about that before, but they have those thick lips and big flat noses. And they're real strong, like the gorillas in the Tarzan movies—just look at Winston. They're not like us. They drive beat up old cars and live in dirty little shacks."

"And would you say this holds true for all Negroes?"

"Sure—most of them. Just look at those shacks down in the ravine..."

"Have you ever been inside a Negro's house?"

"Well, no. But I've heard stories about them. And they're mostly janitors and garbage men. They're poor, and wear old clothes. They don't take many baths; and lots of them, especially the garbage men, don't smell very good. And they're hard to understand—it's like they have their own language. They don't read books like we do, and it doesn't seem like they're as smart as white people. I sure wouldn't want somebody in my family to marry one."

"I see. What else did you and Mr. Estes discuss?"

"Well, he explained there are colored people who are Communists who are going around to all the churches stirring up trouble, and that they may be coming here on a bus. I've heard Horace talking about that too. Horace says he's worried."

Cordelia beckoned to me. "Harry, come sit on the steps here. The sherbet's almost done, so you can take a break. There are some things you and I need to talk about." I sat down beside her, and she wrapped an arm around my shoulders. "Now, Harry, this may be a little hard for you to understand, but you can't believe everything adults tell you—even if they are important people in the community, like Mr. Estes, or even Horace, for that matter. Mr. Estes may know something about religion, but I doubt he's ever had a course in anthropology or sociology. So when he talks about the evolution of the human species or racial differences in intelligence, or politics for that matter, he's just giving you his opinion—his unscientific opinion. He's entitled to that of course, just as you are, but he's no expert. And you don't have to believe him just because he's a minister.

"In fact, some of the biggest messes in history, including wars and people being tortured and burned at the stake, were caused by ministers or priests who were sure they knew the truth and that everyone who disagreed with them was condemned to hell. I hate to have to tell you this, Harry, but you can't even take everything you read in the Bible literally—as a historical fact. Mr. Estes told you that parts of the Bible approve of slavery. Did he also tell you that the Bible says we shouldn't eat pork? Or that women should keep quiet in church? Or that Joshua ordered the sun to stop in the sky? You see, Harry, many of those stories were written for people who lived thousands of years ago in primitive, pre-scientific cultures. They relied on religion to explain the mysterious forces of nature, like what causes people to get sick, or why we have different seasons. They reassured themselves that God preferred some groups of people to others. And strangely enough, it seems God always approved of the ones who were telling the stories. Why back in the Great War the German army wore belts with 'God is With Us' inscribed on the buckle."

I paused and thought about this. "So, if you can't believe what other people tell you and you can't believe the Bible, then how do you know what to believe?"

"You learn how to think for yourself. You learn how to look up your own answers to important questions and how to put the pieces together to form a whole that makes sense. That way, when you read something or when someone tries to convince you that something is true, you don't have to believe it until you've reasoned it out for yourself. It doesn't matter that they may be older than you. Truth is no respecter of age. They should have good reasons for their position. If they don't, then just politely tell them you're not convinced."

"Cordelia, are you a Christian? Mr. Estes says that's the most important thing in the world. That unless you believe in Jesus you'll go to hell."

She looked calmly down at me. "What do you think, Harry? Reason it out for yourself."

"Well," I hesitated, "you go to church. And you say your prayers before you go to sleep and when you get up in the morning."

"Anything else?" she asked.

I thought a minute.

"Well, you seem like you care about other people—the students you had at school, Tommy and L.Q.C., me and Winston, Robert and Senatobia, and Horace. And I've heard you say it's not fair that colored people have to ride in the back of the bus and can't go to restaurants."

"And what about going to hell if you don't believe in Jesus?" she asked.

"Well, wouldn't that mean that hell is pretty full? I mean, what about all the people in China and India—good people—who've never even heard of Jesus? And what about Moses—he died before Jesus was even born. Wouldn't it mean that Moses is—"

"How's it coming out here?" We turned to see my mother watching us through the screen door.

"Oh, Ellen, it's you. Harry and I were just having a little talk."

"Cordelia, you're not filling Harry with more of those radical ideas of yours, I hope."

"On the contrary. But he's a bright boy and old enough to know that things aren't always as simple as they seem."

So my mother had been listening to our conversation. I was aware that she and Cordelia didn't always agree, particularly about politics and religion, and that she might not have been pleased at all she had heard. I felt uneasy when they occasionally argued. But Cordelia had certainly given me a lot to think about.

While it was nice to have my mother visit for a little while, her over-protectiveness had quickly begun to get on my nerves. She was still insisting that I take a nap every afternoon, followed by a bath. I looked forward to her departure when we would once more have the run of the town, answerable only to Cordelia's benevolent dictatorship.

"Let's see," Cordelia said. "I think we need a little more ice for the sherbet. Harry can keep turning while I run down to Carlisle's and get us another bag."

"I'll tell you what; let me just drive us all down there," my mother countered. "Harry needs a break, and it's too hot for either of you to walk all the way to Main Street. We'll be back in ten minutes. The sherbet will keep that long."

We turned out of the driveway and headed down the steep incline toward Main Street. Far below us at the bottom of the hill, directly opposite the point where Lee Street intersected Main Street, stood Carlisle's Drugstore, just as it had since the early 1900s. We parked in front of the store. "Now, I'm going to pay for this," Cordelia stated with authority.

"Oh, no, Cordelia, this is my treat," replied my mother, reaching for her patent leather purse.

"I really must insist," repeated Cordelia, "This sherbet is my project— mine and Harry's that is—and I'm in charge of financing it."

"You know perfectly well that you paid for yesterday's groceries, and that makes it my turn. But I'm not going to sit here in this hot car arguing about it. Come on, Harry, let's go inside where it's cool!"

As we neared the entrance, my mother pointed to the display window. "Cordelia, do you remember that little miniature model of the Taj Mahal you brought home from your trip to India? And Mr. Carlisle offered to put it right there in his window where the whole town could admire it."

But Cordelia was fumbling in her purse. We marched into Carlisle's, my mother in the lead, and stepped up to the high, ornately carved soda fountain.

"Why, hello there, Miss Cordelia, Miss Ellen," called the balding man behind the counter. "What can I get you today?"

"Martin, you remember my nephew, Harry, from Memphis, don't you?" asked Cordelia. She pronounced it "nev-vew." "Harry, I know you've heard me speak of Martin McCrory. He was one of my students."

"Sure, Harry and I know each other. He's one of my best customers. Harry, I've knowed Miss Cordelia all my life. She may've been the librarian, but she's the one what learned me proper English."

My mother was reaching into her purse, but Cordelia was faster. "We'll have a bag of ice, Martin. Here's a five. I haven't got anything smaller." My mother gave Cordelia a look.

On the drive back up Lee Street, Cordelia turned to my mother. "Ellen, when you mentioned that little model of the Taj Mahal in the drugstore window, it reminded me of something. Harry, that drugstore is the reason your mother doesn't like me to drive," she announced cheerfully. My mother rolled her eyes.

"Our parents' first car was a Model T Ford, one of the first ones in Tuckalofa. One day I had driven it over to Grenada to shop for a new dress. I remember that it was back when Richard Watson and I were going together, and there was to be a big Okra Festival dance that night. As I was driving back up Lee Street, I remembered that I had promised to drop off a pair of shoes for Mary Clark Bell to wear to the party and had forgotten to take them with me. I was in such a hurry to run inside for the shoes that I left the car parked at the curb facing down the hill instead of in the driveway like we usually did.

"I ran upstairs and then hurried back down and out to the street. Well, that car was just nowhere to be seen. What I didn't know until later was that at that very minute, my mother and daddy were sitting inside Carlisle's at the soda fountain. There was a great crash, and the entire plate glass front window shattered. They stared in amazement at the empty Model T Ford that had come to rest in the front of the drugstore, not five feet away. The place was a perfect shambles, but that model of the Taj Mahal in the window wasn't even scratched. My mother turned to my father and said, 'I declare, George, that looks like *our* car!'"

10

You only turn thirteen once, of course, and I had been eagerly anticipating my birthday for weeks. The official entry into young adulthood carried with it the promise of adventure, independence, and a world of largely unknown delights involving the opposite sex. Now that it had arrived, I found it difficult to think of anything else. Thankfully, I had slept through the night without the nightmares that were becoming frequent. I had lain in bed for a long time listening to the world coming alive and contemplating the day ahead. Finally, hearing faint sounds of activity from below, I rushed down the stairs toward the kitchen, pausing at the threshold so as to lend a casual air to my grand entrance.

Horace was spreading the last of the sorghum molasses on a biscuit. Despite the fact that it was his day off, he was wearing his usual vest and tie, held in place by a gold bar and chain. He had been away on the road, but had returned the previous day bringing a renewed promise of a birthday surprise. As I took my seat at the breakfast table, however, he simply looked up and nodded a greeting. My heart sank. Had he forgotten?

My mother, who had delayed her return home in honor of the occasion, smiled prettily. "Well, it's a big day for you, Harry!" she announced. "We let you sleep late, you know. Tommy and L.Q.C. have been up for an hour."

Cordelia, standing at the sink, beamed warmly. "What would you like for breakfast, Harry? How about some hotcakes? Maybe you'd even like to try a cup of coffee. I remember I was thirteen when I began having a cup every morning."

Horace was brushing the biscuit crumbs over the edge of the table and into his hand. He stood and stepped out onto the back porch where he sprinkled the crumbs on the steps. As the screen door popped closed behind him, I watched a blue jay alight and begin to strut and peck at the scraps. A gray squirrel sat on an overhanging limb of the pecan tree barking at the jay.

"I expect that squirrel will be down here in a minute to say hello," he said. "Squirrels just seem to like me." He turned to Cordelia. "I'm surprised you don't like them more yourself, dear. You all have a lot in common. You're both smart and not overly respectful of authority."

What did Horace and Cordelia really think of each other? In public they unfailingly presented the image of the perfect couple, devoted to each other in every respect. But occasionally, a remark or the subtle shading of a phrase would have an edge. I had begun to wonder if there was something more to their seemingly idyllic relationship.

Even though breakfast was over, there was still no sign of the special birthday surprise promised by Horace. Disappointed and mystified, I left the table and prowled around the house, looking for something to occupy the time until the start of the festivities I hoped were to come.

On a hall tree at the foot of the stairs were stacked countless back issues of Horace's *National Geographics*, their gold covers shimmering in the dim light that filtered through the glass of the front door. The time-worn novels of Edgar Rice Burroughs and Richard Halliburton gathering dust in the parlor bookcase held no interest for me today, so I tried to content myself with flipping through the old magazines. Sitting on the cool floor of the hall, inspired by the exotic photographs, I conquered the slopes of Kilimanjaro and basked in the admiring smiles of a bevy of bare-breasted native women with bones in their noses. Next I turned to an article on the swords of the British Empire, exotic ceremonial objects with ornate pommels and gleaming blades of Damascus steel, engraved with rampant griffins, anchors, and mermaids.

We had a sword too. It hung above the front door in the shadows over the transom. The sword had always been there, as much a part of the house as Horace's rocking chair in the front room or the piano that had once belonged to L.Q.C. Lamar with Cordelia's Presbyterian hymnbook lying open on the shelf above the keyboard.

"Hey, Horace," I called out. "Whose old sword is this anyhow?"

After a moment I heard the floorboards squeak, and my uncle appeared in the doorway, a straight-backed dining room chair in his hands. He set the chair next to the front door. "Well, go on; climb up there and hand it down. Let's have a look."

It was much heavier than I expected. The scabbard was plain and black and unlike the swords in the magazine, no gold filigree festooned the hilt. The blade curved like a scythe and glinted dully. Along its arc no mermaids or griffins danced; there was only a sleek, lethal smoothness, like the blade of a butcher knife. It was cold to the touch, a weapon designed for efficient killing, for maiming and amputation, not for the pomp of the parade ground.

"Come in here to the parlor and I'll show you something," Horace said, taking the sword. He pointed at the portrait hanging over the piano. I had glanced at it a hundred times before but as we stood facing it, I studied it more closely—an old oil painting of a middle-aged man in a black suit. From beneath a wide-brimmed black hat an unsmiling, ascetic face peered sternly back at me. The thin lips were drawn in a determined line above a square jaw. The eyes, a frosty light blue, shone with a peculiar intensity, the eyes of a poet or an artist set in the face of a frontiersman.

"That's Thomas Boyd Coltharp, my great-grandfather." I looked at Horace, recognizing for the first time those same eyes, pale blue like the sparks from a dynamo. "This sword belonged to him, and he carried it into battle with Nathan Bedford Forrest's cavalry. It used to hang over the door of the log cabin where my father was born out in Lovejoy County." Now I saw the familiar portrait in a new light. Thomas Boyd Coltharp's gaze was as hard and unyielding as the tempered steel of his sword.

"You see, Harry, old Thomas was a pioneer. He came from a family of Indian-fighters. He was tough and resilient, and he had a strong sense of duty to his country. He had principles he was willing to stand up for. That's a rare quality in life, you know. You're getting to be a young man now, and you should begin thinking about these things. And you should be learning some of the skills that men need to have.

"Cordelia just reminded me that today's your birthday. I know I promised you something special. And I reckon it's time you knew how to shoot. Why don't you step over there and have a look behind the dining room door?"

Joy flooded my heart. I knew that leaning in the corner behind the dining room door was Horace's bolt-action, single-shot .22 rifle. I had been forbidden to touch it until I turned thirteen, but I sneaked a peek whenever I could, transfixed by the sober materiality of the wooden stock, gray steel barrel, and shiny brass trigger. For me the rifle was a concrete representation of the abstractions of justice, adventure, life, and death. Guns were inseparable from the kind of life I aspired to. With such a weapon, I could relive the exploits of the cowboys in the Westerns we watched with Horace on his new television, picking off bandits in hot pursuit of our Wells Fargo stagecoach. Like Ramar of the Jungle, another favorite hero, I could coolly dispatch a charging lion with a single well-placed shot to the heart. Like Thomas Boyd Coltharp, the fearless Confederate cavalryman, I could ward off the marauding Yankees. If only I could learn to shoot.

I rushed into the dining room and pulled back the door. There it stood—a big red bow tied to the barrel. I snatched it up, beaming, waving it about in glee. L.Q.C., who along with Tommy had quietly stepped around the corner to watch me receive my gift, held up his hands in surrender.

"Whoa! Hold it right there!" Horace exclaimed. "It's yours now, but first you've got to learn how to handle it properly. And we'll leave it there behind the door except when we go out in the country for target practice. Here, hand it to me." He took the rifle and expertly snapped the bolt open to see that it was unloaded. Below the rolled-up sleeve of his shirt, the blue veins bulged over the muscles of his forearm. I was always surprised at the strength of my uncle who, before he became an engineer, had spent years shoveling coal into the fireboxes of steam locomotives. Then he cradled the stock under his arm, the barrel an inch from the floor.

"Cordelia," he called, "I think the boys and I'll ride out to the old home place. There're some things I want to show them. Should be back for lunch, I 'spect. You boys had better go put on your blue jeans."

So he had not forgotten after all and had already planned the day. And we would even wear our jeans; this was too good to be true. My mother and Cordelia forbade us to wear them downtown. "Only white trash wear blue jeans on Main Street. It's just so common—a sure sign of a lack of breeding." Out in the country it was a different matter, however, as they reluctantly conceded. The countryside was infested with poison ivy, chiggers, ticks, snakes, and worse; and when one left the confines of civilized society, it was only prudent to go prepared with sensible clothing.

"Here, you'd better take some water; it's going to be up in the nineties again." Cordelia handed me a large Mason jar filled with water and tinkling ice cubes, the glass surface already beginning to sweat. The rivulets rolled down its sides, leaving little wobbly tracks behind, snaking around the raised trademark cast in the surface. I stuffed the jar into the paper sack she offered me and wiped my damp hand on my jeans.

Horace pulled back the seat of his pickup truck and carefully stowed the rifle behind it. "Here. Put these in your pocket." He handed me a small, unexpectedly heavy cardboard box. Opening the lid, I marveled at the rows of brilliant brass cylinders alternating with sinister gray lead domes aligned in perfect regimental formation. The tip of each dome was punctuated by a small black hole.

"These are real bullets!"

"We call them cartridges, not bullets. They're hollow-points. They make a bigger hole in the target. You must be careful with them. We'll keep the box closed until we get there."

Tommy, L.Q.C., Sparkplug, and I all piled into the open bed of the truck. Horace backed around to head down the driveway. We bounced out of the driveway, scraping the bottom as usual, and headed down the hill and across the tracks to Main Street. Horace dangled his long, tan arm out the window to signal the turn, then downshifted and spun the wheel. We peeled smoothly around the corner past the Albemarle Hotel, cruising slowly through town with Horace touching the brim of his straw hat as people on the sidewalk nodded.

Then it was out of town and into the country. Here the roadside was shrouded in masses of the kudzu vines imported from Japan and planted throughout the South in an attempt to control erosion. Years later the unintended consequences included a fantastic landscape of leafy green giants, craggy mountains, plunging valleys, and cities with turreted castles and minarets. Sparkplug sat with his nose held high in the air, the wind full of the smell of manure and freshly cut hay. We crossed the muddy Skuna River, seemingly immobile, imprisoned in the swampy bottom where the cypress trees erupted from the bogs. Gray and gaunt, contrasting against the emerald lawn of duckweed, the trees reminded me of tombstones in a newly mown cemetery.

By the time we turned onto a gravel road, the windshield was covered with the innards of smashed grasshoppers. We rumbled across nameless dried-up creeks on ancient bridges of weathered boards that creaked ominously. Then we headed through pine woods, the dust-coated underbrush along the shoulder close enough to touch from the back of the truck. After ten minutes of white cotton fields alternating with black pine forests, we pulled up in front of a tiny wood-frame church set in a grove of oaks and hickories. "Mt. Pisgah Methodist Church" read a sign above the door. Nestled alongside, a little cemetery dozed in the shade, the mossy gravestones dappled in grays and olives. Although the church appeared to be utterly deserted, it was freshly painted and the grass was neatly trimmed. A pair of dragonflies buzzed around me, looping and rolling in a lazy courtship dance.

We spilled out of the truck, and Sparkplug immediately sprang after a squirrel with Tommy in pursuit. Horace yelled after them but they seemed not to hear. "That dog is incorrigible," he muttered.

With Horace in the lead, L.Q.C. and I passed by stones engraved with many of the Scots-Irish surnames familiar to me from gossip around the dinner table—Polk, Cates, McCorkle, and Harris. At the far side of the cemetery stood a moss-encrusted limestone marker in the shape of an obelisk. Bending close, we could just make out the weathered inscription on Horace's great-grandfather's grave.

Thomas Boyd Coltharp

1823–1899

"That's my great-grandmother next to him," Horace observed. "And right over there are two more of my great-grandparents, Iredell Holston Johnston and his wife, Emma. When the war came, he fought for the Confederates too.

"My daddy was born not more than a half-mile from here in a little cabin built by Thomas Boyd Coltharp. In a minute we'll go see if we can find what's left of it. About the same time, he and the neighbors built this church too. That was before the government built the dam and the reservoir and flooded most of our farm."

"Was Thomas Boyd Coltharp born here too?" asked L.Q.C.

"Nossir. He came here from Tennessee when he was a boy before the Civil War. He was one of the first pioneers in this part of Mississippi. Got here about 1840, not long after most of the Indians were either killed or marched off out west and the land was opened up to white settlers."

"Before the late 1830s," added L.Q.C., "there were still lots of Indians in Mississippi. But then the government rounded them all up and shipped them out to Oklahoma. That's when the white pioneers began arriving from Tennessee and the Carolinas. I've got an atlas at home that traces the major migrations of North America and—"

"Hold it, L.Q.C.!" I interrupted. "Let Horace finish. You might learn something! So what did he do when he got here, Horace?"

"Well, he built a log cabin for himself and his wife. He farmed and helped build the new Mississippi and Tennessee Railroad. After the war, they moved over here to Lovejoy County. Come on; let's round up Tommy and that no-good Sparkplug and I'll show you where they lived."

I was growing impatient with all this ancient history, although I found it intriguing that the present could be more completely understood in terms of the past. We bounced and rattled for another mile or so through the dense forest along the remains of a road once paved in gravel. The clearing was sudden and unexpected, and Horace pulled to a stop beneath a huge oak at the edge of a rolling meadow. The shell of an ancient wooden farmhouse peeped from a thicket of sumac. "This is where my father grew up, before he married and moved to Water Valley," Horace said.

It's not much, I thought in my suburban smugness, secretly embarrassed at Horace's humble origins. An open breezeway extended through the middle, separating the house into two halves united by a sagging front porch covered with a rusting tin roof. An abandoned well stood next to the steps, the remains of a galvanized metal dipper hanging from a nail in the rough-sawn wooden boards that lined the shaft. Just beyond the far end of the house a small orchard was crowded into a corner of the pasture. The boughs of the trees sagged with overripe apples, and a bird sang sweetly somewhere among the leaves. I could hear the faint buzz of wasps circling and diving toward the fallen fruit rotting away in the tall grass.

I was about to burst with anticipation thinking about my new rifle stowed behind the seat of the truck. Finally Horace sauntered over to the pickup and retrieved it. He walked to the corner of the porch and took a small sheet of Cordelia's light blue notepaper and a thumbtack from his pocket. He pinned the target to the weathered clapboard and stepped off thirty paces back in my direction. Tommy and L.Q.C. watched with poorly concealed envy.

Then he turned to me. "First rule: always assume a gun is loaded until you check it yourself." He showed me how to pull back the bolt and peer into the chamber where oil glistened on the steel.

"Second rule: never point a gun at anything you don't plan to shoot." He showed me how to carry the rifle under one arm with the muzzle down.

"Okay, now load it."

My fingers shook as I fumbled with the first cartridge, withdrawing it from the box with my nails, clumsily managing to squeeze it into the chamber. Tentatively I closed the bolt and locked it. I looked up at Horace, who nodded solemnly.

"Now cock it. That's right, pull that plunger out until it catches. And keep your finger outside the trigger guard. Put the butt tight against your shoulder. No, it's got to be snug. There, that's better. Now close one eye and sight at the target. You should just barely be able to see the tip of the front sight over the little notch in the rear sight. Take one deep breath—hold it—and let it out again. Then take another breath and ever so gently, squeeze the trigger. Squeeze, never jerk it."

The report was louder than I expected, and the stock lightly slapped my cheek. I blinked and inhaled a whiff of cordite.

"Let's take a look." He strode to the target with me at his heels, and we stared at the immaculate sheet of paper. "Okay, let's try it again. Take your time; you'll get the hang of it."

But I couldn't seem to. Over and over I fired at the scrap of blue without success. I was not feeling at all like Ramar of the Jungle, and L.Q.C. was becoming visibly impatient. "Let me try it, Horace," he pleaded. "We're going to be here all day at this rate."

Horace hesitated. Then he walked over to the target and removed his straw hat. He tacked it to the wall over Cordelia's notepaper and returned to where we stood. "Okay, Harry, since you can't seem to stop jerking the trigger instead of squeezing it, I reckon my new hat will be perfectly safe up there. Go ahead, take a shot!"

I felt slightly humiliated, but something in me rose to the challenge. I raised the rifle and sighted with all my concentration while squeezing imperceptibly with my index finger. Nothing happened. I kept sighting and kept squeezing for what seemed like a full minute when finally the rifle barked and kicked.

Horace strode to the target, untacked the hat and turned toward us, a frown on his face. He held it up, and I gaped with astonishment at the neat, round perforation in the middle of the dark blue hatband.

After an hour of practice we had gone through several sheets of Cordelia's notepaper. L.Q.C. and even Tommy had taken a turn as well, and together we were hitting the target three out of four times. The ground at our feet sparkled with the brass of spent shell casings. It was my turn again. "Okay, Harry, let's try it this time from further back," instructed Horace.

At that moment, something small and red darted across the clearing, and I saw a bird alight in the top of the apple tree forty yards away. It sat there, silhouetted against the sky, and began to sing. I glanced toward Horace, his back to me, tacking up a new paper target on the porch. Without thinking, in the grip of some primal urge, I wheeled and took aim at the bird. There was only a slim chance, I knew, but this was an opportunity for my first kill. Like Ramar of the Jungle, like old Colonel Thomas Coltharp.

My heart was racing, but I remembered to take a long breath and release it. I squeezed the trigger ever so slowly. The rifle cracked, followed by the slightest time lag, until where there had been a bird I saw a shapeless mass wheeling and pirouetting down through the tree, bouncing off branches and disappearing in the tall grass among the rotting apples. I lowered the rifle and turned toward Horace, who stood staring at me in disbelief.

I knew by his expression that something was terribly wrong. Wordlessly, he stepped over, took the rifle from me, and then began walking toward the tree. I followed in confused silence.

At first there seemed to be only fallen apples on the ground. But the buzzing of the wasps had gone silent, and then I saw the lump of scarlet lying broken in the grass. A single feather floated lazily down from the tree. Horace bent down and gently lifted the cardinal in his hand. One leg hung limply from between his fingers. He held it out so we could see. Where there had been a head there was now only the stump of a neck. A bright rivulet of blood ran down Horace's wrist, intertwining with the veins in his arm, like the tracks of condensation on the Mason jar.

11

We waited in silence until L.Q.C. returned from retching in the tall grass after taking one look at the headless remains of the bird. Then we made our way back to the truck, Horace carrying the rifle. As he opened the door, a flash of white erupted at his feet. Sparkplug pounced from underneath, like a wolf on an unsuspecting rabbit, and grabbed his pants leg in his jaws. Horace let out a muffled curse and shook his foot angrily. Sparkplug released his death grip and hopped nimbly onto the passenger seat in the cab. Horace evicted him and motioned to me to climb into the front seat.

I kept hoping he would say something as we bumped along home, but he stared straight ahead at the road. The exhilaration I had expected from bagging my first kill was absent, and instead I was overcome with horror at the sight of the mutilated remains of the bird. Only a moment before it had sat singing its heart out in the top of an apple tree. I felt a new, unfamiliar sense of shame and self-loathing at having wantonly destroyed a thing of such innocence and beauty.

We passed a pasture where a committee of Black Angus had convened an orderly meeting in the shade of a giant cottonwood on the edge of a tiny creek, the tops of old tires protruding from the red silt near the bank. I thought again about those hardy pioneers, Horace's ancestors, who first settled here and lived side by side with the few remaining Indians, clearing these fields by hand, hunting bears and panthers in the bottoms. I imagined his grandfather galloping over the hills and through these woods with General Forrest, jumping creeks on his horse in pursuit of the retreating Yankees.

A little further along, Horace braked in the wake of a tractor inching along directly ahead of us, half-obscured in a cloud of dust, blocking the road. We slowed to walking speed as it became clear that we would be forced to wait until the tractor turned off into some pasture. Finally we pulled to the shoulder and stopped.

"This could take a while," I heard L.Q.C. observe to Tommy in the back of the truck.

We sat there in silence listening to the crickets chirping in the grass. Horace had hardly said a word since I killed the cardinal. He must have understood my dismay because finally he turned to me. "Harry, experience is a hard way to learn a lesson, but it's one of the best ways. Today you will begin to understand that taking a life is serious business—any life, even the life of a bird. It's never to be done without a good reason. It's one thing to shoot a quail or a squirrel if you need the meat. It's even excusable to kill a man in self-defense or to preserve the life of someone you love. But it's something else to kill because you enjoy it."

"I know, Horace. It was stupid. I feel awful. But all that talk about your grandfather and the Yankees…"

"I think maybe you've learned something today. So we won't speak of it again, all right?"

I nodded and looked away.

"Besides, I've been thinking about something else," Horace continued, his tone brightening. "You've learned to shoot now, and I believe it's about time for you to learn to drive too. After all, today is your thirteenth birthday. What better time, wouldn't you agree?"

I gaped at him in astonishment and found that I could say nothing at all.

"Well, of course if you'd rather not, I understand. I know you're not quite ready for your license, but we can't expect you to wait until you're sixteen to even begin to learn, now can we? Your Aunt Cordelia thinks I'm an old stick-in-the-mud because I'm always following the rules, but I've got enough sense to know that some rules should be enforced and others are just there for appearances. Why, there's not a boy in Tuckalofa over twelve who doesn't know how to drive. Besides, Sheriff Fly is entirely too busy playing checkers down at the Sycamore Club to take any notice. What do you say?"

If Horace had invited me to take the controls of his steam engine, I couldn't have been more thrilled. Learning to drive was for me a rite of passage, the pathway to adulthood and to ultimate freedom. "Do you mean right now?" I croaked, beaming.

"Have you ever been behind the wheel before?"

"Sure I have. Well, I mean Mom let me drive around the Kroger parking lot one time—on a Sunday when it was empty, you know."

"So you know the difference between the brake and the accelerator and the clutch?"

"Well. I know about the brake and the accelerator, but Mom's car's a Buick; it doesn't have a clutch."

"Okay, well you'll need to learn how to shift the gears by hand in this old truck."

He demonstrated the complex relationship between the mysterious extra pedal and the accelerator and how to move the lever on the steering column through the sequence of gear positions. "Now remember, when you start off you've got to hold in the clutch, put her in first, then give it the gas, and ease out on the clutch at the same time. Okay, slide on over here and we'll try it."

"But what if I get arrested for driving without a license?"

"Don't worry; we're out in the country. Nobody will care. Just go nice and slow," he replied, getting out and walking around to the passenger's side. I slipped over behind the wheel. He showed me how to slide the seat forward so my feet could reach the pedals and how to adjust the rearview mirror. Swallowing hard, I pushed in on the clutch and, after a couple of grating attempts to find the mysterious sweet spot, managed to work the gear shift into first.

"Now check behind you to make sure no one's coming and release the emergency brake," Horace instructed. But as I reached for the brake, I forgot about my foot and it slipped off the clutch. With a sharp jolt, the truck lurched ahead three feet and died.

"Jesus!" I gasped, then glanced in horror at Horace, who managed to maintain a reassuring poker face. Behind us L.Q.C. and Tommy hooted in derision.

"That's okay, Harry. That old clutch is sort of tight; I really need to get it adjusted, don't you think? Just put her in neutral and turn the key again. That's right. Now push in the clutch, hold it, and shift into first. Give it a little gas—not quite that much—and ease out on the clutch."

I tried to do as I was told. With relief I felt the truck ease smoothly forward and head down the road at about three miles an hour. I managed to shift into second with only a small amount of gear grinding. With deep satisfaction, I realized that I was gliding through the countryside, a plume of dust billowing in the rearview mirror.

After a mile or so, my confidence increased and Horace suggested we speed up a bit. I had made it into third and glanced at the speedometer—a full twenty-five miles an hour. We rounded a curve, and ahead I saw a stop sign marking the turn onto the highway back to town. "Okay, make a full stop. Look both ways. Then take a right, and we'll head on home," instructed Horace.

"But this is the highway to Tuckalofa!" I protested.

"That's okay, you're doing just fine." I managed to get started up again, successfully negotiating the sequence of gears, and found myself in heaven. The world lay at my feet.

"Just be careful to stay on your side of the yellow line and watch for oncoming traffic. When they pass, don't look directly at them; just keep your eye on the right shoulder."

I wasn't at all sure about negotiating any oncoming traffic, but there didn't seem to be many other cars out. We recrossed the Skuna River and passed the county fairgrounds. Not far to go now back into town. With satisfaction I thought of L.Q.C. and Tommy shriveled up in envy in the open truck bed behind me.

"You're doing just fine, Harry," Horace said, glancing in the outside mirror. "Now don't get nervous, but there's a police car coming up back there. Just hold her nice and steady, and he'll pass and keep on going. Nothing to worry about at all…"

But the cop didn't pass us. Instead, he fell in behind, right on our tail, creeping along for a half-mile or so before turning on his flashing red lights. I could feel my knuckles turning white as I gripped the wheel.

"I guess you'd better pull over, Harry. Don't worry; just let me do the talking. This is just Tuckalofa, so you don't need to worry," Horace said. His voice was calm and controlled. I tried to remember that he was an engineer accustomed to emergencies, but I had begun to shake with anxiety. In less than an hour I had committed not one but two major offenses.

I pulled over and, in the mirror, watched the officer stepping out of his car, hitching up his pants with self-importance, and swaggering toward us. I sat up as straight as I could and peered over the sill of the open window as the man in khaki bent over and stuck his face in the window. His breath was rank with chewing tobacco. It was Sheriff Sonny Fly.

"Young feller, I need to see your driver's license," he said, glancing past me at Horace. He didn't sound at all friendly. I eyed the leather holster at his side, a mere twelve inches away, level with my nose.

"Morning, Sonny," Horace said, leaning across in front of me. "You remember my nephew, Harry, from Memphis. He's thirteen today, so he doesn't have a license. But I figured it wouldn't do any harm to give him a little driving lesson."

"I see, Mr. Horace. You'd better step back to the car with me, sir. Your nephew can stay here."

"Don't worry, Harry," Horace said brightly. "I'll be back just as soon as the sheriff completes his investigation." I saw Sonny Fly look at Horace sharply, searching his face for any sign of sarcasm as they retreated to the patrol car. In the side mirror I watched the sheriff prop one of his Red Wing boots on the bumper. Horace faced him, lean and tall, arms folded across his chest.

"Now, Mr. Horace, you ought to know I can't have your nephew driving around out here without a license."

"Okay, Sonny, I agree, I made a mistake; it was my idea, after all. But you and I know every kid in town his age has already learned how to drive."

"I don't care if it was your idea. And I don't care how many others do it. Maybe you think the law don't apply to engineers." He glanced in my direction. "You know, I seen boys arrested and turned over to the child protection authorities for less. Why, if I give the word, they're like to take him away and put him in that home for juvenile delinquents down in Jackson."

This had started badly and was getting worse fast. With a shudder I visualized the home for juvenile delinquents—a brooding Victorian nightmare with bars on the windows. Maybe I should jump out and make a run for it. If I could make it back to town and down into the ravine, I might have a chance to hide. But what if they brought out the bloodhounds?

"Look, Sonny, let's be reasonable," Horace was saying, his voice quiet and calm. After what seemed like a long time, I could hear the sheriff's boots on the pavement as he strolled up to the pickup where I was trying my best to shrink down under the seat.

"Son, I think you'd better get out of the truck," ordered the sheriff.

I climbed out, trying to hold back the tears. In the back of the pickup I heard Sparkplug growl, although Tommy seemed to be holding him tightly. Sonny Fly glowered while Horace stood next to me at the side of the road. I could see the muscles in Horace's neck going taut.

"Now, young feller, you're in real trouble here. Do you know that?"

"Yessir," I whispered, staring down at my Keds. I became acutely aware that one of the strings had come untied and that a ladybug was meandering along the lace. I thought about the black snake on Main Street and the specks of blood on L.Q.C.'s white socks.

"I'm of a mind to teach you and your uncle here a lesson. Nobody breaks the law in my county, you hear me? If you was my nephew, I'd thrash you good—within an inch of your life. Maybe that's just what I should do."

"Sonny," Horace said evenly, although I noticed a vein beginning to bulge on the side of his neck, "I appreciate that you're just trying to do your job. Why don't you let me handle this? I think Harry and I have both learned our lesson. Haven't we, Harry?"

Fly hesitated and hitched up his trousers. He looked down at the pavement, apparently weighing our fate. Then he spat into the grass on the shoulder. "All right, son. On account of your uncle's reputation as an outstanding citizen, I'm going to let you off with a warning. But I think you and him," he gave Horace a look as though he had permanently set his charge on a life of crime, "better head back home and tell Miss Cordelia all about this. And I don't never want to catch you driving without a license around here again. You understand me?"

"Yessir!" I breathed.

"I ain't foolin' neither, Mr. Horace," he snapped. Then he turned and stalked away, slamming the door of his cruiser and laying rubber as he disappeared up the road. I noticed that a small crowd had gathered on the porch of the nearest house, and I felt another rush of shame.

As we drove slowly back up Lee Street with Horace at the wheel, he turned to me. "You know, Harry, that was one of those life experiences we can learn from." I nodded glumly. "And I don't just mean not driving around town before you're legal—which I should never have suggested. I mean knowing when to admit you're wrong and not provoking somebody who has the power to make things difficult for you. You want to be careful of Sheriff Fly. I think he was just trying to scare you today, but I've seen him get pretty mean.

"But I don't see why Cordelia needs to know about this, do you?" I heaved a sigh of relief and managed a half smile. "Okay, then, it'll be our secret," he said. "We'll get L.Q.C. and Tommy to join the conspiracy of silence too."

"And what about the cardinal? Do you think maybe we could get them to keep quiet about that too?" I asked.

"I don't see why not, Harry. That's your lesson to make sense of—nobody else's business, far as I can make out."

I thought about that for a moment. "Horace, do you think it's okay for families to keep secrets from each other?"

He shifted down into second for the climb up the hill. "Well, whether it's right or not, it sure happens. There are more secrets in families than any place else I know of. Is it a good thing? I suppose that depends on who gets hurt and who gets saved from being hurt. But sometimes that's a hard one to call."

"Are there other secrets in our family?"

Horace was silent, gazing straight ahead through the windshield. At last he looked over at me. "I sure hope there aren't any that will ever hurt you or Tommy or L.Q.C." Then I noticed a smile taking shape beneath the bushy mustache. "Happy birthday, Harry," he said cheerfully and wrapped an arm around my shoulders.

Sitting in the kitchen while Cordelia applied rubbing alcohol to a rash of chigger bites that had begun to torment me, I thought of Horace's ancestors—the pioneers, farmers, and blacksmiths buried at Mt. Pisgah—peaceful men and women who built log cabins and churches and raised families of eleven children on the frontier. But now I realized that there was another side to these peace-loving yeomen. They were tough. They wore buckskins and butternut, massacred Indians, and burned villages when they thought they had to. They had transformed themselves from farmers into the fierce cavalry that charged Yankees with reckless abandon, a blood-curdling Rebel yell on their lips.

I was soft and spoiled by comparison, living a pampered city existence most of the year. Could I ever be like them, I wondered. Would I have the courage to stand up against an enemy who was stronger than I was? And what if my adversaries claimed to have the law or the Bible on their side? I thought again about the cold steel saber suspended over the door and of the man with the clear piercing eyes who looked like Horace, glaring down from above Cordelia's piano. I had killed a songbird, but he had killed other men in the defense of his country. What would it be like to kill a man?

"How's he doing?" asked Horace, poking his head in from the hall.

"Honestly, Horace," replied Cordelia. "How could you let Harry run around in all those weeds! He's been sick, you know. What other trouble did you all get into?"

Horace shot me a quick, furtive glance. "I think I'll go pack my bag. We're due to pull out at six tonight, and we won't be home until about six on Wednesday." Apparently even Horace knew when to beat a tactical retreat.

12

It was raining outside, and for a long time I lay in bed, luxuriating in the sound and in the promises of the day—a day to be spent as I chose. My mother had finally returned to Memphis following my birthday, and the prospect of another month away from my parents and our humdrum suburban existence was delightful to contemplate. It had been several days since our ill-fated excursion to the country. Horace would be home that afternoon; I couldn't remember whether he was on the run to Memphis or to Canton. But if the rain stopped, I hoped to persuade him to take us out in the country again, although I wasn't sure about doing any more shooting or driving.

I had been giving the cardinal a good deal of thought. Why had its death affected me so deeply when animals were being routinely slaughtered all around us for food? Wasn't L.Q.C. always smothering beetles and butterflies for his nature collection? Hadn't the sheriff clubbed a harmless black racer to death in the middle of Main Street? It seemed to me that much of the world attached very little value to life.

My regrets were genuine, though, and I had come to see that Horace was right. Taking a life for no reason had been callous and inexcusable. What bothered me the most, however, was that despite my regrets, there was another part of me that had enjoyed it. I had enjoyed the exercise of skill and the sense of power over another living thing, a thing of beauty and fragility.

Through the open bedroom door I watched Robert, Senatobia's husband, struggling up the stair with a stepladder. Except for the ladder, in his white jacket and wire-rimmed glasses, he looked more like a kindly doctor making his rounds than Cordelia's handyman. He knocked at her bedroom door, and when there was no reply, he entered and began setting up to finish the new wallpapering. At first light on cold winter mornings it would have been a similar routine, except that Robert would be making his discreet rounds of the bedrooms, building a coal fire in each of the fireplaces while the household slept.

Everyone except Cordelia that is. She habitually rose at sunup, a habit acquired from her years of running the school library. She knelt by her bed to say her prayers and then hurried down to the kitchen to brew the coffee and begin the day's shopping list. By eight o'clock Senatobia joined her and the cooking got underway. Cordelia telephoned her list to the Jitney Jungle, and by ten o'clock the order would be delivered by Winston, Robert and Senatobia's son. The whole family worked for Cordelia and Horace in one capacity or another.

After breakfast I made my way to the front porch swing, a worn copy of *Journey to the Center of the Earth* I had found in the bookcase tucked under my arm. Just as I finished the first chapter, the crunch of gravel out in the driveway roused me. Craning my neck to see over the porch railing and through the abelia bushes, I watched the battered red pickup with "Jitney Jungle" lettered on the door roll to a stop. I lay down again, listening to the running board creak as the driver stepped out. The tailgate opened and then slammed shut.

Out in the yard came a high-pitched snarl and a growl, and I jumped to my feet. A young light-skinned black man in a white apron, his face partly concealed beneath a folded sheet of newspaper held over his head against the rain, was carrying a carton of groceries under one arm and doing a sort of one-legged jig. It was Winston, shaking his foot madly, trying to dislodge something small and white that had affixed itself to his trouser leg.

"Sparkplug!" I yelled, dashing down the steps. The little white terrier was snapping madly at Winston's ankle but without any real effect, and I grabbed him by the collar, yanking him free from his prey.

"Sorry," I said, looking up sheepishly. "Sparkplug sounds ferocious, but he never really hurts anybody."

"I reckon you right—I'm fine. Little ol' dog just tryin' to sound high and mighty. I got a delivery here for Miss Cordelia."

"Come on. I'll hold Sparkplug." Together we walked around to the back, and Winston knocked on the screen door.

"Oh, hello, Winston," called Cordelia, wiping her hands on a tea towel. "You're just in time. I was afraid we might not have any tomatoes for dinner."

"Morning, Miss Cordelia. I put you first on my run 'cause I knew you'd like these. We got the first of our home-grown tomatoes in this morning, and they look mighty good."

She held the door for him, and as he stepped inside, her hand brushed his shoulder. Then she glanced down and spied me, half hidden behind Winston's mass. "Why, Harry, I didn't see you there. I see you've already said hello to Winston."

"Sure, ol' Harry and me is good buddies, Miss Cordelia," Winston said with a wide smile. "You know, I been meaning to ask; I could use some help with this delivery route of mine. You 'spose he'd want to give me a hand? Maybe a couple of afternoons a week to start off? He could help carry stuff, and I'd pay him a little bit out of my salary."

"Why, I think that's a splendid idea!" exclaimed Cordelia. "These boys need to stay out of trouble, and there's nothing like a job to instill a sense of responsibility. I should call Mr. Pegram down at the Jitney just to make sure, of course. But I imagine he'll have no objection."

My first job! This put an entirely new light on my plans for a leisurely summer. I felt a surge of excitement mixed with a sense of anxiety at the prospect of taking another step into the unfamiliar adult world. Would I be up to it?

And then there was the realization that I would be working for Winston— that a black man would be my boss. What would people say?

Uneasy and self-conscious, I studied my sneakers. My feet had recently gotten entirely too big and I wondered when the rest of me would catch up. Sparkplug squirmed in my arms and tried to nip Winston's elbow.

"Harry, go put Sparkplug in the garage so Winston can work in peace," commanded Cordelia. "And, Harry, since you're gainfully employed now, take this carton to Senatobia in the pantry, if you please."

I met Winston the next afternoon behind the Jitney Jungle where he was loading the red pickup with bags of groceries. Over the tops of the brown paper sacks peeped cantaloupes, stalks of celery, heads of iceberg lettuce, boxes of Wheaties and Ritz crackers, and cans of Campbell's soup and Pet milk.

"Well, if it ain't my new assistant!" he called to me, beaming. "Come on up on this loading dock and grab an armload of this stuff." Although I said nothing, I bristled a little bit at this reminder of my subordinate role.

Our first stop was at Miss Becky Woodman's place on Sumner Street. Miss Becky was a widow who lived alone in the house her father had built. She had been born there eighty years ago, and I had heard it said that she smoked a little pipe set with rhinestones, that her sole occupation was playing bridge for money in the evenings, and that she never lost. She seldom ventured outside for fear that the sun would damage her complexion. When she did, it was always on a cloudy day, carrying a black parasol, wearing a long black Victorian-era dress and a black bonnet that shrouded her features. She explained that she was still in mourning for her husband who had died in a meat-processing plant accident. According to Horace, he had made the mistake of leaning too low over a conveyor belt. His necktie had become entangled in the mechanism, and before the motor could be shut off, he had been sucked halfway into a machine that ground beef. "Miss Becky don't never order no hamburger—I can tell you that!" confided Winston. "But she got to have the pulley bone cut on her chicken or you ain't never going to hear the end of it."

The beds lining the curving driveway were a festival of exotic day lilies. Not just the orange ones I was used to seeing. Some were a pure buttery yellow, while others were bursting with deep ruby red surrounding a fiery orange center. We knocked on the back door and waited. Presently it was answered by Miss Becky's maid, a pretty young black woman in a starched white uniform. "Why look here—if it ain't Winston! And who is this? You got yo'self an apprentice!"

"Morning, Essie. This here's Harry. He's helping me on my rounds— doing all the heavy lifting, you know."

"Hi, Harry," she replied, smiling and giving a little mock curtsy. "Say, Winston, he's cute, but he look kind of scrawny for a delivery man!"

"Don't let him fool you. He's a lot stronger than he looks, be playin' football in the fall up in Memphis," replied Winston. "Ain't that right, Harry?"

I made an effort to stand a bit taller, trying to expand my chest without being too obvious. It had not occurred to me that I might be able to make the football team. But maybe Winston was right. Maybe I should think about it.

"Why, look. He embarrassed!" Essie exclaimed in delight. "Hey, you got that chicken Miss Becky called for? And did you remember to get that pulley bone cut? She havin' her bridge group in and we makin' fried chicken, potato salad, tomato aspic, and cornbread. I's in charge of making sure everything just like she like it."

"It's all here, just like the boss lady ordered," Winston assured her as we turned toward the truck.

"Hey, Winston," she called. "Who you takin' to the church picnic? Why don't you let me come with you? We could have a real good time, if you know what I mean!"

Wilson grinned and shook his head. "You more'n I can handle, girl. I knows trouble when I sees it!"

We headed down the driveway in the truck and turned up the hill. "Who's next?" I asked.

"Well, let's see. We got a box of dog biscuits—nothing else—for Mr. Quigley's beagle, Bubba. Seems like that's all he ever orders. Wouldn't surprise me none if he eats 'em hisself. And then there's the Peyton sisters over on Locust Street. Miss Babe, she don't eat nothing but vegetables; we got a sack of broccoli and cauliflower for her. But Miss Jane, all she wants is her bottle of that peach brandy she gets up in Memphis—that and sit and play her piano. Lord, I been by there late at night and heared her playing. She'll have all the lights out except one little one on the piano. You can see her there through the front windows. I don't know what it is she plays, but it's just the saddest music you done ever heared in your life. I figure she musta had a tragic love affair and never got over it."

"Winston, you got a girlfriend?" I asked.

"Me, naw, not now. Had plenty of 'em in my time, though. No point in getting all tied up with somebody; I don't aim to stay round this old town much longer. I'm saving my money, and when I get a little more, I'm heading for Chicago or maybe Detroit."

"You're leaving Tuckalofa? Why?"

He stared at me in disbelief. "You really something, Harry. You think there's a future for a colored man in this town? Sure, I could keep on drivin' this old truck for the rest of my life—long as I stay on the right side of the law, of course. I could get married and have children too. Then I could watch them step aside on the sidewalk whenever a white man come along or have to go without a restroom or a drink of water 'cause of a 'whites only' sign. I could watch them breaking their backs picking cotton to help make ends meet, sitting at the back of the bus up in Memphis, not being able to vote, not allowed to sit down at the soda fountain at Carlisle's. Sure—there's lots of reasons to stay in Tuckalofa!"

"But what about Robert and Senatobia?" I asked.

"It's different for them. They're part of the old Mississippi, where everybody knows their place. It's all they got, and I guess they're used to it. I'm different, Harry. Sometime I feel like I'm just gonna explode. I gotta find a way out. I want to learn a trade. I even sent for a brochure about an auto mechanics school up in Detroit."

We drove on in silence while I pondered Winston's point of view. It hadn't occurred to me that it was such a burden to be black. Didn't he know that we whites didn't dislike black people? That the separation of the races and the rules that governed us all were just the natural order of things? Like Mr. Estes said, that's just the way it was. Why did he seem to take it so personally, to feel so angry? All the white people I knew were fond of him, and it seemed a little ungrateful of him not to acknowledge that.

As we made our rounds, I began to pay attention to how Winston was received by his white customers, watching carefully for some sign of hostility. But they all seemed genuinely glad to see us. Mr. Quigley stepped out on his back stoop and then sat with us on the steps, scratching his old beagle's ears. He offered Winston one of his cigarettes and chatted about the Cardinals game the night before.

Miss Babe Peyton inspected her sack of broccoli and cauliflower and then passed the time of day in a perfectly civil manner, discussing the spring rainfall and the impact on the summer's watermelon crop. She invited us into her kitchen for a glass of ice water. I saw her sister, Jane, peeping at us from the dining room, but she quickly disappeared as soon as I caught her eye.

But then we came to our last stop at the Foster place out on the edge of town, a run-down old pile of unpainted wood clapboards with a sagging back porch occupied by a rusting refrigerator. As we bounced into the yard—there was no driveway as such—three or four mangy dogs appeared from under the house. The dogs surrounded the truck, barking their heads off as we pulled to a stop.

Winston ignored them, walking briskly up the steps and tapping on the screen door. I eyed the dogs nervously as I followed—a sack of Vienna sausage, Velveeta cheese, Crisco, tomatoes, and cucumbers in my arms. It was beginning to occur to me that you could tell a lot about people by the groceries they ordered.

After a while Mrs. Foster appeared at the door. She was a big-boned woman with curlers in her hair, wearing a tattered old apron and bedroom slippers. "Oh, it's you," she said, sounding irritated. "I've been wondering what was taking you so long. You got my Vienna sausage? My Ralph's going to be home any minute looking for his dinner." She rummaged around in the sack, then glared at Winston. "Where's the giblets? I distinctly told them to send me a package for the gravy I'm making! There ain't any giblets in here, Winston!"

Winston looked stricken. "I'm sorry, Mrs. Foster. I don't take the orders, I just delivers them. They packs 'em up in the order department."

"Don't you talk back to me! Why, you're lucky Ralph isn't home yet. Honestly, why the Jitney hires some uppity nigger to drive their truck is just beyond me. I might have known. You people can't get anything right!"

"I'm awful sorry, Mrs. Foster. I'll tell them about it soon's we get back, and we'll get your giblets to you right away."

"Oh, go on now, get out of here! You've already ruined everything. I'm going inside and call Mr. Pegram and complain. He needs to know the sort of person he has working for him!"

"Yes, ma'am. We're goin'. Come on, Harry."

As we climbed into the truck, I glanced back over my shoulder. Mrs. Foster stood on the porch glaring at us as we departed. The dogs surrounded her, their teeth bared, raw-boned hatred gleaming in their yellow eyes.

13

My back ached, my feet hurt, and I was exhausted. My first day making deliveries was finally over and as soon as Winston dropped me off I collapsed on Cordelia's porch swing. But I was proud too. I had earned a little money—my own money. I had seen more of Tuckalofa, and I had gotten to know Winston better.

He seemed to like me, and it looked like we were on the way to becoming friends. I was coming to see that he wasn't just the big, kind-hearted, black grocery store delivery man known by everybody in town. He was becoming more of a person to me, a complicated person. Underneath the placid, cheerful front was an intelligent, thoughtful man with hopes and ambitions. But I was shocked to discover that he harbored deeply felt resentments about the role he was forced to accept in Tuckalofa. It made me sad to think of him leaving; although, after the way Mrs. Foster had treated him, I was beginning to understand why he might want to go.

Why had I not noticed that side of life before, the side of life lived by Winston and every other black person? There seemed to be a blindness that went with being white, an insensitivity to a whole group of people who were all around me. At least the blind people I had occasionally encountered on the street knew they were blind. But I realized that I was blind, too. Despite the fact that they were everywhere, black people were invisible to me. I just took their presence for granted, almost like the furniture in a familiar room. You didn't really see furniture most of the time, although, of course, it would immediately be missed if it were removed.

The more I thought about it the more little things occurred to me. They seemed to fit into a pattern. Take names, for instance. The black people in town were careful to refer to my aunt as "Miss Cordelia Coltharp," or just "Miss Cordelia" when addressing her. But they certainly knew her last name. On the other hand, I called blacks by their first names only, even if they were much older. I didn't know Winston's, Robert's, and Senatobia's last name, and it had never even occurred to me to wonder about it. I remembered reading that their old African names were taken away from slaves by their masters and replaced by fanciful new ones like Pluto or Hera. It seemed that ignoring a black person's surname was a way of denying their family ties and making them a little less than human. And even though there were no more slaves, in a way the same practice was still going on when, as a matter of course, their last names were never used.

I had to admit that, like most white people, I felt that in many ways blacks weren't really the equal of whites and didn't deserve to be treated the same. But now, for the first time, I began to be ashamed of those feelings. I had seen that Winston knew his job. He handled his customers with skill and tact. I felt embarrassed to have questioned whether he should be my boss.

And then there were the baffling inconsistencies in the system. On one hand, blacks were forbidden to use the "whites only" drinking fountain and lunch counter at the bus station. But if they carried some mysterious, unmentionable disease that we were afraid of catching, then why was Senatobia allowed to prepare our food? Why were black maids allowed to wash our clothes, and black nurses entrusted with the care of white babies?

Wearily I climbed the stairs to wash up for supper. "Oh, Harry," called Cordelia from the kitchen. "Try to find your brother and cousin and tell them we'll be ready to sit down in five minutes. And don't dawdle. Horace left a little while ago and it'll just be the four of us."

I found them together, under the house. There, in a back corner, was a dusty, lattice-enclosed space, which we had converted into our lair. It was a cool, shadowy place filled with old furniture, rusting rakes and shovels, and corrugated cardboard boxes.

"Come look at this," urged L.Q.C. as soon as he saw me, pointing to a makeshift display case made of boards supported by cinder blocks we had found in a forgotten heap. On the shelves stood row after row of Mason jars pirated from Cordelia's pantry. In each was displayed one of his creepy specimens of spiders—ten different species, he boasted—roaches, a huge centipede, and a half-dozen black and yellow bumblebees.

"This is my prize exhibit." Reaching into a cardboard carton, he retrieved another jar, larger than the others. He held it up for us to see, but at first all I could make out was something that looked like a piece of large black rubber tubing wound into a coil. Then I saw the head and the gaping mouth.

I gasped. "It's a snake!"

"Correction, my dear Harry," he replied with scholarly precision. "It's not just any snake. It's that black racer the sheriff bashed in down on Main Street. After everybody left, I sneaked around to the back of the Jitney Jungle and fished it out of the trash bin where Winston threw it. It's quite a handsome specimen, don't you think? I even got some alcohol down at Carlisle's to preserve it. I'm considering donating it to the Smithsonian or something—as soon as I complete my autopsy, of course."

After supper, despite my fatigue from the day's work, I was wandering aimlessly around the house looking for something to do when I spied L.Q.C. in his room, bending over his telescope where it stood on a tripod next to the window. "Hey, if it's not the mad scientist in his observatory. I thought you were going to be a biologist or something, chopping up dead snakes under the house.

"Say, what can you see through that thing anyway?" He looked up, annoyed at the interruption, but I barged in anyway and began examining the instrument. A smaller telescope was mounted on top of the larger one. A series of weights and wheels inscribed with cryptic numbers attached to gleaming stainless steel shafts bristled from the top of the tripod like the antennae of a giant metallic insect. I stepped around and pressed my eye against the large glass lens.

"Hey, don't touch the objective!" he scolded. "You'll scratch the optics."

"Jeeze. Sorry, L.Q.C. Don't be so touchy."

"I'm planning to take it outside tonight, if you want to know. It looks like the sky will be clear, and we'll be able to see Venus. It's the so-called evening star, although it's actually a planet, of course. And one of these nights about midnight I want to look for the Horseshoe and the Trifid nebulae in Sagittarius. Here, I'll show you." He opened his dresser drawer and pulled out a blue cardboard wheel depicting the night sky, the stars shown as white dots connected by lines to form constellations. Around the rim were inscribed the months and days of the year and the hours of the day.

"Look," he said, "what you do is turn the wheel until the date lines up with the time of night, and it shows you how the constellations will look.

Today's what, June twenty-fifth? If you set it for midnight on the twenty-fifth, Hercules is right overhead, Pegasus is over here in the east, and Sagittarius is due south. Venus is in Cancer, so it'll set about eight-thirty," he explained, turning the wheel again until Cancer touched the western horizon.

"Hey, Harry, L.Q.C. Have you guys seen Sparkplug?" Tommy burst into the room wearing an anxious expression. L.Q.C. looked annoyed at the interruption in his lecture. "I put his breakfast out this morning, and he didn't eat it. I searched everywhere—out in the yard, behind the garage, and in the coal shed. He's not here. Cordelia and Senatobia haven't seen him either."

"Oh, he'll turn up," I replied. "He's probably down in the ravine or under the porch waiting to jump out and bite the postman. Sparkplug really got him good yesterday—made him drop all his mail in the bushes. I heard him up on the porch complaining to Horace about it."

"Nah, I looked under the porch, and I stood on the edge of the ravine and called him. He always comes when I call him. It's not like Sparkplug to miss his breakfast."

"Okay," I offered, "after supper let's go see if we can't find him down the street. He's probably been chasing cars again."

There was some daylight left as we mounted a search, calling and whistling, even venturing up to Cedar Crest, the deserted old place next door. Now fallen into ruin, it was a magnificent, ramshackle affair. "I feel sure it must be the oldest house in town," Cordelia had said. "It was built before the Civil War. Slaves made the bricks and hand-hewed the floors and joists from heart of pine. They say there's an old cistern somewhere up there. Senatobia says Cedar Crest is haunted. But that's rubbish, of course."

It stood half-hidden from the street in a grove of ancient red cedars, but we could make out an array of galleries and balconies accented by Tuscan columns and cornices with egg-and-dart moldings. We sometimes dared to approach the front porch in daylight, cautiously peering through the decaying lace curtains into the living room where armchairs and sofas shrouded in white sheets crowded together in conspiratorial groupings.

"What if Sparkplug fell in that old cistern?" asked Tommy. "He could be up there right now, starving to death!"

We searched the grounds as well as we could, using a rake from the garage to probe the untended beds of ivy for the cistern and listening for faint yelps of distress. But Sparkplug was nowhere to be found. Finally, as it grew dark, we had to admit that Sparkplug was lost.

"Come on, Tommy, don't worry. We'll find him in the morning," L.Q.C. said at last. "In the meantime I have something to show you."

Under L.Q.C.'s supervision we set the telescope up in the front yard where we could have a good view of the horizon to the west and south. It was dusk and the lightning bugs were out, drifting slowly, punctuating the purple shadows under the dogwood and magnolia trees with little sparkling exclamation points. In the west, just over the steeple of the Baptist Church, the evening star was suspended like a drop of liquid mercury.

"That's Venus," L.Q.C. informed us, swiveling the telescope and peering through the small finder scope. Then he bent over the main eyepiece, adjusting the focus knob. "Ah, yes, there she is, the ancient goddess of love and beauty—and sex." He turned to Tommy, "Come on, have a look."

Tommy took a quick peek but remained nonplussed. Then, I stepped up, covered one eye, and squinted into the eyepiece. I don't know what I expected, but I wasn't prepared for the small, bright sickle of white, like a tiny crescent moon. For a moment I was transfixed by its majesty and tranquility, perhaps the most beautiful thing I had ever seen—with the exception of Blair Estes, of course. As I stared, Venus drifted to the edge of the field of view, and in a few more seconds, it was gone.

"I don't have the clock drive operational yet," L.Q.C. explained, "so the earth's rotation causes objects to move beyond the field of view quite rapidly at higher magnifications." Next we inspected Jupiter, rising in the east. We could make out four of its moons, lined up in a neat row like tiny diamonds as they orbited the slightly egg-shaped disk, banded with tan and yellow clouds.

A strange thought came to me. Was it possible that millions of miles out there in the cold, empty vastness of space some amateur astronomer could be staring back at us from his front yard? What would his house be like? Would it have a front porch and a turret like ours? Was his family gathered around him or were they dispersed like ours? Horace was out there alone somewhere on the railroad sitting at the throttle of his locomotive. Both my aunt India, L.Q.C.'s mother, and my mother had returned to their homes, leaving L.Q.C., Tommy, and me in Tuckalofa with Cordelia. Our fathers were preoccupied by their businesses. Sparkplug, wherever he was, must be alone too, wondering why we hadn't come to rescue him.

Tommy had shown little interest in the telescope, and now he and Cordelia were sitting together in the swing up on the porch. Although I couldn't see them in the dark, I could sense her there, a comforting presence in a cold, lonely universe. Often at night I missed my parents and was thankful we had Cordelia. She was interesting and good company. She never talked down to us, and she didn't mind explaining things when we asked questions, even L.Q.C.'s stupid ones.

L.Q.C. was preoccupied with his search of the heavens so I wandered up on the porch. I was surprised to hear sniffling. Cordelia had her arm around Tommy, and he was crying softly. "What's wrong?" I asked.

"Tommy just misses Sparkplug," explained Cordelia. "I'm trying to explain to him how dogs sometimes just wander away for a little while; they get sort of absent-minded, you see. They usually come back though."

"But Sparkplug's never wandered off before," lamented Tommy. "He likes it around here."

"Aw, don't worry," I said. "He'll probably be sitting right here on the porch in the morning.

"I know!" I added, trying to change the subject. "Tell us a story, Cordelia. Something funny that happened, you know, maybe when you and Horace were young."

"Or how about a ghost story?" suggested L.Q.C., stepping up on the porch behind me.

"Well, now, let me think," mused Cordelia. "Hmm, well, it's not exactly a ghost story, and it's certainly not funny, but have I ever told you about Catherine and Helen Ringwald? They lived just across the street—where that vacant lot is, in a big old three-story house with four turrets at the corners. That was before it burned down in a terrible fire one night. Why, I remember the next day the neighborhood children combing through the ashes and finding pieces of the family silver completely melted so that you couldn't tell a knife from a fork.

"We were close friends with the Ringwalds. Dr. Ringwald and his wife had two little girls, twins, named Helen and Catherine. They were about your mother's age, L.Q.C., and India and the twins used to dress up in Mrs.

Ringwald's old dresses and hats and play up in their third-floor ballroom. You could hardly tell the twins apart, except that Helen had a birthmark on her neck. Catherine was very vivacious, but Helen was more introverted; they say that one twin usually dominates the other. Anyway, they were inseparable.

"When they were about ten, Catherine became ill. No one could find anything wrong with her, but she got weaker and weaker. There were times when she lapsed into periods of unconsciousness, a deep sleep from which no one could rouse her. Little Helen was afraid—convinced, even—that her sister would go into a coma and everyone would think she had died and she would be buried alive. I don't know where she could have gotten such an idea, but Helen was quite high-strung and she refused to give it up.

"Well, after lingering on for months, Catherine did die. No one ever knew what the matter was, since in those days there was a great deal the doctors didn't understand. Helen was inconsolable, of course, but it was worse than that. At the funeral she began telling everyone that her sister was not dead and that they were burying her by mistake.

"The adults all tried to talk her out of that idea. But she couldn't sleep and spent most of the day up in the ballroom wearing the old dress-up clothes, talking to her sister as though she were alive and standing right there next to her. They took her to Memphis to be examined by a psychiatrist, but nothing would convince her that her sister was really dead and she became more and more distressed.

"Finally, after about six months, in order to appease her and try to end her suffering, her parents came up with a desperate idea. They got permission to have Mr. Harris, the sexton, exhume Catherine's body so that Helen would see that her sister had died a natural death and would accept the truth. But of course, the prospect of opening a grave after so long was not a very pleasant thing to contemplate."

"I once saw a movie where they did that," interrupted L.Q.C. "It was about vampires. There was this one vampire lady who would rise from her grave at night. And when they opened her coffin, she had rosy cheeks and looked like she was just asleep. And then—"

"Shut up, L.Q.C.!" exclaimed Tommy with unexpected authority. "You're ruining the story!"

"Yes, well," continued Cordelia, "Mr. Harris wouldn't agree to the idea at first, but he could see the terrible shape Catherine was in, so after consulting with our minister, he finally gave in.

"One Sunday afternoon after church, the Ringwalds all drove up to the cemetery. Since our family was so close to the Ringwalds, they asked us to come along too for moral support. Helen was wearing a long, blue ball gown from the attic. We all stood around as Mr. Harris began to dig. We watched as the hole got deeper until finally all we could see were the clods of red clay being thrown up out of the grave. Then we heard a noise I'll never forget. It was the hollow sound of his shovel striking the wood coffin.

"Mr. Harris climbed back out of the grave, his overalls all covered with dirt, and knelt down on one knee in front of Helen.

"'Now, Miss Helen,' he said, 'I'll only do this on one condition. When I get the coffin open, I'll be the only one to look inside, you hear? Nobody else will look but me. Then I'll come back up and tell you what I've seen. I'll tell you the truth, but I don't want you looking at your poor sister's body. Will you agree to that?'

"Helen was trembling and crying softly, a wild, feverish look in her eyes. But she nodded her head, and he climbed back down the ladder, a crowbar in his hand. We could hear the creak of the coffin lid as he pried it open.

"We stood there waiting. Finally, after a few minutes, he emerged from the open grave and walked slowly over to Helen. We all crowded around. He was a big, hard, red-faced man, but he gently took her little hands in his. 'Miss Helen,' he said very softly, 'I had a good look at Miss Catherine down there. And I want you to know that she died a natural death. She's just asleep, child.'"

14

"Hey, Harry, wake up!" L.Q.C. was shaking me. I opened my eyes and saw that it was still dark. I realized I had been dreaming about premature burials and exhumed coffins and that the sheets were damp with perspiration.

"Go back to bed, you moron. It's the middle of the night!"

"Shh! Be quiet! Come on, get up. It's one o'clock and the viewing conditions are perfect. I've already been out and set up the 'scope. Come on, Harry! Tommy's getting up too. Just be quiet so we don't wake Cordelia!"

Grumbling to myself, I pulled on my shorts and shirt, and we padded down the stair, taking care to step over the third tread from the bottom—the one that always creaked.

Tommy was sitting outside on the steps. Over the front lawn the stars wheeled, each one an unimaginably remote atomic oven, its fierce radiance unchallenged by the glow of city lights. Venus was long gone behind the westerly hills, and I realized the sky had changed completely since I last studied it after sunset two nights before. Unfamiliar stars had replaced those I was becoming familiar with, and now, directly overhead, the Milky Way had been flung from one horizon to the other.

"That's the Summer Triangle—Vega, Deneb, and Altair," whispered L.Q.C. pointing to three bright stars. "And down there on the horizon, that's Sagittarius; see, it looks like a teapot."

I had never before found myself one of the only waking souls in a town dead to the world, and a sense of exhilaration overtook me. The possibilities were limitless. If I chose, I could even walk down the middle of the street naked and no one but the three of us would ever know.

"Come on, let's look at M8, the Lagoon Nebula. See, you can just make it out above the top of the teapot; it's that little hazy patch of light."

I followed his outstretched arm toward the southern horizon. Sure enough, after a moment of confusion I could make out a group of seven or eight stars shaped like Cordelia's battered old teakettle, dented from being dropped too many times on the kitchen floor. It was tilted, seemingly by some invisible hand pouring tea onto the vacant lot across the street where the Ringwald house had stood. Just above the lid I spotted the fuzzy patch. "Look, Tommy, there it is." I turned him by the shoulders and pointed.

"What? That little smudge?" he asked, clearly unimpressed.

L.Q.C. fumbled with the telescope, changing eyepieces, tinkering with the focus knob. "Ah, that's better," he muttered at last. "I find that lower magnifications afford the best view of wide-field objects, you know."

"Naturally," I muttered, stepping up to the scope. "Come on, let's see."

I felt his hand on my arm. "Wait!" he whispered, pointing down the hill toward Main Street. "There's somebody down there on the sidewalk."

I looked up from the telescope and then down the tree-lined street. Between the occasional pools of yellow spilling from the streetlights, the empty sidewalk was draped in shadow and the white-painted front porches of the houses glowed ever so faintly in the starlight. The street was deserted except for a single car parked at the curb far down the hill. Then I saw a slight movement—a figure in white coming up the hill toward us. We watched without speaking. There was something undeniably eerie about the figure's slow, steady gait and the silence of its approach; I felt the hairs on the back of my neck stand on end. None of us were eager to encounter a sinister stranger at this hour. "Quick!" I hissed. "Get back in the bushes by the porch before we're seen." Crouching, the three of us scuttled across the damp grass to the abelia bushes. I wondered if the bumblebees that infested them during the day took the nights off. We crouched there in the darkness as the figure in white grew closer.

"It's a lady," whispered L.Q.C. into my ear. "Looks like she's wearing a nightgown, and she's got something over her head like a shawl."

As she passed the telescope, which we had left standing on the little terrace above the sidewalk, she stopped. Then she turned and stared in our direction. We sat there in the bushes, frozen, not knowing whether we could be seen. Slowly she extended her arm and beckoned to us, just once, then turned and moved noiselessly away up the sidewalk.

"Holy shit!" whispered L.Q.C. "Did you see that?"

"What now?" I asked, not sure I was ready for the answer.

"Let's go back inside," urged Tommy.

"No, I think we should follow her—from a distance—so we can see what she's up to. Come on, Harry!" L.Q.C. stepped cautiously out of hiding, gesturing to us to follow.

"Okay, let's go, Tommy," I said. "It's all right. Just stick with me. We won't go close to her. It'll be an adventure." Trying to remain in the shadows, we fell in line, keeping well back from the woman in white now a half-block ahead, gliding up Lee Street. Once I glanced down the street behind me. The solitary car was still back there, parked at the curb, although it seemed that even though we had walked an entire block, it was no further away from us than it had been before we started. But the headlights remained switched off, and I could not make out anyone at the wheel.

At the next corner, she turned and headed down an alley into a little hollow. The alley led back up to Manassas Street, parallel to Lee Street a block away. There she turned, and following her, we saw ahead the stone portals and wrought iron fence that enclosed Elm Grove Cemetery.

"Wait here," ordered L.Q.C. "Let's see if she goes inside." As we watched, the woman in white glided between the pillars and was swallowed up by the gloom. L.Q.C. turned to us and in a somber tone pronounced, "Gentlemen, the evidence seems conclusive. A woman wearing a long, white shroud, wandering around town alone in the middle of the night, heading into a cemetery. I strongly suspect that what we have here is a vampire at large."

"Oh, L.Q.C., right! A vampire!" I replied, my voice dripping with contempt. "You just got that idea from Cordelia's story about those twins, Helen and Catherine. Why do you have to be such a cretin?"

"Scientists have often been scoffed at by the uninformed, my dear Harry. Galileo endured ridicule and persecution until experimentation proved him right. You'll see. Tomorrow I shall produce additional evidence to support my theory."

We turned back toward Lee Street, glancing at an anemic sliver of moon peeking above the eastern horizon. Somewhere far across the valley a solitary dog howled. The town was lost in thousands of dreams, and only the shadows seemed awake. I shivered. *Come on, Harry, shape up*, I thought to myself. *You're letting L.Q.C.'s wild theories get the best of you.*

It was only as we turned down the alley that, glancing back over my shoulder, I caught a brief glimpse of red taillights disappearing through the gates of the cemetery.

When I finally dragged myself down to the kitchen the next morning, Tommy and L.Q.C. were already seated at the table. L.Q.C. was poring over a leather-bound volume of the *Encyclopedia Britannica* from the parlor bookcase.

"Sparkplug's still missing, Harry," Tommy said. "I'm really getting worried about him. It's been two days now."

"I bet he'll turn up today," I said, trying to sound optimistic, although it was beginning to look like the little dog might really be gone for good.

"Maybe he's been kidnapped," Tommy said.

"You mean dognapped," corrected L.Q.C., glancing up from his research with an owlish grin.

"Well, good morning, boys," Cordelia said, stepping into the kitchen from the back porch, a little bouquet of multicolored zinnias in her hand. "Harry, I thought you'd sleep forever."

"Hey, did you tell Cordelia about your vampire?" I asked L.Q.C., who frowned and placed a warning finger to his lips. A little while later I heard Horace coming down the stairs. He had gotten in before sunup and headed to bed for a few hours after the long night run. He would now be in search of the morning paper. Cordelia poured him a cup of black coffee as he took a seat beside L.Q.C.

"What are you studying so hard?" he asked.

"Look, Horace, it says here that the belief in vampires is still prevalent among Slavonic peoples," replied L.Q.C. "What do you think? Any reported cases of, you know, unexplained illness or undead people seen walking around late at night?"

Horace looked thoughtful for a moment. "Well, as far as I can recall, the Slavonic community has been real quiet of late. In fact, come to think of it, I don't recall hearing of a single Slav ever setting foot here in Tuckalofa. Where did you get that idea?"

"Oh, I don't know. There's a whole article on it here. It says that in Romania they still dig dead people up and cut off their heads and burn their hearts if they're suspected of being vampires."

"He thinks he saw a vampire last night," I explained, rolling my eyes.

"Well, if you're really interested," suggested Cordelia, "why don't you go pull out that old copy of *Dracula* in the bookcase?"

"You have a copy of that? Here?" exclaimed L.Q.C.

"Certainly. I wasn't a high school librarian for almost forty years for nothing," she replied a little indignantly.

15

Ten o'clock. Already the heat seemed to rise from the sidewalk in waves and everyone was keeping to the shady side of Main Street.

L.Q.C., Tommy, and I had been drafted to help Cordelia make another freezer of the orange sherbet for which she was justly famous. I had offered to walk down to the Jitney for the ingredients, leaving L.Q.C. alone in the parlor, holed up with *Dracula*, and Tommy out in the backyard calling Sparkplug.

I had volunteered for the errand mainly for selfish reasons, knowing that I could duck into Carlisle's Drugstore on the way. There were two good things about Carlisle's. Other than the picture show, as the Skuna Theater was known, Carlisle's was the only place in town that boasted air-conditioning. And Martin McCrory, the clerk, didn't care if we sat in one of his booths reading comics all day, especially if we bought something at the soda fountain. We almost never actually purchased a comic book. When we finished, we just returned it to the rack. Occasionally, if it were a particularly good issue, we'd drop a dime on the counter and take it along, rolled up in a back pocket of our shorts. It was a Wednesday—the day the new editions appeared on the revolving metal rack near the front door. I checked my pocket to see if the four quarters, my weekly allowance plus the remainder of my earnings from Winston, were still there. The oranges, pineapple, and sugar for the sherbet could wait a little while before anyone would miss me.

"Howdy, Harry," Martin smiled. "Must be Wednesday, and, yep, they come in last night. Let's see—there's a new *Superman*, a *Batman*, and a *Donald Duck*—the usual."

I plopped down a quarter for a chocolate soda, and, with the new *Batman* under my arm, I took a seat in my favorite booth. The green vinyl was smooth and cool against my bare legs. The day stretched ahead, hot and clear and empty of obligations beyond assisting with the sherbet. There was no one around to remind me that it was a bit unseemly to slurp away at a soda at 10 a.m. or to chide me for preferring a comic to one of the classic tomes in the dusty bookcase in the living room.

"Why, Harry, what are you doing here?" The voice was playful, teasing. I looked up and into the dark eyes of Blair Estes. She was wearing another tennis skirt—a striking light blue one that emphasized her suntan. "Mind if I sit down? I'm just dying for a Co-Cola."

I almost panicked, remembering with anguish that the last time Blair had seen me I had been propped up in bed reading a *Superman*. She was bound to think that comics were all I was interested in. I was on the brink of demonstrating myself to be a childish moron. I fumbled with the comic book, but it was too late to hide it under the table. Why couldn't I have picked up something respectable—*Popular Mechanics* or *Field and Stream*? Anything but a stupid *Batman*.

"Oh, hi, Blair," I squeaked. "I…I was on my way down to the, er, library, but I just thought I'd drop in here to kill a few minutes 'til they open, you know. I'm looking for a copy of, um, *The Brothers Karamazov*." Somehow it was the first title that leaped to mind, although, of course, I had no intention of reading it, and I instantly regretted the choice. How pompous I must sound to her.

"What're you reading now?" she asked. And then, in one fluid motion, she slid into the booth beside me, her bare leg touching mine under the table. In the frigid air-conditioning it felt like a high-voltage cable.

"Oh, this? Oh, I don't know—I just picked it at random. I admire the artwork, even though it's pretty silly. You can't read Russian literature all the time!" I was digging my own grave, but somehow the absurdities kept tumbling out.

"Do you read a lot of Russian literature? Wow—I'm really impressed! I tried *Crime and Punishment*, but I couldn't get past the first chapter."

I could see that the conversation was moving into increasingly dangerous territory. What if she asked me my opinion of *War and Peace*? As I was about to reply, I sensed someone standing at the soda fountain, a gawky figure in khaki shorts, watching us. It was L.Q.C. He caught my eye and smirked, then turned away and sauntered out the door, no doubt to report me to Cordelia for dawdling.

I was relieved to see that Blair had not noticed. Instead, she was gazing at my hands. "Harry, did you know you have the hands of an artist? Your fingers are so long and slender. I'll bet you can draw or play the violin."

"Who, me? Oh, yeah, well, I do have a sketchbook. Would you like to see it sometime?"

"Oh, yes, that sounds very interesting, Harry. You certainly are versatile! I'd love for you to show it to me."

We sat there for a long agonizing moment as I searched for something non-idiotic to say. At length it occurred to me that I could just ask her about herself. "Um, I see you're playing tennis again today. Do you play a lot?"

"Oh, yes, I love tennis! I'll be on the girl's team at school in September. Look, see how tan I'm getting?" She slipped one of her shoulder straps off her shoulder to show the band of white beneath. I tried not to drool into my soda. She looked directly at me. "Do you like tennis too? Why don't we play together sometime?"

"Well, sure...why not?" I stammered. I had played tennis exactly once in my life, but this didn't seem the time to mention that.

"Why that would be wonderful! Why don't you give me a call?" She smiled at me and then her dark eyes bored deep into mine. Under the table I felt her take my hand and give it a little squeeze. "Besides, Harry, I think it's about time you were my boyfriend, don't you?"

I floated down Main Street in the hot sun, too dazed to notice the little groups of farmers sitting on the fenders of their pickup trucks parked at the curb, gossiping about crops and weather. I was dimly aware of a lady—some friend of Cordelia's—speaking to me as she passed, then continuing on her way with a puzzled look when I simply stared straight ahead, oblivious to the world. Finally I remembered my errand at the Jitney.

Between the five-and-dime store and the Jitney, an alley opened off Main Street and ran toward a parking lot in the rear. As I passed it, a small blur of white disappeared around the corner at the far end. Could it be Sparkplug?

I sprinted down the alley. On the far side of the gravel parking lot I spotted a white mongrel sniffing in the high grass; it was not Sparkplug after all. I was about to return to Main Street when I heard a low moaning coming from a deep recess in the rear of the Jitney where the dumpster stood next to an old coal chute. I moved closer and then edged around the corner.

In the shadows, out of sight from the parking area stood a cluster of three older boys, their backs to me. They were dressed in blue jeans and T-shirts, the sleeves rolled up to the shoulder, and one sported a black leather jacket despite the heat. A fourth boy stood against the wall, moaning and grunting. At first I didn't understand. But then I saw his trousers bunched around his ankles, and the bare white legs wrapped around his waist, and the face of the young woman staring vacantly at me over his shoulder. There was something wrong with those eyes.

"Hurry up, Eddie, that's enough. Give the rest of us a turn, too!"

Fascinated and repelled, I hesitated a moment too long. One of the boys turned toward me. His face was an odd, light shade of pink, and his fine, wispy hair and eyebrows were a pure white. Colorless, malevolent eyes bored into me.

He gave a low wolf whistle.

"Well now, if it ain't ol' Winston's little friend! Hey there, white meat!"

"Yeah, I seen him drivin' around all over town with that big coon," said another, as they all turned to look. Horrified, I saw that like his comrade, there was no color to their faces, only deathly pale skin, white hair, and eyes the color of water.

"Wow, look at them legs! Hey, Roy Ray, you wouldn't mind gettin' a piece of that would you?"

"Maybe he wants some of ol' Wanda Lynn, too. One more shore won't make no difference to her!"

In a surge of panic, I turned and raced back up the alley toward Main Street. I tore around the corner and plunged through the door of the Jitney, my heart thumping. Glancing back over my shoulder, I saw with relief that no one was following.

Even without air-conditioning it was much cooler inside, almost frigid by contrast to scalding Main Street. I stood there, trying to catch my breath, trying to think clearly and make sense of what I had seen. I felt disgusted, as though my little town had somehow been soiled by those alien creatures in the parking lot, with their blank faces and eyes like the disembodied souls in some Saturday horror matinee.

The unhurried pace of the shoppers pushing their baskets along the calm, orderly rows of vegetables and fruits slowly helped me regain my composure. I remembered my errand and began shuffling along the aisles absent-mindedly looking for the oranges. Then I thought about Blair, and my spirits instantly soared. It actually looked as though I had a girlfriend. The most gorgeous creature in Tuckalofa had singled me out instead of some townie hood—even though I wore shorts and read comic books. Perhaps this was what Mr. Estes had meant in last week's sermon when he talked about "grace."

As the full significance of my encounter with Blair crept over me, I was seized with a new kind of panic, even worse than what I had felt in the alley. What a delicious catastrophe! But what was I supposed to do now? I had never even had a real date—certainly I couldn't count the sixth grade ballroom dancing class I had been forced to attend in Memphis. Here I was involved in what was already beginning to feel like a torrid, secret affair with an older woman. The next move was mine; I was going to have to act the part of the suave man of the world. I was going to have to invite Blair to play tennis or go to the picture show with me. The prospect was both crushing and exhilarating.

"Well, look who's here—and on his day off, too!" The familiar bass voice coincided with the appearance of Winston rounding the far end of the aisle.

"Oh, hi, Winston. Cordelia just sent me down here for some oranges and stuff to make sherbet."

"You look kinda serious, Harry, like you got the weight of the world on your shoulders," he replied, smiling.

"Oh, I'm okay. I've just got a problem I have to solve, that's all."

"I'm on my way across the street to Dempsey's; Mr. Pegram, he need some more cardboard cartons. Come on over there with me; we'll talk on the way."

I charged the groceries to Cordelia's account while Winston waited. We walked outside together, colliding with a wall of heat. I was greatly relieved to find that there was no trace of the boys from behind the Jitney. "It's sure enough hot today!" Winston said.

I was silent at first, trying to think how to tell him about what I had seen in the alley. Finally I worked up my courage and recounted the scene. "There they were, Winston. I, er, that is, I think they were doing it—in broad daylight, standing around taking turns!"

"Them's the folks from Irish Bend, Harry. They what they call 'albinos.'

Been living all to theirselves out in the bottoms for years. Generations, they say. They done all interbred with each other so's now they all related. Don't hardly know their brothers and sisters from their mamas and daddies and aunts and uncles. Never come to town except when they run out of cornmeal, beans, and molasses. And every one of them mean as a snake. You want to stay clear of them, hear?"

I imagined a squalid camp hidden away in a canebrake on the edge of town, overrun with filthy, albino children who belonged to no one and to everyone. I had once read a science fiction story about parallel universes, the existence of each unknown to the inhabitants of the other, where multiple realities coexisted. Tuckalofa was beginning to remind me of such a place, where one could stumble on an utterly foreign and unexpected reality. It was as though there were another unseen, unimagined side of life in this town, running alongside but invisible to our sheltered existence on Lee Street. I had thought I knew Tuckalofa well, but the place was beginning to seem like an iceberg, only the exposed tip of which I could see. What else was going on in the back alleys and behind the closed doors of the houses and shops I passed every day?

"But something else's eating you, Harry. I got a feeling there's something you ain't mentioned."

I hesitated. "Women," I answered in mock disgust, trying to sound like Humphrey Bogart. "There's this girl, see, Blair Estes, our minister's daughter. She's three years older than me—although she must think I'm older than I am. She's gorgeous, and, well, she thinks I should be her boyfriend."

"And you upset 'bout that? Sound to me like a good problem to have. Most of the time the ones what like me look like something the cat drug in."

"That's not the problem. I just don't know what to do next. I've never had a girlfriend before."

Winston considered this for a few moments. "Now look here," he said, "that's easy. You just call her up and say can you take her to the picture show or down to Carlisle's for something cool to drink. After all, you a working man now; you got money to spend on women!"

"Yeah, I guess you're right. Maybe I'll do that." I didn't feel much better, but I knew Winston was trying to help. I needed to change the subject. "You got a lot to deliver this afternoon? It's awful hot today!"

"You right about that." He pulled out a bandanna and mopped his forehead. "I sure would like a big old glass of ice water 'bout now."

Outside Dempsey's, a few steps away, stood a public drinking fountain, one of several along Main Street, cast from bronze, weathered to a deep golden brown color. Without thinking I walked over, stood on the foot pedal, and took a long, satisfying series of gulps of the cool water that came burbling up. I wiped my mouth with the back of my hand and stepped back to make room for Winston. He stood there staring at me. At first I didn't understand. Then he slowly shook his head and turned away, a look of deep sadness in his eyes, leaving me alone on the blistering sidewalk.

With the sack of groceries in my arms I shuffled forlornly up Lee Street toward the big house at the top of the hill, deep in thought. I felt like an insensitive clod. Just as we were becoming fast friends, I had managed to humiliate Winston. What was I thinking? Of course a black man couldn't use a whites-only drinking fountain on Main Street.

I decided to avoid the parlor and the front porch. L.Q.C. was likely to be there reading *Dracula,* and he was the last person I wanted to see. After all I had experienced, I knew I would have no patience for his crackpot vampire theory, and I certainly was in no mood to share the details of my encounter with Blair. I set the oranges on the back steps next to the ice cream freezer and wandered into the backyard. I stood at the edge of the ravine, contemplating the new and terrifying world of romance and the increasingly baffling mystery of segregated society.

It was cooler here in the shade of the silent oaks, and below me the creek murmured softly. I thought about seeking a few moments of solitude on its banks. But even though it had been weeks since my near drowning, the prospect of venturing near the water again for the first time made me cringe, like a dull knife blade drawn slowly across the skin.

I needed to be away from the house, though, to have time to think. Behind me the screen door on the back porch slapped, and I turned to see L.Q.C. descending the steps. If I did nothing, it would be only a matter of moments until he would notice me standing there in the trees, and then he would try to drag me along on his latest dumb adventure or give me the third degree about Blair. I stepped tentatively onto the path that led down into the ravine. He was still coming and was bound to spy me at any second. Which was worse, dealing with L.Q.C. or returning to the scene of that terrifying brush with a sucking, watery death? I hesitated another moment and then plunged down the dark trail toward the creek.

With my first glimpse of the creek, I became aware of a tightening in my chest. Unable to go any closer, I froze. Just ahead, towering above the under-canopy of dogwood and magnolia, the Sweetheart Tree stood silent as an obelisk, branches drooping low over the rippling current, its shadow shifting over the sandy bottom. Once more I could feel the tug of the quicksand. I couldn't breathe. I wheeled and ran back up the hill in the direction of the house, stumbling through the undergrowth, trying desperately to hold back the tears streaming from my eyes, in the grip of an unreasoning panic.

I didn't run into L.Q.C. after all. Instead I ended up sitting on the back steps of Cordelia's house, sobbing, with Senatobia's arm wrapped around my shoulder. My shirt was torn, and my bare legs were covered in scratches where I must have plunged through a patch of brambles.

"Come here, honey," she said softly, pulling me to her and dabbing my eyes with her apron. "Now you just sit right here while I gets you a big glass of ice water. Then we got to put something on those legs and get you a new shirt 'fo Miss Cordelia come back from her book club. She be fit to be tied she see you like this! What done got into you, anyhow? You been down in dat ol' ravine again, ain' you? An' after all you done been through. Sure no good gon' come of dat! Dat place full of snakes, not to mention dat quicksand hole. Probly haints down dere, too."

16

The early evening light was rapidly fading as Cordelia, Tommy, L.Q.C., and I gathered in the parlor for another installment of *The Adventures of Huckleberry Finn.* Senatobia had stuck Band-Aids all over my lacerated legs, which were too sore for long trousers, and now my shorts exposed my wounds to full view. It was embarrassing, and I had been forced to make up a story about straying off the path and becoming momentarily lost. Thankfully neither L.Q.C. nor Tommy had made anything of it, and Cordelia had only admonished me briefly about the dangers of wandering around in the ravine alone. My panic attack had subsided but had not been forgotten.

Cordelia began to read, and I tried to concentrate on the story. I had begun to identify with Huck and his friend, Jim, the runaway slave. My growing understanding of Winston made me more conscious of the sense of being an outsider, always vigilant, that was felt by both Jim and Winston. This was a story that seemed much more relevant to life as it really was than did the romantic *Knights of the Round Table,* and I had previously been anxious to see how the story turned out. But tonight, only L.Q.C. seemed enthusiastic. Tommy was quiet and withdrawn, in mourning for the missing Sparkplug. I was preoccupied with Blair Estes, trying to work up the courage to call her for my first real date.

It had been several days since our chance meeting at Carlisle's, and I sensed that if I failed to act soon, my first romance would be doomed before it began. I had managed to get as far as looking up the Estes' number in the thirty-page Tuckalofa telephone directory, but when it came to picking up the receiver, my hand refused to obey the order. Besides, what would I say? What could I ask a girl to do in a little place like Tuckalofa? I needed an idea, something imaginative, apparently spontaneous, so as to disguise my anxiety. I had taken to hanging out at Carlisle's even more than usual and to prowling up and down Main Street, always keeping a lookout for dangerous townies, on the chance of bumping into Blair again. But so far my efforts had come to naught.

"Harry, what's wrong? You don't seem to be paying attention," Cordelia remarked.

"Oh, he's just in love. All he can think about is his new sweetie!" exclaimed L.Q.C.

"Yeah, he just sits around all day with this stupid look on his face," added Tommy.

"Don't push your luck, you cretins!" I snapped. "You're just jealous—all you want to do is read comics and invent idiotic games. Why don't you grow up?"

"You boys shouldn't be so hard on Harry," Cordelia said, coming to my defense. "He's been through a difficult time with that awful episode in the creek and now the bramble patch. Give him a little time to recover. Now let's get on with our reading, shall we?"

But she had not read more than three or four pages when she was interrupted by L.Q.C. "Hey, Cordelia, Huck and Jim are asking for trouble to run off down the river together like that, aren't they? I mean, one is white and the other's colored. We heard some of those old guys down at the Sycamore Club talking about 'integration' today. That's what they meant, isn't it? They said it was going to ruin the country."

She put down her book and considered him thoughtfully. "Well, yes, that's what they meant. "Integration" means a change in the laws that keep Negroes and whites from mixing together in public places. No more white and colored water fountains or bathrooms. No more separate schools or bus station waiting rooms. The men at the Sycamore Club are resentful because they're threatened. Their world is disappearing, a world where just being white entitles them to feel superior. You see, boys, integration is coming and times are changing—for the better I would say, although as you heard there are many who disagree."

"Yeah, Mr. Estes says it's in the Bible that whites and colored people should stay apart," I said.

"Well, what about Senatobia and Winston and Robert?" asked Tommy. "They're colored, but Senatobia practically lives here, and Robert and Winston are around all the time."

"That's different; they work here," L.Q.C. retorted.

"Yeah, well then why do they live in that little house in the ravine? Isn't that your property, Cordelia? Horace said it is."

Cordelia looked at Tommy but said nothing.

"Mr. Estes says there's a bunch of colored people who are riding around the state on a bus, and they're going to come to church in Tuckalofa some Sunday soon and demand to be let in. He says he's not going to stand for it," I offered.

"Yeah, I'll bet you got that from your new girlfriend, that old Blair," Tommy said.

"You mean that group from Rice College up in Holly Springs. Yes, that's the rumor going around," replied Cordelia. "I hope it doesn't have to happen that way; it'll split the church, I'm afraid. But at the same time, boys, ask yourselves what is right—what is just. Is it fair to exclude people from the church just because of their skin color? Sometimes it's not easy to do the right thing. I have a feeling that if the issue gets forced, we'll find out there aren't many people with the courage it takes to stand up for an unpopular idea.

"In fact," she said, almost to herself, "I see a great period of trial ahead for us all here in Tuckalofa—and all over the South, for that matter. I don't think it will ever be the same again. Not that change is a bad thing entirely. But the world will be an utterly different place before you boys are grown. I'm afraid there is to be wailing and gnashing of teeth like the Bible said, and it will fall to your generation to make a better world. Mine is too old and set in its ways and blinded by tradition."

She sighed and set the book aside. "Let's continue another night. Nobody seems to be in the mood tonight."

L.Q.C. had been scribbling something with a pencil on a slip of paper. "Come on, Tommy," he said, folding the paper and handing it to me. "Let's go look through the telescope. Just leave old lover-boy here by himself where he can think sweet thoughts about his girlfriend." He mugged a big kiss accompanied by an obscene slurping sound and a contemptuous laugh, then turned away.

"L.Q.C., you're such a jerk!" I called after him.

Cordelia and I sat there in silence watching them out in the yard setting up the scope. "Harry, I know you like Blair," Cordelia said. "She's a very pretty girl. But be careful. Don't push things too fast."

"What do you mean?" I asked. Moving too fast was the least of my problems; I couldn't even figure out my first move.

"I just don't want you to get hurt," she said. "Blair is rather, well, mature, you know. She's fifteen and that's a big age difference between the two of you."

"Don't worry, Cordelia, I'll be fine. I just think I'll go upstairs and read some. Did you know I've started *Gone with the Wind*? I found it in the bookcase. It's about the Civil War."

"Yes, Harry. I read it when it first came out. It caused quite a sensation. 'After all, tomorrow is another day!' Isn't that Scarlett's favorite saying?"

"I'm glad you're reading it; it's a wonderful story and you'll enjoy it. But you need to try to read it critically, too."

"What do you mean?"

"Remember our conversation over the ice cream freezer? About learning to think for yourself? The author of a novel always has a point of view. Sometimes it's very easy to spot, but other times it's more subtle. You need to ask yourself what the author is trying to say, what she believes, and not just what the plot is about. You learn to read between the lines, so to speak.

"*Gone with the Wind* is a romanticized picture of the old South, especially the relationships between whites and Negroes. But remember that the Negroes were slaves, and the whites were their masters. That relationship affected everything, and the way the author imagines plantation life is a product of the fact that she is white and from the South. You might want to ask yourself how the book would have been different if it had been written by a Negro. Or by someone from the North. Or by a man instead of a woman, for that matter."

As I sank into the easy chair in the corner of the tower bedroom, I tried to begin reading between the lines in *Gone with the Wind*, as Cordelia had suggested. It wasn't easy at first, so I tried to imagine the main characters as people I knew. The beautiful, willful Scarlett was Blair, of course. Try as I might, however, I could not see myself as Rhett Butler. Instead of bold and decisive, I was timid and sickly. Why, I couldn't even figure out how to invite Blair on a date.

The thought brought me back to my current predicament. I remembered the note from L.Q.C. crumpled and stuffed into my pocket. I unfolded it, smoothing it out on the cover of the novel. I stared at the crude sketch. That's it, I thought. That's the next move!

From across Main Street I saw her emerging from the five-and-dime store.

She was wearing pedal pushers and a white, sleeveless blouse. Trying not to break into a run, I walked as quickly as I could after her, weaving and dodging between the oncoming shoppers, until, after half a block, I had overtaken her.

"Oh, hi, Blair! I thought that was you," I said with elaborate nonchalance. She turned, and for just a moment I wasn't sure she remembered me. I was prepared to be dismissed with a casual "fiddle-dee-dee" as Scarlett O'Hara would have done. But instead she smiled.

"Hi, Harry. Where've you been hiding?"

"Oh, nowhere, I just had a lot of stuff to do, you know."

"I've been hoping you'd call me, Harry. I thought that after the other day I might be hearing from you."

"Oh, well, listen, Blair, I've got something I want to show you. Have you got time?"

"When? Not right now. I'm supposed to be home to help Mama fix dinner."

"Oh, come on, it won't take very long. It's just over by Buzzard Bottom. Come on, Blair. It's a surprise!"

"Buzzard Bottom? But that's where all the nigras live, Harry."

"Oh, it's okay—I go over there all the time. It's right near Senatobia's house on the creek, you know."

She hesitated. "Oh, all right. Lead the way—but this better be good."

As we walked past the tarpaper shacks that lined Sourwood Street, an elderly black woman shelling peas on her little front stoop stared at us. What was it in her eyes? Curiosity? Suspicion? Resentment?

"Harry, I don't think this is a good idea at all," Blair said. "I don't feel very welcome here." She took my hand and edged closer against me.

"Don't worry. Look, that's Senatobia and Robert and Winston's house right up there at the edge of the creek. We'll just cut through their yard."

The little cabin was quiet. Senatobia was up at Cordelia's, and Winston would probably be at the Jitney Jungle. I assumed Robert was out too, doing odd jobs at some white family's place. We walked quietly through the little yard past well-kept beds of pink and blue hydrangeas and orange daylilies. Behind the house stood the spirit tree, the bottles glowing with an other-worldly radiance in the summer sun. Just beyond, at the edge of the ravine, the creek gurgled. I felt the tightness in my chest. We stopped at the bank, my anxiety increasing by the moment. What had I gotten myself into?

"Well, here we are," she said. "What is this big surprise anyway?"

"We have to wade across; it's on the other side," I replied. "Let's just take our shoes off. We can leave them here."

"Oh, all right, but let's make it fast. I'm supposed to be home by now!"

She slipped out of her sandals and stood there waiting as I fumbled with the laces of my tennis shoes. It seemed to be taking me a long time, and I realized my fingers were paralyzed. Finally I stood up, my pulse racing. "Look, Blair, maybe this isn't such a good idea after all. I'm feeling a little strange."

"This is where you got stuck in the quicksand, isn't it, Harry?"

I hesitated, staring at the ground. "Yeah, it was right down there by that fallen tree."

Her impatience seemed to give way to something softer. She smiled at me. "Come on, Harry. Come on; I'll go with you. You know what they say about getting right back on a horse after you get thrown."

"I don't know; it looks okay, but you can't tell the quicksand from the regular stuff just by looking at it."

"Oh, Harry, honestly! It's just a little old creek! Come on." She stepped into the water while I held my breath. She took three or four steps to the middle, stopped, and glanced back at me. "Look, it's just fine!"

I willed my foot to step into the stream, but nothing happened. She waded back to where I stood immobilized on the bank and took my hand. "Come on, Harry, we'll go together. I really want to see your surprise."

Somehow her touch broke loose the thing that had frozen inside me, and I felt a surge of courage. I stepped into the current, feeling the fine brown sand squish between my toes. Together we waded the creek and stepped out on the far bank at the base of the Sweetheart Tree. Blair was looking at me and smiling.

"That was brave of you, Harry," she said. "Now show me your surprise; I didn't get all wet and muddy for nothing, you know."

"Blair, I need to ask you something first." I hesitated, afraid of what her answer would be. "When you said you wanted me to be your boyfriend, were you just teasing me?"

She squeezed my hand. "Why, Harry, you're shy, aren't you? You're cute and very mature too. Do you know that? And, yes, I really meant it. Now where's my surprise?"

"Well, okay, come around here to this big tree. You don't have to cross the creek to get here if you come the back way down the path from Cordelia's, but I didn't want to bring you that way; it's really steep, and we'd have probably run into my cousin, L.Q.C." I started to confide to her that it had been L.Q.C. who gave me the idea in the note he had written, but quickly reconsidered. Why share the credit for my inspiration?

"I started thinking about this old tree where people—you know, sweethearts—have been coming for so long. So I came down here yesterday and I carved this…"

I pointed to the silver trunk of the old beech tree where the freshly carved initials, enclosed in a heart, glinted brightly in the dappled sunlight: "HP + BE."

"Oh, Harry, that's us! It's wonderful!" she cried. Then she took my hand again, this time edging closer. She moved quickly, expertly; it later occurred to me that this was certainly not the first time she had kissed someone on the lips.

I was stunned. Until then, a kiss had been a sharp peck planted on my cheek by an elderly relative, something to be avoided at all costs. Now I understood what all the fuss was about—how my heroes like Bogart could indulge in such a thing. Blair's lips were soft, warm, and yielding, and her kiss was no sharp peck. It lingered, not long, perhaps, but longer than absolutely necessary, as though she were enjoying it too.

There was a little embarrassed silence between us. She turned back toward the tree, studying the other names and initials closely. Then she pointed to another set just above ours. "Oh, look; it says, 'BG loves MR.' I'll bet that's Billy Grover and Mary Rollins. They've been going together since the third grade."

"Yeah, and look over here," I added. "Here's old Sonny Fly and somebody named Helen."

"Gross! Can you imagine that old sourpuss in love?" she giggled.

"Yeah, Helen was probably his pet pig," I added.

"Just look at all these old romances. They go up the trunk higher than you can reach—right up into the branches and leaves. You can't even read them all. It's like they just keep going on and on right up to heaven.

"Come on, Harry, let's sit under the Sweetheart Tree," she said, pulling me down beside her on a bed of moss. It was cool there next to the creek far beneath the lofty canopy of beech, the understory of dogwood enveloping us in our own leafy pavilion, a thousand miles away from the rest of the world. She pulled me to her, and this time I kissed her.

We leaned back together against the trunk. I gazed into her eyes and then kissed her again. She responded, kissing me deeper this time, and for a moment I felt her tongue. I couldn't believe this was happening to me.

"Hey, who that over there?"

I felt her freeze in my arms. Startled, I looked through the trees and across the creek to the back stoop of the little cabin where Winston stood. Blair pushed me away and stood up.

"Oh, hi, Winston," I called, jumping to my feet, trying hard to sound normal. "It's just me, Harry."

"Hey, there, Harry. What you doing? Why don't you drop in for a nice glass of sweet tea or ice water? It sure is a hot one today, and I got the afternoon off."

"Uh, sure. Just a minute," I called. Then I turned to her. "Come on, Blair," I whispered. "We have to go see Winston."

She drew back. "Oh, Harry, I couldn't! He must have been standing there watching us. And besides, I've never been inside a nigra house! They say they're dirty, and they smell bad," she whispered.

"Oh, I don't think he could have seen anything," I protested. "The house is all the way on the other side of the creek, and just look at all these bushes. Let's go! We'll just sit on the porch for a few minutes." And then to my own astonishment I took her hand and stepped into the creek, giving her a playful little splash as we waded back across.

But I could see she was not happy. When we reached the other side, I helped her clamber up the bank where we had left our shoes. She said nothing as we made our way past the spirit tree to Winston's door.

He stood there, smiling his welcome. "This is Blair—my girlfriend!" I blurted, close to exploding with pride.

"Welcome, Miss Blair. Too hot to sit on the porch today; you all come on inside. Daddy's here, and he'd like to say hello, too."

I had visited on the porch before, but never inside the house. The room was cool and dim, lit only by the light from the open door and a single window. It took a moment for our eyes to adjust and for me to absorb the impact. The walls of the large room were covered from the floor to the raftered ceiling with bookshelves, crammed to overflowing until not an inch of space remained. On the floor mounds of books were stacked, and on a large dining table, more books were piled, leaving only a foot or two of clear space at one end where meals could be served. At the table sat Robert, a large volume open in front of him. In his wire-rimmed reading glasses, Cordelia's handyman looked like a college professor. He smiled at Blair and me and stood slowly.

"Uh, Blair, this is Robert," I said.

"Welcome to our home, children," replied Robert. "Won't you please sit down?" He pulled an ancient ladder-back chair from under the table and held it for Blair, who took the seat wordlessly, staring straight ahead. Winston set a tray down with two tall glasses of iced tea, a sprig of mint in each. He placed one in front of each of us, and I immediately drained half of mine. Blair sat in silence, ignoring hers. I looked around in wonder.

"I see you're surprised by my collection," Robert said softly. "Not many people have ever seen it, I suppose; we don't get many visitors. But reading is my reason for living."

I got up and stepped over to the nearest bookcase, inspecting copies of *Brave New World*, *The Grapes of Wrath*, *Nicholas Nickleby*, and *A Tale of Two Cities*. On the next shelf I found *Gulliver's Travels*, *Life of Samuel Johnson*, and *Pilgrim's Progress*. On another I encountered Plato and a collection of Euripides' plays next to a matching set of *The Iliad* and *The Odyssey*. On the table a large, leather-bound volume of *Paradise Lost* lay open to a Gustave Dore illustration of the banishment of Adam and Eve from the Garden of Eden. Piled here and there were other large volumes on gardening and geography, astronomy and astrology, anthropology and anatomy.

"I never went to school, you know, at least not past the fourth grade," explained Robert. He picked up a small emerald-green book from the table. Holding it gently like an ancient love letter, he turned it over, examining the spine, then opened the front cover. "This was my first." He handed it to me. "You might be interested in what's written inside."

It was *Vanity Fair*. I turned to the title page and stared at the inscription, written in faded blue ink with a fountain pen: "To Robert with affection and admiration, on the occasion of his 'graduation.' –C. Coltharp, Christmas, 1929."

I must have looked puzzled because Robert gently reached for the volume and set it back on the table. "Your Aunt Cordelia taught me to read, Harry. Your Uncle Horace was away a lot one winter—the railroad sent him to work up in Chicago. Miss Cordelia got so lonesome that she took to reading aloud to me after I had finished helping her with her chores. Lord, she read everything under the sun—*The New York Times*, *Harper's*, Mark Twain, William Faulkner, Rudyard Kipling, the Bible—you name it. I guess I took to it, because one day I asked her to teach me.

"She did, too. And by the time Mr. Horace came back home, when she figured I had learned enough to appreciate it, she gave me that book. That started me on my own little library, and I've been adding to it ever since, just one book at a time whenever I get a little spare cash. Sometimes I get Winston to drive me up to Oxford or Memphis to the second-hand bookstores."

He reached for a battered ledger book of the sort accountants use. "This is one of my notebooks I use to keep up with what I've read." He opened it and showed us the contents—page after page of neat entries recording book titles and dates. "I make a note when I start one and when I finish it. Let's see; I'm reading Joseph Conrad's *Heart of Darkness* right now, and when I finish, it'll be number 941."

"Harry, I really must be getting back now," Blair said, a bit abruptly it seemed to me. She stood. "Thank you for your hospitality, Robert, Winston. But I'm expected home."

As we walked back up Sourwood Street, Blair was silent. I tried to hold her hand, but she pulled away from me. "What's wrong?" I asked.

She stopped and whirled around. "What's wrong? I've never been so embarrassed in my life!" she exclaimed. "What do you mean, taking me into those lazy nigras' house like that?" She glared at me and angrily stamped her foot. "How could you? You took me in there when you knew Winston had been standing there spying on us! You even drank their tea. How do you even know they washed those glasses?" Tears welled in her eyes. "Honestly, Harry, I don't want to see you any more until you grow up and start acting like a white gentleman!

"And another thing—I don't want my initials on that old tree with yours, so you'd better just go right back over there with your knife and fix it!"

My heart aching and my ego shattered, I stalked around the house looking for L.Q.C. or Tommy—anybody so that I wouldn't have to be alone with the pain and humiliation. There was a rising anger, as well. It was Winston's fault that I had lost Blair. If Winston and Robert had been at work where they belonged, or if Winston hadn't been spying on us, or if he hadn't insisted that we visit their run-down old cabin, none of this would have happened.

The house seemed deserted. Where was everybody anyway? The door from the dining room to the kitchen stood partly closed, and I gave it an impatient push. I felt it bump something on the other side, and a moment later a crash followed. I stepped into the kitchen to see Senatobia standing on a stool in front of the little pantry just inside the door looking down at the remains of a shattered pottery bowl on the floor.

"Look what you made me do, you damned old nigger!" I exploded. "What's the door doing closed like that? Now get down and clean up that mess before I call Cordelia!"

A look of pain and astonishment filled her eyes. But she said nothing. She simply climbed down from the stool, slowly got to her hands and knees, and began retrieving the broken shards.

If only she had lashed out at me, accusing me of being the racist I was, it might have been bearable. Immediately ashamed and disgusted with myself, I rushed to the cupboard, grabbed Cordelia's big butcher knife, slipped it into my waistband, and bounded out the back door. I ran stumbling down the path into the ravine and then along the creek bank to the Sweetheart Tree. With a pent-up fury I stabbed and hacked away at my carefully carved inscription until nothing was left but a gaping wound in the silver bark.

17

That evening after supper I sat on the front steps sucking sugar water from a tiny wax facsimile of a Coca-Cola bottle, scanning the indigo sky for bats, trying to appear calm. Inwardly though, I was still fuming from the altercation with Blair. Even worse, I was humiliated and angry with myself for the way I had spoken to Senatobia. Dear old Senatobia, who had comforted me and patched me up after I plunged in panic through the briar patch, and who had not told a soul about it. What a cad I was, what a miserable excuse for a human being. I was selfish and vicious, a disaster with women, a puny little boy pretending to be grown-up.

I tried to think of something else. The lightning bugs never failed to put on a show out in the front yard, and we had all gathered on the front porch to cool off and watch the performance. The dark green wicker chairs, dressed up with white cotton seat cushions, stood cool and inviting. Horace had returned home that afternoon. He had taken a long nap, and now he and Cordelia sat together in the swing. L.Q.C.'s mother, my Aunt India, who had arrived for a long weekend visit, had settled down across from them, fanning herself with a copy of the *Tuckalofa Tattler*. A large blue pottery bowl filled with cold green grapes beckoned from the wicker coffee table, and the perfume of honeysuckle hung heavy in the twilight.

Mr. Quigley from up the street rolled by on his bicycle, his beagle along for the ride, its ears hanging over the rim of the wicker basket mounted on the handlebars. The old man waved to Horace, who reciprocated with an almost imperceptible nod and a slightly raised finger. Tommy seemed to have momentarily forgotten his sorrow about the missing Sparkplug as he ran about in the front yard brandishing a Mason jar that glowed like a railroad lantern from a steadily expanding collection of lightning bugs. L.Q.C. sat apart, reading near the window that opened into the living room, the book illuminated in a stripe of yellow thrown across the quickly darkening porch by the lamp inside.

Gradually the sound of Cordelia's soft voice began to restore my sense of equilibrium. She was catching Horace and her sister up on the news of the town—who was in the hospital, the candidates for Queen of the Okra Festival, the latest rumors on whether there would be another round of railroad layoffs or a strike at the Hollingsworth plant. I knew that if I waited, eventually the gossip would end, and the stories would begin. But the conversation could not be hurried. It had to be allowed to find its own course, like the creek that meandered through town, twisting and looping, disappearing temporarily under bridges and into tunnels. So I sat patiently, trying not to think about Blair, listening to the katydids snap and buzz.

Without warning L.Q.C. leapt to his feet. "Arghh!" he moaned. Then he took one faltering step forward, dropped his book, and collapsed, crashing into the coffee table, shattering the blue bowl, and propelling a hundred green grapes across the porch floor like billiard balls.

India rushed to his side. "Cordelia, he's fainted! Look! He's white as a sheet." She knelt, holding his head in her lap, and began to fan him with her newspaper.

"Harry, run to the kitchen and bring us a cold, damp cloth," ordered Cordelia, "Go on; don't just stand there."

By the time I returned, L.Q.C. had regained his senses and was laid out on the settee with a cushion lodged under his feet. He was very pale. Bending over him I draped the cloth over his forehead. "Poor baby," I whispered in his ear.

Cordelia had picked up the fragments of the bowl and had managed to scoop up a few loose grapes. Tommy had dropped his jar of lightning bugs and sprinted to the porch, where he stood staring, his eyes wide, at the sight of the stricken L.Q.C.

Horace stood by, shaking his head. "Look what he was reading," he observed, handing the book to Cordelia.

"It's that old copy of *Dracula*," she replied. "It's plenty gory—a bit suggestive, too—for the Victorians."

"Old L.Q.C. never could stand blood, you know," Tommy commented.

"Honestly, Cordelia, what possessed you to give him a copy of that?" asked Horace.

L.Q.C. was now sitting up and looking vacantly around with a confused expression. "Wow—what a great book!" he finally exclaimed.

Reassured that he had recovered, everyone resumed their seats. "Goodness me, now where was I?" asked Cordelia. "Oh, yes, we were talking about the Hollingsworth plant...."

"Hey," I interrupted, "Did Sheriff Fly ever have a girlfriend? Somebody named Helen?" I was annoyed with the unwarranted attention L.Q.C. had received, bored with the gossip, and still preoccupied by the incident with Blair in the ravine. I had been thinking about the initials carved in the Sweetheart Tree, trying to connect them with people I knew or had heard of.

Cordelia looked quizzically at me, and for a moment there was silence. Then India spoke up, "Oh, Harry, you must mean poor Helen Ringwald. But that was years ago. What made you ask about that? And how did you know about her and Sonny?"

"I saw their names down in the ravine—on the Sweetheart Tree."

"Oh, my, yes, the Sweetheart Tree," India said. "Half the people in Tuckalofa must have carved their initials there. Why, my name is even there somewhere. What about yours, Cordelia? What stories that old tree could tell."

If you only knew, I thought to myself.

"Let me see," began India. "I understand Cordelia has already told you about Helen...."

"Yeah, it was her twin sister they dug up at the cemetery after Helen thought she had been buried alive," interjected L.Q.C., apparently recovered from his experience at Castle Dracula.

"Well, there's more to the story than you've heard so far," India remarked. We all waited for her to continue.

"After her sister was exhumed, Helen was never completely all right. She wasn't crazy exactly. More sad and lonely, I expect."

"Really, India, don't you think the boys are a little young for this?" asked Horace.

"Oh, Horace, I really don't see the harm. I've always believed in bringing up young people without hiding the truth. They're almost teenagers, and besides the whole town knows what happened."

Horace sighed.

"Well," she began, taking his lack of further objection for tacit approval. "Helen and I were best friends all through elementary school and high school. She was quite beautiful in a pale, delicate way, even though she had a bright red birthmark on her neck. She was funny and bright and was always teasing and playing little jokes on people. But then, when we were seniors, she fell in love with a young man in our class—Sonny Fly."

"You mean the sheriff?" asked Tommy, and India nodded.

"They say opposites attract. He was the star of the football team, but he could be a little crude. 'A diamond in the rough,' Helen used to say. I remember him as someone to feel sorry for. As I recall, Cordelia knew him as a student. He was plenty bright, but his parents thought school was a waste of time. His father was an alcoholic and would beat Sonny mercilessly over the smallest infraction. Some people said Sonny had a mean streak too, and maybe he did. But it was no wonder, coming from that sort of background. His family were all members of a little country church and lived in a run-down place out on the old Hayesville road. Helen's father was a doctor, and they were Episcopalians—a different sort of people altogether—so their love affair was probably doomed from the start. You could say they were a sort of modern Romeo and Juliet.

"Her parents forbade her to see Sonny, but Helen wouldn't listen. She began sneaking out of the house late at night to meet him and then slipping back in again early in the morning. She would tell me all about their escapades, driving over to some juke joint in Calhoun County on a Saturday night and then parking on a dark road out in the country. It was fun and exciting for a while.

"But then she went into a decline and began to look ill. She stopped eating and was tired all the time. Her father, poor old Dr. Ringwald, examined her but couldn't find anything wrong. This was the winter of our senior year, and it should have been a happy time. But one day, Helen told me she thought she was going to have a baby. I was the only one who knew what was going on. I was her best friend, but Helen had sworn me to secrecy, and so I couldn't say a word to anyone.

"She grew pale with dark circles under her eyes, and anyone could see something was seriously wrong. She didn't want to get married, but she didn't want to give the baby up for adoption either. She began crying almost all the time, and when her pregnancy began to show, her parents were forced to take her out of school. By then it was just a month or two before graduation.

"They decided that she needed more help than was available in Tuckalofa, so they took her to Whitfield down in Jackson. They may call it a sanitarium, but it's the state hospital for drug addicts, the emotionally disturbed, and the criminally insane. Those institutions—even the best, privately run ones—were places of desperation. They could be brutal, not much better than prisons, and once you were committed and locked up there, you were totally at the mercy of the ward nurses and doctors. The treatments could be barbaric—cold baths, straightjackets and shackles, solitary confinement, and experimental drugs and surgery that reduced some patients to walking corpses.

"I went to visit her when she came home. When I went into her room, I was just mortified. She had always had sparkling, mischievous blue eyes, but now it seemed like there was nothing behind them any more. They had given her some sort of treatments—whether shock or drugs or something else, I never knew—and she had become a zombie. She couldn't remember anything about what had happened and had lost all her old spirit. Like Gertrude Stein said, 'there was no there there.'

"For a little while Helen got better. But since everyone could see that she was pregnant, people were beginning to talk. Her parents wanted her to go live with relatives in Memphis until the baby came, but Helen insisted on staying home in Tuckalofa. She told me Sonny was very angry. He wanted her to get rid of the baby—to have an abortion—but she wouldn't agree. Besides, where could she go to have that done in those days except some old root doctor out in the country who would probably kill her? She told me Sonny had hit her and had even threatened to kill her and the baby if she didn't do as he said. It was just an awful situation."

"He sounds really mean. Why didn't you just turn him in to the police?" asked Tommy.

"Oh, I don't know why I didn't say anything. It was just that I had promised not to reveal a word of what Helen had told me. I was trying to be a loyal friend, I guess." India paused, extracted a tissue from her pocket, and dabbed at her eyes.

"Then what happened?" asked L.Q.C.

"Well, Helen finally just couldn't take it anymore, I guess. She had what they called a nervous breakdown, and they had to send her back to Whitfield. They decided that the treatments weren't doing any good. Even though she was pregnant they recommended an operation, a prefrontal lobotomy, they called it. In those days it was still a new procedure and no one really understood the risks. They rarely do that operation any more because it's very dangerous and hurt about as many people as it helped. Lobotomies were also performed on some young, unmarried women who got pregnant as a way of dealing with their promiscuity, and Helen's parents may have even seen it as a way of getting rid of Sonny Fly. But to operate on a pregnant woman like that seems barbaric; I'll never forgive them for that. They told the family, though, that there really wasn't any choice if they didn't want her to be institutionalized for the rest of her life."

"Yeah, I read about lobotomies," interjected L.Q.C. "They take this ice pick and stick it through your eye socket and twist it around until they squish your brain all to pieces. Then they vacuum it out through your ears."

Leave it to L.Q.C. to know all about brains, I thought. I had one last grape left over from the handful I had taken from the bowl. Placing it between my thumb and forefinger, I flipped it through the darkness in the general direction of his head. There was a small but satisfying thunk.

"Ow! Who did that?" he yelled. Cordelia jumped a little, and we could hear the grape rolling across the floor under the swing.

"Anyway," India continued, "while she was on the operating table, something went wrong. Maybe they cut the wrong nerve, but they couldn't get her to wake up from the anesthesia. So they decided to take the baby. I don't think it lived—she wasn't due to deliver—but I'm not sure about that. Some people in town think the baby survived and was secretly put up for adoption.

"So they sent poor Helen back home to the big Ringwald house on Jackson Street where they had moved after their house on Lee Street burned. They put her to bed in the front upstairs bedroom. That was years ago, and ever since, she's just been lying there, a vegetable. They say she sleeps all day long but that sometimes in the middle of the night she'll wake up and cry out for her baby. They still talk to her and read the newspaper aloud, just in case; no one knows whether she hears and understands or not. I've heard that Sonny Fly still visits her; he never married, of course. They say he always remembers her birthday and brings her flowers on Valentine's. Of course, she doesn't know him though. But if you drive past the house at night, no matter how late it is, there's always a light burning upstairs in her bedroom window."

"India, I think we've heard enough about Helen for one night. You're going to give these boys bad dreams," Horace said.

"Who wants the last of the green grapes?" asked Cordelia. "And, Harry, don't think I didn't see you throw that one at your cousin!"

Later that night, after the house had grown quiet, I lay in bed thinking about how cruel and unfair life was turning out to be, the more I learned about how things really are. What could one count on in life? Surely not love, as the story of Sonny and poor Helen demonstrated. Not to mention my disastrous breakup with Blair.

Friends? I had thought Winston was my friend, but look at what had happened after he saw us under the Sweetheart Tree. Blair had been right about him. He really had been spying on us, and it was Winston's fault she had ditched me. Just when you thought a colored person was a real friend, he forgot his place.

And what about families? Could they be depended on? Wasn't ours fragmented by distance and disagreements over race and politics? Weren't families always prying into your private life and telling you what to do? Weren't they full of annoying eccentrics like L.Q.C.?

For the first time, I realized I was getting sick of Tuckalofa with its treacherous women, comatose lobotomy victims, sadistic sheriffs, snakes crawling around loose in the streets, and albino sex fiends. I was ready to resume a normal life and was surprised to find that I was actually looking forward to the start of school. I missed my friends back in Memphis, our own house, my own room with the Rebel flag and model airplanes, the country club and the black waiters in their starched white jackets who would bring you a hamburger while you lounged around the swimming pool leering at the girls...

All at once a commotion erupted from somewhere downstairs; it was the sound of a dog barking wildly. Then I heard the ragged clip of paws on wood flooring as something charged up the stairs, followed by a whoop from Tommy's bedroom. As I jumped up, the lights flashed on in the hall, and a moment later L.Q.C., India, Cordelia, and I stood gaping through Tommy's door. Horace appeared with a flashlight in his hand, pointing it into the darkened bedroom. Tommy was sitting up in bed, and in his arms he held Sparkplug. The little dog was delirious with glee, yelping and licking Tommy's face. We all stared at each other in astonishment. Where had he been? How had he gotten back into the house?

Then Sparkplug looked up and saw us standing there. He bounded out of the bed, flew across the room to Horace, and began growling and nipping at his pajama leg.

18

As usual on Sunday, Senatobia presented us with a breakfast of waffles served with melted butter in a little pitcher along with Log Cabin maple syrup. Horace had risen early and was down at the depot checking on his engine for the run he was to start that afternoon. So it was just Cordelia, Aunt India, L.Q.C., Tommy, and me at the table. All anybody could talk about was the return of Sparkplug.

"He sure is skinny," Tommy observed, "and kind of scruffy too. It looks like he's been living out in the woods alone with nobody to take care of him."

L.Q.C. gulped down a mouthful of waffles. "I read an article in *Reader's Digest* once about a dog that ran away from his family on their vacation to the Grand Canyon. They lived in New Jersey, and this dog made it all the way back home on his own. Some people think animals have a homing instinct—you know, like carrier pigeons."

"You sure right about that," Senatobia said, refilling the orange juice glasses. "Animals is smarter than lots of peoples. They just got a way of knowing things—things a lot of folks should know and don't." She glanced in my direction, and I knew she was referring to my inexcusable behavior over the broken bowl in the pantry. Ever since the incident she had avoided direct eye contact and no longer initiated any conversation with me. If I spoke to her, she only nodded or answered as briefly as possible. Senatobia had once been my friend, my confidant, and these subtle rebuffs stung, even though I knew they were well deserved. I knew that I should go to her and apologize. But I still had my pride, and in my arrogance, I reminded myself that she did work for us, after all.

"Sparkplug is plenty smart," I said, attempting to let her know I had not taken her remark to heart. "But what I can't figure out is this. Suppose he did run away or get lost. And suppose he did find his way back home all by himself. When he showed up last night, everybody had already gone to bed, right? The doors were all closed. So how did he get into the house?"

A few minutes later, after Senatobia had disappeared into the pantry in search of the butter dish, we heard her exclaim, "Oh, Lawd! Miss Cordelia, come here! Look what I done found."

Her voice carried such a note of amazement that immediately chairs scraped across the pine floor as we all flew from our seats and rushed toward the pantry—all except the dignified Cordelia, who refused to budge. "What is it, Senatobia?" she called.

In the pantry Senatobia stood holding something disturbingly fleshy aloft between her thumb and forefinger. We stared in wonder as she stepped into the dining room and set the thing down on the table. To my horror I saw that it had teeth. Two rows of grimy, ivory-colored molars, bicuspids, incisors, and canines protruding from dust-covered gums that had once been pink.

"Human teeth!" exclaimed L.Q.C. "In the pantry? Maybe there's a body buried in there."

"Lord, have mercy," breathed Cordelia, "those must be my grandmother's dentures! Now how could they…" She paused, considering the mystery.

"Why, I declare! I think I remember. Let me see…India Roberta Beauchamp, my grandmother, died in 1928. They must have been in there for thirty years."

"Fascinating," breathed L.Q.C. in a clinical tone.

"Gross!" cried Tommy with unconcealed delight.

"But how did they get there?" I asked.

"You boys have probably never heard my grandmother's story; it's one you should know," replied Cordelia. She thought for a moment. "And it reminds me about those trips Horace has been taking you on out to Mt. Pisgah and wherever else you go. I think it's a very good thing that you're learning some family history. But you need to hear about the other side of your family as well. Tomorrow morning we'll go for a ride. I wonder if we could still find the old Beauchamp place? I've been meaning to go back out there for years, and I just feel like some exploring. And since Senatobia has managed to find my grandmother's teeth, on the way I'll tell you about her and my grandfather.

"And I've been thinking that we need some more irises in the front yard. They've always had lovely irises at the old Mount Airy cemetery—not far from the Beauchamp house. Maybe I'll get Winston to ride out there with us and dig up some of the rhizomes and replant them here in the yard; it's his day off from the grocery. Senatobia, would you please put some tea and some of that leftover chicken in a basket in the icebox before you leave tonight? We'll have ourselves a picnic."

"Can we take Sparkplug?" pleaded Tommy, and Cordelia smiled.

"Can I drive?" pleaded L.Q.C. Although I had not mentioned to Cordelia my run-in with Sheriff Fly, she had somehow heard that Horace had let me take a turn behind the wheel. L.Q.C. was only a few months younger than I, and ever since, he had begun badgering her to let him do the same.

"We'll see," Cordelia said. "Maybe on the way home."

Early the following morning as the picnic was being packed, Winston appeared on the back porch, a shovel in his hand. I had, of course, continued to help him on his grocery deliveries. I felt distanced from him. Since the day he invited Blair and me into his cabin and my resulting breakup with her, I no longer felt sure about whether he was really my friend and protector. But I had thought a lot more about whether he bore any responsibility for our breakup and was coming to the conclusion that, based on the evidence, none of it could really be blamed on him. I had been the one who insisted we accept his invitation. And Blair was the one who reacted so strongly to what had been a sincere gesture of hospitality by Winston and Robert. Blair was the one I should blame. It was sobering to realize that a person who was so attractive on the outside could harbor such hostility inside. Perhaps I was lucky to be rid of her and lucky to have Winston as my friend, even if he was black.

That was really what it came down to, if I were completely honest with myself. Because he was black, I held Winston to a higher standard than my white friends. With them you expected lapses and were willing to look the other way. Take L.Q.C. for instance. He was nerdy and pretentious, and his harebrained ideas were annoying. But that didn't stop me from appreciating his other qualities—his intelligence, imagination, curiosity, and initiative. I liked him, warts and all. So why should it be harder for me to give Winston the benefit of the doubt?

I was itching to get started. Winston began to climb into the backseat of the Packard. Black men didn't belong in the front seat with a white woman, of course. But Cordelia stopped him. "Ride in the front if you like, Winston. You've got long legs, and there's more room. It's just fine with us."

Wearing a gauzy print dress, Cordelia sat at the wheel, regally erect, silver-gray hair fluttering in the wind from the open windows. I closed my eyes and breathed in the perfume of the countryside—hay and honeysuckle, mud and manure. Tommy held Sparkplug in his lap, the terrier's nose poked out the window sampling the fragrant slipstream.

"I remember you taking Frank and me out here once, Miss Cordelia," Winston said. I had never known Frank, Horace and Cordelia's only son, but I knew the story of how he had been killed in the Pacific during a kamikaze attack on his ship. It was something nobody ever seemed to want to talk about, and I had learned that it was just another one of a hundred things in Tuckalofa one really shouldn't bring up. It was like Helen Ringwald in her never-ending sleep. These were all things that seemed to be best forgotten. I knew, though, that Cordelia hadn't forgotten Frank. She kept his old letters tied up in a bundle in her desk, and sometimes she would sit reading them alone in her room.

"Oh, yes—Frank loved to drive out in the country," she replied. "And he always wanted you to come along too, Winston. I never saw two boys so close, even though you were a good bit younger." *And even though you were colored, I thought.*

"Yeah, I guess I done looked at him like he was a big brother," Winston said, turning to us in the backseat. "Him and me, we'd build these forts down in the ravine. Tried to dam up that old creek, too. The water always broke through, but that'd just give Frank a new idea to try the next time. That Frank, he could figure out how to most build anything, you know, a lean-to or a bridge. Always said he wanted to be an engineer or an architect. He'd a been a good one, too, if it hadn't of been for the war.

"After them Japs killed him I wanted to sign up and fight, too, but I was too young and anyhow they didn't want us colored boys. Wouldn't let us join no combat units. Said we couldn't be trusted when the going got tough."

As the Packard rumbled across a bridge above a muddy creek, Cordelia turned to us. "We're close to the route General Grant's army took chasing the Confederates toward Grenada."

"I believe that was in the winter of 1862," intoned L.Q.C. "I've been studying that campaign. Grant was trying to make his way from Corinth down to Vicksburg, figuring he would cut the Confederacy in two; near here there was a little skirmish before the Confederates fell back."

"Yes, well, thank you, L.Q.C.," Cordelia said. "It must have been an awful time; it had been raining for days, and the mud was so thick the cannons sank over the wheels of the caissons. The men on both sides were soaked to the bone and couldn't stop to sleep for days. But it was nothing, of course, compared to what the Confederates would later have to endure at Vicksburg."

We drove on through the hill country, finally turning onto the road to Coffeeville. "We're in Calhoun County now, boys. With any luck, we'll find the place where my grandmother was born.

"And I mustn't forget to finish the story that started all this, the one about those old false teeth in the pantry. You know India and Ellen were much younger than I, and when they were growing up, we all lived on Lee Street together—India, Ellen, Frank, my parents, Horace, and I. And for the last few years of her life, my grandmother, India Roberta, lived with us as well. India and Ellen loved to play pranks on her. She was quite old by then and didn't see well. She wore dentures and would take them out at night and leave them in a glass of water on her bedside table. Their favorite trick was to make off with her teeth while she was asleep. We would turn the house upside down looking for them until we finally caught on that they would always run downstairs and hide them in the back of the pantry. Right next to that bottle of Old Crow that Horace likes to keep stashed back there that he thinks nobody knows about."

After several miles, Cordelia slowed down, scrutinizing the cotton fields and patches of pine forest. "We're looking for an old dirt road on the left—wait, look—that's it up there! We'll turn in and walk from here."

The overgrown path had once been a narrow, unpaved farm road. We struck off along it on foot toward a low ridge covered with trees, pausing to push the briars aside as they clutched at us. Cotton fields lined the path, the white bolls just beginning to show through the green leaves. The heavy air became slightly cooler once we reached the trees and began to climb. The contours of the old road grew more distinct now, and I stumbled in the ruts worn by ancient wagon wheels. A startled cottontail ran from underfoot to seek the safety of a hollow tree.

After about ten minutes, as we neared the crest of the hill, the trees grew smaller and the sky brighter. L.Q.C., who was inclined toward chubbiness, was puffing. Cordelia signaled a halt then looked around. "I declare," she said in wonderment, "the house is completely gone. The last time I was here—it's been twenty years, I imagine—it had fallen into ruin, but it was still standing. It was right over there—I'm sure of it—right below the crest of the hill. A big two-story house with a balcony over the front door and brick chimneys at each end."

We wandered over to the spot she indicated, a small clearing, and began rummaging among the fallen leaves and pine needles. I stubbed my toe on something hard—a fragment of red brick covered in moss. There were other shards too, a crumbling pile of them half buried in loamy soil. "This must be all that's left of one of the chimneys," I observed.

"I believe this would be a productive site for my first excavation," pronounced L.Q.C. "I've been thinking of pursuing graduate studies in archaeology, you know."

Tommy and I looked at each other and rolled our eyes.

"Well, we may as well have our picnic here. Besides, there's something I want to show you all," Cordelia said, spreading an old quilt on the pine needles. We unpacked the chicken and tea, and I grabbed a drumstick a half second ahead of Tommy, who glowered at me. Cordelia reached into her purse and produced a single large sheet of thin gray stationery. It had been folded and sealed to create an envelope. There was no stamp, but the address, written with sepia ink in a flowing copperplate, read "Mr. Joseph King, Bonny Doon, NC."

"My great-grandfather, Caulfield Beauchamp, and his wife were some of the first pioneers to settle here in Calhoun County. They left the Beauchamp family homestead back in Halifax County, North Carolina, for Mississippi when Caulfield was a young man in his twenties. They cleared the land themselves and built a house here on this hilltop about 1850. It was called 'Bonny Doon,' a reference to a poem by Robert Burns, the Scottish poet. The house once enjoyed a beautiful view and lovely cool breezes before the trees took over again. This old letter was written from this very spot by my great-grandfather to his brother-in-law back in North Carolina.

"If you read between the lines, there's a sense of excitement about living on the frontier in what he saw as a land of promise. They say that in 1850 Mississippi was the wealthiest state in the country." She paused a moment and began to read.

Bonny Doon, 18th Oct. 1850

Dear Joseph:

I received your letter bearing the date of the l6th of last month, which afforded us a good deal of pleasure to hear that you all are well. All of my family are well and have been all of this summer and fall. In fact I hear of no sickness in this country anywhere, scarcely.

I was at Grenada day before yesterday and saw Carfax Bingham. He had just returned from North Carolina and came through Tennessee and stayed a week or two. He said he never expected to see old Halifax anymore—it was too poor a place for him.

Mississippi seems to me a dark country. The earth, the forest, and the negroes, of course. But it's something else, too. It is dark in spirit, primitive, even threatening, not like Halifax.

But there is much profit to be made, I think, and so we are happy. I am busily engaged gathering cotton and the prospect for the planter is very encouraging. Everything is high. Cotton is 12 cents per pound.

Negro fellows are worth $1,000, and if I can pick up a few strong young bucks at auction I believe I could double next season's crop. I would like for you to come out to this country next spring and join me as a partner. I think we could make money.

My best respects to your family, also inquiring friends.

Most Respectfully,

Caulfield Beauchamp

"This was written in 1850, and thirteen years later Caulfield Beauchamp was dead. The war came along, and by 1862 the Confederates were on the defensive with Grant sweeping through Mississippi on his way to Vicksburg, ripping up the railroads and burning houses and farms. Caulfield joined the Confederate Army and could have been part of that retreating force that fell back from Holly Springs to Oxford and finally to Coffeeville. They made a strong stand there, though. They used to say that the Battle of Coffeeville was fought under a full moon and that from town you could hear the shooting way out here in Calhoun County.

"The Yankees turned around and ran back up to Oxford, where my friend

Miss Callista Oglethorpe's family lived in a big house on Lamar Street. The Oglethorpes had hung a Confederate flag on the balcony and refused to take it down in open defiance of martial law. Her mother was in labor waiting for Miss Callista to be born when the soldiers marched up to the house. They picked up the bed with her mother in it and carried it out into the front yard. Then they set fire to the house. Miss Callista was born there in the yard while the house was still in flames.

"Grant eventually made it all the way to Vicksburg, of course, and Caulfield ended up there, too. He and the other defenders held out against the Yankees for six weeks, living in trenches and caves under constant artillery bombardment."

"Yeah, I read they had to eat mules and rats to survive," interjected L.Q.C.

"Yes, well, it's true that a large proportion of the Confederates who died either starved or succumbed to scurvy or Yellow Fever," continued Cordelia. "When at last Vicksburg fell on July 4, 1863, Caulfield was released from the army and started back home the only way he could—on foot. It was around 150 miles from Vicksburg—but he made it.

"When he finally reached Bonny Doon, he must have realized that his family had not heard a word from him since before the start of the siege and that they would be surprised by his unexpected return and shocked by his gaunt and filthy appearance. So he paused to bathe in an old hollow tree full of rainwater that stood somewhere around here near the house. A short time later, he fell seriously ill, and, of course, there was little to be done except watch him waste away.

"Some thought he had contracted Yellow Fever in Vicksburg, while others thought he must have gotten chilled and caught pneumonia from the cold rainwater in that hollow log. Maybe he was just exhausted by the horrors he had experienced in the war. Whatever it was, it killed him, like so many who died in that awful war. What a tragic end for a young man in his early forties who just wanted to carve out a peaceful life for himself and his family here on the frontier."

Our next stop, the cemetery at Mount Airy—about a mile further along the main road—reminded me of Mt. Pisgah where Horace's side of the family was buried. A one-room clapboard church stood in a clearing. Outside, a long, sagging, picnic table made of rough-sawn, weathered boards threatened to collapse from old age. The tiny, neatly mown graveyard was shaded by mournful cedars, their trunks delicately tinted with moss. Most of the tombstones were inscribed "Beauchamp," and Cordelia pointed out the graves of her great-grandparents, Caulfield Beauchamp and his wife.

"We should come back out here on the first Sunday in September," Cordelia said. "That's when they have the annual picnic on the grounds and the Sacred Harp singing. It's a very old form of music that was brought from the Carolinas by the first settlers."

Arranged in a border just beyond the gravestones, the leaves of the iris beds, faded and past blooming now, drooped in the dappled sunlight. While Winston dug in the beds, Tommy produced an old tennis ball. Sparkplug's pointed ears stood up as he watched Tommy wind up and launch a soaring pitch down the gravel road. "I don't know why you even bother throwing him that ball," L.Q.C. remarked. "He never brings it back. All he'll do is run off with it into the woods." Sure enough, Sparkplug streaked after the ball, nabbed it on a single bounce, and headed off in the opposite direction with his prize.

I had been thinking about the letter Cordelia had read to us, a letter so old it pre-dated postage stamps. "Caulfield Beauchamp said something about buying Negroes—young bucks. He meant slaves, didn't he?"

"Yes, Harry," she replied. "Your great-great grandfather was a slaveholder, like all the other large planters in Mississippi. There was no modern agricultural machinery in those days, and it was the only way you could profitably raise cotton in large amounts; the whole economy was built around slavery, I'm sorry to say."

It sounded just like *Gone With the Wind* to me. "In the war was he fighting to keep his slaves?"

Cordelia hesitated and glanced at Winston, bent over the iris beds on the far side of the little graveyard. "I expect he was fighting to keep his way of life. Of course, that way of life depended on slaves, so, yes, I suppose he was fighting to defend slavery. But it wasn't that simple. He probably felt that his country was being invaded by people from the North who were burning down whole farms and towns and who were trying to tell him how to live. A lot of Southerners thought that was why the American Revolution had been fought against the British in the first place.

"You see, when Southerners lost the war, much of their world was destroyed. Many people still haven't gotten over the memories of that awful experience passed down to them. It was the only time Americans had tasted defeat in a war, and many people in our part of the country still feel angry about that. Others feel ashamed and guilty—not because they were beaten fighting for independence and defending their homes against invasion, but because their cause included defense of the right to own slaves."

"I'm glad we don't have slavery any more. It doesn't seem fair," Tommy observed.

"Boys, I'm going to tell you something. We may not have slavery anymore, but we are still feeling its effects a hundred years later. Harry, you told me Mr. Estes said Negroes are lazy and ignorant. And you've even heard Horace say that they are physically strong but show no initiative. Those are what we call 'stereotypes,' broad generalizations about a whole group of people, and they go back to the days of slavery.

"When you enslave people, you take away more than their freedom. You take away their self-respect, too, and along with it their initiative. They learn that no matter how hard they try, things won't get any better; they'll always be slaves. So eventually they just give up trying.

"If you're a slave and you call attention to yourself by physical weakness, or by trying to learn to read, or by showing any sign of intelligence, you're likely to be severely punished and maybe even killed. And so, as a matter of survival, you pass that lesson along to your children and to your children's children. After a few generations, you end up with a people who have never known freedom or the benefits of education or initiative. They have come to believe that in order to survive you have to be docile, to 'keep in your place,' to act like you don't understand, and that the only thing you're fit for in life is manual labor.

"So even today, when white people see some Negroes acting like this, it just confirms what they already want to believe—that they are an inferior race who deserved nothing better than slavery and who can still be looked down on and denied equal rights.

"It took generations for those attitudes to get established, and it's going to take generations for them to change. So even though slavery was abolished, in a sense, it is still with us today. I want you to remember that the next time you hear someone saying that Negroes are inferior. It was we who made them feel and act that way."

I remembered the way I had humiliated Winston at the water fountain on Main Street. And my visit to Winston's cabin with Blair, the hatred she had expressed and that I had felt myself when I stormed back to our house. And how I had mistreated Senatobia. How black people seemed invisible to me and how easy it was for me to hurt them without giving it a second thought. Was I simply acting out a pattern that went back all those years to my great-great grandfather, the slaveholder?

In a little plot apart from the other grave markers, Cordelia pointed to a short row of unhewn fragments of brown sandstone protruding from the ground. "Those are the graves of the slaves. Lots of them lived so close to their masters that they were almost members of the family. But when they died, there was no money for carved marble tombstones for them. So even then they were second-class citizens."

Winston had harvested a dozen or so rhizomes, and had carried them back to the Packard where Cordelia had lain newspaper across the floor of the trunk. I realized that he had heard most of Cordelia's account of slavery. We started piling back into the car, but Cordelia stopped us. "You boys entertain yourselves for a few minutes. I think I'd just like to be by myself for a little bit." Then she wandered slowly back toward the church.

Tommy was still preoccupied with Sparkplug, and L.Q.C. wandered over to sit against a tree trunk with a book. Winston and I sat together in silence perched on the fender of the car. I was thinking about the letter Cordelia had read to us, about how my great-great-grandfather had described his Mississippi as a "dark country" and about the horrors he had experienced in the war. I wondered if the future could hold anything like that for me.

"Say, Harry," Winston said, interrupting my thoughts. "You ain't said anything 'bout your girlfriend, Miss Blair, recently. Everything goin' okay with you two?"

It was the first time Blair's name had come up between us since she and I had visited his cabin. Given my ambivalence about him, I wasn't sure how Winston might be feeling about me. How much of the truth was I willing to share with him? So I equivocated. "Naw, we broke up. That is, she broke up with me. But I don't mind. I don't think she's really my type."

"Aw, that's a shame, Harry. I liked her, although you gots to watch out for them older women. Uh huh. They'll play with your mind if you lets 'em."

I decided to change the subject before it was too late. "It seems so sad, all the things that happened out here, all those old family stories. Do you think that's why Cordelia wants to be alone?" I asked Winston. "Maybe she's thinking about Caulfield Beauchamp walking all the way home from Vicksburg or about his slaves."

Winston nodded solemnly. "I think your aunt carries more on her heart than we knows."

This family does have its share of secrets, I thought to myself.

"Say, Winston, do you ever think about the possibility that my great-great-grandfather could have owned your great-great-grandfather?"

It was the wrong thing to say. I realized it as soon as the words were out of my mouth. Winston didn't reply. He just looked away.

Once more I had wounded him. Would I never learn?

19

"Oh, come on—please! You said I could drive home, Cordelia," insisted L.Q.C. as she returned to the car where we sat, slapping at gnats.

"Well, I didn't exactly say that," she replied. "But I suppose it'll be all right out here in the country. But you'll need to pull over and let me take it before we get back into town."

"Better put on your crash helmets," I muttered under my breath.

The Packard had a smooth transmission, so L.Q.C. had none of the battle with the gears I had faced in Horace's pickup. After bumping along the gravel road for a mile, he made a broad sweeping turn onto the paved highway, swinging across the dividing line in the process. An oncoming semi sounded its horn in alarm, and L.Q.C. swerved back to the right. Sparkplug, his head out the window, responded with an indignant frenzy of barking as the truck barreled past.

We cruised along in nervous silence, all of us watching the road intently as L.Q.C. labored to guide us between the shoulder and the centerline, weaving and then over-correcting.

"Whoa there! You ever driven a car before?" cried Winston.

"Certainly," replied L.Q.C. indignantly. "Mother lets me drive our Dodge all the time back at home."

"I'm going to remember to ask India about that," replied Cordelia.

"It's not me," he protested, twisting the wheel sharply. "I'm just not accustomed to such a massive automobile. The Packard's greater momentum makes it tend to resist any change in velocity or direction, as Newton pointed out."

"Oh, right—so it's going to be Newton's fault when we're all killed," I commented.

None of us was sure how long the other car had been tailing us, but it could have been a long time since L.Q.C. was too preoccupied with keeping us out of a ditch to glance in the rearview mirror. What was clear to me, though, was that we were still in Calhoun County. That didn't stop the cop from switching on his siren though.

"Holy shit!" muttered L.Q.C. He turned an ashen gray and looked like he was about to faint again.

"For goodness sake, L.Q.C., pull yourself together," commanded Cordelia. "Just slow down and ease over to the side of the road. That's it. Don't worry; let me explain to the officer." I didn't like the look of this. It was all too familiar.

We heard the car door slam behind us and after a moment the sharp command, "All right, everybody out. And keep your hands where I can see 'em. Then line up over here on the shoulder."

All of us—even Cordelia—meekly obeyed. As I stepped out of the backseat and turned to face the officer, I froze. The sun was directly behind him, so at first all I could make out was that he was very tall, dressed in khaki, and wore mud-caked boots. It couldn't be, not again.

We stood there in the blazing sun watching the heat waves rise from the blacktop while Sheriff Fly slowly walked around the Packard, as though he were inspecting the paint job. Tommy held Sparkplug in his arms.

"Why, Sonny, I didn't expect to meet you way out here," Cordelia said in a pleasant tone.

"Open that trunk," Fly commanded.

"Now, Sonny, let's not overreact," began Cordelia. "I'll admit that L.Q.C. here is a little short of his sixteenth birthday. But we're not even in Dancing Rabbit County. You have no right to stop us."

The sheriff turned and stepped up to Cordelia. He stood a little too close, staring down at her. There was sweat running down the back of his neck, and the armpits of his khaki shirt were stained a dark brown. "Maybe you didn't hear me, Miss Cordelia. I said open that trunk."

"Oh, very well, Sonny. Here, L.Q.C., hand me the keys."

She stepped over to the car and raised the trunk lid. The sheriff peered over her shoulder at the mass of green piled on the newspaper. "There you are, Sonny, I admit it. You've caught us smuggling irises. I imagine there's a stiff penalty for that!"

"Don't you mock me, Miss Cordelia! I got more'n enough on you to teach you a lesson you won't forget. Reckless driving by a minor under your supervision. Suspicion of transporting possible contraband plant materials. And all with a uppity nigger along for the ride! That, Miss Cordelia, is what is known as 'probable cause.'

"Now listen here—all of you. I want Miss Cordelia and you, young feller," he pointed a blunt index finger at L.Q.C.'s nose, "and the big buck here, all in the backseat of my car. You other boys can sit in the Packard and wait 'til I come back."

"What are you saying, Sonny?" Cordelia's tone was sharp.

"What I'm saying, Miss Cordelia Coltharp, is that I'm placing you all under arrest. I'm taking the whole bunch of you in, and we'll just let the judge sort this all out. I'm fed up with your whole damn family—always actin' so dignified and above it all." He reached out and seized Cordelia by the arm, but she jerked away.

"Unhand me, you vulgarian!" she demanded.

Fly's face turned bright red, and then something dark descended across it. He reached for her arm again. "I ain't one of your high school students no more, Miss Cordelia, and out here you don't make the rules—I do!"

"You're hurting me!" she cried, but he was already hustling her toward the patrol car. We stood there, immobilized in terror—all except Winston, who took a menacing step toward Fly.

But before Winston could make a move to stop him, I heard Tommy shout, "Get the sheriff! Get him before he hurts Cordelia!" He flung Sparkplug to the ground. There was a low growl and a blur of white as Sparkplug charged for Sonny Fly, hugging the ground like a homing missile. At the last moment he snarled and vaulted three feet into the air, just as he had attacked Caruso the peacock, and sank his teeth into the back of Fly's thigh. Then he hung there by those sharp little teeth, his feet and tail thrashing in mid-air, growling and chomping.

Fly screamed and let go of Cordelia, snatching wildly behind him at the dog. He grabbed Sparkplug with one big hand and with a mighty pull wrenched him loose and threw him hard to the pavement. A dark bloodstain had already begun to seep through his trousers.

Sparkplug lay there, momentarily stunned, as Fly reached for the long black nightstick stuck in his belt. He stood over Sparkplug just long enough to glance at Tommy, then at Cordelia, before he raised the club and brought it down across the dog's back. Sparkplug gave a little high-pitched yelp. Then Fly raised the stick again and smashed in Sparkplug's head with a sickening crunch. The little dog never uttered another sound as Fly hit him again and again and again.

We stood there in horror, staring at the unrecognizable red and white pulp lying on the blacktop. Finally Fly backed away, and Winston silently knelt and picked up Sparkplug and laid him in the open trunk on top of the irises. When he turned back toward us, his white T-shirt was stained with blood.

For the first time I could remember, I saw tears in Cordelia's eyes. Tommy, L.Q.C., and I stood frozen at attention there on the shoulder, as helpless as marble soldiers in front of some county courthouse. Fly bent down, his free hand grasping his wound. He was obviously in pain and seemed unsure what to do next.

"Sheriff Fly," Cordelia said, "we are going home now—back to Dancing Rabbit County, if you catch my meaning. If you have an ounce of judgment left, you won't try to stop us. You're right; you were one of my students. And do you remember who else was in your class? I'm referring to John Calhoun Coleman, the city attorney. There are laws against false arrest—especially outside your jurisdiction—and against brutalizing law-abiding citizens. If you stand in our way, I'll go straight to John. I've known him since he was in high school, and he still drops by to see me. I think he'll believe me when I tell him about this outrage.

"Come along boys, Winston. We're taking poor Sparkplug home."

Fly stood glaring at us as we climbed into the Packard. "Oh, Miss Cordelia," he called at last, his voice high-pitched with pain and anger. "I reckon you think you done won this time. But if I was you, I'd keep those boys of yours on a real short leash—and that goes for the big nigger too!"

20

That afternoon we buried Sparkplug beneath the Sweetheart Tree at the exact spot of my romantic encounter with Blair, although, of course, only Winston and I knew about that. Winston produced an orange crate from the Jitney Jungle. Tommy removed Sparkplug's collar and tag, wrapped the little terrier in a blanket, and carefully laid him in the box. Then we processed down the path with Winston carrying the shovel and Cordelia clutching a bundle of the irises from Mount Airy. After the grave had been filled in, Tommy took Sparkplug's silver dog tag from his pocket, along with a small hammer and a couple of nails. Weeping softly, he knelt and tacked the little silver tag to the base of the tree. Then we planted the flowers in a circle around the fresh mound of red clay. A couple of drops of dried blood, black against the green, spotted the leaves where Winston had lain Sparkplug on the irises in the trunk.

"Sparkplug wasn't exactly a good dog," Cordelia observed, "but he was there when we needed him."

I was still in shock over what had happened to Sparkplug. But even worse was the recognition that I had done nothing to prevent it. Paralyzed by fear of Fly, I had just stood there. Winston had been about to intervene, once more confirming his courage and loyalty to us. But it had been Tommy—my little brother—who had the presence of mind to act, while I had once more confirmed my lack of backbone.

When Horace came trudging up the street late that afternoon wearing his suit and carrying his overnight bag, Cordelia was waiting for him on the porch. He had only a short layover in Tuckalofa and was to head out again in the early evening. I watched from the yard as he bent to kiss her in his old-fashioned, formal way, and she took his hand. Then they sat down on the swing together and talked for a long time.

At supper, the conversation was subdued. L.Q.C. tried telling a couple of dumb jokes, but nothing would cheer Tommy up. "Do dogs go to heaven?" asked Tommy at last.

"Well, like Will Rogers said, if they don't, then I want to go where they go," replied Horace. I could see that he was just trying to relieve the tension, but Cordelia shot him a disapproving glance.

"Why, I expect they do, Tommy," she said. "God is love, you know. And He knows how much you loved Sparkplug. That love didn't die today. Maybe when you get to heaven, Sparkplug will come running out to meet you."

"And then I bet he take a bite out of yo' new white robe," added Senatobia, clearing away the plate of leftover cornbread.

"Be sure and take some of that home with you, Senatobia," Cordelia said. "I know how much Robert likes cornbread."

"Yeah, well at least Sparkplug didn't die by himself way out in the country. At least he found his way home before that," I observed. "And by the way, I still can't figure out how he got inside the house that night after everybody was in bed."

I lay awake long after the household had turned in. Every time I was about to drift off to sleep I was jarred back to wakefulness by some creak or thud as the old house adjusted itself and settled down for the night. I was keyed up and kept picturing the scene as Sheriff Fly pulled us over and lined us up on the shoulder, threatening Cordelia. I saw Tommy release Sparkplug and the little dog leaping toward Fly. And I saw him lying crumpled there at the edge of the road, bleeding from his mouth and ears. Finally I slipped off and dreamed I heard him scampering up the stairs.

I awoke with a start. It was still dark, so I lay listening. But everything was quiet. Had I heard a thud and the rattle of loose glass in the front door as it was pulled closed? A thin strip of yellow projected on the wall by the streetlight hung there like a sliver of lemon peel entangled among the wallpaper roses. I climbed out of bed and was peering out the window at the shadowed lawn when I thought I saw something move behind one of the big oaks in the front yard. I waited.

A low voice, the voice of a woman, drifted up to the open window from below. Another voice, that of a child, seemed to reply. Then a figure moved from the shadow of the tree into the glow of the streetlight, and I could see Tommy standing there in his pajamas. After a moment someone else, tall and draped in white, emerged from the shadows. The same ghostly figure we had followed to the cemetery had returned to Lee Street. As I watched, she took Tommy's hands in hers. Then she bent over as if to kiss him. Maybe L.Q.C. had been right. Maybe she was a vampire after all, casting a spell on him.

I was about to yell at her through the window to get away from my brother when Caruso, the peacock, began screaming like a banshee. She gave a start, dropped Tommy's hands, and sprang back, glaring up at the window. Horace was not due back until morning, but I heard Cordelia hurrying down the stairs. Barefooted, I went padding after her and followed her down to the parlor where she stood in her dressing gown, peeping out the window into the side yard. The street was partially blocked from view and dark as a coal bin, but we could hear the chickens squawking and the peacock howling.

"Cordelia," I whispered, "It's—"

"I'll bet it's some old hobo trying to rustle one of my chickens!" she exclaimed under her breath, cutting me off before I could explain about Tommy and the woman in white.

Caruso continued to scream, and, to my amazement, Cordelia went to the dining room and returned with the .22 rifle kept behind the door, the one Horace had given me for my birthday. It was the only means of protection we had in the house, other than the old butcher knife from the kitchen. But Cordelia had an aversion to firearms of any kind. I had heard her plead with Horace to give the rifle away or at least keep it locked up in the attic, but he would not hear of it. From time to time he would suggest that if she would just learn to shoot she might get over her distrust of guns. She always refused, however, and I doubted she even knew how to load the rifle. But that night, she knew the chicken thief didn't know that.

She opened the front door and stepped out into the night. I followed close behind, trying to spot Tommy and the woman in white before Cordelia could mistakenly draw a bead on them. "Now you listen to me, whoever you are," she called out into the dark. "I hear you trying to rustle my chickens! I've got a loaded shotgun here, and I give you fair warning. I don't know the first thing about guns, and I'm a terrible shot, so I'm just as likely to hit you as not!"

There was not a sound as Caruso stopped screaming. Then we saw Tommy sitting on the steps down at the sidewalk—alone. Not waiting for Cordelia, I ran to him and grabbed him around the shoulders, scanning the street in search of the figure in white. He seemed unharmed, and the street was populated only by restless shadows shifting in the breeze and by a single car parked at the curb down the street in front of the Parker house. At first I thought I detected the shadow of a driver behind the wheel. I was about to say something to Cordelia, who was close behind me carrying the rifle, but when I looked again, the car seemed to be empty.

I gently shook him, but he gave a sort of muffled grunt and stared straight ahead. "Tommy!" I said forcefully, "It's me—Harry."

"Harry?" he replied dully. "What are you doing here? I thought I heard Sparkplug. He was down here all alone, trying to get in the house. And when I went to look, that nice lady said she'd help me find him. Has he come back?"

21

"Hey, Tommy, did you have any funny dreams last night? Maybe about a mysterious lady in a long white dress?" He looked at me blankly.

"Harry, what on earth are you talking about?" asked Cordelia. "What mysterious lady? It was just some old hobo in the chicken coop, I'm sure. And Tommy was having a harmless episode of sleepwalking. Honestly, I can't imagine how you boys get all these extravagant notions in your heads."

It was a Saturday, and as the day wore on, I retreated to the parlor to escape the heat, trying to concentrate on *Gone with the Wind*. Tommy and L.Q.C. were huddled together discussing L.Q.C.'s latest project, the mapping of Tuckalofa. The map was being drawn on several sheets of butcher paper spliced together and was now spread out like a white tablecloth over the dining room table.

We heard Cordelia at the front door. "Why, good afternoon, Miss Katie Mae! What a pleasure to see you. Come out here, boys, and say hello to Miss Katie Mae McCarthy."

Sighing and tucking our T-shirts into our shorts so as avoid the inevitable reprimand from Cordelia, we reluctantly assembled on the front porch.

"Why, look at you, Tommy! How you've grown!" exclaimed Miss Katie Mae, pecking my brother's forehead with a kiss. "And Harry and L.Q.C. too! I do declare, Cordelia, those boys—all three of them—are so handsome. You know, I've always thought all the men in your family look so English; it's those dark, deep-set eyes. My goodness it is warm; I just can't remember more of a scorcher than this summer has turned out to be. If it doesn't cool off soon, I believe I may just go into a decline!"

Senatobia appeared bearing a plate of cucumber sandwiches. "Here, Miss Katie Mae, you just help yourself to one of these," she commanded. "They'll sure help cool you off."

"I knew I should have made more orange sherbet," Cordelia sighed. "Nothing like it for a hot afternoon. It's so cold it'll make your teeth ache.

Would you like a pillow for your back? That old swing can get hard. And maybe a nice glass of ginger ale?"

"Oh, no, thank you, Cordelia. I can't stay. Although now that you mention it, I wonder if you might have a tiny drop of sherry? I just wanted to stop by long enough to invite these fine nephews of yours to my Sunday School class. This quarter we're doing Genesis, and tomorrow we'll be studying the story of Joseph and his brothers. I know they would be interested, and we'd just love to have them join us."

"Why, I think that's a splendid idea," Cordelia replied, glancing at us. "Besides, just about everybody in the Presbyterian Church grew up going to Miss Katie Mae's Sunday School class. Her class is quite famous, and it would give you a chance to meet some of your local contemporaries. Now give me a moment, and I'll be right back with that sherry."

Little Miss Katie Mae, as she was known behind her back, was indeed Lilliputian. She was ancient too—at least ninety, I guessed. Every time I saw her on my trips to Tuckalofa she seemed to have gotten even older and smaller. She sat in the swing wearing high-top black lace-up shoes that didn't quite reach the floor. Beside her lay a white straw purse with yellow daises on it that was big enough to carry a kitchen sink.

Following a few minutes of further conversation, she took a last sip of the sherry, then rummaged around in her purse, retrieving a Tuckalofa Funeral Home fan. Her faint little mustache was damp with perspiration. "Well, I really must be off now; I have an appointment with old Jim Rainey to have my toenails clipped, you know. And then I must prepare for my Sunday School lesson, especially since I know I can look forward to having you boys as guests."

She began struggling to climb down from the swing. "Now don't just run off like that," Cordelia said. "Harry, give Miss Katie Mae your arm and help her down the steps."

"Oh! There's just one more thing I forgot to mention," Little Miss Katie Mae said. "We always like to try to get into the spirit of our lessons, and tomorrow we'll all be dressing up like Joseph and his family—you know, with desert robes and sandals and such. I'm sure your aunt can help you find some old sheets, can't you, Cordelia?"

Then she sighed, already weary from the effort to rise from the swing and settled back down with a little plop. "Dear me. I don't suppose you'd have another tiny glass of that sherry, would you?"

It was only seven o'clock the next morning, Sunday, when out in the hall the telephone jingled. Horace rose from the breakfast table, giving us a puzzled look. We had been in the midst of devouring Senatobia's waffles with maple syrup and fresh blueberries and homegrown cantaloupe. There were biscuits with molasses, as well—Horace's favorite—and grits and sausage.

Everyone was dressed for church. Cordelia was stately in a navy pique dress set off by a long string of pearls. Before she and Horace left for church she would add her white gloves and wide-brimmed straw hat. Horace, who had returned home about daybreak, was elegant in his slightly rumpled seersucker suit and white carnation boutonniere.

After a couple of minutes Horace returned and resumed his seat. We all stared at him, waiting for an explanation of the call. "I've got to leave early this morning," he finally announced. "Mr. Estes has called a special meeting of the session for eight-thirty. You boys can walk down by yourselves for Sunday School, and I'll meet you all out in front of the church a little before eleven."

"What's this about a special meeting?" asked Cordelia.

"I'm not sure. He said there was an emergency of some sort. Something about that group from Rice College in Holly Springs planning to show up today."

"Well, if that's what it is, I certainly hope you'll speak up and urge the session to treat them like they would any other visitors. In my opinion the church ought to side with the dispossessed instead of with their oppressors, and if the Southern Presbyterian Church can't be a model of tolerance, then how can we expect it from anyone else?"

"I don't know about that," he replied. "Certainly we should be hospitable to anyone who wants to join us in worship. But I hear this group has other things on their mind, like picketing and disrupting the service."

"What rubbish!" retorted Cordelia. "Horace, you've been listening too much to Mr. Estes and some of those other old fossils on the session!"

"Now, now. We must move cautiously, Cordelia. We must be careful to do things decently and in order. People can't be expected to change overnight."

He stood up to leave. "Senatobia, thank you for another excellent breakfast. I don't believe I've ever had such fine waffles."

He paused at the door. "And, Cordelia, I must say I resent being called a fossil!"

"Well, then, stop acting like an old dinosaur!" she replied. "These boys are watching you. Why, everybody in the church is going to be watching."

We sat listening as Horace stalked off down the hall, and I noticed that he had not chosen to pursue the argument with Cordelia.

Sunday School began promptly at nine o'clock so as to allow plenty of time before the eleven o'clock service in the sanctuary. As Tommy, L.Q.C., and I marched up the steps, a popping noise filled the air, followed by the scratch of a well-worn 78 recording from the loudspeakers built into the steeple of the Baptist Church down the street. Then Tuckalofa was flooded by a tidal wave of sound as the electric carillon broke into a florid arrangement of "How Great Thou Art." From backyards all over town a chorus of dogs erupted into a collective howl of joyous protest.

"The dogs are always the best part of Sunday," Tommy observed appreciatively.

We filed into the high-ceilinged classroom, nervously surveying the rest of the class. Like us they were dressed in an assortment of homemade Bedouin robes and burnooses. Nobody seemed too happy to be there. "This looks like a real disaster," muttered L.Q.C. under his breath.

The ancient Little Miss Katie Mae, old as Deuteronomy, stood at the door greeting her students, swathed in a small Oriental rug and glass beads, looking like a cross between Salome and a Mardi Gras queen. After a few introductory remarks welcoming the three of us and setting the stage for the lesson, she ordered us all to gather around on the floor in a circle like nomads at an oasis. Then she began to read aloud the story of Joseph and his coat of many colors and his adventures in Pharaoh's court.

It's a fairly long, involved story, of course, and before Little Miss Katie Mae had even gotten Joseph to Egypt, I saw Tommy and L.Q.C. whispering to each other. Then a few minutes later, a plump little girl sitting in front of them yelled, "Ouch!" She whirled around staring daggers, so I knew they were up to something. Little Miss Katie Mae paused and looked up, but then continued reading.

A few minutes later, just as Joseph was getting settled in as Pharaoh's soothsayer, there was another yell. "Ouch! That hurt!" The girl in front turned and pointed accusingly at L.Q.C. "Miss Katie Mae, they..." she hesitated.

"They popped her bra strap!" one of the other girls said indignantly.

We must have been smirking, because Little Miss Katie Mae firmly laid down her book of Bible stories and glared at us. "L.Q.C., Harry, Tommy—I am shocked, truly shocked. I certainly never expected such behavior from Cordelia Coltharp's nephews! If you boys are going to behave like Philistines, then you can just stay here with me after Sunday School is over. I do believe you need a period of quiet reflection on your misdeeds while you beg the Lord for forgiveness. Honestly!"

When the bell finally rang, everyone jumped up, talking and laughing, anxious to shed their robes and escape, hoping to be allowed by their parents to skip the eleven o'clock service and to be released for a leisurely afternoon. But Little Miss Katie Mae held up her hand. "Now, children, before you leave I need to warn you about something that's going on today. As you are on your way to church, you may see a bus and some strangers in front of the sanctuary. It's being said that a group of colored troublemakers from Holly Springs are planning to try to disrupt the worship service this morning.

"You must not go near them, do you hear? Just let Mr. Estes and the elders deal with this. These people are all godless Communists, so I hear. They'll claim they're just here to go to church, of course, but all they really care about is integration."

As L.Q.C., Tommy, and I began leaving the classroom with the others, trying not to be noticed, she stepped in front of us, blocking our path. "Not so fast, boys. I want to have a word with all three of you." Then she walked us up to the front of the room, sat us down, and began a lengthy lecture about decorous behavior where ladies were concerned. Finally she seemed to have reached the end. "Well, now that we've got that straight, I think we should all pray. I want you boys to get down on your knees here beside me."

Meekly, we knelt down on the hard floor. We all closed our eyes, and Little Miss Katie Mae began to pray. First she said the Twenty-third Psalm and then the One-hundredth Psalm. Then we all said the Lord's Prayer.

Just as I thought she was finished at last, she launched into prayers for Mayor Branston, the governor, Mr. Estes, and President Eisenhower, since he was a Presbyterian too. She prayed for the starving masses enslaved by the Communists in Russia and for our colored people that they might be content to keep in their place. And for all the poor ignorant heathens in Africa who didn't know Jesus and for the Presbyterian missionaries who were sacrificing the comforts of home to save souls in the farthest corners of the globe. She asked God to bless the Tuckalofa football team, who had already started practicing for their new season, and to make the price of cotton come back up. She prayed the potluck supper tickets would all sell and that it wouldn't rain since they didn't have a tent this year after the squirrels got into the church attic where the tent was stored. And that Roy Elroy, the guest evangelist coming up from Jackson, would truly bring the Lord's word with him and that all the gamblers, philanderers, drunkards, hobos, liberals, and other lost souls in town would be touched and turn from their sinfulness.

By then my knees were beginning to ache. I opened my eyes a crack. Tommy was kneeling beside Little Miss Katie Mae, both of whom had their eyes tightly shut. I glanced at L.Q.C. and saw that he was watching me. He gave his head a little sideways jerk toward the door, and I nodded. Then he nudged Tommy, silencing him with a finger to his lips.

Little Miss Katie Mae had begun asking that God in His infinite mercy would pity these three wayward and inconsiderate children and lead them to mend their ways now before it was too late. As she was humbly beseeching Him to lead us to grow up into fine Christian gentlemen who would make their parents, their church, and their community proud, L.Q.C., Tommy, and I stole away like Bedouins melting into the trackless wastes of the desert.

We shed our robes and pitched them into an empty classroom. When we emerged from the side door of the Sunday School building, a chaotic scene greeted us. It looked as though half the town were milling around in front of the church. I recognized some of Cordelia and Horace's friends dressed for church. There were others, sunburned white men in overalls and their weather-beaten wives in faded country dresses, who I knew were not members of the church. Had they heard the rumors and come to see for themselves what would happen?

There were black people too, gathered together in a little knot across the street, talking quietly among themselves; I recognized Winston among them. A half-block down the street sat Sheriff Fly parked in his patrol car.

At the curb in front of the sanctuary stood a chartered bus, its engine running, and I saw a succession of young black men and women descending from it. They wore neat white shirts and ties and Sunday dresses and seemed calm but watchful. Behind them appeared several older black men and a couple of white men, all in dark suits. One of the white men was bearded and wore a bow tie. "They look like college students—and some faculty, too," observed L.Q.C. "Must be those demonstrators from Rice College we heard about."

They formed up in a group with the bearded man in the lead and began a solemn procession toward the front steps of the sanctuary. At that moment the double doors to the narthex opened, and a line of white men in suits and ties filed out onto the front portico. They fanned out until they stood shoulder to shoulder across the entire front of the church. I recognized some of them—Mr. Morris wearing his thick green sunglasses, Judge Theodosius Cobb, Mr. Crenshaw, and Mr. McMurray. In the middle stood Mr. Estes in his black vestments, and next to him stood Horace.

"It's the whole session," whispered L.Q.C. "The elders, the leaders of the church."

They stared straight ahead at the students from the bus standing patiently at the bottom of the steps. Nobody in either group spoke or moved.

Then I saw a well-dressed man in a tan poplin suit and his wife coming up the walk. I vaguely recognized them as members of the church, neighbors of Cordelia and Horace from further up Lee Street. They sidestepped the demonstrators without giving them a glance and climbed the steps. As they reached the portico, the wall of elders parted like the Red Sea and allowed the couple to pass. Mr. Estes spoke to them, and they nodded their heads, glancing back over their shoulders at the scene as they disappeared inside. Some other white people in the crowd followed. They too were allowed to pass before the solid wall formed itself again, sealing the gap.

Then the bearded man walked up the steps. He stopped in front of Mr. Estes and said something we couldn't hear. Mr. Estes listened, his face impassive, arms folded across his chest; he shook his head. The bearded man turned and walked back down the steps where he faced the students. We edged closer so we could hear.

"Brothers and sisters," he began, "I have explained to the minister and the session that we are here to worship in peace, that we have no desire to provoke or to challenge. They have listened, but have denied us entry. I explained that, in that case, we would stand here peacefully until either we are admitted or the service is over."

A steady stream of white people was now making its way past the silent knot of demonstrators and up the steps where the phalanx of elders parted to admit them. Some of the local black people had crossed the street and were watching. Winston was among them, standing a head taller than the others. I saw him looking at me and gave him a little nod, but he just kept staring straight ahead.

"Why don't you go back home where you belong, you damn nigger-loving Yankee!" snarled someone behind me at the man with the beard, just softly enough so that only the demonstrators and those of us nearby heard. I turned and saw a tall blonde boy wearing a madras sport coat and penny loafers. Next to him stood Blair. She was wearing a red sundress that made her arms and shoulders look even browner than usual. I saw her take the tall boy's arm, and together they started up the steps. As they passed, she looked my way, but she just kept going, disappearing between Horace and her father into the sanctuary.

Finally Mr. Estes turned and disappeared inside, leaving the elders at their post. "Come on, we don't want to miss old Estes' sermon today," L.Q.C. said with relish, starting up the steps.

"That's okay. You and Tommy go ahead," I replied. "I think I'll just stay here." Much later I came to understand that it was at that moment that my world forever shifted on its axis. Perhaps it was Winston's silently watching me, or perhaps it was the sting of another rejection by Blair and the consciousness that the wound was still raw. But I realized on some deep level that I had more in common with those dignified outcasts standing there baking in the sun than I did with all the God-fearing church-goers filing up the steps into their segregated, sanitized sanctuary.

Even so, I lacked the courage to join the demonstrators. I just stood motionless, a passive spectator on the sidelines, as the heat radiated off the pavement and seeped up through the soles of my shoes.

The demonstrators remained motionless, facing the steps, talking quietly among themselves, as the muffled sound of hymns drifted from inside the church. At the top of the portico, the wall of elders still glared down at them with a collective frown. I didn't notice Sheriff Fly quietly walking up to the bus as it stood at the curb, engine idling.

Finally, after an hour, the doors were thrown open, and we could hear the last strains of "Onward Christian Soldiers" dying away inside. With Mr. Estes standing at the door, smiling and shaking hands, the line of elders parted, and people began spilling out and down the steps. Straight ahead of them stood the demonstrators, blocking the walk. As the first members of the congregation neared, the students fell back along either side of the path. They stood there in their white shirts and ties and summer dresses, watching. Everyone became very quiet.

Out of the corner of my eye, I saw a quick movement and heard raised voices. A member of the congregation—I caught a glimpse of a multicolored jacket—had shoved one of the black students backward onto the ground. As we watched, the tall blonde young man, the one who was escorting Blair, stood over the fallen youth and gave him a hard kick to the ribs.

One of the other students grabbed Blair's new boyfriend in a headlock, and I heard the madras sport coat rip. As they struggled there on the walk, a man in khaki came barreling out of the crowd. Sonny Fly raised the nightstick and swept it down hard across the student's back. The young man groaned and fell to his knees, releasing Blair's boyfriend. Fly raised the club and would have smashed it across the student's skull. But before he could bring it down again, a huge brown arm grabbed his wrist and gave it a hard twist.

Fly cursed as Winston forced him down onto one knee. The big black man's face was like a thundercloud, and there were tears in his eyes, as though all the years of pain and humiliation just wouldn't stay locked up inside any more.

Then I saw Fly reaching for his holster with his free hand, his long red fingers fumbling with the leather flap. But before he could draw the gun, something else happened. Out of the crowd, behind the sheriff, darted a small boy. He made a running dive and grabbed Fly's leg. Then he bit into the back of it at the precise spot where the day before Sparkplug had removed a sizable morsel of flesh.

Fly screamed in pain and spun around, wrenching his arm out of Winston's grip. "Run, Winston, run! Run!" yelled Tommy.

Fly reached down and grabbed Tommy by the arm, dragging him to his feet. "Why you little son of a bitch!" he exclaimed.

"That'll be enough, Sonny! Let him go. The boy's done nothing wrong. Let him go or, by God, I'll thrash you right here in front of the church—even if

I am a member of the session. I may be older than you, Sonny, but I've spent the last forty years shoveling coal, and I believe I can do it. And when I'm through, you can arrest me—if you've got the nerve."

Fly stared in amazement at Tuckalofa's senior engineer standing there in his seersucker suit, his frosty blue eyes blazing like the eyes of old Thomas Boyd Coltharp in the portrait over the piano. For a moment I thought he might try to pull his gun on Horace. But then I saw something come over his big, red face that hadn't been there before. Very slowly he pulled his hand away and released Tommy, who stepped to Horace's side.

"Where's that goddam nigger?" Fly bellowed, searching the faces of the crowd encircling them on the front lawn of the church. But Winston was nowhere to be seen.

22

L.Q.C. and Tommy and I made our way back up Lee Street along with Cordelia and Horace, mostly in silence. I was trying to make sense of what had happened in front of the church. On the one hand there was Horace's conviction, shared by Mr. Estes and the other elders, that the demonstrators had not really come to worship, but only to make a political statement. That seemed reasonable to me. I wasn't so sure any more about Mr. Estes, but how could I doubt Horace?

On the other hand, I knew Cordelia felt equally certain that the elders were wrong to have barred the doors and that the church should have welcomed them without any questions asked. That seemed consistent with everything people had always told me about the church—that it was the house of God, and that God is love. But how could that be if people were going to get beat up just for trying to attend a worship service?

And how could Horace and Cordelia both be right? I remembered what Cordelia had told me that I should try to reason the truth out for myself. I had seen the demonstrators, and they didn't seem dangerous to me. They hadn't started the trouble. It had been started by the elders, escalated by Blair's new boyfriend, and culminated in Sheriff Fly's senseless brutality. To a person, the demonstrators had maintained a quiet dignity. They were clean and well dressed, and all they said they wanted was to be allowed to come inside for an hour just like anybody else. It was true most were black. But would Jesus have been standing out there shoulder to shoulder with Mr. Estes and Horace and the elders? I had to admit that from what I had heard about Jesus, it seemed more likely that he would have been riding on that bus.

But if Jesus would have sided with the demonstrators rather than the church, then the church must not always be right. And if that was so, then didn't it raise a question about whether what the church preached could be taken seriously, much less believed? And whether good, wise people like Horace could be mistaken?

What really worried me was that if Cordelia were right and if I sided with her, then didn't that make the two of us members of a tiny minority of white people in town who had chosen our version of justice over the views of the majority, over the established authority of the church? My search for truth was certainly turning out to be more complicated than I had anticipated. It was becoming clear to me that there was a lot more going on in Tuckalofa than met the eye. Below the sleepy surface, powerful forces were stirring. I began to feel very worried and not a little scared. Several things were becoming clear though. I was being forced to admit that I was surrounded by many people who didn't see the world in the same way Cordelia and I did. They weren't all what I had heard called "white trash" or "rednecks" either. Many of them were respectable people, leaders of the church, pillars of the community, friends of my family. They were everywhere, and it was pretty clear they wouldn't take kindly to having their views challenged by a kid like me.

Could I develop the ability to defend my new ideas against formidable opposition from the likes of Mr. Estes? Could I learn to hold my own, to refute their arguments with facts and logic like Cordelia could do?

It was distressing to realize that I might not always be able to stand on the sidelines like I had in front of the church. Some day I might have to make a decision about which side I was on. I secretly hoped it wouldn't come to that and that I could just quietly pack my duffle bag and head back to Memphis for the start of school. But what if it did? Would I be able to summon up the courage of my convictions, as Cordelia would put it, and take action? Why, even my little brother Tommy had done that when he went after the sheriff, while I just stood there watching.

When we reached the house, we all sat down on the porch, except for Cordelia who headed for the kitchen where Senatobia was rattling around fixing dinner. I could smell the country fried steak. Horace pulled out his pipe and an orange pouch of Sir Walter Raleigh tobacco. With his thumbnail, he deftly scratched the tip of a wooden match so that it burst into flame in his cupped hand. Then he stood up, puffing on the pipe until a cloud of fragrant smoke enveloped him.

"Tommy, that was a courageous thing you did," Horace said. "But you could have gotten badly hurt. Things almost got out of control."

"I was just trying to help Winston," replied Tommy. "That and to pay that old sheriff back for what he did to Sparkplug."

"Won't the sheriff be looking for Winston after he stopped him from hitting that colored student?" I asked.

"Yes, I expect he will, Harry. I just hope Winston can manage to keep out of sight for a day or two until things cool down. And I want you boys to stay clear of Sheriff Fly from now on—especially you, Tommy. All three of you have had a run-in with him this summer. Do you hear me?

"You've got to learn to respect authority if you want to get on in life. I'm not talking about Sheriff Fly personally. Just between you and me, he sometimes uses his authority to intimidate people he doesn't like or understand. But you must respect the uniform he wears. Order is absolutely necessary in a society based on the rule of law."

"But, Horace," I ventured, "were the students from Holly Springs breaking the law? You're an elder. Is that why you were up in front of the church blocking them from going inside?" Horace busied himself fishing around in his coat pocket for his matches. "Well, Harry, it's like this," he said at last. "I am a member of the session, all right, and I have taken a sacred vow to uphold the teachings of the church and to ensure that things are done in an orderly manner.

"Apparently the word got around late last night that we might have visitors this morning. As you know, Mr. Estes called a special meeting of the session. Nobody knew for sure whether the group from Rice College would really show up or what they would do. He had put together a plan, though, and he told us just to stand out there all during the service and not to let anybody pass that we didn't know. Said he'd tipped off the sheriff to be there too, just in case things got out of hand.

"A couple of us listened and then spoke up and said we weren't sure about that approach. I said we were playing with fire, and that I was for peaceful change but that we needed to go slowly. 'Well, I'm not in favor of any change,' old Mr. Howard said. 'This is our church. Why should we have to let anybody else in—much less a bunch of nigra agitators?'

"'Maybe we could just show them up to the balcony,' suggested somebody else.

"'No,' replied Mr. Howard. 'If we do that, they'll create a disturbance like I hear that other group did up in Batesville. Plus we'll have established a precedent, and the next time they come back, we'll have to let 'em in again. We need to stand firm now, draw a line in the sand, so to speak.'

"Mr. Estes stood up then and said that speaking of precedents we should remember that Jesus had driven the moneychangers from the temple and that we should have the same courage to keep out anybody who was just there to make a political point, rather than to worship.

"Well, that sort of got to me. So I asked Mr. Estes if he could see into the hearts of others and tell what motivated people to come to church. I asked him if he was prepared to keep out any members of the congregation whose reasons for being there he didn't approve of.

"Before he could reply, though, Mr. Howard got to his feet. He glared at me and launched into a long speech about how what was really happening here was that the godless Communists and the NAACP were behind it all. He said that if we didn't stand up to them now, pretty soon colored people would be wanting to eat in our restaurants. And if they got away with that, before we knew it they'd want to join the church! They'd be trying to marry our daughters and we'd all have little pickaninnies for grandchildren, and soon our entire American way of life would be a thing of the past. 'Is that what you want, Horace?' he said, looking at me. 'You got a duty to protect the church against these outside agitators!'

"Well, I just sat there while they all waited on me to answer him, not knowing exactly what to say. I felt confused because I could sort of see his point, you know. I knew it was an important decision, one that could affect all of us for a long time to come, and I wanted to get it right. But, boys, sometimes when you don't have much time and the issues are complicated and other people are depending on you, it isn't easy to see what's right.

"Just then little Mr. Peacock, one of the deacons, came running in. 'They're here! They're here!' he shouted. 'A whole busload of 'em—nigras and whites together—parked right out front on Main Street.'

"Mr. Estes stood up. 'I suggest we gird up our loins, gentlemen. We have the work of the Lord to do—let us stand together like a mighty fortress.' It was too late. The debate was over, and I had lost my chance to answer Mr. Howard. I wasn't prepared to take a stand against the majority, and so there was nothing more I could do except go along with the others. We lined up across the front portico, and you know the rest.

"I can feel the times changing, and it's going to be a very different world that you boys inherit. I just hope it'll be one worth living in, but sometimes I have my doubts. There's so much hate—seems like it's just beneath the surface everywhere you turn these days. And now it seems it's found its way into the church, so I guess there's no place left that's safe."

"Horace is right," Cordelia said from where she had been standing just inside the screen door listening. She stepped out onto the porch and faced us. "It is indeed going to be a very different world that you boys inherit. And it can be a better one if decent people speak up. But they had better decide now which side they're on." She was looking straight at me.

"Like Horace says, if you wait until everything depends on your answer or if you hesitate, it may be too late. And if people like us avoid the question, if we just keep quiet and do nothing, then the haters are going to win. They'll win because there are so many of them and because they use fear as their weapon, playing on our suspicions and fear of unfamiliar ideas. They'll use that fear, twisting the truth and inflaming our insecurities until we're ready to deprive others of their rights because we don't even think of them as human beings any more."

Horace sat there quietly for a moment. "Maybe Cordelia's right about the haters winning. I hope not. Because what I'm really afraid of, boys, is that all this division and animosity will grow, and that it'll not just split our little town of Tuckalofa or even the country. I'm afraid it'll split families—families like ours—and that it'll turn children against their parents and brothers against brothers. That's what scares me, because this family's the most precious thing to me there is…" He paused and took a pull from his pipe, but it had gone out.

"Well," Cordelia said briskly, "you all come on in now, or Senatobia's dinner will get cold."

The morning after the demonstration, I spent an hour at Carlisle's Drugstore, pretending that everything was back to normal and that the most pressing matter I had to think about was making my chocolate soda last while I thumbed through a *Green Lantern*. I was keeping an eye out for Winston, who, as far as I had heard, still hadn't been seen. He was supposed to pick me up about one o'clock for our delivery rounds. But I guessed that the sheriff was looking for him too, and I didn't need to be told that if Fly were successful, it would go hard on Winston.

At last the straw slurped against the bottom of the glass, and I got up and replaced the comic book in the rack. Leaving Carlisle's, I passed a little knot of merchants in straw hats standing around outside Guy's Barbershop. They stopped talking and watched me. "There goes that boy from up in Memphis, the one that works with the big buck at the Jitney," I heard someone say under his breath, the words dripping with scorn. "It was his brother that went after the sheriff out in front of the Presbyterian Church yesterday."

Hearing myself and Tommy branded as outsiders in Tuckalofa was something new and disturbing to me. Even though I felt sure that the demonstrators had been right, I wasn't sure I was willing to distance myself from respectable people like these businessmen over an issue that didn't directly concern me. Especially if it carried a price. I still hoped I could just remain neutral and the whole thing would blow over.

I hurried on not looking back, pretending I had not heard, feeling their stares boring into my back. I was almost past the post office when I remembered to check Cordelia's mail box. I had always liked the post office with the big bronze WPA eagle over the door, a symbol of order and stability. It was comforting to spend a few quiet moments in the dim lobby where brass gleamed against dark oak paneling, and where the cool, smooth marble floor and wainscot seemed to lower the temperature a full ten degrees. But somehow, today the post office didn't feel as reassuring as usual.

Back up at the house I flipped through the mail I had collected, absent-mindedly looking for any new commemorative stamps for my collection, and then deposited the envelopes in the little basket on the marble-topped telephone table. Despite the tension in the air on Main Street, here at Cordelia and Horace's it still seemed like the summer would stretch on forever, full of the drowsy hum of electric fans and the slap of screen doors. I lay down on the porch swing to wait for dinner, watching a bumblebee make his rounds amidst the abelia bushes that surrounded the porch, the push-pull rhythm of a lawnmower across the street lulling me into semi-consciousness.

The crunch of gravel was harsh as the red and white Jitney Jungle delivery truck pulled into the driveway, scraping the sidewalk. Winston was back! But he was early for our rounds—we hadn't even had dinner yet. I leapt up and scrambled down the porch steps, anxious to see him and to discuss the events in front of the church. But a stranger sat at the wheel, an older black man I didn't recognize. I hesitated and then sat down on the steps as he walked toward me with a sack in his arms.

Cordelia had heard the truck too and stood on the porch.

"Mornin', Miss Cordelia. I got you the okra and tomatoes, and your ginger ale, and some of that Calumet baking powder too, what we was out of last week. And I even got you your Green Stamps."

"Why, thank you. It's Everett, isn't it? That's very thoughtful of you. The okra's been so good this year!

"But you don't usually make the deliveries. Where is Winston today?"

He hesitated. "Oh, Miss Cordelia, I reckon you ain't heard. Old Mr. Sonny he done arrested Winston last night and got him up in the jail. Say he was drunk and resisted arrest out in front of the church yesterday."

"Winston drunk? On a Sunday morning? Why, Winston's a pillar of the CME Church!" exclaimed Cordelia.

"Well, I 'spect you right about that. But he didn't show up for work this morning, and I heared his neighbor, Bertha, telling about it to her sister-in-law down in front of the bank not more'n a hour ago. She say Winston was at home with Robert, his daddy, just sitting there reading when Mr. Sonny walked up on their porch. Next thing anybody knowed he done handcuffed Winston and put him in the backseat of his po-lice car and then they just drove off."

My heart sank, and a cold sense of foreboding crept over me. As Everett walked back to his truck, I turned to Cordelia. "What'll happen to him? I saw the way the sheriff looked at him yesterday, like he really wanted to hurt him bad!"

"Now don't you start worrying, Harry," she said. "I'm sure it's nothing serious—Negroes have rights, too, you know. He's probably out on bail already."

"Well, why didn't he come pick me up for our deliveries instead of Everett?"

"Why don't you go wash up?" she answered, avoiding the question. "And then go round up Tommy and L.Q.C. and tell them dinner will be ready in just a few minutes."

We took our seats at the dining room table. "Tommy, won't you try this good summer squash? Here pass it down to your cousin," Cordelia said as though it were just another big, lazy noontime dinner and she were looking forward to making a new batch of sherbet on the back porch after her afternoon nap. But the air felt dead and heavy with a sort of electric charge hanging about us, as though a storm were blowing in from somewhere over the hills.

Finally she looked down the table to Horace. I had overheard her upstairs filling him in about Winston as he packed his bag for the overnight run up to Memphis and back. "Obviously we can't leave poor Winston locked up in jail, if that's where he is," she stated with authority. "As soon as we finish dinner, I'm going to march down there and make sure he's been let out on bail."

"Now, Cordelia," he replied, "you always want to rush into these things. I'll be back tomorrow night. Why don't we just wait until then so I can come with you?"

"Nonsense!" she retorted. "The Apostle Paul says we should think of the poor and those in captivity. Why, I'll bet that awful Sonny Fly serves nothing but stale bread and water in that old jail of his. I'll just ask Senatobia to help me put together some of that leftover chicken from Sunday dinner, and I'll take it along. She's very upset about all this, of course. She hadn't said a word to me about it until a few minutes ago when I asked her about what Everett told us. She said she didn't want to worry us. But then she became very emotional and said she and Robert have been trying to find out how Winston was ever since he was arrested, but nobody will tell them anything.

"Horace, I want to say something here where the boys will hear me. On Sunday when I saw you out on the porch of the church with the rest of the session, my heart just sank. But I know you're not as impulsive as I am, and sometimes it takes you a while to see that the powers that be aren't always right. But when you stood up for Tommy and Winston against Fly, you showed great courage, and I'm proud of you. We're all proud of you."

I heard the bell in the kitchen ring, the one beneath her chair that Cordelia pushed with her toe, and Senatobia appeared. "Now, Senatobia, let's make up a nice basket of that leftover chicken and cornbread and whatever else is in there so I can take it with me to see Winston. Don't you worry; we're going to get to the bottom of all this."

"I'm going too," I piped up. "I've never seen a jail, and Winston may need me. Don't worry, Senatobia, you just leave it to Cordelia and me."

But Senatobia just turned away and disappeared into the kitchen.

The Dancing Rabbit County Courthouse was set back from Catalpa Street at the crest of a broad lawn. Unlike the stately antebellum courthouses that anchored the squares in Holly Springs and Oxford, it was a squarish, ungainly structure clad in a severe red brick that looked more like a late nineteenth century schoolhouse. On the pediment over the front door hung the face of a clock, its painted hands permanently stopped at sixteen minutes to one o'clock.

"That clock has been there since William Jennings Bryan ran for president in 1896 on the slogan 'sixteen to one,' the ratio of silver to gold he wanted to see in the dollar," Cordelia explained. "They couldn't afford a real clock, and most people supported Bryan, so some wag came up with the idea of painting the hands on."

At one corner of the site, a small structure of the same red brick hid in the shadow of the courthouse, its small windows covered by a lattice of steel plate. We parked the Packard beneath a large pin oak at the edge of the gravel patch separating the two buildings. Beneath the oak, a rusted iron ring, some six inches in diameter, was anchored in the earth.

"See that ring, Harry? In the old days this is where convicted felons were hanged. They would set up a wooden gallows right here under this tree and throw a rope over that big branch. Then the hangman tied a noose in one end and secured the other end to that ring. People used to come from all over the county to watch a hanging. Some would even bring a picnic to spread out here on the lawn."

I shivered, imagining the lawn packed for the ghoulish festivities. At that point it was as close as I had ever come to violent death; even today I sometimes think about that ring in the ground, about the elemental simplicity and economy of taking a life using only a length of rope. "Do they still hang people here?" I asked.

"Oh, no. Now they electrocute them down at Parchman Prison in Jackson. They say it's more humane, of course, but I have my doubts. Somehow the notion of being burned alive along every nerve in your body doesn't sound any better to me than being hanged."

We stepped through the front door into a dimly lit foyer furnished with a gray metal desk and a file cabinet in one corner. The jail smelled of urine. A steel door clad in peeling gray paint with a small sliding view panel was set into the wall opposite the entrance. At the desk sat a shriveled up little man with gray hair, wearing a gray uniform with a patch on the shoulder. There was no indication that he noticed us, so we just stood there in silence. Eventually he glanced up at Cordelia. Then he gave me the once-over.

"No minors allowed in the jailhouse."

"Why, good morning to you too, Ralph," Cordelia said. "Harry, this is Ralph Slatley; he was one of my students. This is my nephew, Harry."

"How do you do, sir?" I said.

"We're here to see Winston," she said. "That is unless he's already been released."

"I cain't let you see him, Miss Cordelia—sheriff's orders."

"What on earth do you mean, Ralph? What's he been charged with?"

"Drunk an' disorderly an' resisting arrest out in front of the church on Sunday—that's what."

"Rubbish! Winston's never been drunk or disorderly in his life!"

"Listen, Miss Cordelia, I don't arrest 'em. I just lock 'em up. All I know is Mr. Sonny says ain't nobody allowed to see him 'til he gives the okay. And you're going to have to tell your boy to wait outside. It's a city ordinance."

"Very well, then. Harry, why don't you wait for me out in the car while Mr. Slatley and I have a little conversation?"

I sat in the Packard for a good twenty minutes before I heard the steel front door slam and Cordelia emerged. When she climbed in and sat down in the driver's seat, her face was as gray as the inside of the jail. "What happened? Did you get to see him?" I asked. I noticed that she wasn't carrying the basket of chicken.

"Yes, Harry, I finally got to see him."

"But how in the world did you convince Mr. Slatley to let you in?"

"Well, you see, Ralph Slatley was just one of the dumbest students I ever had the misfortune to watch trying to use a library card catalog. He finally flunked out, and the only job he could get—with my help, I might add—was sitting there in that jail.

"At first I tried offering him the basket of chicken, but he didn't seem very interested. Then I remembered that he had tried several times to get his high school certificate by taking the GED test, but never was able to pass it. So I told him I'd tutor him if he wanted to try one more time. I also mentioned that I'm friends with the county superintendent of education, which is true enough, and that maybe I could get a little special consideration for his application.

"I suppose you might say I bribed my way in—but it was a case of what's called 'situation ethics,' you see. A small transgression in order to accomplish a larger good. After all, if the end doesn't justify the means, then what does?

"Well, he finally unlocked the door to the cell block and let me in. There's a little hallway with two cells on each side. In the first one I saw old Tom Heron, the town drunk. He spends most nights in there since it's better than sharing the alley behind the picture show with the rats.

"Winston was in there, but, oh, Harry..." She seemed unable to go on. "Harry, Winston's in a great deal of trouble," she said finally, "and I don't know what to do next. Oh, how I wish Horace were here."

23

I don't think any of us saw it coming. Certainly I didn't.

I was startled by a crash from down in the kitchen followed by agitated voices. I crept down the back stairs, and sat in the darkness several steps from the bottom, around the corner where I could overhear without being seen.

"I'm so sorry, dear, truly I am. I do know what he meant to you, what he's always meant to you. It just defies description!" I heard Horace say. It sounded like he was almost choking.

"Oh, Horace, Winston was always the gentlest, kindest, man! He wasn't capable of doing anything like that!" Cordelia's voice broke, on the edge of tears.

"Here, Horace, let me get that. I'm the one who dropped it. It was just such a shock…" I could hear the whisk of a broom and the dry clatter of broken china as she swept the shards into a metal dustpan. Then a long silence fell between them.

Finally, her voice under control once more, Cordelia spoke. "You know, that Sonny Fly's been nothing but a hoodlum for years, as far back as his junior year. He came from such a horrible home, of course. I've told you how his father used to abuse him, and I've no doubt that's what made him the way he is, but even as a boy he was surly and always late to class. He would sulk when I corrected him for returning a book late or disturbing the other students in my library. They had to suspend him from the football team after he got into that big fight with the team from Coffeeville the night Tuckalofa lost the championship. They say he broke the arm of one of those poor boys—hit him with a baseball bat.

"But I will say this for him. When he was with his sweetheart, poor Helen Ringwald, he was just transformed. With her he was always affectionate and considerate—like another person entirely."

She paused before asking, "How did you hear about Winston?"

"We had just pulled in down at the depot; it was about an hour ago," replied Horace. "Everybody's talking about it. It seems Sonny is claiming Winston attacked him in his cell last night when he opened the door to let him go home. Imagine such a story. Why would you attack the sheriff just as you're being released? They say Sonny beat Winston so bad that he died before they could even get him to the hospital. Floyd Rogers says he heard that old Tom Heron was in another cell waiting to be bailed out. Says Tom heard Winston crying out in the middle of the night, 'Please, Mr. Sonny, I didn't mean nothing! Just please don't hit me no more!' They say Winston had a fractured skull and was literally covered in bruises, and his face was so swollen you wouldn't recognize him. Oh, Cordelia, I'm so sorry to have to tell you that."

Sitting alone in the dark on the stairs, I felt something crumple in my chest. I must have moaned aloud because the next thing I knew Horace was peering around the corner. "Harry! What are you doing there?" he sounded surprised, but not angry. "Come on out, son. I guess you heard about what happened to your friend Winston."

I thought I might throw up. My legs were so weak I could hardly make it down the steps into the kitchen. I could tell Cordelia had been crying, which was unheard of, although now she seemed more collected. Anger had taken the place of tears.

"This is all just too much!" she exclaimed. "I do declare I'll just call John Calhoun Coleman myself right now. You remember he was one of my students too. He's the city attorney. It's up to him to do something about this. Don't you worry, Harry. Justice will prevail if I have anything to say about it!"

"Now, Cordelia, why don't we just let the system take its course? There'll be an investigation, of course" Horace said. He paused. "Although I wouldn't expect too much. It's likely to come down to the word of the sheriff against hearsay evidence from the town drunk."

I wondered how Horace could remain so calm, so detached. But Cordelia was not listening. She seemed to have recovered, and her blood was up. She stalked out of the kitchen, and we heard her on the telephone in the front hall. "Myrtle, this is Miss Cordelia Coltharp up on Lee Street. That's right, 250-H. Now you just get Mr. Coleman at city hall for me right this minute. No, I don't know the number, and I haven't got my glasses on. For heaven's sake, Myrtle, *you're* the operator!"

In a moment, Cordelia returned to the kitchen. "Well, they say John's out," she announced. "Horace, I'm going down to his office. I'll wait all day to see him if I have to. John's a nice boy. But he's not the sort you'd expect to become a prosecutor, although his father was a hero in the Great War. Now I guess we'll see what sort of fiber the son is made of."

The sun was low above the crest of the ridge that embraced the west side of the town before Cordelia returned from city hall. We had all felt the tension of waiting for her. I sat on the porch steps watching L.Q.C. and Tommy in the front yard half-heartedly trying out a new balsa wood glider, trying to adjust the wings so it would execute a perfect loop. They had managed to hang it up in the lower branches of the magnolia tree and were swatting at it with the rake. Horace sat on the porch swing reading the paper and puffing on his pipe, outwardly calm, although I noticed how he kept lighting it and then knocking it out again before it was empty.

When at last she came slowly walking up the sidewalk, her face drawn and the line of her jaw set, I knew that her visit had not gone as she had hoped. Horace stood and motioned to her to sit beside him. L.Q.C. and Tommy dropped the rake and followed.

"You just wouldn't believe it," she was saying to Horace. "Finally, after I've been sitting there all day, John comes sneaking out of his office just a half hour ago. I think he must have been in there all along—hiding—hoping I would go away!

"'Why, hello there, Miss Cordelia,' he says, as though he's surprised to see me. 'I'm truly sorry to keep you waiting, but it's been a long day—all this hubbub about Winston and the sheriff, you know.' That's what he calls it—a hubbub! He's wearing his usual white shirt and bow tie and suspenders, and he looks just as fresh as a daisy. 'Would you and Mr. Horace care for some of these tomatoes? They're homegrown. Sally, my secretary, brings them to me. I remind her I'm a bachelor and that I never cook for myself and that they'll just go to waste, but she keeps bringing them anyway. Come on, let's go in here where we can talk.'

"So we step into his inner office and he sits down behind his big desk. Do you know he's got a portrait of Robert E. Lee hanging on the wall right behind him next to his Rotary Club certificate and a big stuffed bass?

"'Now what can I do for you, Miss Cordelia?' he asks with this obsequious little smile, leaning back in his chair, making a little steeple with his fingertips.

"'John, I'm here to talk to you about Winston and to find out when you intend to have Sonny Fly arrested,' I say, trying not to lose my temper.

"'Whoa, now, Miss Cordelia,' he says, 'We got to move one step at a time here. I'm planning an investigation, of course, but the sheriff claims Winston became violent and that he had to subdue him. Says it was self defense.'

"'Rubbish!' I say, and then I tell him about what I saw when I visited Winston in jail. He stands up and walks over to the window. 'Would you be willing to testify to what you're telling me in court—under oath?' he asks.

"'Of course, I would, John,' I tell him.

"'This is a complicated case, Miss Cordelia, and it's important you understand what you could be walking into. Feelings are running high. The whole town's riled up. It's all anybody can talk about. People are already taking sides. Sure, I want to do the right thing. But there's a lot to think about.

"'I'm sure there's a few white folks who think the same as you—that Sonny needs to be locked up and indicted and tried for murder. All the coloreds are really hot about it, of course, and I sure wouldn't recommend anybody step foot down in Buzzard Bottom after dark tonight, but there's also the feeling among many that Sonny was just doing his job and that Winston got what's been coming to him. A lot of folks seem to think Winston had gotten awful uppity, driving around town with your nephew, interfering with Sonny at that demonstration, and all. And to make things worse, they're saying down at the Sycamore Club that if Sonny's indicted, the Citizens' Council, and even that silly group of night-riding hooligans—what do they call themselves, the Cyclopes—are likely to get involved. God forbid, we certainly don't need any of that here in Tuckalofa, especially after what happened with that Emmett Till case over in Tallahatchie County. I'm sure you can see that side of it too.'

"Well, I'm really burning mad by that point, but I manage to thank him for his time and I stand up to leave. But just as I get to the door, I turn back around to him. 'There's just one more thing I have to say to you, John. It's a story I once heard about General Lee,' and I point to the portrait on the wall behind him.

"'Lee was senior warden of the Episcopal Church in Lexington, Virginia, where he took a position as president of little Washington College after the war.

One Sunday morning, so the story goes, as the congregation was kneeling for prayer, in walked an old Negro man, a former slave. The old man walked down the aisle as the white parishioners stared in horror until he came to an empty pew. Then he knelt down and began to pray.

"'The congregation was visibly upset, as nothing like that had ever happened before, and people began to whisper to each other. The whole service came to a standstill. Then Lee, who had been watching from another pew, slowly stood. He went over to where the Negro man was still praying, and he knelt down beside him.

"'John, I think you would do well to be asking yourself what General Lee would do if he were in your place.'"

24

We rolled up to the Mount Zion CME Church about twenty minutes early. Horace nosed the Packard into the circle of shade beneath a pecan tree outside the little white clapboard building. Winston's funeral was to begin at two o'clock, but Cordelia wanted to be sure we weren't late.

The ushers, dignified black men in dark suits and bright white shirts, were already at their posts in the little narthex. They greeted us with grave respect, shaking hands all around and then handing us each a fan imprinted with a color illustration of a white, blue-eyed Jesus kneeling in prayer outside a rocky grotto. Angels with black faces and red and yellow wings hovered about him.

The other mourners soon began to arrive, some of the men in suits and others in worn but freshly pressed coveralls. Most of the black women wore elaborate dresses set off by wildly improbable hats. There were gold lame turbans and black extravaganzas with wide brims and veils, flashing sequins, and dramatic bows. A group of women clad entirely in white positioned themselves strategically about the perimeter of the room, ready to offer first aid to any emotionally overwrought mourners.

A few other white people were sprinkled here and there, more than I had expected. But then, everybody in town knew Winston. Even my mother had driven down from Memphis for the day, while Aunt India had sent Cordelia a note explaining that she would be unable to attend. I was surprised my mother had come; when I inquired, she explained that she knew how close Winston and I had become. She had seemed about to add something else as well, but then she stopped and refused to say more, and I saw the beginning of tears.

We packed ourselves into a pew with Horace seated on the end and Cordelia next to him, then my mother, Tommy and me, and finally L.Q.C. With a sigh, a large black woman fanning herself eased down next to L.Q.C.

Winston's open casket stood at the end of the center aisle at the base of the pulpit. The casket's interior was lined in white silk ruffles, and from where we sat, I could just make out the tip of his nose.

As everyone got settled, the pianist, a reed-thin old man with a cane who looked close to eighty, teetered in from a side door near the front. He was helped onto the bench with the assistance of the ushers and then looked for a signal from the preacher.

As he began a mournful dirge tinged with the blues, we all stood and turned toward the back of the church where the procession, headed by the preacher, Brother Daniel, was making its way down the center aisle. He was followed by Robert, Winston's father, accompanied by a woman I didn't know. Then came the choir in their emerald green robes. As they passed, I saw Cordelia take Horace's arm.

With a start I recognized the woman with Robert. It was Senatobia, transformed by an iridescent navy blue dress and a magnificent black wig. I had never seen her dressed in anything but an old housedress. She and Robert took seats in the front pew. The preacher mounted the pulpit and motioned the congregation to be seated. The little sanctuary was growing quite warm with so many mourners packed together, enthusiastically fanning themselves. All at once L.Q.C. gripped my arm. The woman next to him had begun to moan softly. Then she gave a terrifying wail and half stood, arms waving toward the rafters. Her eyes rolled back in her head, and the pew shook as she collapsed backward into her seat, slowly toppling over into L.Q.C.'s lap.

"Holy shit!" he breathed, struggling to dislodge himself beneath her considerable mass. Before he could do so, though, two of the older ladies in white nurses' uniforms materialized from the aisle. Two pairs of strong dark arms firmly yanked her upright to a sitting posture and began to beat the air with their fans. The victim moaned softly and opened her eyes. After a moment she seemed to regain contact with her surroundings. She looked around at L.Q.C., who cowered against me, pale with terror, and smiled.

"You okay, honey?" she asked him. "You don't look so good."

Brother Daniel's remarks were delivered with a quiet dignity that could not conceal the passion that lay beneath the words. "Brothers and sisters, do not think that we alone mourn the loss of this brother in Christ who has been taken from us by the cruel hand of oppression. The Lord God Almighty Himself mourns with us. He who neither sleeps nor slumbers mourns with us. The

Lord of Abraham, Isaac, Jacob, and Moses mourns with us, and He shall not be mocked!"

"Amen!" exclaimed someone behind us.

"'Vengeance is mine, I will repay, saith the Lord,' and the day will come, says the Lord, when the meek shall inherit the earth and the righteous shall be vindicated. He will come like a mighty wind, and the wicked shall be driven out before Him, and they shall be scattered like chaff.

"I say to you, my friends, that day is coming. Yes, that day is coming soon! A day when good men, kind men, strong men like Brother Winston will be free to walk the streets of America without fear. When they will be treated with respect and dignity. When they will be free to take any seat on that bus. When they will be free to use that public restroom, drink from that water fountain, or order a meal in that restaurant.

"And when that day comes, it will be because the strong arm of the Lord has parted the waters of injustice and lifted up men like Brother Winston to lead the rest of us on the way to the Promised Land."

"Thank you, Jesus!" someone called out. "You say it, brother! Praise the Lord."

"Praise the Lord!" answered a chorus of voices as the ancient pianist slammed into a rousing gospel number. The congregation jumped to its feet, singing, swaying, and clapping. From the pulpit, Brother Daniel joined in, singing and clapping in time to the beat.

Swing down, chariot comin', let me ride
Swing down, chariot comin', let me ride
Swing down, chariot comin', let me ride
I got a home on the other side!

When the music subsided, Brother Daniel announced it was time to view the body of the deceased. Robert and Senatobia took the lead, followed by the rest of the congregation. We were seated near the front, and when the ushers came and stood at the end of our pew, motioning that we should follow, I didn't want to go. I was afraid of what I would see, remembering Horace's description of what had been done to Winston in the jail. But I forced myself, and we all got up and moved toward the open coffin.

It was my first time looking at a dead man. Even before we got there, I could tell Winston looked pretty good considering all he had been through. His light brown face was unmarked, although I thought I could detect a bit of swelling around his jaw.

Robert and Senatobia were just a short distance ahead of us, and both had been weeping. As she approached the casket, Senatobia's legs seemed to give way. Horace stepped quickly to her side to support her. "Oh, honey," she cried, bending over Winston, "you is my baby, sure enough!" Then she turned to Horace and embraced him, and I heard her say almost in a whisper, "And you, Mr. Horace, you is one good man."

"On the contrary, Senatobia," replied Horace, "it is we who owe you a debt of gratitude." He paused, waiting for Cordelia, who was next in line. She stood at the casket for what seemed like a long time gazing at Winston. Then she reached down and softly caressed his cheek, and I saw that her hand was shaking. Horace wrapped his arm around her, and she looked up at him with tears in her eyes. Then they moved away back to their seats.

L.Q.C. was ahead of me, and after his reaction to reading *Dracula*, I was afraid he might pass out when he reached the casket. I was ready to catch him, but he just made a little noise in his throat and kept on going.

Something uncontrollable was welling up inside me as I stepped up to where Winston lay. I remembered his strength as he delivered me from the quicksand, his tenderness as he placed Sparkplug's battered corpse in its grave, and the look of courage and defiance as he stood there in front of the church twisting Sheriff Fly's arm. I thought about Winston standing next to the whites-only drinking fountain on Main Street, about the grief and humiliation in his eyes. About how I had doubted his loyalty and even blamed my breakup with Blair on him. About how I had asked him what it felt like to consider that his ancestors could have been my ancestors' slaves. And about my own unbelievable stupidity and insensitivity.

Tommy gave me a gentle nudge, urging me to move on, and I realized that I was softly sobbing.

When everybody had taken a look and returned to their seats, four old white-haired black men slowly made their way up to the front of the church. They stood together facing the congregation. One of them led off a cappella with the first line from an old field song. Cordelia later explained that it was the kind of song sung by the slaves in the cotton fields and that it could well be two hundred years old. One of the others followed with the reply, which echoed the first line. Then the others joined in, each refrain answered by another, until a complex pattern of overlapping verses reverberated through the little church, melding together in the sweetest, saddest music I had ever heard.

The words were about Pharaoh and the children of Israel, but I knew that it was really about the long bondage of another people, the people who surrounded me there in the church. In the dark rhythms and the repeating cadences I thought I could catch a glimpse of what it meant to be enslaved, to be treated like a beast of burden, systematically beaten and starved and raped. To have your family sold away, never to be seen or heard from again. To be kept in ignorance and superstition and then condemned for your stupidity by the very people—my people—who had seen to it that you never even learned to read.

It occurred to me that except for the accident of my skin color, it could have been my story instead of theirs, and that this was why what was going on in Tuckalofa mattered. Because if one group of people could get away with persecuting others, then it might just be a matter of time until it was I who was the victim.

I looked around me at the kind, dark faces that bore witness to the collective pain of countless generations of oppression. I marveled at the realization that my family and I could not only be allowed to come to this sacred place but that we could be welcomed like honored guests.

Next, Brother Daniel announced that it was time for the testimonials. The head of the deacons went first. He talked about a side of Winston I didn't know, about how Winston visited all the sick people in the congregation every Sunday afternoon. We heard how Winston had led the other men in rebuilding an old lady's house that had burned and how he loved to read the scriptures at the Sunday service.

Then Mr. Clarence Pegram, the manager of the Jitney Jungle and one of the other white people present, stood up. He was a big, red-faced man; he looked nervous, talking to a church full of black folks, but he seemed to speak from the heart. He talked about how Winston had never missed a day of work and how he would always remember that Miss Becky Woodman preferred to have the pulley bone cut on her chicken, and to include a box of paper doilies on Saturdays for the Coltharps' Sunday dinner, and to add a box of Milkbone dog biscuits to the Quigleys' order for Bubba, their beagle.

Then to my surprise Horace stood up. Everyone turned and looked in his direction. "For those of you who don't know me," he began, "I'm Horace Coltharp. I knew Winston and his family all his life. Why, his father, Robert, has worked around our house for over thirty years, and Robert's wife, Senatobia, has been our cook for just about as long. They are some of the finest people I've ever known.

"Winston was just about my son Frank's best friend growing up. Winston and Frank used to swim in Persimmon Creek together. They went fishing together. I remember how he and Senatobia carried Frank's duffel bag down to the depot the morning he left for the war. Why, Winston was just like a...." He paused and glanced down at Cordelia. "Winston was just like a member of our family.

"Most of you don't know that not long ago Winston saved my nephew's life when he almost drowned in the creek behind our house. My family and I owe him a debt of gratitude for all he did for us. Now I have a confession to make, and this seems like as good a time as any to make it." People looked at each other. White men didn't often make confessions to black folks.

"I've felt confused. And I've been slow to see that the times are changing. There have even been occasions when I worked to see that they didn't change— to see to it that the status quo was preserved—all in the name of order— although I knew in my heart it wasn't just. What I want to say is that I see that now." A murmur rippled through the congregation.

"Sitting here today, I felt something I haven't often felt before. It was a sort of stirring, a cool breeze blowing over my heart, and my confusion seemed to clear away. I became very calm and sure of what I should say to you all on this occasion.

"I've lived in this town most of my life, but I didn't fully realize that there are really two Tuckalofas, the colored one and the white one. And when I came in here today, I thought the same thing most of my friends do—that we whites shouldn't let ourselves be pressured by any outsiders to change the way we've always run our community. I'm an engineer, and my profession is all about respecting the rules of the road. I've always supported law and order, and I've always believed in changing society by evolution and not revolution.

"But lately I've been listening to many of my friends going on and on about all the reasons we should take a hard line against any change in the relationships between races. About how people aren't ready. And I've been thinking about some of the things in the Bible—how the mob called for the crucifixion of our Lord and how Pilate washed his hands and gave in to them.

"I sure hate to say this, but some of my friends have started to remind me more of the Pharisees than of Christians. If we don't see it in our hearts to change our ways, we are going to regret these days for a long time to come. Some people may think taking a hard line will put an end to the agitation. But it won't, and I'm afraid that this is just the beginning of the trouble unless we find another way.

"I see now that unless people like me—the white people who decide what happens and what doesn't happen around here—unless we are willing to work for justice, there won't be any peace. So I'm going to try my best to work for change from now on. For justice for Winston and for justice for all the rest of us here in Tuckalofa.

"That's all. But you can have my word on that."

"Amen!" called a voice from the far side.

"Lord, bless that man!" came another.

"Amen, brother. You tell it like it is!" cried another, and another, until there was a chorus of shouts from the little congregation.

After Brother Daniel's closing prayer, the ushers stepped forward and slowly closed the lid of the casket. Then they rolled it back up the aisle, the choir raising the roof with another spiritual. At the ushers' direction we fell in behind and processed out of the church into the parking lot, squinting against the blazing summer sun. Cordelia edged up beside me and took my hand and squeezed it softly. I looked up at her. "I can't believe Winston's gone," I said. "I liked him so much. Why did he have to die? Why does anybody have to die?"

"I don't know, Harry," she replied. "I don't understand it, either. There's so much I just don't understand."

We all drove in procession up to the cemetery, through the gates, past the marble and granite slabs and obelisks of the white graves, and into the black section. Next to a mound of red clay, the open grave, like a fresh wound in the green hillside, waited for the pallbearers to arrive with the casket. Everyone gathered around while Brother Daniel offered a final prayer. Then the ushers passed a couple of ropes under Winston's casket and slowly lowered him down into the cool darkness until he was out of sight. It was very still except for the birds twittering in the treetops and the crickets chirping away out in the high grass.

As we were walking back to the Packard, Tommy asked, "Hey, where's Cordelia?" Most of the congregation were piling into their cars and trucks. As we looked around the dusty cemetery, I spied Cordelia not far from Winston's grave where the sexton was already shoveling in the dirt. She stood very close to a black man whose back was turned to us. They didn't seem to be talking to each other exactly. It was more as though they were just standing there, each absorbing the other's unspoken thoughts. It was not until he turned slightly that I could see who he was. It was Robert.

25

In the days following Winston's death, the ensuing speculation over whether the grand jury would indict Sonny Fly for murder galvanized Tuckalofa in ways I could not have foreseen. Understandably, Senatobia seemed to be able to think of little else.

"Lawd, Miss Cordelia," I heard her ask after breakfast, "what you reckon going to happen if they lets Mr. Sonny off? I hear talk at church that all the colored folks is fixin' to boycott the stores on Main Street. They even got the NAACP sending down lawyers from Chicago. If there's one thing we don't need, it's no Yankee lawyers messin' with our business."

"Oh, for heaven's sake, Senatobia," replied Cordelia, "*I'm* a member of the NAACP!"

Senatobia stared at Cordelia in amazement before continuing. "Well, if all that ain't bad enough, I heard down at the telephone office that if he do stand trial, them ole Cyclopes is like to get stirred up. Them boys is just mean white trash—they even worse'n the Klan—and ain't no telling what'll happen once they get into this."

"Now, listen to me, Senatobia. I don't want you worrying about a bunch of small-time thugs and rabble-rousers who imagine they can dress up in sheets and intimidate the people of this town. I know we have our problems, but things haven't reached that point, and I'm sure they won't. Justice may seem to move slowly, but we must all keep calm and give it a chance."

"Well, I sho hope you right, Miss Cordelia, but I is scared. I been thinking of going to visit my sister over in Lovejoy County until this all blow over. I would, too, 'cept Robert say we ain't going nowhere, so I guess I just got to stay put for the time being."

One morning, a week or so after Winston's funeral, I was sitting in my favorite booth at Carlisle's. Now that Winston was gone I had no more delivery duties, and the days seemed long and empty. As I was contemplating the future, Mr. Ernest Crabtree from the real estate agency next door rushed in waving a copy of the *Tuckalofa Tattler*.

"Lookee here!" he hollered to no one in particular, "It says here the sheriff is gonna stand trial for first degree murder! Been indicted by the grand jury and arrested! They set the trial for August, and the jury's coming from Lovejoy County. Sonny's lawyer done convinced the judge he can't get no fair trial with a Tuckalofa jury! First degree, by God, and all that happened was some nigger got hisself beat up in jail!"

All the other customers stared at each other in silence.

"Now, Ernest, you just hold your horses for a minute, there," Mrs. Tootie Carlisle said from where she stood behind the counter. "Winston was a good, honest, hardworking colored man. Everybody in town knows that, and I for one am not surprised to hear that Sonny Fly got mixed up in this. I heard he belongs to the Cyclopes and the White Citizens' Council too. I just hope they keep him locked up 'til time for the trial." Several of the other patrons nodded in agreement as she finished polishing a milkshake glass and glanced at the clock on the ornately carved soda fountain with "Tuckalofa" emblazoned in gold letters across the cornice above the mirror. "Goodness, it's almost noon already. I think I'll just go make myself a tomato sandwich."

So for a little while at least it did look like there was a chance that justice might roll down like mighty waters. That same day, though, the judge released Sheriff Fly from custody on his own recognizance. Although he was suspended from his official duties, the next morning he was hanging out as usual next to the fire station, playing checkers in the shade at the Sycamore Club. His buddies laughed and joked with him, and anyone would have thought he had been elected King of the Tuckalofa Okra Festival.

None of the black people in town were laughing though. During the night someone had taped bright yellow posters to the lampposts all along Main Street. The city maintenance crews had begun moving down the street tearing down the signs, but it was too late. Everybody had already seen them. In large black letters they announced the possibility of a boycott:

STRIKE FOR JUSTICE IF FLY IS ACQUITTED!
DON'T PATRONIZE MAIN STREET MERCHANTS!

"What'll happen if they go through with the boycott?" I asked Cordelia.

"I honestly don't know, Harry. Some people are saying they'll have to call out the National Guard to keep order. I hope that things won't get out of hand, but I have a feeling Tuckalofa could be in for a hard time."

Sheriff Fly lived alone up the street from us in the same little bungalow where it was said John Dillinger had once hidden out briefly. Horace had recently referred to the place as doubly cursed. Since his suspension, Fly could no longer frequent his office in the courthouse, so we had begun seeing him out at the curb checking his mail after dinner or strolling down to the Sycamore Club, always wearing his khaki shirt and trousers and Red Wing boots. Cordelia and I had ventured downtown shopping that afternoon, and as we walked back up Lee Street, Cordelia grasped my arm. I followed her gaze up the sidewalk where, some fifty yards ahead, Fly was coming toward us.

It had been drilled into me that when passing on a public sidewalk it was inexcusable—even worse, it was "common"—to fail to speak to a fellow citizen, no matter if he were an enemy, or how poor or disreputable he might be. Under Cordelia's tutelage, speaking had become as automatic as choosing the right salad fork at dinner. As he drew nearer, I waited to see whether she would hold true to her mannerly principles or perhaps pass with an icy stare that communicated her contempt. I was surprised when, without a word, still holding my arm, she steered me across the street before we got close enough to be obliged to exchange greetings.

Around four o'clock it finally began to cool off, and by five Cordelia had taken her bath and sat for a little while on the porch in a fresh dress. As usual, supper was at six, and by seven we were all back on the porch, the dishes washed and put away.

"I declare—it's been just like a furnace all day. Let's go get an Eskimo Pie!" she suddenly exclaimed. "It'll be nice and cool driving around. What do you say, boys?"

We needed no second invitation. Despite the tension that lay everywhere beneath the surface, the summer seemed to be dragging toward its conclusion at the same imperceptible crawl as Persimmon Creek twisting through town. I tried not to think about the inevitable return home to Memphis and the start of school after Labor Day. But I was sick of our dusty clubhouse under the house and L.Q.C.'s over-ripe nature collection, which had begun to gather a greenish mold and to stink to high heaven so that Cordelia had inquired about the peculiar odor that sometimes rose from beneath the floorboards of the pantry. Preparations for Fly's trial seemed to be moving at a glacial rate, and we were even becoming bored with most of the gossip about strikes and boycotts, and a rumor that the National Guard might be called out to keep the peace.

Blair had disappeared, no doubt spending all her time on the tennis court flirting with her latest tall, blonde conquest. Tommy was getting on my nerves, the way he was always tagging along after L.Q.C. and me. L.Q.C. annoyed me as well with his crackpot pseudoscientific goings-on. Horace had been on the road ever since the funeral, and so there had been no target practice or expeditions out in the country. Cordelia seemed distracted by the heat and the local political upheaval, and it was even hard to get her to sit and finish reading aloud from *Huckleberry Finn* in the evenings.

It had been weeks since anybody had seen the mysterious woman in white, even though I had tried to assign L.Q.C. and Tommy to a rotating schedule for keeping watch between bedtime and midnight. When they resisted, I lay awake for hours in the dark of the tower bedroom, surveying the street for signs of her. Staying awake wasn't hard for me. I dreaded falling asleep and the dreams it would bring. Despite my efforts, eventually I would drift off to sleep without spotting anyone outside on the sidewalk, only to awake after midnight in the grips of a nightmare about headless songbirds, quicksand, Sparkplug, Winston, Fly, or enormous black snakes holed up in the sewers under Main Street. The next morning I could remember none of the details, however, and another tedious day stretched before me, filled with the vague tensions of the approaching trial and the faint echoes of my secret night terrors.

Everyone must have shared my ennui, for Tommy, L.Q.C., and I all jumped at Cordelia's offer to take a drive around town. We cruised up Main Street in the Packard, the windows down, drinking in the cool air. Opposite the park at the north end of town we pulled up in front of the little ramshackle convenience store run by a Mr. Crain, a wild-eyed semi-recluse who sold mostly bread, cigarettes, Moon Pies, and Cokes—the generic name we used for all brands of soft drinks from Nehi to NuGrape. Cordelia explained that it was said that if he were in an accommodating mood and if one had the cash and could be trusted, Mr. Crain could and would produce most forms of illegal alcohol from beneath the linoleum-covered counter.

He was not only the local bootlegger. Crain's other claim to fame was that he was the only denizen of Tuckalofa known to have flown over the Pure Oil station in a pickup truck. This unusual feat, admittedly an inadvertent accomplishment, occurred when he had been caught along with his mother-in-law at the pumps during the tornado that had struck some years before. The funnel cloud reportedly levitated the truck over the roof of the station, gently setting it down, with Crain still at the wheel, in a nearby field. The only damage reported by the terrified driver was that the vacuum inside the funnel cloud had drained the gas tank.

Crain also offered the only Eskimo Pies in town. I admired the Eskimo Pie. Unlike other brands, which were dull and flat as a pancake, the Eskimo Pie was distinguished by its crisp angularity and its elegant silver foil wrapper. In my considered opinion, it was the king of ice cream bars.

Refreshed after our stop at Crain's, we resumed our journey back down Main Street. The street lamps winked on, and the profiles of steeples and cornices began to stand out against the twilit sky. "This is just my favorite time of day," Cordelia remarked. "The French refer to it as *l'heure bleu,* the blue hour."

"Let's drive by the Ringwalds' and see if Helen's still up there asleep with the light on in her bedroom," urged Tommy as we neared the corner of Jackson Street.

The big house was set well back from the street in a grove of oaks. As we glided past, we all craned our necks out the windows. Sure enough, a solitary light gleamed in an upstairs window. Just then the front door opened, and a tall, thin man in a coat and tie stepped out and descended the porch steps. "Look, it's the sheriff!" I cried. It was the only time I had ever seen him dressed in anything but khakis and boots.

"Why, as I live and breathe, I do believe you're right!" whispered Cordelia. "He must have been to visit Helen. I've heard he does that—they say he brings her a little bouquet of violets—but I just never believed it. It seems so unlike him."

I imagined poor, helpless, Helen lying alone up there, dreaming of her lost baby, a vase of violets on her nightstand.

Once we were back on Main Street, instead of turning up Lee Street, Cordelia looked around at us and suggested, "It's such a pleasant evening. Why don't we just drive out to Stonewall Jackson School and back. You know, it's out past the west side of town."

That was fine with me. I loved listening to the rattle of the katydids and the gurgle of the occasional bullfrog in the grassy bogs by the roadside. And I liked to hold my arm out the window in the slipstream, changing the angle of attack of the palm and causing my hand to swoop and dive.

"That's Jackson School up ahead," Cordelia said after we had gone a few miles. "It's the new county school, named for the famous Confederate general. It was paid for with tax dollars from both Negroes and white people, but it's for white children only, of course. The school's symbol is the Confederate battle flag, and they call themselves the Rebels. Some people seem to think that's what the Confederacy was all about—segregation and 'keeping Negroes in their place,' as they say."

"The Rebels–that's the same as Ole Miss," I put in. At that point, I was still a Rebels football fan and had decided that I would attend the University of Mississippi, like most of my family before me. I had even picked out my fraternity. I would join Phi Delta Theta like Frank, Cordelia and Horace's son.

"Yes, they're the Stonewall Jackson Rebels, just like Ole Miss," continued Cordelia. "But you see, Harry, what began years ago as genuine patriotism and Southerners' love of their home has now begun to be twisted into something altogether different. When I was a student at Ole Miss, I used to stand up when the band played 'Dixie,' just like everybody else as a sign of respect and love of all that's special about the South. But I don't, anymore. The associations have changed.

"Too many people who do that now are really saying they agree with all the hatred and racial division, with segregation and repression. We live by our symbols, boys. But the meaning of our symbols can change. They can be appropriated by radical elements of a society and transformed into something entirely different. Hitler understood that when he used the tune of the old German national anthem for the new Nazi theme song. So you'd better stop and think before you casually put a Rebel flag decal on your car window or wave one at some football game."

"Hey, look over there!" cried L.Q.C.. "Somebody's got a big bonfire!" It was almost dark now, and the orange glow off to the right was hard to miss. Cordelia slowed the Packard, and we all stared across the pasture to a little grove of trees in the distance. In the dying light we could make out a cluster of cars and pickup trucks drawn up under the trees and figures moving back and forth, silhouetted against the flames. A little dirt lane turned off the highway toward the gathering, and about ten yards down it was parked a dust-covered truck. Next to the truck stood a solitary figure in a purple robe, a pointed hood with black eye holes covering its head. Held across its chest was a double-barreled shotgun.

The Packard was moving very slowly as we passed the entrance to the lane, and everyone fell silent. Then we felt Cordelia brake to a stop. She turned, looked back over her shoulder, and threw the car into reverse.

"Cordelia!" I cried, "What are you doing?"

"Yeah, let's get out of here!" seconded L.Q.C.

But the big car continued to back up. As we neared the lane, we saw the hooded figure walking toward us. Cordelia came to a stop and waited while the figure slowly moved across the glare of the headlights and around to the driver's side. Then it bent down and peered into the open window. It struck a wooden match and held it up to illuminate the driver's face.

"Why, good evening," Cordelia said, as though she were about to order a hamburger from a carhop at a drive-in. "That looks like an interesting meeting you're holding out there. My nephews and I were wondering if you might allow a few visitors—strictly for educational purposes, you know. As it happens, we've just been discussing participatory democracy and political science."

"Cordelia! Are you nuts?" breathed L.Q.C. in alarm, but she ignored him.

"Lady," the pointed hood snarled in a thick twang as the reek of whiskey filled the car, "where you all from anyhow? Cain't you see this here's a meeting of the Cyclopes? Ain't nobody allowed in here—leastways no goddam fancy-talking Communist liberals!"

"I see. In other words, nobody but a few hooligans who have to hide behind sheets out in a cow pasture, spouting a lot of white-supremacist mumbo-jumbo."

I couldn't believe my ears, and apparently the creature in the robe couldn't either because it seemed momentarily taken aback. Then it extended its arm through the open window and dropped the burning match into Cordelia's lap. She slammed the gearshift into drive and gunned the engine. The Packard roared and leapt forward, and the hooded figure disappeared in a cloud of dust and a shower of flying gravel.

She briskly brushed the smoldering match onto the floor. "I do believe Falstaff was right, boys," she reflected, her eyes focused on the rearview mirror. "Discretion is, in fact, the better part of valor."

26

The hooded monster was bending over me, thrusting a lighted match in my face. I tried to swat it away, but he pushed it closer and I could feel the flame singeing my cheek.

"Harry, wake up!" I was instantly awake, squinting into the beam from L.Q.C.'s flashlight held an inch from my face.

"Turn off that damn flashlight!" Angrily, I thrust it aside.

"You were right! She's down there again with Tommy! The lady in white!"

"What? Tommy's with her? Where?" I jumped from my bed and peeped through the window. Sure enough, Tommy and the woman in white were standing huddled together at the foot of the front steps. He wore his pajamas and slippers. Bathed in the watery glow of the streetlight, the scene had a hallucinogenic quality, and I wondered briefly if I might still be dreaming.

The dark-haired woman stood so that I could see a pale face with high cheekbones. She was neither young nor old and was wearing a vacant expression. As we watched, she took Tommy's hand. She pointed up the street, and together they began to move up the sidewalk. Something about it made my flesh crawl.

I had related to L.Q.C. the first of Tommy's sleepwalking episodes, the one Cordelia and I had witnessed, but he had been skeptical. Maybe now he would believe me. "Let's go! He thinks she's going to help him find Sparkplug." I whispered, rummaging around for my jeans and tennis shoes.

The night was unexpectedly crisp and cool, and for the first time that summer, a touch of fall quickened the air. A chalk-pale gibbous moon balanced on the treetops, the chill making it seem to shine brighter, and it was easy enough to see. A block ahead and up the hill we could make out the two figures.

"They're headed for the cemetery," L.Q.C. said softly. "We've got to be careful. I read that you should never wake a sleepwalker; it can give them permanent brain damage."

Keeping well back, we followed as Tommy and the woman crossed the street and headed down the dark alley that wound through the little hollow and then up to Manassas Street. I glanced over my shoulder several times to see if we were being followed by the car I had seen before, but behind us the street stretched away still and empty.

In the hollow, it was surprisingly cold. From far away down in the valley we could hear the rumble of an approaching train. A moment later a long, mournful whistle reverberated across the hills. What was it about that whistle that summoned up such complex feelings? There was in it loneliness and longing certainly, but also the siren song of a faraway world. I wondered if that world was beset by the same heartaches and injustices that besieged us. A big part of me was coming to detest Tuckalofa. And yet I still felt an undeniable affection for this little town despite all its intolerance, cruelties, absurdities, and contradictions. It occurred to me for the first time that it might be possible to both love and hate something at the same time, and I shivered.

We emerged from the alley onto Manassas Street, which afforded a clear view to the cemetery gates at the top of the hill. As we watched, Tommy and the woman slipped through them and vanished into the graveyard. "Come on," I hissed. "We can't lose them now!"

We broke into a trot and quickly covered the distance to the white limestone piers that supported the wrought iron gates. The gates stood open as usual, framing a view of the rolling, moonlit landscape punctuated by the faintly luminescent tombstones. Fifty yards away we could make out Tommy and the woman, gliding along between the rows of obelisks, crosses, and weeping Victorian angels.

It was a fairly simple matter to creep closer, slipping from the cover of one gravestone to another until we caught up with them. In the glow of the moonlight we could now see quite clearly, and from no more than twenty feet away we watched as the woman in white guided Tommy up a small flight of steps and into a family plot enclosed by a low wrought iron fence. There they stopped in front of two small, simple stones of the sort that marked the graves of children. Then as we watched in horror, she bent over Tommy, who stood rigid as if in a trance. She pulled him to her in an eager embrace, her dark hair falling across his shoulders.

"Look out, Tommy, she's going to suck your blood!" cried L.Q.C., jumping to his feet. The woman's head jerked toward us, eyes blazing in terror. A scream like a cornered animal echoed across the cemetery.

Suddenly we were blinded by a beam of light from the opposite side of the plot. "Get back, you little bastards! You hear me? Get back, I said!" snarled a man's voice, and in the glare we saw a man step from the shadows. He swung his legs over the fence, stepped into the enclosure, and moved slowly toward Tommy and the woman. "It's all right, now, Sweetie," we heard him say to her. The imperious tone was gone. "Time to go back home."

Gently he pulled her away from Tommy and swept her up in his arms. He glanced down at my brother, standing dazed at his feet, and then at us. Without another word, Sonny Fly turned, stepped over the low fence and strode rapidly away, the woman's silky nightgown billowing softly behind them.

I ran to Tommy, grabbed him by the shoulders, and shook him. "Wake up!" I cried. He mumbled something and stared at me blankly.

"Harry?" he finally said, "Go away and let me get back to sleep."

I felt L.Q.C.'s hand tighten around my arm. "Look, Harry," he hissed, "the name on the steps!" I squinted at the crumbling pavement leading up into the family plot. Carved into the first tread was a single faint word, but in the moonlight I was unable to decipher it. I knelt down and traced the letters with my index finger.

"It says 'Ringwald!'"

"You remember—the story we heard about Helen Ringwald and her twin sister, Catherine, the one Helen was afraid had been buried alive. Look, there's a child's grave right over here."

We bent over the small marble stone topped by a carving of a tiny lamb. The surface was partially obscured with a light coating of moss and lichen, but there was no mistaking the inscription:

Catherine Ringwald
Daughter of Fontaine and Eleanor Ringwald

"So this is where they dug her up and reburied her with her family and ours all standing around watching," I whispered. "And, look. Here's another grave right next to it. Let's see; all it says is 'A little one.' That must be Helen and Sonny's baby."

L.Q.C. grabbed my wrist. "Holy Shit!" he exclaimed. "Don't you see? The lady we've been following is Helen. And all this time Sheriff Fly's been following her too. He visits her at home and keeps an eye on her when she gets out at night. He must still be in love."

"But why has she started coming to see Tommy?"

"Don't you get it, Harry? Helen thought her sister was still alive and now she thinks her baby is, too. Helen thinks Tommy is her little lost son."

"Can we go home now?" asked Tommy, still half-asleep. "I'm cold."

"Yeah, we'd better be getting back," replied L.Q.C. "Tommy's shivering. And old Sonny Fly may be nice to Helen, but I didn't like the way he looked at us."

27

On the first day of Sheriff Sonny Fly's trial, dozens of white men, their eyes small and hard like little chunks of gravel, stood around in shirtsleeves outside the Dancing Rabbit County Courthouse smoking cigarettes and speculating on the outcome. "I heared that if Sonny's convicted or if them niggers try a boycott, the Cyclopes is gonna rise up and the governor's gonna call out the National Guard to keep order. I got a brother-in-law what's in the Guard an' he oughta know!"

"I tell you what. I better not catch any more of them sorry-ass coons from Buzzard Bottom hanging around on Main Street after dark, or there's gonna be some more up there in the cemetery with that Winston."

"I'm sure glad they didn't call me for this jury. Lookee here, they convict the sheriff and not a one of 'em'll be able to show his face in Tuckalofa again. Why, be lucky if he make it home to Lovejoy County in one piece!"

Not all the sentiment was pro-Fly, however. In an editorial the same day, the *Tuckalofa Tattler* pointed out that the grand jury had found sufficient evidence against Fly to justify the trial and called for all citizens to allow justice to run its course and to respect the verdict, whatever it might be. But it also urged the black citizenry to cease the threats of a boycott. For the first time in its eighty-year history, the newspaper began printing daily editions, instead of the usual one per week, with the latest on the trial in headlines Cordelia could read without her glasses from across the porch.

Based on her conversation with John Calhoun Coleman about her visit to Winston in jail, Cordelia had received a subpoena to testify. Horace had requested vacation leave from the railroad to attend the trial. I sensed that there was more to his presence than supporting Cordelia in her testimony and that something had changed in his character. He was still "Main-line Horace," very much the dignified senior engineer, of course, but lately he had seemed softer somehow, more vulnerable. I could see that Winston's death had affected him deeply, and ever since, he had seemed to be reconsidering his world, including much that he had seemed sure about before.

And so on the third day after the jury had been bused in from Lovejoy County and after the opening arguments had been completed, we all put on our Sunday clothes and marched down to the courthouse together. Tommy had protested, but Cordelia insisted that it was all part of what she referred to as our "liberal education."

"I feel confident the jury will do its duty and find the sheriff guilty. The evidence just seems so clear cut. But regardless of the outcome, this will be an important lesson in civics for all of you. This is exactly what those ignorant, racist members of the so-called Cyclopes are most afraid of—impartial justice by a jury of one's peers. It's why Justice is always depicted as blindfolded, holding a sword and a scale."

The courtroom on the second floor of the red brick building was filling up rapidly as we entered. It was already stifling hot, even though the tall double-hung windows were raised at the top and bottom. The ceiling fans rotated lazily below the schoolroom light fixtures, throwing flickering shadows across the tile floor. We found seats on the main level with the other white spectators. Behind us I could see that the balcony was already full of blacks, and I noticed Robert and Senatobia taking seats near the railing.

"There's John Calhoun Coleman at the prosecution's table," Horace commented. "And over there on the other side next to Sonny Fly is Clancy Sneed. He's Sonny's defense attorney. He's also a member of the White Citizens' Council. If you ask me, they're mainly a bunch of bigots masquerading as respectable businessmen. I hear he's taken this case on for free."

Just then a buzz arose among the spectators and we turned to look. Down the aisle came a half-dozen men, all dressed in starched khakis, all with silver stars pinned to their chests. They found seats together not far behind us, a row of sunburned, unsmiling faces. "I don't believe it," whispered Horace. "Those are all sheriffs—they must be from the neighboring counties. They're here to support Sonny."

"And to intimidate the jury, no doubt," replied Cordelia.

After a couple of minutes the jury was led in through a side door and took their seats in their box, separated from the spectators by a low wood railing. They were all white men, some wearing shirts and ties, others in denim coveralls. The bailiff ordered everyone to rise, and the judge took his seat on the bench. I recognized him. It was Judge Theodosius Cobb, and I had last seen him standing shoulder to shoulder with the other elders across the portico of the Presbyterian Church.

After some initial business between the judge and the lawyers, Mr. Coleman called the medical examiner to testify about Winston's injuries, which were severe. He had died of a brain hemorrhage caused by blunt trauma consistent with a severe beating.

Following the doctor's statement and a brief cross-examination, Mr. Coleman addressed the judge. "Your Honor, the prosecution calls Mr. Tom Heron."

There was a titter as old Mr. Heron, known to everyone as the town drunk, shuffled down the aisle and took the stand.

"Now, Tom," began Mr. Coleman after Tom had been sworn in, "on the night Winston was arrested you were in the jail too. Is that right?"

"Yessir," answered Tom in a voice as hoarse as a crow.

"And did you see Winston as he was brought in by Sheriff Fly?"

"Yessir," croaked Tom. "It was late, sometime after ten o'clock, and I seen him get locked up."

"And would you say Winston was drunk?"

"You're sure askin' a real expert about that, John!" someone in the audience called out, and the courtroom erupted into laughter.

Judge Cobb whacked his gavel and glowered. "Now let me tell you all for the first and the last time. There'll be no more comments or outbursts like that in this courtroom, or you'll all sit out the rest of these proceedings on the front lawn!

"Now you may continue, Mr. Heron."

"Nossir, Winston seemed sober to me."

"Well, would you say he was disorderly?"

"Nossir. He was real quiet and, you know, passive. I didn't hear him say nothin' at all."

"And then what happened?"

"Well, then I heared Sheriff Fly go into Winston's cell and shut the door. I couldn't see into his cell from where I was, but I could sure hear. Sheriff Fly, he just laid into Winston. Sounded like a baseball bat hitting the ball—a sort of a crack, you know—over and over. It went on for a good five minutes, I'd say. And then the sheriff come out, and I heared him lock the door behind him. Winston was moaning and whimpering, like he'd been hurt real bad. I remember I laid there awake just listening to him. I couldn't go to sleep after that."

"All right, Tom, let's move ahead to the next night, the second night Winston spent in jail, the night he died. You were still in your cell, is that right?"

"Yep. I was free to go. But it had been raining off and on all day, and I didn't have no place to go to stay dry. So the sheriff, he told me I could just stay another night if I wanted.

"Well, sometime in the middle of the night I heared a ruckus and Sheriff Fly yellin', "You goddam uppity nigger!" And then I heared ol' Winston cryin'. He kept sobbing, 'Please, Mr. Sonny, I didn't mean nothing! Just please don't hit me no more!' I could tell he was being beat up again, except this time, it seemed even worse'n the night before.

"After a little while it just got real quiet, and I heard the sheriff go out. I pretended to be asleep, but as soon as it got light outside I called to Ralph to unlock the door. And then I got out of there as fast as I could."

"Now, Tom, the medical examiner has testified that Winston died of a fractured skull and severe bleeding of the brain. He also mentioned multiple contusions—bruises, that is—along with a broken collarbone and a broken nose. Would you say that what you heard was consistent with those kinds of injuries—caused by a ferocious beating?"

"The defense objects, Your Honor!" cried Mr. Sneed. "The witness lacks the expertise to offer an opinion on such a matter."

"I'll sustain that. Mr. Coleman, please confine your questions to factual matters."

"Yes, Your Honor. Well, thank you, Tom. I have no more questions. Your witness, Clancy."

Mr. Sneed stood up and walked over to the witness stand. "Tom, would you tell the court what you were doing in jail?"

"Well, I, er, I mighta got into the sauce a little bit, and Sheriff Fly, he suggested I'd be more comfortable there."

"So you were drunk? And you have testified you didn't actually see Sheriff

Fly strike Winston. Isn't it possible, Tom, that you didn't hear exactly what you thought you heard, either?"

"Oh, nossir, I heared it all right."

"Tom, how many nights would you say you've spent drying out there in jail in the last month?"

"Oh, I don't rightly know about that. I guess I'm no stranger, though, truth be knowed."

"Just one more question, Tom. When Sheriff Fly arrested you, did he harm you in any way?"

"Oh, nossir, he was real friendly—said he had my regular room reserved for me."

"That's all I have for the witness, Your Honor."

The next witness for the prosecution was Mr. Clarence Pegram, the manager of the Jitney Jungle. After some initial questions, Mr. Coleman continued. "Clarence, you've testified that Winston had been a reliable employee for almost four years, that he was never late for work, and that you trusted him to make your deliveries all over town. I know your time is valuable and I have just one more question for you. Did you ever see Winston drunk?"

Mr. Pegram sat up a little straighter, as though he was offended at the very thought. "Drunk? Winston? Why he was a deacon at the CME Church! He wouldn't have touched a drop if his life depended on it. Most upright, respectable colored man I ever knew."

After a short recess so the judge and the jury could have a smoke, the trial resumed. Cordelia was called to the stand. Standing there tall and straight and poised in a gray linen suit, a yellow rose from her garden pinned to her shoulder, calmly taking the oath with her hand on the Bible, she could have been Ingrid Bergman or Katharine Hepburn in one of the picture shows we had seen down at the Skuna Theater. Mr. Coleman led off by asking her to tell the court how long she had known Winston.

"Why, I knew Winston all his life. He was my own son's playmate growing up. Both Robert and Senatobia, his parents, have worked for us for years. Winston and my nephews had become friends too, and he actually saved one of them from drowning earlier this summer."

"So is that why you decided to visit him in jail the day after he was arrested?"

"Yes, partly. Everyone in our family felt a debt of gratitude to him. He was very special—smart and gentle and always anxious to help other people in any way he could."

"All right, now, Miss Cordelia. Would you just tell us about your visit to see him the day before he died?"

Cordelia began her account of what had happened inside the jail after they sent me out to the car. She told how Ralph Slatley, the jailer, wouldn't let her in at first, although she didn't bother to mention bribing him. She told how she had seen Tom Heron in the first cell and then at last had come to the cell in the back.

"It was very dim, and I didn't think there was anyone else there. I was about to go ask Ralph when I heard something, a sort of a low moan, from the cell in the far corner. So I stepped back down the hall and looked through the bars. At first I thought there was just a big pile of old clothes in the corner on the floor. The cell was empty except for a toilet without a seat or a lid and a little bare steel cot attached to the wall with chains. But then the pile of rags moved a little, and I could see that it was a man lying there on the floor all doubled up into a little ball—in the fetal position—like he was trying his best to just disappear. 'Winston?' I called out. 'Is that you?'

"He moved again and turned toward me a little bit, and I could see that where his face had been there was just a mask of dried blood. He moaned again and tried to say something, but I couldn't understand him.

"So I went storming back out to the foyer where Ralph was sitting there flipping through a girlie magazine like it was all just another routine day in the jail, and I threw the chicken basket in his face. I know I shouldn't have done that, but I was furious. I called him a barbarian, and I don't know what all.

"I ended by telling him to be sure to tell Sonny Fly I had been there. 'And you tell him, too,' I said, 'that he can't beat up Negro men like he does poor, defenseless little dogs and expect to get away with it!' And then I rushed out, slamming the door in Ralph's face."

Then it was Mr. Sneed's turn to cross-examine her. "Good morning, Miss Cordelia," he said, smiling pleasantly. "Would you tell us how long you've known Sheriff Fly?"

"Most of his life, I suppose. Sonny Fly once dated my sister's friend, Helen Ringwald. I was older, of course, and he was a student when I ran the high school library."

"I see. Would you say he was one of the better students?"

A round of muffled chuckles filled the air, but Cordelia ignored them. "Sonny was no student at all. All he could think of was football and girls."

The crowd tittered again, and the judge banged his gavel.

"So you and he were not particularly close?"

"No, but that wasn't the reason. He was a bully. He liked to pick on students who were smaller and weaker. And he once beat up a boy from Coffeeville with a baseball bat. And everybody saw what he would have done to that Negro student at the demonstration in front of the church if Winston hadn't—"

"Miss Cordelia," interrupted the judge, "please limit your answer to the question you were asked."

"Very well, Your Honor," she replied.

"Isn't it fair to say, Miss Cordelia, that you actually despise Sheriff Fly?"

"Why, no. I don't despise him—"

"Now when you saw Winston in the cell, what was he wearing?" asked Mr. Sneed, cutting her off.

"Well, I don't remember, exactly. I believe he was wearing a T-shirt and khaki trousers."

"Did you see any bruises on Winston's body?"

"Well, no, not on his body, but—"

"Now then," continued Mr. Sneed, "the last time I was in that jail—on a professional matter, of course," he looked at Judge Cobb and gave a little wink, "I seem to recall that the lights were pretty doggone dim. Why, back in the corner of those cells it's almost dark, even during the day. Isn't that right?"

"Yes, but as I said," replied Cordelia, "I could see that his face was covered in dried blood."

"Might I respectfully suggest," Miss Cordelia, "that you were looking into a dark cell from a distance of what, eight or ten feet away? You couldn't tell exactly what he was wearing and you couldn't see any bruises on his body. Dried blood is black. Winston was a colored man with a black face. Isn't it possible that you are mistaken about the blood?"

"No, I don't believe I am—" she protested.

"No more questions, Your Honor," concluded Mr. Sneed.

It was almost noon so court was recessed. We all walked home together. Cordelia had arranged for our dinner to be brought over from Mrs. Watson's boarding house so that Senatobia could attend the trial. There were collard greens, baked ham, squash, fried okra, the last of the homegrown tomatoes, and hot cornbread.

"It'll be interesting to see whether they call Sonny Fly to testify," Horace observed. "The defense doesn't have to call him, you know, and if they don't, the prosecution won't have a chance to cross-examine. This could be the end of the testimony.

"By the way, I thought you did well, dear."

"I don't know," replied Cordelia. "That business about the dark cell may have raised some doubt in the jury's mind."

"But you told the truth!" I exclaimed.

"Unfortunately, Harry," she replied, "the truth isn't all that matters. What really matters is what the jury believes and whether they have the courage to act accordingly."

28

The courtroom was even hotter and had become quite still. As the judge conferred with the lawyers at the bench, I noticed five or six spectators and one member of the jury nodding off. But everyone sat up and paid attention when Mr. Sneed announced, "The defense calls Sheriff Sonny Fly."

Fly climbed slowly to his feet, turned and nodded to the row of sheriffs from the other counties, and strolled across the room to the witness box. He was wearing a blue suit and a Western bolo tie instead of his usual khakis.

"I do, so help me God," he said in a loud voice as the bailiff finished reading him the oath. As he sat down, he unbuttoned his jacket so that everyone except the judge could see the silver badge pinned to his shirt. Then he crossed his legs and leaned back in the chair.

"Now, Sheriff," began Mr. Sneed as soon as he had asked Fly a few preliminary questions about how long he had been in office, "what was your professional opinion of the deceased? Had you ever had occasion to have dealings with him before his last arrest?"

"Who, Winston? Sure. Now there was a troublemaker. He would fool you at first, though. Always seemed real quiet and almost shy on the surface, but underneath he was mean. Real mean. No respect for authority. Didn't know his place neither, riding around town in the front seat of Miss Cordelia's Packard and all.

"Take that demonstration at the Presbyterian Church. I seen him talking to those outside agitators before they all marched up to try to infiltrate the worship. Then after it was over and I tried to make a lawful arrest of one of them Communists for disturbing the peace, why he interfered with the performance of my official duties. I woulda arrested him then and there except some other high an' mighty busybodies got in the way." He glared at us from across the room.

"So after the altercation at the church, you considered that you had probable cause—a reason to be looking for him? And then you caught up with him later that same night at his house?"

"Yep. There he was, just sittin' on the porch steps, like he was expectin' me. So I cuffed him and put him in the car and brung him up to the jail. Booked him and locked him up. Just a routine arrest. Then I left to attend to some personal business."

"You didn't return to Winston's cell that night and assault him?"

"Nossir, I did not."

"And then the next day what happened?" asked Mr. Sneed.

"Well, I come in about eleven o'clock after my morning patrol. I heared from Ralph that Miss Cordelia had been there. I looked into the cellblock to make sure everything was okay, and I told Tom he was free to go. Then I left to go home for dinner while the judge was deciding about Winston's bail. I was back again for a while later that afternoon, but everything was still real quiet.

"That night after supper, I got a call from some nigger lawyer. He had a Yankee accent, but I could still tell he was a nigger—tellin' me that Winston's bail had been paid by the NAACP. So I went down to let him out. I had some errands to run first, so I guess it was about eleven before I got there.

"Well, when I opened the door of his cell, he jumped me. He was a big, strong buck, and it was all I could do to subdue him. I tell you, I was afraid for my life. We had quite a tussle, and I finally had to tap him a couple times on the shoulder and on the ass—on his backside, I mean—before he give up.

"After that I figured he could just spend another night in jail for his trouble. He seemed okay to me. When I nudged him with my toe, he was still breathing. I checked that. So I locked him up and went back home. It wasn't 'til early the next mornin' that I come to find him layin' there dead."

"Thank you, Sheriff. Your witness, John," Mr. Sneed said, taking a seat at the defense table. Fly looked over at the jury and raised a single finger in greeting, and I saw one of the jurors give him a little nod in return.

"Good afternoon, Sheriff," John Calhoun Coleman said. "I regret the necessity of asking you a few questions—I sincerely do—but I hope you'll indulge me."

"Sure, you just fire away, John," replied Fly.

"Thank you; I'll try to be brief. Now, Sheriff, when Winston stopped you from striking the young student demonstrator in front of the church, had the demonstrator broken any laws? I mean, I understand there had been a brief fracas with a local white boy, but was it anything more serious than that?"

"Listen, John, there was a potential riot about to break loose. I was outnumbered by those radicals, and it was clear that it could have become a real bad situation."

"I see. Now later, when you arrested Winston at home, did he offer any resistance?"

"Nossir, not at that time. Like I said, he could fool you into thinking he was a real nice, quiet nigger who knew his place."

"And when you booked him and locked him up, did he resist you in any way?"

"Nossir, he did not. Like I said, it weren't 'til the next night that he give me any trouble."

"Well, Sheriff, Mr. Heron has testified that you attacked Winston in his cell that first night."

"Well, ol' Tom must of been drunker than I thought then."

"Now, Sheriff, you testified, I believe, that the next night, the night Winston died, you got a call from a lawyer telling you that his bail had been paid. You said that before you went down to the jail to release him you ran some errands and that it was about eleven before you got there. What sort of errands did you run?"

"What do you mean, John? It was just a little personal business I needed to attend to."

"Tuckalofa shuts down pretty early, Sonny. By eleven o'clock it's closed up tighter than a tick. Where were you just before eleven?"

Fly shifted in his chair and looked at the judge. The judge nodded at him to answer the question.

"Well, I don't rightly remember all the details. I probably went by home, and then I mighta taken a little walk—"

"Sonny, you said just a moment ago that you had some personal business to attend to. That doesn't sound like taking a walk, do you think?"

"Well, what if it don't? I can't see how that has nothin' to do with—"

"Sheriff," interrupted the judge in a stern voice, "I'll decide what testimony is relevant. Now, I'm instructing you to give a straight answer to Mr. Coleman's question."

Fly's expression changed, and the cockiness seemed to evaporate. He leaned forward, and his chair settled on all four legs with a thunk. He hesitated for what seemed to be a full minute before he finally looked back up at Mr. Coleman.

"Okay, John. It's like this." He paused again, as though he were trying to control his emotions. "Years ago I had a girl. Miss Cordelia's already mentioned her to you—Helen Ringwald. I reckon just about everybody here knows about her brain operation. The doctors blew it, and she lost her baby. After that she was never the same. She's been an invalid ever since, and I visit her when I can, and…"

He stopped and looked around the courtroom, blinking like a man who has just awakened and can't remember exactly where he is. "Go on, Sonny, you were telling us about your visits to Miss Helen Ringwald," Mr. Coleman said.

When Fly spoke again, it was in the voice of a different man altogether. "Her doctors say she's asleep most of the time. But sometimes—usually in the middle of the night—she wakes up. She starts calling out for her baby. Sometimes she even manages to slip out of the house and go off looking for her poor dead child. She doesn't know where she is, I guess. I think they call it a 'fugue state' or something like that. It's been going on for years. Usually she ends up wandering up to the cemetery—to the baby's grave.

"I try to look out for her. When her family discovers she's missing, they call me. I keep an eye out for her on my patrols. When I see her wandering around town, I follow her from a distance. Usually she comes back by herself, and nobody's the wiser. No harm done, I figure. That night, before I went back to the jail, I had been keeping watch over Helen."

"I see," Mr. Coleman gently said. "And when you got to the jail would you say you were upset, Sheriff? It must be difficult seeing your old sweetheart in such a sad condition."

"Well, maybe I was, a little. I worry about her a lot. I guess I just never got over her, if you know what I mean."

"So that night when you say Winston attacked you, Sheriff, you were already upset. Were you armed?"

"Well, I had my nightstick, of course," replied Fly, appearing to regain his composure and confidence. "But you never go into a prisoner's cell wearing your sidearm. That's standard procedure."

"So you had a nightstick? Is that what you used to subdue the prisoner?"

"Why, sure. I had no choice. I was afeared for my life."

"And how many times would you say you, er, 'tapped' him with your club, Sheriff? The doctor has testified that he sustained multiple severe injuries."

"Oh, maybe two or three—four at the most. Like I said, he was strong, and he just kept coming at me."

"Okay, Sheriff. That will be all."

Fly pushed his chair back and rose.

"Oh, just one more question," Mr. Coleman said, turning back to face the witness. "Don't you think it odd that a prisoner would wait to attack you until you came to release him from jail?"

Fly glared at Mr. Coleman. "You know as well as I do, John, that there's no figuring why those people—them niggers, I mean—do the things they do. Sometimes they're just animals. Why some of the stories I could tell you about what goes on down there in Buzzard Bottom on Saturday nights…"

"Thank you, Sheriff, I really don't think that'll be necessary," replied Mr. Coleman.

29

We decided to walk home together, and Cordelia invited Senatobia and Robert to join us in waiting while the jury began its deliberations. Cordelia predicted it could take at least another day for a verdict and argued that we all needed a break. "The jury are people from Lovejoy County," she reminded us. "Most of them don't know the sheriff, so it's entirely possible they haven't already made their minds up. Meanwhile, let's try to relax. We have to have faith in the jury system, boys. It's all we've got, you know."

But despite Cordelia's efforts, the tension that filled the town seemed to have seeped into the house. She became uncharacteristically silent, busying herself browsing through her cookbooks. Horace fidgeted and puttered about, filling his pipe, lighting it, knocking out the partially burnt tobacco, then refilling and relighting it all over again.

It felt strange to have him around the house so much after his frequent road trips. He seemed at a loss as to how to occupy his time, and I suppose inventing odd jobs was his way of responding to his grief and rage, of trying to fill the void in his heart. He finally drafted Robert, who had been sitting in silence on a stool in the kitchen, to help re-hang the squeaking door between the dining room and the kitchen. Robert agreed without enthusiasm, and they began working silently together, each lost in his own thoughts.

They were soon summarily evicted by Senatobia, who claimed they were disturbing her preparations for supper. We all felt her unease at the absurdity of the situation. "Lawd, Mr. Horace," she had protested. "How you 'spect me to serve supper with you mens taking that ol' door off the hinges right in the middle of my kitchen. That door been squeaking for twenty-five years an' you got to fix it today?"

I could tell by her tone, heavy with apprehension, that she just wanted to be left alone to grieve and wait for the verdict in her own territory.

L.Q.C. and Tommy pretended to be oblivious to the proceedings at the courthouse. But from their short-tempered spats over a half-hearted game of

Parcheesi, I could see that even they were affected by the speculation over the outcome of Sonny Fly's trial.

I sat alone at the open window of my bedroom watching a thunderstorm build in the southwest. As the wind freshened, I savored the aroma of oncoming rain mixed with the metallic tang of the window screen. The visibility rapidly shrank to a few hundred yards, and the landscape of distant treetops, punctuated by church steeples and framed by the hills beyond, seemed to vaporize as a wall of gray obliterated the view of the valley. Just as the thunderstorm passed overhead and a sweeping curtain of rain dragged across the town, the telephone under the front stair rang.

I could hear muffled footsteps and Cordelia's voice, so I stepped to the top of the stairs. "What do you mean? How could they, so fast?" she was asking the caller. "Oh, no, surely he didn't say that? And did the judge have any comments? Yes, yes, I see…Well, Myrtle, thank you for calling. I expect we'll all remember this day for a long time to come."

Before she could hang up, I was down the stairs. Horace, Robert, and Senatobia surrounded Cordelia, while L.Q.C. and Tommy stared up from the living room floor. "That was Myrtle at the telephone exchange," explained Cordelia matter-of-factly. "The jury has acquitted Sonny Fly of Winston's murder. They returned the verdict in exactly 32 minutes.

"The judge just thanked the jury and told them they could go home in time for supper. And he told Sonny he was free to go too. Sonny just strolled up to the evidence table and picked up his nightstick. 'Now, by God, I can get back to rounding up niggers,' he said.

"It's all over," sighed Cordelia.

"I only wish it were," replied Horace. But before he could say anything more, Senatobia gave a little moan. She sagged against the doorjamb, and her eyes disappeared somewhere back into her skull. Horace moved quickly. But before he could reach her, she slowly slid downward, collapsing in a crumpled heap on the floor.

The rain stopped before suppertime, so L.Q.C., Tommy, and I headed down the hill to Main Street. The narrow storm ditch that paralleled the sidewalk was still thick with a torrent of muddy water plunging toward Persimmon Creek.

"Did you see how poor ol' Senatobia just sort of melted like a stick of butter?" asked L.Q.C. "I thought maybe she'd had a coronary or a cerebral thrombosis."

"Shut up, L.Q.C.," I retorted. "I'm just glad Horace revived her. And it was good of Cordelia to tell Robert to take her on home. Winston was Senatobia and Robert's son, after all."

It was impossible not to notice that not a single black face was to be seen on Main Street, although little groups of whites had congregated in front of Carlisle's and down at Dempsey's Dry Goods. Even though it had been less than two hours since the verdict, every lamppost now displayed a new poster announcing the boycott.

STAND UP FOR JUSTICE!
RESIST RACISM IN THE COURTS!
STOP TRADING WITH MAIN STREET MERCHANTS NOW!

We edged closer to the front of the drugstore where a skinny little man I recognized as a teller at the Bank of Tuckalofa was holding forth. "Well, I'm not sure it was the right decision—not sure at all. Winston wouldn't have attacked Sonny like that. But even so, we can't have the county sheriff getting life in prison, or worse, just for beating up a colored man in jail. How'd we ever maintain law and order if we did?"

"If you ask me, the Communists are behind the whole thing," offered a shriveled old man in a tie secured by a gigantic VFW tie bar and chain. "They've got a world-wide conspiracy to sow dissension, you know."

"That's Mr. Floyd Turnipseed," whispered L.Q.C. "I heard he got shot in the ass in World War I."

"Well, I for one say it's just a travesty of justice," exclaimed a lady in a wide-brimmed straw hat. "Why, everybody knows that Sonny Fly is a sadistic brute. That jury had its mind made up the minute they heard Winston was a colored man. I tell you, it almost makes me ashamed to live in Mississippi."

"Let me tell you a thing or two about them Communists," continued Mr. Turnipseed.

"Hold on, I'm gonna tell you all something," interrupted Mr. R.C. Williams, who owned the Pure Oil station. "If this here boycott by the coloreds comes off, we're all going to be in a heap of trouble. Why, half my trade is with colored. I already heard the Cyclopes is getting organized to stop it, and my brother, Roy—he's in the National Guard—he says they been told to be ready to mobilize on twelve hours' notice. I seen the lights on up at the armory last night. I 'spect they're up there getting ready to issue weapons and making plans for just this kind of eventuality."

"Like I was saying, them Communists. . ." insisted Mr. Turnipseed.

"Well, all I'll say is this," interrupted the lady in the hat. "If Sonny Fly tries to sit next to me at church, I'm just going to stand up and move to another pew! And you won't catch me speaking to him on the street either, just like nothing has happened."

Further down the sidewalk the little crowd in front of Dempsey's was mostly young men in blue jeans and T-shirts, hands shoved into their pockets, cigarettes hanging from their mouths. At first they didn't notice us, and I overheard one of them, a small, wiry, hard-muscled fellow with a blond flat top. "Eight o'clock you say, at the park? Sure I'll be there—wouldn't miss this for the world."

"Whooee—I guess some niggers are gon' learn a thing or two about boycotts tonight!" another said. The accent was hill country cracker nasal, metallic.

Then one of them spotted us standing there. He threw his cigarette to the sidewalk and brought the heel of his brogan down on it, grinding it into powder against the pavement. He nudged the man next to him who turned and glared at us through narrowed eyes. "That's enough talk for now, Billy Ray. Lookee who we got comin'."

"Why, them's the little pussies from up on Lee Street. I seed 'em with that lady what testified against Sonny," replied his companion. Without warning he spat, and with admiration I watched L.Q.C. hop nimbly to avoid the dark gob of chewing tobacco arcing toward his tennis shoes.

"Come on," whispered L.Q.C., "just keep walking. Don't make eye contact with them."

"You shittin' me?" sneered another young man in a sleeveless T-shirt that revealed a multicolored tattoo of a naked woman on his upper arm. His hair and eyebrows were pure white and his transparent eyes shone like ice water. "That lady's hubby's that ol' engineer what got into it with Sonny out in front of the church? The one what tried to help out Winston and that little black bastard from Holly Springs? I hope that nigger has the nerve to come back down here on another goddam bus crusade. I got a brand new carton of double-ought buckshot that's just itchin' to make his acquaintance!"

He took a menacing step toward us, then crouched down. Grimacing and extending his arms like an ogre, hands grasping at us like claws, he pantomimed seizing Tommy in his clutches. Tommy dodged and broke into a run with L.Q.C. and me close behind, our dignity forgotten. Instead of coming after us though, the man with the tattoo stepped to the curb. Behind us, I heard the boycott poster being ripped from a lamppost, followed by high-pitched jeers and laughter.

30

That evening supper was late. No one seemed to have any appetite, and we all sat around in the parlor pretending to read or work crossword puzzles. Cordelia seemed so distant and preoccupied that Horace finally inquired about the lack of activity in the kitchen. "Why just look at the time! Of course, dear," she replied absently, "I expect we must have some leftovers from Mrs. Watson's boarding house. I'll heat them up in just a jiffy."

At the table she was uncharacteristically quiet. When she finally asked Horace to pass the cornbread, she dropped the silver basket, scattering the golden yellow sticks across the floor. Had she foreseen all that was about to happen, just as she believed she had foreseen her son Frank's fate in the Pacific?

The days were growing noticeably shorter already, even though there were still two weeks until the dreaded start of school, and by the time supper was over, it was almost dark. L.Q.C., Tommy, and I were sitting on the front porch steps when Tommy spotted the orange glow in the distance. "Look! Down there on Main! It looks like some kind of parade!" he cried.

From our perch near the hilltop we could see indistinct figures moving along Main Street. "Come on—let's see what's going on," urged L.Q.C., jumping to his feet and bounding down the steps. We followed, sprinting away down the sidewalk, ignoring the sound of Cordelia's voice calling for us to stop.

Tommy was right. It was a parade—like an unholy procession from the days of the Inquisition. Down the center of Main Street they came in ranks of three or four abreast, marching at a measured, funeral pace. The purple robes and peaked hoods glinted in the light of torches, and the stench of kerosene drenched the sultry air. Several marchers wore capes of bright, contrasting colors over their robes; others carried Confederate battle flags or placards with crudely lettered slogans denouncing the boycott, the NAACP, Earl Warren, and the federal government. Many carried pistols tucked into their sashes while others were armed with deer rifles or shotguns. Some had only lengths of chain or tire irons. But the thing that made my blood run cold, that sent us cowering into the shadows of the alley next to the bank, was that the parade was absolutely silent. Only the slow, rhythmic clomp of heavy shoes and boots disturbed the night.

"Holy shit—it must be the Cyclopes! The same bunch we saw around the bonfire the other night," breathed L.Q.C.

"What are they up to?" I wondered aloud, afraid to voice my fears.

"Careful," whispered L.Q.C. "Don't let them see us!"

We waited in the alley until they had passed. Peeping around the corner, I saw that the sidewalks were as deserted as one would expect to see at three in the morning. Nowhere could I see another spectator. Keeping against the building façades we fell in far behind the marchers, a hundred yards or so separating us as they turned up Sourwood Street. "They're headed for Buzzard Bottom," exclaimed L.Q.C.

"Right—let's cut them off!" I replied, my heart rate already beginning to accelerate. "We can go through the ravine, down along the creek past the railroad yard."

Barely enough twilight remained to allow us to scramble down the steep bank that fell off into the darkness of the ravine and then navigate along the edge of the creek. Invisible saplings slapped our faces as honeysuckle and wild berry bushes tore at our legs. Up ahead we could make out the cluster of houses that faced onto Sourwood Street and backed up to Persimmon Creek. "That's Robert and Senatobia's place straight ahead." I panted, breathing hard. "I can just make out the Sweetheart Tree across the creek. Come on!"

At the mouth of the ravine, the point where the flood plain opened out into Buzzard Bottom, we paused in the shadows between Robert's cabin and a neighbor's. It was quiet except for the buzz of cicadas and the intermittent croak of a bullfrog down by the creek. I heard Tommy slap a mosquito.

"Look—here they come!" L.Q.C. said, pointing toward Main Street, a block away. The first ranks of ghostly marchers were rounding the bend in the road, torches flaring in the gloom.

"What are they going to do?" cried Tommy. "Let's get out of here while we still can!"

But we just stood there, watching. There was something mesmerizing about the approaching mob, undeniably sinister, but fascinating as well. Perhaps it was the same paralysis a cobra is said to inflict on its prey, hypnotizing it into immobility. We just stood there as they reached the little community of unpainted clapboard cabins intermingled with tarpaper shanties and gathered in the street facing Robert and Senatobia's. They were still silent, their torches flickering and casting long inky shadows that flowed into the blackness of the ravine.

A dog barked, and the curtains of the house next door were drawn back by an unseen hand. Behind us, a screen door banged and the cicadas went quiet. I turned and looked toward Robert's where a tall figure had emerged from the house. The man stood on the porch, arms crossed, staring at the mob in the street—the same pose he had assumed on the steps of the Presbyterian Church.

"Look!" gasped L.Q.C. "It's Horace!"

As Horace waited, the leader of the Cyclopes, arrayed in a red satin cape, stepped forward. He moved up the little path to the edge of the porch and stopped. Horace just stood there, still wearing the dark suit he had worn for the trial. He looked as though he had just showered and stepped out of the depot after the run down from Memphis.

"I'm giving you fair warning, Mr. Horace Coltharp," snarled the Cyclops. "You'll get yourself down from there and back home if you know what's good for you. These boys ain't playing around, and this don't concern you." He spoke in an artificially high, strained timbre, as though trying to disguise his voice. But one look at him, and I knew who he was.

"This is my town, and it does concern me," replied Horace. His tone was even, reasonable, but he spoke loudly enough for everyone to hear him. "You fellows are about to make a big mistake. Can't you see that anything you start tonight won't end here? Times are changing. Can't you see that you can't terrorize people and get away with it any more?"

"Listen here," growled the Cyclops. "We ain't about to let this town get overrun by niggers or liberals or Communist sympathizers trying to shut down our businesses and take over our way of life. You think we goin' to just sit still and let that happen?"

"You think things are bad now?" asked Horace. "Why, all it will take is one little incident tonight, and tomorrow Tuckalofa will be swarming with federal marshals and National Guard. You won't be able to set foot outside your house after dark or walk down Main Street without getting a bayonet stuck in your face!"

I heard the hiss of the first rock as it soared over our heads toward the house. There was a crash as it shattered Robert's front window. A cheer erupted from the mob, the first sound they had made. Horace turned his head and was peering into the darkness at the far side of the crowd, where we cowered in the shadows as the second rock smashed into his temple. He stiffened and fell straight backward like a big tree crashing to the floor of a forest. He lay there on his back on the porch in an odd, rigid posture, as a satisfied murmur spread through the crowd.

We crouched in the bushes in terror, waiting for Horace to get up. But he didn't get up. He didn't move. Then the front door opened, and Robert stepped out onto the porch, followed by Senatobia. They looked very old to me. Ignoring the mob, they bent down to Horace and tried to lift him.

The sight of the two black people seemed to inflame the crowd.

"Torch 'em!" came a shout. Out of the mob emerged a single hooded figure running toward the house. When he reached the front bedroom window, he smashed the glass and thrust a torch inside. Senatobia's lace curtains burst into a white sheet of flame like the mantle of a Coleman lantern. The mob cheered, and I heard scattered Rebel yells.

"Come on," I yelled, "we've got to help Horace."

Without looking to see if the others were following, I burst from our hiding place and sprinted to the porch of the cabin. Robert looked up from where he knelt beside Horace. "Harry, what are you doing here? I can't get him to move! And he's awfully heavy. Can you help us lift him?"

I could already smell smoke from inside the cabin. Then I heard L.Q.C. and Tommy running up the steps behind me. "Okay, we'll take his legs. You and Senatobia grab his shoulders," I ordered.

We managed to bundle Horace down the steps and off into the side yard where we laid him in the grass. The large swelling on the side of his head was impossible to miss. We tried to revive him, but Dr. Elliot told us later that he must have died instantly.

"Oh, precious Jesus!" exclaimed Senatobia. We looked up and saw flames burst from the open window of the cabin's main room.

"My books!" wailed Robert. Before anyone could stop him, he was running back toward the porch.

"Robert!" I screamed, but he ignored me. All we could do was watch as he scrambled up the steps and disappeared into the conflagration.

Now that the cabin had begun to blaze, the Cyclopes seemed to have lost interest. They turned and started down Sourwood Street toward the next little house. A family with two small boys cowered on the porch as the father and mother pleaded with the men in hoods. But from where I stood next to Horace's body in the tall grass I could hear the breaking glass and see the torches disappearing through the windows.

31

Early the next morning, Robert's charred body was pulled from the smoldering remains of his library. The firemen covered him with a blanket and laid him in the grass. At first light, the ambulance, accompanied by Dr. Elliot, was allowed to retrieve the bodies. They found Cordelia still sitting at Horace's side in the grass, where we had all spent the night together. She had refused to let us carry him home.

"I want them to see what they did," she explained.

When the attendants arrived, she was clinging to Senatobia, two widows trying their best to console each other. Senatobia was rocking slowly back and forth, softly singing a spiritual.

The only book to survive from Robert's library was a scorched copy of *A Tale of Two Cities*. Senatobia handed it to Cordelia. "Here, you keep this, Miss Cordelia. I ain't much on reading, and Robert, he'd want you to have it after all you done for him and after…well, you know."

Cordelia opened the volume and in a low voice began to read, almost to herself.

It was the best of times, it was the worst of times, it was the age of wisdom, it was the age of foolishness, it was the epoch of belief, it was the epoch of incredulity, it was the season of Light, it was the season of Darkness, it was the spring of hope, it was the winter of despair…

Tuckalofa awoke to find itself under occupation. The National Guard had pulled in during the night, and as we sat over a silent breakfast in the dining room trying not to stare at Horace's empty chair, the house began to shake. A moment later, an olive-drab half-track lumbered up Lee Street spewing oily black smoke.

The sidewalks of Main Street were dotted with young, fresh-faced soldiers in camouflage fatigues and steel helmets, rifles slung over their shoulders. Officers cruised up and down in jeeps, walkie-talkies pressed to their ears. Stenciled signs in the store windows announced a curfew at sundown and banned public gatherings of more than three citizens. The *Tattler* suspended publication until further notice, and the Bank of Tuckalofa closed—to prevent a run, it was said. At the corner of Sourwood Street sat a hulking Sherman tank, engine idling with a deep, pent-up power. A trooper stood in the turret manning a black .50-caliber machine gun, a belt of gleaming brass cartridges dangling from the breach.

A sad plume of gray smoke hung over Buzzard Bottom. As the day advanced, it drifted over the town and into the houses to be absorbed by upholstered furniture in sedate Victorian parlors, overcoats in hall closets, and down pillows in bedrooms.

The fire station stood deserted, the volunteer firemen still away on duty keeping watch over the smoldering ruins. An unconfirmed rumor circulated that as many as a dozen houses had been torched by the Cyclopes and that when the fire department arrived, some of the firefighters simply stood around and watched them burn.

By mid-morning an endless stream of neighbors, pillars of the community, railroad men, and residents of Buzzard Bottom had begun descending on Lee Street. Cakes and pies and casseroles of every conceivable flavor began to pile up in the kitchen and pantry, spilling out onto the sideboard in the dining room. Apple cobblers, peach cobblers, lemon meringue pies, and coconut cakes were heaped on the dining room table. Tomato aspic, tuna fish casseroles, squash casseroles, green bean casseroles, and chicken pot pies, along with mounds of fried chicken, surrounded by baskets of biscuits and cornbread, weighted down the pine planks of the old kitchen table. Pitchers of iced tea and lemonade, streaked with trails of condensation, clustered on the counter.

That afternoon my parents pulled into the driveway along with Aunt India and Uncle John, L.Q.C.'s parents, who had flown into Memphis. They had driven together straight to Tuckalofa, successfully talking the military police into allowing them through the roadblock at the edge of town. My mother and India assumed command of the logistics of a death in the family, while my father and John sat on the porch, smoking and greeting the visitors.

Cordelia had somehow obtained special permission from the officer in charge of the National Guard to hold Horace's funeral at the Presbyterian

Church despite the ban on public assemblies. She had also prevailed on him to allow Robert's service to be held at the CME church. Robert's funeral had been scheduled for the following afternoon, with Horace's service to be held the day afterward.

The next day, Cordelia announced that she wanted to attend Robert's funeral alone, which seemed strange to us. India and my mother both offered to accompany her, but she refused. "I want to be there with Senatobia, just the two of us together. I can't explain it to you. Just grant me this one favor."

When she returned, Cordelia immediately withdrew into her upstairs bedroom, where the door remained closed. She did not appear for supper, nor afterward, as the family sat around in the parlor.

Early the next morning a Cadillac hearse pulled up in front of the house. Supervised by Mr. Leonidas Lovelace, the funeral director, four pale men in ill-fitting suits carried Horace's pewter-gray casket up the front steps, across the porch, and into the parlor. They laid it across sawhorses draped in velvet in front of the fireplace where it would repose until time for the funeral.

I was standing there alone, contemplating the closed coffin, when I looked up to see Cordelia slowly descending the staircase. Something about her was different, and it took me a moment to realize that her silver-gray hair had gone snow white overnight. She seemed to float down the stairs, as though up in her room alone she had somehow become weightless. She drifted over to the casket, her summer dress flowing softly in the breeze from the open window, and gently put her arm around my shoulders.

"Horace and Robert were both so fond of you. You know that, don't you, Harry?"

"I guess so," I replied.

"I saw him last night. He came back to say good-bye to me."

"You saw Horace?"

She made no reply, though, and it was not until later that I began to wonder if I had understood her correctly. She was smiling at me, and her face reflected a serenity I had not seen there before—certainly not three nights before when I had run home through the ravine to summon her. I had told her that Horace had been injured standing up to the Cyclopes, but in my agitation had included no details of how it had happened. I had told her about Robert disappearing into the burning cabin, and she had turned pale and stared off into the distance. "Robert is dead, and Horace too. Horace was struck in the head by a rock, wasn't he? I begged him to stay here and not go down to Robert's, but he wouldn't listen. After he left, I was sitting here in the parlor, but I saw it all as clearly as if I had been standing there on Robert's porch."

Then it hit me—I would never see either of them again. Horace was dead. Robert was dead. Cordelia would die, too. I would die. Death was real.

I was terribly sad about Horace, of course. He had been more than an uncle to me. He had been my friend. And I began to understand that the most memorable thing about him was not that he was an engineer: it was his character. Certainly he routinely performed a dangerous job with great skill. But he was also a leader. He was there when he was needed. People looked up to him because he could be trusted, because they knew he would level with them, and because they knew he cared about them. He had died—sacrificed himself—standing up to a mob in the service of other people who were weaker than he was. His life, as well as his death, had meaning.

I decided that I would try to become like Horace. I would do my best to be brave. I would try to take care of Cordelia. And I would have the courage to tell the truth about how I saw things, even to people who I knew did not agree with me.

As I stood there with Cordelia next to his casket, we were interrupted by subdued male laughter from outside on the front porch where someone seemed to be telling a story. I sensed that she might want to be alone, so I excused myself and walked out to join them.

"Hey, Harry, come over here and see Jethro Claypool," my father said. "You remember Jethro—he was your Uncle Horace's fireman on 857 for as long as I can remember. He was just telling us about how Sparkplug tormented Horace."

I had met Jethro down at the depot. He was a big, kindly man in his early thirties. He was wearing clean, freshly pressed coveralls but seemed uneasy as everyone waited for him to continue his story.

"Yes—well, you all know that Sparkplug and Mr. Horace, they didn't exactly get along. I reckon Sparkplug just aggravated the stew out of him, the way that dog was always carrying on—chewing up slippers and rugs, barking at cars, going after the postman, chasing Miss Cordelia's peacock. Mr. Horace would go on and on about Sparkplug until finally I just asked him why he didn't do something about it instead of talking my ear off all the time.

"Well, one day when we was going on a trip, Mr. Horace bundled Sparkplug up and took him along with us in the cab. Told me not to say a word to anybody. Took him all the way down to Durant. And when we were still way out in the country, he stopped the engine and dropped him off there on the tracks."

Tommy and L.Q.C. and I exchanged glances.

"Well, Mr. Horace didn't think little Tommy would take it so hard—thought he'd get over it after a day or two. But then he told me he saw that wasn't happening.

"And about that time we started seeing Sparkplug again. Sometimes outside Durant we'd catch a glimpse of white in the weeds along the roadbed, and there he'd be, running along sniffing the ground on the trail of some rabbit or squirrel. And sometimes he'd stop and just look at us as we drove by, like he was watching us up there in the cab and wondering why we just kept on going.

"Finally, one evening, just as it was getting dark, we were headed back to Tuckalofa when we saw him up ahead—this little sad spot of white just sitting there by the tracks like he was waiting for us to come along. I guess Mr. Horace just couldn't stand it any more 'cause he put on the brakes, and, with Sparkplug chasing along beside us, old 857 finally rolled to a stop.

"Well, Sparkplug took one look at us and then jumped onto the steps, up into the cab, and just sat there, tongue hanging out, tail wagging. Seemed like he was sort of grinning at us.

"On the way back home I asked Mr. Horace why he had changed his mind about Sparkplug after the way that dog seemed to torment him. 'Well, Jethro, I've learned that you can't just think of yourself in life,' he told me. 'I'm as selfish as anybody else, I reckon, but I've slowly come to see that the happiness of other people is as important—more important, even—than having things exactly like I'd choose for them to be.

"'There's something more crucial,' he said. 'It's your duty. When somebody relies on you to always do the right thing, to be a certain kind of person, then you're under a solemn obligation not to let him down, even if it means you give up some of your own happiness. When you promise something to somebody—to spend your life with your wife, for instance, no matter what comes along—well, then you've made a sacred vow. You've assumed a duty. You didn't have to, but you did. And later, if you break that vow, even if she has it coming, even if she has hurt you deeply and has broken a vow to you, then you've diminished yourself.'

"After we got to the depot and Mr. Horace had changed clothes, he carried Sparkplug up here to the house. He told me later that just before he got home he stuffed him in his bag and, when no one was looking, carried him out in the coal shed with a bowl of water.

"Then that night after everyone was in bed, he went down and let him into the house. All he had to do was open the door—Sparkplug made for the stairs, headed straight for Tommy's room, and jumped into bed with him, barking his old head off as usual."

About an hour before the funeral, Mr. Lovelace and his men returned, carried Horace's casket out to the hearse, and drove it to the church. The sanctuary was full, and the balcony was overflowing with black people. It was hot and stuffy, even with the slowly turning ceiling fans, so Mr. Lovelace's men passed out hand-held fans decorated with a picture of the Tuckalofa Funeral Home.

The casket had been rolled down the aisle to a spot in front of the pulpit. I was glad to see it was still closed. Mr. Lovelace had tried to talk Cordelia into having it open for the service, but I had heard her tell him that was "common,"—that nobody in our family had ever had an open casket and we weren't about to give in to vulgarity at this late date. I wondered whether Horace would have a big bruise on his temple where the rock had struck him or whether Mr. Lovelace had been able to cover it up with makeup or plastic putty of some sort.

The service opened with a prayer followed by a grand old hymn. At first I joined in the singing only half-heartedly, my mind wandering to thoughts of Horace. Then we came to the fourth verse. Something washed over me and I couldn't go on; I just stood there trembling.

Time, like an ever-rolling stream, Bears all its sons away;
They fly forgotten, as a dream Dies at the opening day.

When the hymn was over, Mr. Estes stepped up into the pulpit and began his eulogy. From where we all sat together in the pew, we could hardly see him through all the flowers that surrounded the casket.

"My friends, Horace Coltharp loved his family," he announced in a dramatic voice. "He loved Tuckalofa. He loved this church. He loved his locomotive, old Number 857. But he loved his savior more. And when his engine pulls into that heavenly station, guess who's going to step out of the depot. Why, it'll be none other than Jesus Himself. And he'll glance at his gold pocket watch and say, 'Welcome home, Horace. I see you're right on time as usual!'" I saw Cordelia roll her eyes and cringe.

He looked out over the congregation. "Now, some of you may not associate railroad men with poetry. And most of you probably don't know that Horace was very fond of it. When I asked Miss Cordelia what his favorite poem was, she gave me this, which I'd like to take a moment to read for you. I'm sure most of you who remember Miss Cordelia's poetry readings in the high school library are already familiar with these lines from 'Death Be Not Proud' by John Donne. She tells me that in honor of Horace, she has arranged to have them inscribed on the gates to the cemetery."

Death be not proud, though some have called thee
Mighty and dreadful, for thou art not so;
For those whom thou think'st thou dost overthrow
Die not, poor Death, nor yet canst thou kill me.

When the service was over, we all filed out to where the hearse was waiting at the curb. Mr. Estes stood there with us at the top of the steps, and I saw him say something to Cordelia. Then he turned to me.

"Harry, please accept my condolences for your great loss. Your uncle was a fine man—although there are some of us who didn't agree with his recent position on the racial issue. I had always thought of him as a solid biblical Christian and a supporter of that wise doctrine of 'separate but equal.' You're a perceptive young man, and I feel sure you agree with me on that."

I suppose something finally snapped in me. Before all that had recently happened to turn my world upside down, I would have muttered some inane reply and turned away. But instead, I stared straight back into those cold, black eyes. "Mr. Estes, let me tell you something," I said, my voice quavering.

"Horace was twice the Christian you'll ever be! He wasn't afraid to take a stand. He could admit it when he made a mistake. He said what he thought, not just what everybody wanted to hear, and he stood up for the people in this town who don't have a voice. He was twice the man you are. And if what you stand for is what it means to be a Christian, then you can just count me out!"

We were alone for a moment, the others having moved down the steps toward the waiting funeral procession. I was shaking slightly but was determined to stand my ground, waiting for his reply. He stood there in silence for a long moment, glaring at me. A vein in his temple was beginning to throb.

"Well, Harry, I suppose we both know where this new attitude of yours came from." He glanced in Cordelia's direction. "I suppose it was inevitable, living in such a liberal environment, that you'd—"

"And you're wrong about Cordelia, too!" I blurted. "She understands more than you ever will about justice and what it means to care about other people!"

I thought I detected a strange clouding in his dark eyes. Instead of looking directly at me, he gazed just past my ear, as though he were focusing on a speck on the wall behind me. "I'm truly sorry to hear you feel that way, Harry. I'll pray for you. And for your aunt."

Then he turned away, back toward the church, leaving me standing alone. What was it I had seen in his eyes? The old fire and brimstone had vanished, replaced by something else. I would never know what it was, and it would be more than thirty years until I spoke with him again.

What I did know, however, was that our brief conversation had changed me. For the first time, I had stood up to a bully who wielded power over me. And in the process, I had been emancipated from a sort of slavery. So although I was overcome by grief at the loss of Horace, I felt a strange exhilaration as well.

When the pallbearers—Jethro Claypool, John Calhoun Coleman, Martin McCrory, Thurmond Honeycut, Jesse Morris, and Judge Theodosius Cobb— had loaded the casket into the back of the hearse, we all stuffed ourselves into Cordelia's Packard with my father at the wheel. We pulled out into the street, following the hearse at the head of the procession. As we rolled down Main Street, people stopped and stood in silence, the men with their straw hats pressed over their hearts. In front of the depot a small crowd had gathered, and as we passed, I realized it was composed of all the black firemen, brakemen, and porters. On a siding stood Horace's engine, number 857, the boiler fired up, headlight gleaming, the cab draped in black crepe.

As we turned up the hill for the cemetery, Cordelia gasped, pointing straight ahead. "Look at that!" she cried, "The license plate on the hearse!"

We all leaned forward, peering through the windshield. The number on the hearse carrying Main-line Horace to his grave was 857.

32

We were all exhausted and stuffed full of casseroles and cobblers. The telephone had finally stopped ringing, and by nine o'clock everyone else had turned in. I found myself unable to sleep, though, the emotion of saying goodbye to Horace and the confrontation with Mr. Estes still fresh in my mind. The house was dark and had begun to creak as it settled down for the night when I heard a soft knock at my bedroom door. It was L.Q.C. "Come on, Harry!" he whispered, an unfeigned urgency in his voice. "Get dressed. You don't want to miss this!"

My curiosity aroused, a few minutes later I followed him and Tommy silently down the stairs and out onto the street. Under the streetlights moths fluttered like lost souls. "Come with me, you guys," L.Q.C. whispered, "But you have to swear not to tell anybody. Ever."

He led the way up Lee Street, pausing in the shadows every few yards to check the deserted sidewalk for anyone approaching. Sonny Fly's house was set back from the street, and a single light burned in an upstairs window. Taking a small flashlight from his pocket, L.Q.C. crept up to the mailbox standing at the curb. He motioned to Tommy and me to come closer, and then slowly pulled open the door of the box. A powerful odor assaulted us. As he directed the beam inside I let out an involuntary gasp and leapt backward, while Tommy stifled a scream. Inside, a foot away, mouth gaping, coiled and ready to strike, lay the preserved remains of the great black snake Sheriff Sonny Fly had killed on Main Street.

Later I understood that at that moment, Fly must have looked out the window and seen us standing there at his mailbox, although he would have been unable to anticipate the horror that awaited him. That, at least, remains some small source of satisfaction.

At about ten o'clock the next morning Caruso, the peacock, began to scream. A few moments later the doorbell rang. Senatobia was away in mourning for Robert at a sister's house in the country, and I heard Cordelia walking to the door. She stepped out onto the porch and I could hear a stranger speaking in a raw hill country twang. Then came her voice issuing an indignant denial, followed by an imperious summons directed up the staircase, "Boys, you'd all better come down here. It's Sheriff Fly, and he has something to say to you."

My blood ran cold, but I knew better than to ignore a command from Cordelia. As soon as L.Q.C., Tommy, and I stood facing her and Fly on the porch we knew what he was about to say.

"Very well, Sheriff, tell these boys what you told me," she said.

"Them little juvenile delinquents of yours," he glared at Cordelia, "they done put a goddam big dead snake in my mailbox last night. Liked to scare me to death."

I glanced at L.Q.C.

"Boys, is this true?" she asked skeptically.

Silence.

"Is it true? You heard me! Harry, did you have anything to do with this?"

I stared at the floorboards, looking for a crack large enough to crawl into. "Well, not exactly," I mumbled.

It was Tommy who broke the silence. "I did it, Cordelia. It was my idea!"

Fly began to say something, but L.Q.C. cut him off.

"No, he didn't! I did it—he had it coming."

"No, L.Q.C.! You know you didn't do it!" I objected, suddenly shamed into confessing my share of responsibility. "I was lying, I did do it. That was Sheriff Fly the other night with the Cyclopes. He's the leader, the one Horace took on. Sure, he was wearing a sheet, but I could tell it was him. I could tell by the steel caps on his boots!"

Fly glared at me, his bony face going reddish purple with anger. "Why, you little bastards! I'm placing you all under arrest for vandalism and malicious mischief!" He pulled out his handcuffs and took a step toward us.

"No!" screamed Tommy and charged, head down, straight at the sheriff, plowing into the big man's groin. Fly roared in pain and staggered backward into the porch railing. There was a sharp crack as the railing gave way, and Fly disappeared into the abelia bushes.

"Shit! Goddamit!" We heard him roar in pain and fury as a half dozen black and yellow bumblebees flushed from the bushes like a miniature covey of quail, buzzing indignantly. He was on his feet in a moment, waving one arm wildly, his other hand holding the back of his neck. He retreated in panic to the sidewalk, flailing at the bees, while Cordelia, Tommy, and I stood on the porch, unable to move. I hardly noticed that L.Q.C. had disappeared inside.

It was less than a minute until the swarm dispersed and Fly recovered. Then he strode back up the steps to where we stood speechless with terror. I saw him reach for his pistol.

"Hold it, Sheriff! Hold it right there or I'll blow your brains out!"

In amazement, I turned to see L.Q.C. pointing my .22 rifle straight at Fly's chest. Fly stopped. Slowly he moved his hand away from the holster.

"L.Q.C., no!" cried Cordelia. She turned back to Fly. "Sheriff, you are not taking these boys off my porch."

"You badly mistaken about that, Miss Cordelia," he snarled.

I remember—I'm sure I do—what happened next as though it were yesterday. Cordelia turned toward L.Q.C. "Give me the rifle," she commanded. L.Q.C. hesitated, then lowered the gun and Cordelia took it from him. Fly seized the moment and reached for his sidearm once more. But Cordelia was faster. She raised the rifle to her shoulder. He froze.

"I want you to know, Sonny, that I'm not going to shoot you for what you did to Sparkplug. I'm not even going to shoot you for what you and those thugs did to Horace, although you deserve it. She hesitated. "But I am going to shoot you for what you did to Winston."

Then came the sharp report, the smell of cordite, the little puff of silver smoke, and a small, perfectly round hole appeared in the center of Sonny Fly's forehead.

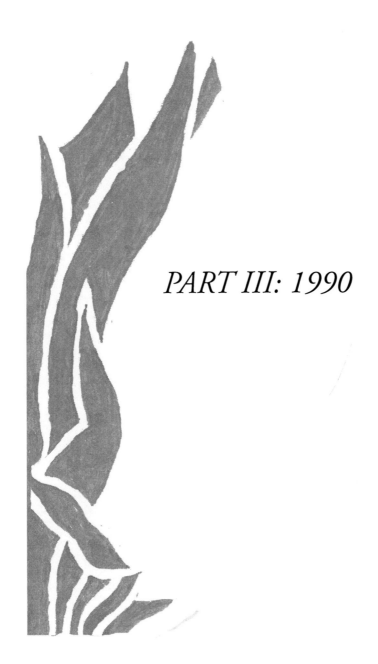

PART III: 1990

33

Slumped over Cordelia's desk, I awake with a start, disoriented, groggy from lack of sleep, and still stuck in 1958 on the day after Horace's funeral. With a pang of grief I remember—thirty years have passed, and today is the day of Cordelia's funeral.

So they are both gone now, first Horace and now Cordelia. The guard has changed, and now I am in charge. It seems preposterous. Only yesterday I had just turned thirteen.

The big house is cold and silent, but through the window I can see a sky tinted with the rose of a clear December dawn. My back aches, my fingers are stiff from a whole day and night of writing, and the fountain pen is running on empty again. The floor beneath the pull-down desk is littered with yellow sheets from the legal pad. There, I have finished it, my long overdue account of that summer.

Or have I? On the desk-top Cordelia's unopened will stares at me along with the diary and the ancient handmade valentine with the intertwined heart inscribed, "CC + RW, 1929." Who is or was the mysterious RW? I am still no closer to solving the riddle. It occurs to me that in a town the size of Tuckalofa it would be unlikely for me never to have heard his name. I make a short list. There was R.C. Williams who owned the Pure Oil station; Rodney Willingham, the mechanic down at Chester's Garage; and Ray Wheatley, who sometimes substituted for Jethro as Horace's fireman. Richard Watson, her old flame from Ole Miss, briefly occurs to me, but there is no reason to think their relationship continued. I think back over the list. With the exception of Watson they were all plain men. None of them seems like Cordelia's type, and I have no memory of her ever having mentioned any of the others.

I retrieve my scattered notes from the floor, and as I leaf back through them, the unwelcome thought again intrudes. Perhaps I haven't finished the story after all. Something is missing. I throw on my jeans and a sweatshirt and make my way down to the kitchen by the back stair, past the spot where I had overheard the news of Winston's death. Fumbling in a cabinet, I manage to find the coffee. Seated at the breakfast table, munching on a slice of toast, I try to analyze this odd feeling of incompleteness.

It is still early; Cordelia's funeral is not until eleven o'clock—plenty of time to visit the ravine one more time. This is not a rational impulse, I tell myself. Why should I feel drawn back there?

Descending the steep path, I feel certain it is not only that I have left something out. I cannot write the rest of the story because I have forgotten something. What is this odd, hollow place in my memory, a place I cannot bring myself to visit? There is more to tell, and it needs to be told now that she is gone.

The silver bark of the Sweetheart Tree glows brightly with the cold, clear sunlight of winter as the sun peeps above the ridge that borders the ravine. The creek burbles sedately, and I contemplate the passage of time. Were the Greeks right? Is it really impossible to step twice into the same river?

At the base of the trunk something shiny catches my eye. I stoop and brush away the fallen leaves. At the spot where I embraced Blair for the first and last time, the small silver dog tag that Tommy tacked to the tree marks Sparkplug's grave.

I gaze upward. Perhaps it is the low angle of the light or the absence of leaves on the bare branches, but the tree seems somehow different. It is even larger than I remember as a boy, which is hardly surprising given the passage of three decades. The bark, shining in the sun, is still tattooed with lovers' names, of course. And the old wound is still there, left by me on that day when, consumed by fury, I obliterated my own and Blair's initials. But now I notice that the carved inscriptions extend up the trunk. Where in summer they were obscured by leafy branches, winter has exposed the upper reaches to view. As I walk slowly around the trunk, craning my neck, I spot it. High above the ground, impossible to reach without a ladder balanced precariously on the edge of the creek bank, is carved a heart, the two halves intertwined like the tendrils of a vine. Inscribed in the center are the initials CC + RW.

The Presbyterian Church anchors the corner of Main and Jefferson Streets. Built almost a hundred years ago in the Romanesque Revival style, the broad gables of gray limestone, stained glass windows with round tops, and a broad portico across the front give the building an austere, respectable air. Once, before it was struck by lightning and burned, it was said that a tall steeple soared above the entrance, visible for miles. The deacons, fearing that the lightning might have been a sign of the Almighty's disapproval of their pride, never replaced it.

I am dreading Cordelia's funeral. I know I will have to endure my aunt's well-meaning, long-forgotten friends who will no doubt fuss over me as the sole representative of the family. I am having second thoughts too about the decision to follow Cordelia's wishes with respect to embalming. What if Mr. Lovelace was right? What will I do if, in the midst of the service, a strange aroma begins to permeate the sanctuary? Most of all though, I worry about the eulogy. I remember Mr. Estes' inane remarks at Horace's funeral. What will he say about Cordelia and her life—a life that represented the antithesis of everything the old preacher represents? A life that took the Gospel to heart every day.

So I am caught completely off guard by the hearty voice that greets me in the church narthex. "Hey, there, cretin!"

I spin around and stare at the heavy-set figure in the rumpled three-piece suit and bow tie grinning at me from the doorway. For a moment I draw a blank, but then it hits me. I have not seen L.Q.C. in what—twenty years?

As we shake hands, he explains. "I should have called to let you know I was coming after all, but the plane from New York was late, and I missed my flight to Memphis. I finally got there this morning and barely had time to rent a car and hotfoot it down here.

"Say, Harry, you're looking a bit peaked. Are you all right?"

"Sure, L.Q.C. I just didn't get much sleep last night. You look, er, well-fed!"

He laughs. "That's the life of a museum director—wining and dining the nouveau riche, fawning over their dreadful private collections, trying to squeeze donations out of them."

I feel another hand on my arm. "Harry, is that you?"

The dark eyes—her father's eyes—have kept their fire, although now a few fine lines surround them. She is as tan and trim as ever and looks as though she has just stepped off the tennis court.

"Blair!" I exclaim, surprised at how genuinely glad I feel to see her.

"You haven't changed a bit, Harry. Well, maybe a little bit taller than when you were thirteen." She smiles up at me.

"You look wonderful! Do you still live in Tuckalofa?"

She shakes her head. "We live in Jackson now—my husband, John, my daughter, and I. My father called to let me know about your aunt. I was always fond of her, you know."

"You remember my cousin, L.Q.C., don't you, Blair? The one with the telescope and the nature collection? Look, the service is about to get started, and your father wants me to meet him in his study. But I hope we'll see you again afterward.

"Come on, L.Q.C., we need to have a word with Mr. Estes. Something about the service. I don't know exactly what he wants."

The pews step down like an amphitheater toward the high pulpit that rises above the communion table and dominates the room. L.Q.C. and I make our way down the sloping side aisle and through the passageway that leads to the minister's tiny study just off the chancel. As we enter through the open door, Mr. Estes, dressed in his black vestments, steps from around his desk to greet us. Seated next to the desk is a younger man, also robed in black and wearing a clerical collar, who stands and turns to greet us. With a start, I realize it's Tommy. It has been at least five years now since we've seen each other. He has gained weight, and his temples are graying. I had completely forgotten his promise to try to find someone else to handle his big wedding in Atlanta so he could attend the service.

He and L.Q.C. shake hands, but as I give him a brotherly hug, I am unexpectedly overcome. Even as a child, Tommy, unlike me, found it easy to make a commitment. It was Tommy who was devoted to Sparkplug and who unleashed him against Fly, who didn't hesitate to attack Fly himself to save Winston in front of the church, and later to shove him off the porch when he tried to arrest us. And now, here he is at the funeral, after all. As the youngest, L.Q.C. and I had often discounted him, while in fact, Tommy was the bravest, the least selfish, the most loyal of the three of us. What begins as a perfunctory hug becomes a sincere embrace, and when I step away Tommy looks at me in surprise.

Recovering, I inquire about his wife, Melanie, and he explains that she is down with the flu and sends her regards. Then the three of us stand there grinning awkwardly at each other as Mr. Estes looks on. "I tried to call you to let you know I was coming, Harry," he explains, "but I couldn't get an answer at Cordelia's. Still no answer machine, I guess. You know, I had misgivings about coming back here, but I finally decided to just get in the car and drive over. Now that I'm here, Mr. Estes has asked me to help with the service—if that's all right with you guys, of course."

L.Q.C. and I make our way into the packed sanctuary and take our seats in the reserved pew at the front. Blair is already seated in the pew directly behind us. The pine coffin in front of the communion table is closed, just as Cordelia instructed. I take a careful whiff but detect no suspicious odor.

The organ strikes up "Faith of Our Fathers," and everyone stands. I half-expect to see Miss Mary Francis Hollowell still at the console, but then realize she would be in her late eighties by now. Instead, a young man occupies her place.

After leading the opening prayer, Mr. Estes welcomes the visitors. "Here we go," I whisper to L.Q.C., "the tried and true come-to-Jesus sermon."

But instead of beginning his homily, he turns to Tommy, seated in the high-backed armchair next to the pulpit. "Friends," he says, "today on this sad occasion we have a special visitor. Dr. Thomas Polk of St. Mark Presbyterian Church in Atlanta, the nephew of our own Miss Cordelia Coltharp, is with us. Dr. Polk has graciously agreed to say a few words about Miss Cordelia."

"Tommy told me he'd never come back to Tuckalofa," I whisper to L.Q.C. as my brother rises and steps to the pulpit. I note how tall and handsome he has become and how with his graying hair and steady gaze he resembles Cordelia. He pauses a moment and looks out over the congregation.

"We are here today to celebrate the extraordinary life of Cordelia Cunningham Coltharp," he begins. "As you have heard, Cordelia was my aunt. Although I never lived in Tuckalofa, I spent many a summer here. Those summers included some of the most formative events of my life. And they all seemed to center around Cordelia.

"She was the first liberal I ever knew in a time, not unlike our own, when that was not a fashionable label. By liberal I don't mean she was radical, strident, or took part in demonstrations. She was too much the old-fashioned lady for that. I mean that she was open to change and embraced new ideas. And that she was passionate about justice. And that she was optimistic, believing that the world could be made a better place if only men and women of goodwill worked to make it so. She passed those values on to her family and to generations of her students.

"How many of you ever visited Miss Cordelia's library at Tuckalofa High School and heard her reading aloud from the classics? Let me ask those of you who did to raise your hand." Virtually every hand in the sanctuary goes up. Tommy waits a few moments for the impact to sink in and then continues.

"Many of you knew her well or believed you did. But did you know, for instance, that she graduated with honors from Ole Miss? Did you know that she and her college roommate once swam in the reflecting pool in front of the Taj Mahal at midnight? That for years she subscribed to the *New York Times*, *The New Republic*, and *Vanity Fair*, as well as *The Saturday Evening Post*? That she won a graduate scholarship in drama, moved to New York, and once had the lead in an off-Broadway production of O'Neill's *Long Day's Journey into Night*?

"Did you know that she was descended from some of the earliest pioneers to settle this part of Mississippi—slave holders and, when the war came, Confederate soldiers—and that she felt she had somehow inherited the stain of slavery?

"Did you know that for years she was the only white female member of the NAACP in Mississippi? Cordelia had a passion for many things in life, but none of them surpassed her passion for justice. She worked for it tirelessly, but quietly, behind the scenes.

"As some of you will remember, many years ago, she was involved in the violent death of the sheriff of this county. She was, of course, cleared of any wrongdoing, since it was determined that she had acted in self-defense. Following that terrible day—I was there and so I know what happened—Cordelia always maintained that she had had a hand in bringing about justice. Justice that had been denied by due process, by a legal system that had become corrupted by the poison of racism.

"She taught us—her nephews, her sisters, her husband—to have the courage of our convictions and not to shrink from the moral complexities that we all encounter in life, but which were so much at the forefront during the turmoil of the fifties and sixties. She never lost her moral compass.

"And finally, she loved us and willingly sacrificed for us—including risking her own freedom in ways that even today are not fully known or appreciated, even by some members of her own family.

"Hers was a life fully lived, a life of passion, energy, risk, and love. There can be no clearer illustration of what it means to be created in the image of God. And so, friends, if this community of Tuckalofa is a better place today, if there is more tolerance here, more freedom here, more justice, then I believe it is in large measure due to the life of Cordelia Cunningham Coltharp."

It is not until after the burial at the cemetery that L.Q.C., Tommy, and I are finally alone. We stand together on the crest of the ridge, gazing down at the rooftops and steeples that punch through the barren treetops below us. The mourners are dispersing, back to the cars that line the little asphalt lane, grateful to be out of the wind that sweeps through the valley. I shiver and turn up the collar of my overcoat.

"Have you ever been back to Winston's family's graves since their funerals?" asks Tommy. We both shake our heads. "Well, neither had I until this morning. I came up here when I first got to town to see where Cordelia would be buried. Come on, I want to show you something. They're over there in the black section, of course."

We make our way through the forest of gravestones, across the rolling hillside, and through the gate in the chain link fence that separates the white and black sections of the cemetery. "With that fence it looks like somebody's afraid the black folks might climb out of their graves, cross over, dig new ones for themselves, and integrate the place," L.Q.C. dryly observes.

Tommy leads us to a row of three graves, two of the markers beginning to show a dusting of moss, the third obviously newer. In silence we contemplate the inscriptions:

Robert Winston 1896–1958
Robert Winston Jr. 1930–1958
Senatobia Winston 1900–1976

"Winston? Their *last* name was Winston?" exclaims L.Q.C. "I always thought Winston was his first name."

"So did I; so did everybody, I guess," replies Tommy. No one ever used their full names. They were just Winston and Robert and Senatobia to us."

But I am staring at the elder Robert's gravestone. And then it all fits together, and there on that wind-swept hill overlooking the town I understand.

My brother and cousin have started back toward the car, not noticing me still standing alone next to the graves. Finally they stop and turn toward me, waiting. Recovering, I hurry after them.

"Come on back to the house," I manage to say at last. "We'll have a shot of Horace's Old Crow. It's still there in the back of the pantry, if you can believe it. It might even be drinkable. Then there's something else I need to show you."

34

The kindling crackles in the fireplace, and the coal catches and begins to flare. We sit together, sharing a glass of Scotch—Horace's whiskey is long past its time—savoring the faint aroma of anthracite, so powerfully redolent of Christmases past and vanished steam locomotives.

I begin by holding up Cordelia's diary. "I found this in her desk. You can read all of it for yourselves if you like." I thumb through the little leather book until I come to the first passage I have marked. "But first I want to read to you some of her entries from 1929."

July 12. Today RW spent the afternoon reading Keats aloud. He is so bright and often sees more in a passage than I do...

September 1. Horace is gone again; this time it will be for a month, up to Chicago to work in the I.C. main office. The nights alone are hard for me.

September 5. RW read to me again and when we finished it was almost dark, so I asked him to have a bit of supper with me. He is a gentle, kind man, and it comforts me so to be with him.

October 5. Horace is to be gone again, for six weeks this time...

October 10. We should not have done what we have done. I am wracked with guilt, and yet I cannot wait to see him again tonight. Horace always says nothing is more important than family, but for me nothing is more important than love. Poor Horace. Poor, poor Cordelia.

November 30. I am pregnant, and I have admitted to Horace the child is not his, as it is obvious it must have been conceived while he was away on the road. It will also become obvious enough to everyone else once it is born, of course. He was deeply wounded, inconsolable even, and insisted on knowing the identity of the father. When I finally told him, he almost collapsed in grief. What am I to do?

December 24. Tonight is Christmas Eve, but there is little joy in our home. The day after tomorrow I am to go away, to a place in Asheville, N.C., a sanitarium called Blue Ridge Hospital, where I will have the baby. We shall tell people I have suffered a nervous breakdown, and indeed, this is not far from the truth. We have found a bright young colored woman from the country who used to work for Mama, and she and RW have agreed to marry. We will provide a stipend, and they will raise the child. It has all been arranged with Horace's help. He has taken the front bedroom, and when I return, we are to sleep apart. But he will not seek a divorce. He says he feels partly responsible for what has happened since he has been gone from home so much. I do not know how he can bear to speak to me.

"My God—Cordelia had a lover? It doesn't seem possible!" exclaims Tommy as I put down the diary.

"There's something else," I add, producing the valentine taken from the secret compartment in Cordelia's desk. My brother and cousin examine it, seeming puzzled. "It's obviously handmade. Now look at the heart. Did you look closely at Robert's gravestone up in the cemetery? The same motif is carved there. I also found it on the Sweetheart Tree down in the ravine. CC has to be Cordelia Coltharp, and RW has to be Robert Winston. There's only one possible explanation. Cordelia and Robert were lovers back in 1929."

We sit in silence for a long moment. It does seem incredible.

"Let's see," begins L.Q.C. "Cordelia was born in 1898. That would mean she was thirty-one in 1929. She and Horace were married—when—around 1920 or so?"

"Then they must have been married for nine or ten years by then," interjects Tommy.

"But what about the illegitimate baby? What became of it?" asks Tommy.

"It seems obvious, don't you think?" I respond, laying aside the valentine.

"He was around all the time, after all. I delivered groceries with him. He saved my life. He was Winston—Robert Winston Jr., that is—the son of Robert and Cordelia—our black first cousin. He grew up in the cottage at the back of Henry and Cordelia's lot down in the ravine, playing with Frank, neither of them knowing that they were half-brothers. Senatobia was the 'bright young colored woman' Cordelia mentions who agreed to marry Robert and help raise Winston as her own son.

"Remember the way Robert spent so much time around the house when Horace was away, building fires and hanging wallpaper in the bedrooms and so forth? He told me that Cordelia taught him to read, and they must have enjoyed reciting poetry as well. And don't you remember how Cordelia was always inventing odd jobs and errands for Winston that would let them go driving together—like the time he went with us out to her family's place to dig irises? And how she rushed down to see Mr. Coleman after the sheriff arrested him?"

"Yes, and remember how Robert and Senatobia were always so glad to see us at their house, just like we were all family?" adds L.Q.C., apparently warming to the idea.

"And how it was Winston who buried Sparkplug," says Tommy. "I wonder if Winston ever knew who his real mother was?"

Finally, feeling a bit like a solicitor in a Dickens novel, I unseal Cordelia's will and begin to read it aloud. "It's dated 1954."

"That would be before Winston, Robert, and Horace died," observes L.Q.C.

"'…to my dear husband, Horace Coltharp,'" the will begins, "'I bequeath all my worldly possessions. Should he predecease me, I bequeath to my sisters, India Maxwell and Ellen Polk, my home on Lee Street. To my nephews, Harrison Beauchamp Polk Jr., Thomas Beauchamp Polk, and Lucius Quintius Cinncinatus Lamar Maxwell, I bequeath one half of the residue of my estate. To my son, Robert Winston Jr., I bequeath the remaining one half of the residue of my estate. Finally, to my dearest friend, his father, Robert Winston Sr., I bequeath the valentine in the hidden compartment of my desk drawer.'"

It has grown dark. No one has thought to switch on a lamp, and the fire's shadows dance across the high ceiling. The whiskey has taken effect, smoothing the distance that time has set between us, and now it is our turn to retell the old stories. Stories about Cordelia and Horace, rides in the lofty cab of old number 857, constellations wheeling over the ravine on a winter's night, Sparkplug, and premature burials.

As though by unspoken agreement, though, little is said about that summer of 1958. About Helen Ringwald, the quicksand bog, Sheriff Fly, the Cyclopes, or the night Sourwood Street was burned to the ground and Horace and Robert died.

And nothing is said about the fatal standoff with Fly on Cordelia's front porch. As the evening wears on, it begins to seem that Tommy and L.Q.C. are purposely avoiding the subject. Every time I bring it up, they seem a little too eager to move on, and I sense a growing tension among us.

Finally something compels me to force the issue. "Hey, what about the snake in old Sonny Fly's mailbox? Do you remember that smell—like a punch in the nose? And later on the porch with Cordelia and Fly, I always thought that was brave of you, Tommy, to try to take the blame when it was all L.Q.C.'s idea."

I catch the brief glance exchanged between them before Tommy replies. "Oh, it was nothing, Harry. You tried to do the same. But L.Q.C. wouldn't have any of it; he owned up to it, himself."

"Something has always bothered me, though, about what happened when Fly came down to arrest us," I continue. "I didn't think Cordelia knew the first thing about guns. As I recall, she detested them. Remember the night we thought we heard the chicken thief outside and she called out that she'd be just as likely to hit him as not? That was nothing but a bluff. But she wasn't bluffing with Sonny Fly. It's always been a mystery to me how she could have hit him right in the middle of the forehead like that."

Tommy and L.Q.C. look at each other again, but neither speaks for a long time. Finally Tommy leans across and puts his hand on my knee. "Harry, do you remember what I said in my eulogy about how Cordelia had sacrificed for us, how she had risked her own freedom for us in ways that some members of her own family don't even know about?"

"Yeah, I wondered what you meant by that."

"Harry, Cordelia didn't shoot Fly."

"What do you mean? I saw her do it. We all did!"

"Try to remember, Harry," he insists. "She didn't do it."

"The hell she didn't! She snatched the rifle away from L.Q.C.," I stammer, totally bewildered. "Just one cartridge in that rifle, and she drilled him right between the eyes. Then we all agreed to swear it was self-defense so she wouldn't be prosecuted, and John Calhoun Coleman dropped it. That's all there was to it."

"No, Harry," says L.Q.C., shifting uneasily in his chair. "Tommy's right. Try to remember. She didn't do it."

"Well, who did?" I protest.

"You did, Harry. It was you who grabbed the rifle from me, not Cordelia. You were always a good shot. Remember that day out in the country when you nailed that cardinal in the top of the tree? You shot Fly. It was you we agreed to protect.

"It was Cordelia's idea to take the blame. She thought she might be able to get away pleading self-defense, and she didn't want you to have to go through the trauma of a trial. So we concocted a cover story. 'Situation ethics,' she called it. We all stuck by our story, only it began to be obvious that you really believed it."

"You had just blanked out the truth," says Tommy. "It's called 'repression' or 'selective forgetting.' The psychiatrists explained it to us; it's not an uncommon reaction to severe stress. The truth is pushed down into the unconscious. But it's not really forgotten—just denied admission to consciousness. In your case you became severely anxious and depressed. You stopped eating and couldn't sleep. When you did sleep, there were nightmares. Finally Mom and Dad had to hospitalize you. I know you remember the psychiatric ward where you spent a month or so.

"When they let you out, they told us the depression had lifted but that you still had the memory loss. The doctors advised us all never to mention the episode. They said the trauma of killing Fly had been severe, but that one day you might recover the memory on your own. Until then, it was better to protect you by not forcing you to confront the truth.

"I'm sorry, we were just doing what we thought was best for you. But maybe it's better to have it come out at last."

It was as though I had been slammed against the wall, and for a moment I could hardly draw a breath. I found it impossible to say anything, so I just sat there staring at them. I was supposed to believe that I had intentionally killed a man and didn't know it?

It was Tommy who finally broke the silence. "I'm sorry, Harry. We didn't plan to mention any of this. But you kept bringing it up, almost as though you sensed there was something you had forgotten and that you wanted to know about."

Could there be anything to what he said? Hadn't I been worrying about precisely that, about something I couldn't remember, ever since I began writing my account of that summer? But it was just too ridiculous. "Look Tommy, L.Q.C., I'm not prepared to buy a word of this. It's absurd.

"But just for the sake of argument, let's say you're right. Suppose you tell me exactly what you think really happened on the porch that day. Go on, let's have it. I'm not sick any more!"

"Okay, Harry," began Tommy, hesitating, "the way I remember it, Fly stormed down to Cordelia's, threatening to arrest us for putting the snake in his mailbox. We all tried to take the blame at first. Then he pulled out his handcuffs…"

"And then you butted him off the porch into the bushes," interrupted L.Q.C. "At first I thought I was going to die laughing. The old bastard was covered with bees!"

"Yeah, but he didn't just beat a retreat and go home," continued Tommy. "We saw that he was headed back up on the porch. That's when L.Q.C. ducked inside and grabbed the rifle. It was pretty quick thinking, too, because the next thing we knew Fly was about to draw his pistol. But L.Q.C. was faster and got the drop on him. He told Fly he'd blow his brains out.

"Then Cordelia spoke up. She told Fly he wasn't going to arrest anybody, but he said that was exactly what he was going to do. And that's when you reached over and snatched the rifle out of L.Q.C.'s hands, Harry.

"I remember how cool you seemed. You even remembered to cock it—L.Q.C. had forgotten, and it wouldn't have fired. Then you put it to your shoulder and aimed at Fly's head. You told him you weren't going to shoot him for what he did to Sparkplug, or even what the Cyclopes did to Horace. But you were going to shoot him for what he did to Winston.

"And then, before anybody could move, you pulled the trigger. Fly's head jerked back and he stumbled backward and fell off the porch again, right back in the bushes with the bees. Only this time he didn't move.

"We all turned and watched as you calmly propped the rifle against the wall. Then you sat down on the swing and just stared ahead. Nobody said anything at first. Then Cordelia told us to sit there while she called her friend Mr. Coleman, the city attorney who had prosecuted Fly at the trial.

"In a minute she came back and picked up the rifle for a moment before leaning it back against the wall. I wondered if that was in case anyone checked it for her fingerprints. Then she told us what she was going to say, that it had been she who had shot Fly in self-defense. She asked us if we would go along. L.Q.C. and I agreed, but we couldn't get you to say a word. It was almost as though you had gone into some sort of trance.

"A few minutes later Mr. Coleman drove up. By that time two or three of the neighbors had arrived, too. I guess they had heard the shot. They were all standing around out in the front yard looking at Fly still lying there in the bushes. For some reason I remember watching a bee crawling into his ear.

"Mr. Coleman asked Cordelia a few questions, but he seemed satisfied that she was telling the truth. He didn't bother to ask us anything at all. Then he said he'd better call the medical examiner and for us to go inside and not to worry."

Tommy reached over and gently placed a hand on my knee. "That's the way it was, Harry. But there is one more thing I need to tell you. Something I couldn't tell you before.

"When we were boys, you always seemed so serious and thoughtful to me. But you were tentative and overly cautious, too, as though you could never decide exactly what was right. Or even who you were or what you believed. But that day on the porch, you weren't tentative. You took a stand. You showed great courage and you did the right thing. Horace and old Colonel Thomas Coltharp would have been proud of you. And you made me proud to be your brother."

Epilogue: 2012

Now that Cordelia is gone, there is no reason to return to Tuckalofa, and yet I do so from time to time. The old anxiety has faded, and somehow I feel drawn there. It is hard to believe it has been more than twenty years since Cordelia's funeral and more than fifty years since that summer in Tuckalofa. I never spent another summer there; although, once I grew older, I tried to make an occasional day trip to check on Cordelia, alone in the house on Lee Street. But even for those short visits it was hard for me to bring myself to return.

Except for Tommy, the rest of my immediate family is gone too, vanished through the stone gates of the cemetery at the top of Manassas Street inscribed with the lines from "Death Be Not Proud" that Horace loved. Our mother is buried there next to our father. L.Q.C.'s mother, India, is there too. Cordelia now lies next to Main-line Horace along with their son, Frank. A pecan tree planted by Tommy and me in the family plot has matured into a favorite playground for rambunctious squirrels and blue jays. With his fondness for anti-authoritarian critters who enjoyed a freedom he could never permit himself, Horace would be pleased to see them cavorting over his grave.

And, of course, not a hundred yards away, over in the black section, are Winston, Robert, and Senatobia. I did not see Senatobia again after the summer of 1958. She moved away from Tuckalofa to be with relatives out in the country. I never even attempted an apology for my vicious outburst after she dropped the bowl in Cordelia's pantry. Like so much else, it remains a heavy piece of baggage I carry with me, one I am still unable to set down.

There was a half-hearted investigation into Horace's death, but when no one would come forward to positively identify any of the Cyclopes, the case was dropped. They say poor harmless Helen Ringwald, the mysterious woman in white who was given to roaming the town in a fugue state, lived on for years, the light burning by her bed all night. She died without anyone knowing whether she ever heard a word of the newspapers read to her by her mother or ever saw the flowers brought to her by Sonny Fly. John Calhoun Coleman continued to be elected city attorney until he was past eighty and finally keeled over of a heart attack fishing for crappie on Grenada Lake. Blair Estes Reynolds is married to a prosperous attorney. They have a daughter, who recently won the Country Club of Jackson's women's tennis championship. Mr. Estes eventually developed Alzheimer's and died in a nursing home for ministers near Black Mountain, North Carolina.

On my trips back to Mississippi, I always take the old road through the hill country. Even though I-55 cuts time off the drive, it fails to move me like the old route. Cruising slowly down into the valley and onto Main Street, I pass the Baptist Church, the WPA-era post office and the office of the *Tuckalofa Tattler*. The Presbyterian Church at last boasts a new steeple, a hollow fiberglass version of the original, with a microwave antenna concealed inside. Whenever I pass it, I remember Cordelia's indignant reaction to the congregation's decision to pull out of the national church at Mr. Estes' urging because of what were considered excessively liberal leanings.

The handsome old Bank of Tuckalofa is gone now, replaced by an undistinguished pastiche of pseudo-historic architecture. But the Albemarle Hotel across the street and Carlisle's Drugstore don't seem to have changed.

On this visit—another summer has come—I drop in at Carlisle's and take a seat at the soda fountain. A striking teenage girl with coal black eyes and a suntan takes my order, a chocolate soda for old times' sake. She reminds me of Blair at that age. I try to make conversation. "Fifty years ago you could have found me sitting on this very stool reading comic books," I explain, and she smiles vacantly in response. What does fifty years mean to a sixteen-year-old?

"I don't suppose you ever heard of the Coltharps—Cordelia and Henry?" she shakes her head apologetically. "Well, back around 1920 their Model T Ford crashed through that very same plate glass window and came to a stop just about where I'm sitting."

"A Model T?" she asks with a blank look.

Carlisle's has added Tuckalofa souvenirs to their inventory, and I purchase a commemorative coffee mug with a photograph of the old railroad depot, long-since demolished. "Thanks. I'll send this to my brother in Atlanta."

"No problem," she chirps, ringing up the sale.

I amble up Lee Street, automatically speaking to an elderly man with a cane as we pass on the sidewalk. Cordelia would be proud.

Across the grassy scar that is all that remains of the once-proud Illinois Central main line, upstream from the old bridge, Persimmon Creek has been channelized for flood control, and downstream it is now buried in a concrete culvert beneath an asphalt parking lot. But the biggest change is the trees. Once there were mature oaks lining the street, their canopies almost meeting overhead. Another tornado uprooted most of them—gone in a couple of minutes after a hundred years. They have never been replaced, and even though that was twenty years ago, without the trees, the genteel old neighborhood has the raw look of a suburban subdivision.

Behind the houses though, where the terrain falls sharply away, I can make out the dense greenery of the ravine, its ancient trees largely spared by the storm. I remember with an odd combination of dread and longing the secret hollows with the quicksand bogs, spirit trees, and a sunlit glade where boys used to quest for the Grail. Cedar Crest next door to Cordelia's has become a rotting hulk, probably decayed beyond restoration even if anyone were interested in a haunted house in a depressed real estate market.

Cordelia's house still rears proudly above the crest of the hill, the corner tower surveying the valley below. Someone has bricked up the old latticework skirt that enclosed our secret basement clubhouse. The abelia bushes where Sheriff Fly was stung in his final minutes have grown bigger now, but otherwise everything looks the same.

Did I really kill a man on that porch when I was still a child, struggling to make sense of the world, daring to think for myself for the first time? How did a memory like that become denied, buried? Is it really possible to utterly wipe an experience of that magnitude from one's consciousness? Perhaps it is; the psychologists tell us the mind is still largely *terra incognito.*

To this day, I have no recollection of seizing the rifle from L.Q.C., although I must admit to a strange aversion to firearms of any sort, and the smell of gunpowder makes me nauseous. Perhaps L.Q.C. and Tommy are the deluded ones, victims of some shared hallucination. And what would Cordelia's version of those events be?

But whatever the truth is about that awful day on her front porch, I can say that the terrible nightmares I began to suffer that summer have diminished over the years. And somehow since that evening spent with Tommy and L.Q.C. after her funeral, a weight seems to have been lifted from my shoulders.

The three of us—L.Q.C., Tommy, and I—still don't see much of each other, and when we do, the subject of Fly's death doesn't come up. A year or so after Cordelia's death we met in Tuckalofa to finalize the sale of her house to an energetic young couple with ambitious renovation plans. We said nothing, though, about tiny Mr. Nobody in the coal shed or the Sweetheart Tree in the ravine. And we said nothing about that day in 1958 when a man died on the front porch. Some things are best forgotten.

What will become of Tuckalofa? The railroad—the town's principal *raison d'être* for a century—will probably never return, and, so far, even Walmart has passed the town by. And yet there are a few signs of hope. I am told that housing has become so expensive up in fashionable Oxford that some of the other hill country towns have begun to attract retirees, and the Chamber of Commerce has begun an ad campaign touting Tuckalofa's small town charm and low cost of living. With the high price of gasoline there is even a rumor of a future rail line to be built along the abandoned Illinois Central right-of-way, providing a light-rail connection all the way to Memphis. In the summer, tapered green banners shaped like pods of okra wave from the lampposts, proclaiming that the long moribund Okra Festival has been revived.

On the site of the old Jitney Jungle, I spy a campaign poster for the county sheriff's race taped to the window of the new hardware store. The smiling face on the poster is that of a young black man who reminds me of Winston. What would Sonny Fly say? I step inside to buy a pair of clippers to tidy up the family plot in the cemetery. They seem to be doing a brisk business dispensing everything from weed killers to power tools. The clerk offers to show me the clippers, and we strike up a conversation.

"Sure, I've heard of Miss Cordelia Coltharp. She was a legend, the librarian up at the old high school. My parents used to talk about her sitting on a stool reading to any students who dropped by during lunch. Did you say you used to live here too?"

I explain that I grew up in Memphis, but that I sometimes wonder how my life would have been different had I lived in Tuckalofa, instead of just visiting for the summers as a boy.

"You know," replies the clerk, "it's beyond me how anyone can bear to live in a big town like Memphis when they could live down here instead. I hear Miss Cordelia's house is going on the market again. The folks who live there now have been transferred to Batesville. They've done a nice job fixing up your family's old place; you ought to go up and have a look at it." He is cordial, trying to be diplomatic, but I detect a sincere note of pity in his voice for me, for anyone who lives in Memphis.

The road home winds north, past the old familiar towns, their names still proudly emblazoned on the water tanks that occasionally interrupt the gentle roll of the hills. Except for Oxford, though, most of the little towns seem to have fallen on hard times, barely managing to hold on. The decaying sidewalks of the Main Streets are lined with boarded-up storefronts and populated by small groups of sullen young black men.

I drift along wondering about my complex feelings for Tuckalofa, the place where, in the space of one summer, I learned that love and hate could be neighbors. The words of the clerk in the hardware store keep coming back to me, asking how I can bear to live in Memphis when I could live in Tuckalofa instead. For an absurd moment I allow myself to seriously consider the possibility. What if I purchased Cordelia's house and retired there? After all, things do seem to be changing. I could simply turn around at the next gas station, drive back to town, look up the real estate agent, and make an offer.

Surely it would be lovely to gaze again at the dipper from Cordelia's bedroom on a cold, clear winter's night, following the pointers to the North Star hanging immobile over the ravine. But what would it be like to rock in her swing on a summer evening, watching the lightning bugs come out on that porch where a man died a violent death? And what about the ravine, that chasm separating blacks from whites, the living from the dead, and me from my youth? Would I regularly make the trek down that twisting, overgrown path, to the sandy creek where I almost drowned, and where people I loved and admired were murdered by a hooded lynch mob?

Could I live surrounded by those memories, in the very midst of the ghosts of those I loved and hated, reminded every day of that summer that did so much to make me who I am? No, the Greeks were right after all; it really is impossible to step twice into the same river. Some things, once confronted, are best forgotten again—or at least laid to rest where they can do no more harm. The past should remain a dark country, largely inaccessible, inhabited by the shadows of both unbearable grief and unsustainable joy.